P9-DGR-396

LESSER EVILS

WITHDRAWN
Baldwinsville, NY 13027-2578

Joe Flanagan

LESSER EVILS

Europa
editions

Europa Editions
214 West 29th Street
New York, N.Y. 10001
www.europaeditions.com
info@europaeditions.com

This book is a work of fiction. Any references to historical events,
real people, or real locales are used fictitiously.

JUN 0 9 2016

Copyright © by Joe Flanagan
First Publication 2016 by Europa Editions

All rights reserved, including the right of reproduction
in whole or in part in any form

Library of Congress Cataloging in Publication Data is available
ISBN 978-1-60945-310-7

Flanagan, Joe
Lesser Evils

Book design by Emanuele Ragnisco
www.mekkanografici.com

Cover photo © kickimages/iStock

Prepress by Grafica Punto Print – Rome

Printed in the USA

LESSER EVILS

1

In green shallows, the ocean's lesser creatures showed themselves. Bland minnows appeared at the edge of clearings in the sea grass, their fish eyes wide with astonishment at having survived another tide. Hermit crabs like long-suffering old refugees hauled their burdens across the bottom, and ragged jellyfish drifted like souls passing through limbo.

On the beach there was a scattering of people in motionless torpor, fully under the spell of the July sun. Reclining mothers in Ray Bans watched the sluggish movements of their children. Elderly couples peered out from beneath the brims of their hats as though deep in the heart of an old, old dream where even longing and regret had been dulled by the sweltering haze.

The little colony made a spray of color on the beach with their swimsuits, umbrellas, and coolers. Sometimes a faint breeze came in off the water and touched their cheeks, ruffling the pages of their paperbacks and magazines. It carried a rumor of the wild breathless Atlantic—fish and death and oblivion—and caused people to glance for a moment out to the horizon.

Between long stretches of wooded desolation were crude clam shacks and lonely houses collapsing in weedy yards, turned into summer souvenir shops without much enthusiasm. Liquor stores appeared, new motor courts, and seafood restaurants. They crowded the road—now a small highway—in a welter of neon and plastic. The theme was maritime kitsch: talking fish, cartoon sea captains, grinning crustaceans, draped fishnets decorated with buoys and painted shells.

Within a mile, the commercial activity faded. Reeds appeared, a glimpse of ocean, the smell of decay, and then another strip in another town: Eastham, Brewster, Orleans, Chatham.

In Hyannis, the road formed a wide boulevard of low storefronts. Down a side street there was a block of weathered buildings, dead and empty remnants of the maritime trade, their windows smeared, their gutters sprouting grass. Beside this, a bus station and a small cemetery surrounded by a picket fence.

From his open window in the police station, Lieutenant Warren watched the stillness. The ticket clerk at the bus station was visible as a phantom behind the glass, a frozen specter that moved only occasionally to turn the page of his book.

There was a knock on the door and he turned to see Sergeant Garrity push his head in. Garrity looked at the floor and paused before speaking, which meant that the sergeant was delighted to be the bearer of bad news and was savoring it for a moment before passing it along. "Someone to see you, lieutenant."

Warren got up and went into the hallway. On the bench across from the sergeant's desk was Jane Myrna, his son's summer school teacher, and his son, who went by the name of Little Mike. The young woman looked up. "Mr. Warren," she said, "We had an accident."

Little Mike suddenly became absorbed in a book he had in his lap. It was a primary reader for toddlers with textures you could touch. He was small for his age. His legs stuck out straight from the bench seat, and Warren saw that he had a towel wrapped around his gray flannels. Garrity was a looming presence to the left, rustling papers and closing drawers. Warren motioned for them to follow him into his office. Little Mike trailed his teacher, gathering up the book and the loose ends of the towel, trying to keep it wrapped around his waist.

In Warren's office there were no mementos, photographs, or anything to suggest a personal history. He had posted only bulletins, shift rosters, and a calendar from Cameron's boatyard where he sometimes got extra work as a carpenter. This month showed a poorly composed snapshot of a red-hulled workboat up on jacks and, beyond it, a rough wilderness of pine trees.

Jane Myrna took a seat in a chair against the wall, while Little Mike sat on the floor behind his father's desk and opened *Pat the Bunny*. Warren stood in front of Jane with his hands on his hips and his feet spread apart, then realized it was not the attitude to take and tried for something more relaxed. The demands of his work made social conventions difficult. He was fond of Jane Myrna because she had been so good to Mike and because he believed her to be genuine and virtuous. That was the truth, he assured himself. But the knowledge that it was not the entire truth made him blink and shift his feet. He tried not to gather in the details of her there in his office as she crossed her ankles beneath the chair and looked up at him with an open face. "The boys were teasing him," she said. "He brought his book to school with him and they saw it. We really try to keep an eye on him but this time they got him off to himself."

"Did they hurt him?"

"I think they just pushed him around a little bit, but you know how he is."

"Yes."

"He wet his pants."

Little Mike was out of sight. Only his soft murmuring could be heard from behind the desk. Jane said, "I would have brought him home to change but I have to get back to my classroom. I figured it would be best to bring him here."

Rage and sorrow, by now familiar afflictions, filled the cavity of Warren's chest like a sudden illness. It came with each incident involving Little Mike, but it never lost its power. He was at a loss now at how to stand before Jane Myrna, once again the aggrieved father, and appear appropriately angry, judicious, compassionate, in command. He didn't know which it should be. Once they had made the boy eat dog shit. They had talked him into snipping his eyebrows off with scissors in art class. They practiced the wrestling moves they saw on Saturday morning TV and nearly dislocated his shoulder. Mike's inability to cry was unsettling. It was as if he had received a divine message, one to which his father was not privy—that this was the way it was supposed to be.

"I think that will be enough for today," Warren said.

"I'm sorry, Mr. Warren."

"It's not your fault."

"I try to keep an eye on him."

"I know, Jane. I'm grateful."

Jane Myrna went over to Little Mike and said goodbye. On her way to the door, Warren said, "Who were the boys involved?" Her face registered dismay. She had the door partway open, then closed it. "It was . . . Danny Freitag, Shaggy Hilliard. You know. Those kids."

He wrote the names down. "Anyone else?"

Her distress seemed to deepen. "Ken Reich. Fred Finn. Matt Langella."

When she had gone, Warren dropped the sheet of paper on his desk. It wasn't the first time he'd made such a list. After the episode with the dog shit, he had visited each family. He showed up in uniform, and while it was strictly a personal matter, he did nothing to dispel the impression that he was there on official business. Unspoken insinuations, the ambient atmosphere of threat, and the influence of his position seemed to have had the desired effect. But it had left him with a queasy, shameful feeling and there were rumblings around town later that he had overstepped his bounds.

Warren sat down behind his desk and looked at the boy. He had the mental capacity of a three-year-old. He had no idea how to camouflage the things about himself that made him stand out and invite abuse. He seemed impervious to the humiliations he suffered regularly, more concerned, it seemed, with the effect they had on his father. Now he held his father's hand to his chest. "Dad," he said. "Don't be sad." It was his sheer, innocent witlessness that Warren found devastating. That and the uncanny perception of a boy so impaired. It was as if after each episode, he had to audition for his father's acceptance, just to make sure he still had it, to make sure the latest abuse hadn't caused a seismic shift in the only sure thing he knew. He seemed to feel that after each humiliation he could face the ultimate rejection: that his father, his only friend, wouldn't want him anymore; and these heartrending gestures were his appeal for mercy to the source from which he needed it most.

"Dad," he said. "Is there any bad guys here?"

The sadness that was bearing down on Warren's center expanded into his throat and stung his eyes. "We might have a couple."

"Can I see them?"

"What do you want to see the bad guys for, Mike?"

"Dad! *Bad guys!*"

"Come on. Let's go home."

Out in the hallway, it was silent, a slow weekday in the middle of summer and no one about. The police station smelled of Pine-Sol and new leather. Warren went out into the bright afternoon with Mike, and when the heavy varnished doors closed behind them, the police station was filled with quiet again. The desk sergeant, who had the florid complexion of a heavy drinker, looked down at the blotter, a sad and sinister little narrative of a brief span of time in a small seacoast community. The hidden life, the appetites, delusions, and mishaps that seemed pettier, dirtier, and more tragic somehow because of the postcard seaside setting. The corners of his mouth turned upward as he ran his fingers over the previous night's entries: a drunk and violent husband on Willow St. An elderly woman with dementia struck by a car and killed on Route 149 in Mashpee. A six-year-old boy gone missing in Truro.

At American Legion Post 1124, the bubbles rose in amber beer, the liquid suffused with light from the big picture windows behind the bar overlooking Route 132 and the municipal airfield. The lounge was cool with refrigerated air, and at the three o'clock hour, a lazy frat house conviviality prevailed.

Denny Nelson was behind the bar polishing glasses. A former Navy cook, Nelson's routine was comprised of raunchy commentary and tales of his military incompetence. He had become an institution at Post 1124, his oversexed patter and general harmlessness essential to the experience. His brisk motions slowed to a stop as he watched a new Ford two-door pull into the lot. Nelson considered himself a sketch, and while his comments were normally intended for the whole room, he now lowered his voice so that only the men seated at the bar could hear him.

"General quarters, general quarters. Heavy ordnance coming in the door."

A chorus of murmurs traveled down the bar.

"Oh yeah."

"Look at that."

"Look who's here."

The man striding across the parking lot was built like a stevedore, massive through the chest and shoulders, legs like tree trunks. His hair was short, spiky in a tight crew cut. He wore a lightweight powder gray suit, a white shirt, and a bright blue tie. In his blazer pocket was a matching blue handkerchief. When he walked into the lounge, Nelson put his heels together and executed an elaborate salute. The newcomer walked through the lounge with his eyes straight ahead in the kind of indulgence sometimes practiced by people who know they are watched. A few men chose not to look at him at all, like the roofers, with their windburned and feral appearance, their bare forearms blackened with tar, who lowered their heads as he passed.

At the bar, someone said, "He looks just like Aldo Ray, don't he?" The visitor went to a booth in the dim recesses of the lounge. Once he was seated, Denny Nelson arrived with a dry martini. "Captain Stasiak, sir," he said. "How are you?"

"What do you say, Nellie."

Dale Stasiak had the uniform tan of a film star, even down to his scalp, which shone through the fine bristles of his crew cut. While there was little transition between his shoulders and his head and he was a bit thick in the lips, he did not have the face of an extraordinarily stocky man. His features were those you would see on a man of finer proportions, yet the whole assembly composed a look that was hard and authoritative. His eyes were a soft hazel color, which produced a troubling effect, so prominently located, as they were, in the face of the essential man.

Denny Nelson made a hasty retreat to his place behind the bar. Stasiak slowly unwrapped a panatela and waited for the district attorney. When he arrived, he stood at the entrance and looked around the lounge with a defensive, mistrustful expression. Elliott Yost was a small, slight man who couldn't seem to find a suit that fit him. The unhealthy-looking strands of hair he'd plastered across his bald dome with pomade in the morning were rebellious by afternoon. Stasiak chuckled as he watched Elliott cross the room with his satchel. "Dale," he said, as he pulled up a chair across from Stasiak.

"Hello, Elliott."

Elliott had been the district attorney for the Cape and islands since 1951. His caseload over the years had been made up mainly of unremarkable thefts and crimes of impulse. There was generally only one killing a year and they all got neatly resolved without much effort on his part. Elliott lived with his wife and two teenage sons in Sandwich, a serene little village that had somehow retained all the charms of the last decade while taking on few traits of the current one. It was the ideal place for someone like Elliott, who was distressed by disorder and lived with an uneasy sense that a great turmoil was under way in the world and that somewhere west of the canal its distant surging could be felt in the air. Dale Stasiak's arrival on Cape Cod seemed a validation of his feelings, though Elliott didn't know whether it was cause for celebration or worry. The decorated state trooper had made a name for himself in a campaign against the mob in Boston—the now famous Attanasio case. It was understood that Stasiak was given command of Troop D, headquartered at the Yarmouth barracks, as a reward. But Elliott was not the only one who thought the posting a little surprising. It was possible that the assignment was not about prestige. Elliott wondered if Stasiak's arrival was a portent of things to come or a hedge against things that might. He was not well connected with the attorney general's office in Boston and he felt he'd been kept in the dark.

He had worked a few minor cases with Stasiak since his arrival. He seldom showed up at Elliott's offices, preferring to send a couple of the new men he'd brought down from Boston with him, who were taciturn and not very helpful. And Elliott didn't like conducting business in a bar, but he supposed it was part of the rough and freewheeling cop culture in Boston and what Stasiak was used to.

The first few times he met Stasiak, Elliott tried to make small talk, which wasn't his style, but he didn't want to come off as aloof and it was important that Stasiak like him. As it turned out, the policeman had no use for small talk, and Elliott found him inscrutable in any case, so now when they met, Elliott just got straight down to business. He was beginning to think that Stasiak did not care for him, and figured the no-nonsense approach was something he might look favorably upon.

This particular meeting had the district attorney more uneasy than usual. A young boy had gone missing in Truro and four days had passed with no sign of him. That morning, Elliott had discovered that the family had retained an attorney and there were complaints about Stasiak's handling of the investigation.

Denny Nelson materialized in his peripheral vision and startled him. "What can I get for you, sir?"

Elliott fussed with his satchel and cast his eyes around the room, across the Marine Corps plaque mounted on the pine paneling, across the red and gold regimental banner. It was only 3:15.

"I'll have a Schaefer," Elliott said.

When Denny Nelson was out of earshot, Stasiak said, "So, what's going on, Elliott?"

"Well, primarily the missing boy out in Truro. What's the status with that?"

"We start dragging the ponds tomorrow," Stasiak said. "There's a bunch of them out there."

"I understand you interviewed the parents."

"That's right."

"At the barracks?"

"Yeah."

"Dale, I'm not going to question your expertise in any way. I wouldn't do that. But you need to know there was a complaint about it. They went to the board of selectmen to protest the way they were treated. And they've hired a lawyer. He called me this morning."

"The parents are distraught."

"They say they were treated like suspects."

Stasiak looked at the district attorney in such a way that Elliott was glad when Denny Nelson arrived in that moment with a brimming pilsner glass on a round tray. He made a show of receiving the beer, loosening his tie, and taking what he hoped looked like an eager first drink. When he looked up, Stasiak's eyes were on him, dead in their sockets like a pair of marbles. "I understand you've got your methods, Dale. But a complaint to the selectmen . . . We don't want to get off on the wrong foot with this."

Unsettled by Stasiak's silence, Elliott quickly moved on to the upcoming trial of a car theft ring and evidence against a foreman in the department of public works who was under investigation for selling supplies out of the state barn. Elliott made repeated assaults on his beer, his will diminishing with each one.

"I think I might have evidence," Elliott said, choking back the bitter, malty taste that was rising up his throat, "that there is an illegal moneylending operation going on."

"Here? I doubt it a lot."

"What would you say if I told you I know of a man who borrowed a hundred and fifty dollars at ten percent interest a week—compounded—and got beat up when he couldn't make the payments?"

"I'd say he should borrow his money from a bank. What's this guy's name?"

"Russell Weeks."

"Who's got that one?"

"The locals. Barnstable police. Lieutenant Warren. Do you know him?"

Stasiak shook his head. "So what does Russell Weeks say?"

"Not much. His wife is doing most of the talking. She's a domestic over at the DuPont place in Oyster Harbors."

"DuPont?"

"Right. Of DuPont chemical. Some lawyer they keep on retainer called my office. Apparently, the woman has been with the DuPonts for more than twenty years, so there's a relationship there. I guess she went to Mrs. DuPont with her problem—or her husband's problem—and they took up her case."

"Have they given you any names?"

"Not yet. The husband didn't even want to report it at first. He's too scared to name names right now, but I think he'll come around."

Stasiak sipped his drink and looked around the room, whether lost in thought or boredom, Elliott couldn't tell.

"We probably ought to take a look at that one, too," Stasiak said.

"Thank you. I was going to ask you if you would."

When they had finished their business, Elliott said good-bye, sneaking a glance at the mostly full pilsner glass. Stasiak ordered another martini and watched the evening come down over the sleepy airfield across the road. He left the VFW and drove east, down Cape toward his house in Wellfleet. It was dark now, and fog was coming in off the ocean, invading the woods and the hunched forms of the little towns.

Stasiak thought about the parents of the missing boy—the Gilbrides. They had come up from Tennessee and were staying in a cottage in Truro. The boy disappeared around 10 A.M. Monday, July 9, three days ago. Stasiak had gone at the parents hard. He impounded their car, photographed them, and had his men showing their pictures at service stations, restaurants, and any other place where they might have been seen around the time of their son's disappearance. In the end, he had to let them go but he still wanted to have a go at the mother. She had been so delicate the first time around that the most general questions set her off to sobbing and tearing her clothes. He understood they had a lawyer on the way from Knoxville. Stasiak wanted to get to her before they arrived but he didn't think he was going to get the chance. If Elliott didn't have the stomach for this, Stasiak would have to straighten him out. He knew how far he could go before a confession could be considered coerced. And he would tell Yost he didn't give a shit about whatever niceties they operated by down here. He could tell him a few hair-raising tales that would change his thinking, like the discovery of the Derry child in a basement cistern in Worcester.

He pulled into a small gravel lot where there was an A&W stand. But for Stasiak and his Ford, the lot was deserted. The

A&W glowed orange and white, suffusing the fog around it with electric radiance so that it appeared enveloped in an aura. The kids who worked there had the sliding service windows open and he could hear them talking inside in dreamy, lackadaisical tones, like the voices of people who are just beginning to drift off to sleep.

Stasiak walked over to a phone booth and shut the door behind him. He deposited a dime and dialed.

"State police, Detective Heller."

"What's the situation, Heller?"

"The situation is good."

"Anything I need to know about?"

"No. Everything is quiet."

"We need to find Russell Weeks," Stasiak said.

"Russell Weeks."

"Yeah, Russell Weeks and Mrs. Weeks. Are you familiar?"

"Yes, sir."

"Get in touch with Stevie."

"When?"

"Now."

2

The rented house where Warren lived with his son was a simple two bedroom A-frame in a hastily constructed postwar development called General Patton Drive. Intended as affordable housing for returning GIs, the neighborhood had gradually become a refuge for struggling families and feckless couples. It wasn't like that in the beginning. Warren remembered the bright colored trim on the houses and the newly planted trees, emerald lawns, and crisp-edged walkways, the little neighborhood a declaration of promise and hope. He had been in the Pacific for three and a half years, and even now he remembered the joy and the expectation, even though things had gone so wrong. He recalled how fireflies made semaphore over the lawns on June evenings and the smell of pillowcases that had hung out all day in the fresh air. General Patton Drive was populated by young couples just starting their lives again after the war, but they had all gotten out and now he was here with Little Mike and he often felt like a huge explosion had gone off in his life, gutting it from the inside and leaving just the walls, a vacant hulk inside which he and the boy moved around as if in a dream.

He was grateful for Jane Myrna, who he had hired to watch Mike over the summer and who somehow made his situation seem less desperate. It was not only her presence but the wake it made, the things she left behind, the slight scent of the soap she used, the little art projects with Mike, the hair band that was now sitting in plain view on the table where Warren had put it so that she would see it when she came on Monday, an act that seemed to want scrutiny even as he assured himself of its innocence.

Warren stood in the kitchen at the back door in his T-shirt, smoking. He had ground beef patties sizzling in a frying pan on the burner for dinner, the grease spitting and coagulating on the counter. The house was so small that the living room was just a few steps away. Little Mike was on the floor in his Dr. Dentons, which he insisted on wearing even though he was too old for them. Warren watched him as he lay on his side, playing with his latest toy, the washing machine. He was alternately fascinated and dismayed by the things Mike came up with to amuse himself. They indicated an inventiveness that would never have the chance to develop and manic obsession. For the past few months, Mike had been fascinated by things involving laundry. He was underfoot when Warren did the wash, pestering his father to leave the lid open so he could sit on the kitchen counter and watch the water. He'd fashioned an agitator of sorts from the wheel of a broken Tonka truck affixed to the end of a long pencil, which he whirled around in a mason jar filled with soapy water and little strips of cloth. He occupied himself for hours this way.

Warren looked down at the half smoked Chesterfield in his fingers, and then out over the clothesline and the oil tank. In some ways, staying here seemed like gratuitous penance, not only because of the declining neighborhood but because of the things that had happened here. But the rent was low and while Warren didn't have much money, he was trying to put away enough in case there was some kind of operation or treatment that would help Mike. The doctors had told him that the boy's mental retardation was a permanent birth defect, but they were coming up with new things all the time—like that new polio vaccine—and you never knew.

A week earlier, Jane had told him about a place that was run by the Catholic Church and suggested that it might be a good alternative to public school. Warren knew about Nazareth Hall. He saw the kids sometimes when he drove past the building and he felt compelled to look away. Jane told him that there were professionals on the staff, psychiatrists and nuns who had done graduate work in developmental psychology and mental retardation. Some of them had clinical experience in hospitals. Warren told her he would think about it.

The sun was going down in a milky haze just over the tops of the trees. A sound caught the air, a screech or a cry, it was hard to tell. It could have been a cat or a woman or a child. It occurred to Warren how difficult it was to find respite from the prevailing strain and watchfulness that he felt. He had spent his entire life around men, and for most of it held authority over them, but he did not feel comfortable in their midst. Marvin Holland, the Barnstable chief of police, had suffered a heart attack a month earlier. As the next ranking officer, Warren was acting in his place. The chief was sixty-five, and with a history of health problems, it was likely he wouldn't be coming back to work. There was a good possibility that Warren would be appointed in his place, though there was the fact that he was not a native and had grown up in Boston. It made for the kind of provincial drama that people found irresistible. The subject of Marvin Holland and the chief's position triggered in him an unpleasant alertness. He was wary, grasping, and anxious, the way ambition always made him. He felt unmoored.

What did he want, he wondered. The future stirred like a big animal whose sleep has been disturbed. From the doorway where he stood, he looked into the darkness of the little house, where his police radio sat on the kitchen counter as silent as a stone.

The next day, Warren was in his office going over the call log from the midnight-to-eight shift when the two detectives came in. Ed Jenkins and Phil Dunleavy were tight-lipped and businesslike, and they offered no greeting as Jenkins took up a post leaning against a file cabinet and Dunleavy sat across the desk from Warren. Ed Jenkins was one of those small men whose comportment declares they are someone to be reckoned with. He had a bent nose, an aggressive set to his jaw, and he moved with the exaggerated confidence of someone whose stature makes him doubt himself. Jenkins could be foulmouthed and act the big city wise guy when he needed to, but in fact, Warren knew him to be modest and self-deprecating. Dunleavy was a big, rangy figure with narrow shoulders and a slight stoop in his posture. He had fine, receding blond hair going to white and an impassive face, a bit jowly and aristo-cratic-looking. Warren had worked with Jenkins and Dunleavy long enough to know they were skilled and dependable. At times, he felt overwhelmed running the department and he was grateful for their presence.

A boy had been missing in Truro for four days. It was out-side of Barnstable's jurisdiction but Warren had called the Truro chief of police that morning to see if there was any infor-mation he could work on from this end. The chief was unco-operative, as expected. He had the state police working with him, and didn't Warren have his own troubles over there?

There was a stack of pictures of the child on the desk. A broad grin, freckles on the bridge of his nose, a crew cut with a cowlick in the front. The picture had been given out to all the patrols to post in grocery stores, on street corners, and on phone booths. Warren asked the two detectives, "Have you guys got anything at all figured on this kid?"

"Just what we got on the teletype," said Dunleavy. "That's Truro's thing. We weren't even looking at it. Were we sup-posed to be looking at it?"

"No. I was thinking we could help out if they'd give us some information to work with. I talked to their chief this morning."

"And?"

"Nothing doing."

"He's a horse's ass," said Jenkins.

"If there's anything new, they're sitting on it," Dunleavy said. "The kid probably wandered into a pond somewhere."

"They got the staties working on it, don't they?" Jenkins said. "Let them figure it out. The Truro cops couldn't find the kid if he was standing out in front of the station."

Warren turned the pictures of the child facedown. "What else?"

"Russell Weeks," Dunleavy said.

The Weeks case had originated with a call from Elliott Yost, who had been contacted by an attorney for the DuPont family regarding the plight of a longtime domestic worker at their summer estate in Oyster Harbors.

Miriam Weeks, a favorite of Lois DuPont, had approached her employer with a tale of woe regarding her husband's financial indiscretions and a group of men from whom he'd borrowed a hundred and fifty dollars. Russell Weeks was taken from his home late one night, driven somewhere, and administered a severe beating. He packed a small bag and disappeared, leaving Mrs. Weeks and their nine-year-old daughter alone.

Warren got this information during a meeting in the district attorney's office with the Duponts' attorney, who was skeptical of the story. Dunleavy and Jenkins had driven the winding roads of Marstons Mills in search of Russell Weeks's haunts and acquaintances and turned up not much of anything. There were no reports of him consorting with outsiders or having borrowed one hundred and fifty dollars.

Interviewing Miriam Weeks had proven elusive so far. She consented to a meeting with Warren through the Duponts' attorney, but just the day before, Mrs. Weeks and her daughter also disappeared, leaving no word where they had gone.

Warren drove out to their home. It was faintly dilapidated, weathered and worn just a little past the point of rural charm. He tried the side door and found it unlocked, which was not unusual in that part of town. There was a smell of sour milk, or rancid garbage. He called out and got no answer. The icebox hummed in its corner, a dishrag was hung over the faucet in the sink.

An unfinished breakfast was on the kitchen table, the milk curdled in two bowls. A spoon lay on the floor, and a short distance away, near the cabinets, an overturned box of Maypo. He called out again but the house was silent.

Dunleavy reached across Warren's desk for the day's patrol roster. "Russell Weeks took a powder," he said. "Got tired of hearth and home and lit out for other pastures. If you ask me. Maybe he got into money trouble. *Maybe*. But either way, it's a loser."

"Well the district attorney is very interested in it," said Warren.

"I'm sure he is. It's not every day you get a call from the attorney for the DuPonts. Elliott wants to score some points."

"Weeks doesn't have any family on the Cape?" Warren asked.

"We've looked all over, lieutenant," Jenkins said. "There was talk of a brother in New Hampshire, but so far we haven't found him."

Warren flipped through the thin file on Russell Weeks. "What else have you guys got going?"

"I'm due in court at 11:30," Dunleavy said.

Jenkins said, "I'm going out to that place on Phinney's Lane that got broken into last night. Atomic Liquors."

Warren gathered up the photos of the missing boy. "When either of you gets a chance, swing out to Marstons Mills, see if you can find anything on the wife and daughter." He slid the photos in their direction. "And take these and put them out at the front desk."

3

In the morning, Father Boyle took his breviary and paced the veranda. There had been dreams the night before. From years of now disused practice, he said the first words of an act of contrition and then abandoned it. Prayer, or at least anything more strenuous than reciting the words, was a thirsty walk down an empty highway. He was bored by the featureless landscape of his soul, and sometimes the boredom threatened to turn into a kind of terror, like that experienced by the pioneers' wives, who found themselves under the monstrous sky of the open prairie, who were undone by surreal horizons, relentless winds, and the weight of the void.

Father Boyle suspected he had come to the end of a life of faith. He went through the world trying to do good, though he felt a charlatan and a fraud. He flipped through his breviary. He whistled into the chasm. When he looked at the sum of his years in religious life he was left with a sense of folly. He felt himself surrounded by old debris, the remnants of a discredited past among which he continued to live. He felt oppressed by the sentimental props and tired ritual. There seemed to be nothing left but a generally mystified feeling about the years when he burned from within. He could make no sense of that time and didn't miss it so much anymore.

Back in his room he had dozens of plant specimens lying about, drying on windowsills, laid in rows across the surface of his steamer trunk and tucked into the pages of the thick, musty botanical guides he had pilfered from the library. His hobby as an amateur naturalist gave him the happiness he supposed he should have gotten from his vocation. He dutifully visited the sick, aided the poor, and waited for God to appear at his bedside, but he would have preferred to be left alone with his sketchbooks and the mysteries of the woods and meadows.

Why he continued with it—the cancer patients, the mentally ill, saying the Mass—he did not know. Father Keenan said it was because he had faith still, while he himself suspected it was nothing more than the comfort of the familiar. He put a finger in his mouth, probed the vacant space once occupied by one of his incisors, and wondered if he was headed for a nervous breakdown.

Through the window screens he could hear the housekeeper's voice in desultory conversation with Father Keenan. He entered the kitchen, murmured, "Good morning," and went to the coffeepot.

"Brother Terrance," Father Keenan said. He sat at the table with the newspaper in front of him, dressed in the black short-sleeved shirt with a white collar. Mrs. Gonsalves, who had been leaning against the counter with her arms folded, went rummaging in the refrigerator. Father Keenan was a large man, what might have been described as beefy but now, at thirty-eight, was beginning to head toward portly. He had a great broad plain of a face and a full head of dark blond hair. His nose was flat, and in combination with a cleft lip that was so slight as to be barely noticeable, his face bore the impression of mild disfigurement. "What's the word?" he said, as Father Boyle took a place at the table.

"Not much, really. Going up the road in a bit."

Father Keenan paused for a moment. "Ah. Today is Thursday."

Nazareth Hall, a private school for retarded children, was about two hundred yards down South Street from the church. The priests referred to it as "up the road."

"Weren't you over with the Knights of Columbus last night?" Father Boyle asked as he took a place at the table.

"I was indeed."

"Jolly fellows, the knights."

"That they are." Father Keenan chuckled as he raised his coffee cup to his lips, trying to suppress a laugh. He and Father Boyle had once gotten into a discussion about the Knights of Columbus that took an uncharacteristically irreverent turn. Father Keenan was judicious in his wording but he'd been hinting at them being dolts and boozers. Father Boyle had goaded him on, trying to get him to cross the line. It was a running joke with them now.

Father Boyle finished his coffee, then stood and put his black blazer on. "Will you be in late tonight?" he asked Father Keenan.

"I think so."

"I might be up late drawing."

"I'll stop in and say hello."

Father Boyle went out the veranda door. Mrs. Gonsalves stopped what she was doing and leaned against the counter, looking at Father Keenan. He looked up briefly from the paper. "I would ask you not to start, Lucy."

"Yeah, you don't want me to start, but . . ."

"But what?"

"I don't know what you're gonna do with that one."

"Leave it alone."

"Hm. What time you gonna be home?"

"Ah, let me see." He took a small leather-bound appointment calendar out of his top pocket and opened it on the table. "I don't think I'll be back before seven."

"O.K. I'll leave the dinner out on the counter. Put it at 350 when you get home. About fifteen minutes."

"All right." He was still examining the pages in his booklet.

"Put the bread in tinfoil and put that in too, if you wanna have it warm."

"Mm-hm."

Mrs. Gonsalves sat across from him at the table. "He goes and I don't know even what he does."

"Father Boyle?"

"Yeah. Where does he go?"

"Well, right now, he's going over to Nazareth Hall."

"Yeah, but you know—"

"He goes to the hospital. I know that."

"O.K. When you go someplace. Say on the weekend. I know. You go to Cambridge to St. Anselm's. You go to your sister's in Fall River. I got a number I can call you at. With him, you never know. You don't know where he goes."

"Are you supposed to know?"

Mrs. Gonsalves's mouth fell partway open. "Well, what's the big secret? And yeah, sometimes I gotta get in touch with someone, you know? Someone come here and they need the priest. Like last week when that lady come in here with the drunk husband all crying and everything else, by God. Nobody here."

"I'll talk to him."

"I don't know what you're gonna do with that one."

Warren had forty-two patrol officers, ten cruisers, and two detectives to cover the seven villages and seventy-six square miles that made up the town of Barnstable. Before Marvin Holland had his heart attack, Warren's schedule had been unpredictable at best. Days were fairly dependable but he pulled plenty of evenings and the occasional midnight shift, depending on what was going on and what Marvin's concerns were. He was usually able to get someone in to stay with Mike, if not Jane Myrna, one of the women who lived in the neighborhood. Now that he was acting chief, he worked days only, but the job seemed larger than ever, sitting squarely in the middle of his life and displacing everything else. He kept a radio with him at all times, sat it on the round Formica table in the kitchen while he fixed dinner, washed the dishes, and did the laundry, then took it to his bedroom when he retired, placing it on the nightstand with the volume on low.

Warren had aspirations, half-formed plans that thrilled and embarrassed him simultaneously. He hoped to become an agent with the FBI. It was a cherished wish but it chafed his practical nature and caused some kind of disquiet to his natural modesty even while it gave him a zest for the future that was otherwise absent.

The application sat in the top drawer of his dresser with just the first lines filled in. He had no college but hoped his experience might make him a good candidate. Three and a half years with the state police; three years in the Pacific during the war; Australia, New Guinea, the Philippines; seven years with the Barnstable police.

Three months after the war broke out Warren was in Australia, the staging area for the Pacific theater and teeming with hundreds of thousands of servicemen waiting for orders, performing unglamorous work, or blowing off steam. The Army soon found itself faced with a situation for which it was ill-prepared.

Desperate for officers with police experience, they came personally for Warren one day at his tent in the fields outside Townsville. He was designated to take charge of a stockade where the Army had incarcerated five thousand from its own ranks: murderers, rapists, thieves, mental cases, and every other strain of malcontent imaginable. This was an aspect of the war that no one, it seemed, had considered, and it had, in fact, been Warren's stock in trade for most of his life: behavior outside the social contract, aberrant acts. When his unit finally loaded its equipment onto a train for Port Moresby to join the fighting, Warren was tamping down race fights in Townsville.

It was his great disappointment and the source of no small shame that he missed all the fighting in the Pacific. He had traveled farther from home than he'd ever dreamed he would and had seen things that years later would seem unimaginable, but in the end he shipped back to the States with a deep sense of failure.

It was dusk and the streetlights hadn't gone on yet. He was driving through West Barnstable on his way back from Cameron's boatyard, where he'd gone to see if they would have any work for him on the weekend. Warren drove slowly with one arm out the window, watching the roof peaks and TV antennae float across a sky that was like a broad swatch of flannel, light gray and shading toward charcoal by the minute. The postwar years gathered like a bad weather system on the horizon in his mind. It was a mood, generally, but it produced images, too: interiors of rooms, rumpled bedsheets, a dripping faucet, Little Mike in diapers. There was, briefly, the erotic *frisson* of Ava's thighs and how they had looked in profile as she bent to step into her panties, the graceful swell above the knee. The way the pines swayed when they'd prayed with the baby before the grotto at Our Lady of Victory. The anger, the frustration, the rage at Ava as she changed into something that disgusted and frightened him.

He approached a flashing red light where the road crossed a set of railroad tracks. The roadside was crowded with daylilies and crickets peeped in the descending dark. The radio came on and filled the car with the sound of shouting voices, and then went silent. He sat at the flashing light and looked down at the radio, waiting. Again, the speaker in the dashboard came alive, frantic, unintelligible sounds, obscured in a universe of static. He was about to speak when the dispatcher cut in.

"This is KCA374. Identify yourself."

Warren sat in the middle of the tracks, waiting for a response. People had turned their porch lights on and a sprinkle of stars was visible above the treetops.

"Forty-six Eel River Road! Forty-six Eel River Road!"

As soon as he heard the address, Warren stomped on the accelerator. Eel River Road wasn't far away. He flew down Old King's Highway for a half mile, then cut left into a road that passed through thick woods. There were few houses out this way. It was dark and mosquito-infested, dismal year-round.

Warren radioed dispatch that he was practically there and tossed the mike on the seat. He switched the searchlight on and pointed it through the trees. After repeated calls for the officer to identify himself, dispatch got a response. Warren heard the words "Easy three!" shouted over screaming in the background.

"Easy three," Warren said into the mike, "this is Easy seven. I'm out on the road right now."

"I see your light! You just went past us!"

Warren stopped and backed his unmarked up to the last dirt turnoff he'd passed and then nosed it into the woods. At the end of the track he found a nondescript shingled cottage with the lights ablaze inside, the cruiser parked out front. The place looked threatened with imminent consumption by the woods. Warren took a nightstick from under the front seat and walked across the yard. The door was ajar and he stepped inside. To his left, a summer hire whose name he could not remember was attempting to keep a middle-aged woman pinned to the wall with his forearm across her throat. He was a college kid, like most of what they called the "summer specials," and he looked scared. The woman, a tough-looking local with the pale, doughy look of heavy smoking and confinement indoors, rolled her eyes toward Warren when he entered. There was an iron on the floor a few inches from her reach, and while the rookie pressed her against the wall with one arm, his other was struggling to prevent her from grabbing it.

Chairs were toppled and the sofa was overturned and lying on its back. In the middle of the room stood a huge man, his belly hanging over rumpled trousers that stopped between his calves and his ankles. He was fair-haired and balding, with a great porcine face and massive forearms covered with dense russet fur. Blood was trickling in rivulets down his head and neck. He stood there gaping at Warren, swaying on his feet. "Hit the breeze, fucker," he said.

Warren saw movement in the kitchen and Don Petraglia, whose voice he had recognized from the original call, emerged from behind the stove. "Lieutenant!" he gasped, in what sounded like a combination of surprise, relief, and chagrin. "Lieutenant, he's crazy."

"Where is your weapon, Petraglia?"

"I still got it."

Warren glanced down at the young cop and the woman on the floor, thrashing and grunting, both of them running out of steam. He looked to see that the rookie's weapon was still in its holster, then swept the iron away toward the front door with his foot. "You have that under control, patrolman?"

"I think so." Sweat was pouring off his face.

"I don't want her coming up on my back."

"I think I got it, sir."

The big man's head was covered with knots and lacerated in a dozen places. He took two steps toward Warren. "I said hit . . . the . . . breeeeze, fucker! Get out of my house."

Petraglia said, "Lieutenant, we beat the hell out of him. He doesn't even feel it."

"Come on out here, Petraglia."

The fat man spat a bloody glob at Warren. He shuffled his feet and flexed his fingers and started huffing breath through his mouth. Petraglia froze.

"Petraglia, get the woman cuffed."

The policeman sidled out of the kitchen with his back to the wall, watching the man. His shirttail was out and all the buttons torn off his shirt. He was moving as if he were injured. "Watch him," he said. "He's nuts."

The man rushed Warren. The ceramic knickknacks on the windowsills clinked together as his bare feet pounded across the floor and shook the house. Warren timed the fat man's approach, one, two, three steps, and got into a slight crouch. When the man was about four feet away, Warren launched himself forward headfirst and drove the crown of his skull into the fat man's face. There was a sickening pop. Warren fell off to the side, collided with an end table, and found himself sitting on the floor, covered in the contents of an overturned ashtray. A sixteen-ounce can of Ballantine Ale was spinning across the floor spewing foam. He saw lights, a profusion of them like small detonations in his vision. He had trouble getting up and thought for a second he was about to lose consciousness. The man remained standing, looking down at him. A hot line of pain was beginning to grow in a steady throb across his scalp.

The wife was shrieking at the two policemen as they worked her arms behind her back. Her husband made his way unsteadily toward them. Warren got up, set himself, and went at the man again. He managed to hurl Warren off to the side, sending him crashing into a hi-fi set on the other side of the room. He scrambled to his feet as the man punched Petraglia twice in the face and wrenched his nightstick from him. Petraglia was down and inert. Warren leaped on the man's back. The man wheeled and tottered, flailing with the stick. The summer cop stood gawking at Petraglia on the floor. "Get the stick away from him!" Warren yelled. The kid rushed in and tried to disarm the man, but his movements were tentative and within seconds, the man had him pinned against the front of his own body with the stick against his throat, pulling the cop into himself with both hands, crushing his windpipe.

Warren got the crook of his left arm around the fat man's neck and squeezed with everything he had. Every muscle in his body was contracted to its limit and it was as if he were paralyzed in a seizure. While Warren held on, the man was ramming him against the wall repeatedly. The drywall gave and Warren was driven into the space between two studs. There was a pop, a shower of sparks, and the house went dark. Warren called Petraglia's name, now at the point of desperation. Their radios were crackling with the voices of the responding officers, voices that now betrayed fear as their calls for a location went unanswered. The entire four-to-midnight shift was coming.

Warren heard the stick drop on the floor. The man grabbed a fistful of Warren's hair. Warren was still squeezing but he was at the edge of fatigue. The grip on his hair slackened, then suddenly Warren felt a great release beneath him. He sank toward the floor and emerged out of the wall as the fat man's legs buckled and he went down, taking Warren with him. The man was lying facedown, making a snoring sound. The young officer was partially pinned beneath him. Warren quickly got a handcuff on one wrist but the man's body was too big to bring his other hand around. "We have to get this guy cuffed right now," Warren said.

The patrolman went into a fit of coughing.

"Right now," said Warren. "Before he comes to."

They linked two sets of cuffs together and got the man's hands restrained. Warren found Petraglia sitting up with his head hanging between his knees. "Shit," he croaked. "Sorry, lieutenant."

Cars were rolling up now, filling the house with their headlight beams and flashing red lights. Doors were slamming and there was a commotion of voices. They hog-tied the man with a section of rope from the trunk of one of the cruisers. He let out an occasional series of grunts and halfhearted invective. "Fuckers. Alla you fuckers. Hate you, you buncha fuckers." His wife was just a dark shape in one of the cruisers, sitting still now.

Warren saw the silhouette of a smallish man in civilian clothes moving among the others with a slight bounce to his gait. He recognized Detective Jenkins coming up the driveway toward him. "Everything all right, lieutenant?"

"Yes. Aren't you supposed to be off duty?"

"Me and Gladys were just over at the Neptune Lounge and I seen one of the radio cars go by."

"You didn't bring Gladys out here, did you?"

"No. I left her at the bar where she's happy."

Warren found Petraglia and his partner. "We're sending the husband over to the hospital," he said. "I want you two to go with him. See if they'll lock him in the mental unit until we know what his status is. Make sure he's restrained and no one gets hurt. Let me get a look at you guys." Warren examined their faces, necks, and hands with a flashlight. "I want you both to get looked at while you're there. Call me when you've done it. Don't put it off, Petraglia." Warren clicked off the light and joined a group of officers at the head of the driveway.

Petraglia lit a cigarette, then offered one to the summer special. "How was that for a fucking caper?"

The rookie shook his head and inhaled. His hands were shaking. They smoked in silence for a while. Jenkins joined them. Nearby, a patrolman named Welke was sorting through the contents of the fat man's wallet. Petraglia said, "How about the lieutenant?"

"Shit," said the summer special.

"I mean, yeah, he's got a stick up his ass," said Petraglia, "But he can be one serious son of a bitch to contend with."

"Man. I heard stories," said the summer special. "But I couldn't believe . . ."

They watched Warren talking with the other cops, who were gathered around him in a semicircle at the head of the driveway.

"I heard stories too," said Jenkins. "But I been there for a few of them. I don't care what they say about him. When you walk in on something like this"—he gestured with his cigarette toward the house—"or worse . . . That's the guy you want to see walking in the door." Welke spoke up from off to their left. "Look at this," he said. He was holding up a condom in its square foil packet. "Warren should have used one of these. Then he wouldn't have that kid on his hands."

Jenkins turned to him in the darkness. "Someone ought to bust you in your fucking mouth, Welke."

The officer tossed the packet down on the hood of the cruiser with the scattered contents of the fat man's wallet. "Would that be you, Jenkins?"

Suddenly, the paddy wagon lumbered up the dirt road, its headlights illuminating the bent, knobby trees and the scrubby underbrush, revealing the random details of the little clearing in which they stood, like some kind of subterranean grotto. One of the cops said, "I wouldn't live out here if you paid me."

Warren woke with a headache, his scalp tender to the touch. When he got to his office, he fumbled through the contents of his desk drawers in search of aspirin. Jenkins came in, closed the door, and sat down. "We got a call from Elliott Yost this morning. He's giving the Weeks case to the state police."

Warren stood. "*What?*"

"He wants the staties to take it over. He says he thinks they got the experience. They got that new guy, you know, Stasiak, and he was a pretty big deal up in Boston. But we aren't a bunch of amateurs down here, you know what I mean? And that's what burns my ass. I told him that, too."

"Don't hand over any files just yet."

"What are you going to do?"

"I'm going to see Elliott."

At the courthouse, Warren walked down the hallway to Elliott Yost's office beneath high vaulted ceilings. The floors shone with new wax and there was a long procession of gleaming dark wooden doors. The effect was ecclesiastical. Warren found the district attorney in his office.

Elliott led Warren into a conference room. Mounted on the wall were large framed photographs of President Eisenhower and Governor Furcolo. "Why did you take us off the Weeks case?" Warren said.

"Lieutenant Warren, it is not a reflection on you or the department. I simply chose to have it followed up by people whom I happen to believe have the most experience with this sort of thing. That's all."

"What is it you think we do down here?"

"Well, you don't handle missing persons cases every day."

"And the state police don't either. Not down here."

"Captain Stasiak has handled several. Not to mention his experience with the rackets."

Warren opened his mouth to speak, but Elliott cut him off. "It's got nothing to do with you personally, professionally, or any other way. It's a matter of using the best tools at my disposal. I have a job to do."

"It's a slap in the face, Elliott."

"I wish you didn't feel that way."

"It makes me look bad. It makes my department look bad."

"That wasn't my intention. I have a man at my disposal who has done this kind of thing, not once but several times. I'd be a fool not to use him. And forgive me for pointing this out, lieutenant, but it's not your department. Not yet."

Warren felt his temper rise instantly. "I'm acting chief, Yost. That means I'm chief right now, while you're taking my responsibilities away from me." He was almost shouting.

Elliott spoke back sharply. "I have discretion on how this thing gets handled."

"Well, maybe you forgot that I have a couple of experienced investigators and it's not the first missing persons case they've seen either."

"I'm not going to argue this with you."

"My men know the Cape and they know the locals."

"Then you'll be a valuable resource to the state police. I can let them know you'll be at their disposal. Let's not let our pride get in the way."

Warren looked at the district attorney. He was on the verge of saying something about personal ambition, about Elliott wanting to put on a good show for the DuPonts because they were rich and powerful and could lift his standing and his career. "I don't like this a bit, Elliott. I think it's wrong."

"Point taken."

On his way back to Hyannis, Warren drove beneath an overpass whose abutments were subsumed by honeysuckle and ailanthus and he experienced the futility that sometimes came over him and which made him feel defeated and panicked at the same time. He once responded to a suicide at a cut-rate beach cottage where a young woman had hanged herself and he often saw her in his mind, her head twisted off to the side at a grotesque angle and a surprised look on her blue face, as if this wasn't what she had expected at all. At moments like this, in the shadows beneath the overpass, he found himself gripping the steering wheel and shaking his head and wondering what could drive a person to do such a thing. But what troubled him just as much was the young woman's appearances in his vision—the types of things that prompted it. There was a correlation there, he suspected, if he took the time to trace it out.

When he got back to Hyannis, he closed himself in his office and paced. He spotted the list of names he'd taken down the day Jane Myrna brought Mike by. The father of one of the boys who'd abused his son was David Langella, a concrete contractor who had some kind of connection to the head selectman through marriage or something, so Warren had heard. He happened to know that Chief Holland had fixed a drunk driving arrest for Langella a few years ago. Langella had a reputation as a drinker and a brawler who was never held responsible for his behavior, whose antics were almost appreciated, Warren believed, as an expression of local color.

He looked at the phone, his anger rising. Warren picked up the receiver and called the clerk over at the Barnstable courthouse. He gave her Langella's name and asked for a records check. He noted with satisfaction that she was quiet for a moment and then asked him to repeat himself. Warren knew that there was a better than even chance that she would talk about his request and that word would get around. The clerk told him that it would take her some time—she was alone and handling the switchboard at the moment. He requested that she call back and leave the information with Sgt. Garrity at the desk, who he knew was even more likely to spread the gossip.

5

The girl lay on her back in a faded purple and lavender checked shirt and denim overalls. She was tomboyish, with short coarse hair, dirt beneath her nails, and long, slender limbs she hadn't yet grown into. With her soiled clothes and her smeared skin, the androgynous child looked like she'd climbed into the bathtub and fallen asleep after a long day of playing outside.

The porcelain was streaked with the blood of her mother, who had been dismembered in the tub before her. The air in the bathroom was moist and smelled of freshly opened shellfish. And there was, too, an indeterminate musky scent that could almost be taken as part of this world, but its evanescent quality kept it halfway in the realm of the imagined. Leaning against the wall at the foot of the tub was a man of about twenty-three, dressed in a butcher's smock and smoking a cigarette. He was looking down at the girl with a troubled expression. On the floor by his feet was a pair of bloody aqua-colored rubber gloves. An older man sat on the toilet across from him, also in a smock. Their bare arms were flecked with gore and bits of skin and tissue.

The older man took a long drag off his cigarette and, squinting through the smoke, watched his companion. He leaned over the tub with his cigarette held between thumb and forefinger and planted the lit end in the center of the girl's forehead.

"Jesus Christ, Steve."

Tendrils of smoke rose up and, for a few seconds, came dense and fast before dying out altogether. The skin blackened and shrank away, leaving a glistening crater around the cigarette end. Steve took his hand away and the cigarette stood straight up on its own. He sat back on the toilet. "Look at that," he said.

"Fuck."

"We're going to need more oilcloth."

The young man stood as if in a stupor, smeared from knees to elbows in varying shades of red, purple, and brown. "Is this about that guy who wouldn't pay?"

Steve swept his foot across a pile of tools, which spread with a clatter across the tiled floor. There were assorted knives, saws, and cleavers, a pair of metal snips and a set of bolt cutters. "It's connected, Bobby. There's a connection there, O.K.?" Steve picked out a pair of surgical scissors and handed them to the young man. "I'm going out to get the oilcloth. Cut the clothes off."

They took six bundles out of the apartment and down an outside stairway to a step van. Each was double lined with old bedsheets taken from the laundry room that occupied the first floor of the Starlight Cottages, an old resort from the 1920s that had closed down long ago.

They drove the step van to the dump on the outskirts of town. Branches scraped the sides of the vehicle as it entered the woods. The road ended in a clearing, where the smell of raw earth and garbage was overpowering. They each took a bundle and disappeared into the brush, heading in the direction of the dump. They made three trips and when they emerged sweating at the tree line with their final load, they saw that they were being observed by a row of seagulls, perched silently atop the mountain of trash and silhouetted against the misty sky.

A stout nun in a habit appeared on the other side of the screen door and looked out at Warren and Little Mike. "Come in," she said. They stepped into the front hallway. Boxes lined the walls on either side, full of toys and books. "You must be Mr. Warren."

"I am. This is my son, Mike."

"Come with me."

They walked down a corridor with classrooms on either side. They could hear children's voices, laughter, an adult trying to speak over the din. The nun led them to an office at the end and rapped twice on the doorjamb. "Mr. Warren is here," she said. She motioned for them to go inside. Seated behind a desk was a large, masculine-looking woman in heavy framed spectacles. She, too, wore a full habit, and though her overall appearance was formidable, her face was open and pleasant. "Hello," she called out. "Come in."

Warren took a chair, Mike clinging to him, attached to his knee.

"And this is Michael?" the nun asked.

"It's Mike. We call him Little Mike. It's because he was so small when he was born and there was another Mike in the neighborhood . . . Anyway."

The nun introduced herself as Sister John Frances and made small talk with Little Mike. "And how do you like school?" she asked, finally.

Warren said, "He's had . . ."

"Mike can answer, Mr. Warren." She cut him off without looking away from the boy. Little Mike evaded the question, fidgeting and murmuring. She turned back to Warren. "As you probably know, we work with handicapped children from kindergarten through eighth grade. We're operated by the Catholic Church but you don't have to be Catholic to bring your child here. We don't follow the same schedule as regular schools. We're in session year-round because the kids need the attention and the structure. We don't have grades, per se. Instead, we master certain skills and we have the children work their way up—if they can—to fourth-grade-level math, fifth grade, sixth, as far as we can get them. So instead of grades we have skill levels, and no time requirement to get there. We focus on the basics—reading, writing, arithmetic. But we also work on practical things: hygiene, getting dressed, buying things at the store. Everyday problem-solving. We get them as far along as we can so that by the time they're high school age, they can more or less function like other young people. Ultimately, we'd like them to have more options besides complete dependence on a caretaker or institutionalization."

The offhanded reference to such a possibility awoke in Warren both a sudden fear and a resolve. He would do everything in his power to ensure that Mike was never taken away from him or put in a home somewhere, but as he summoned this determination, he felt an inexorable tide rising around him: things for which he could never prepare, the possibility of Mike getting worse, of financial trouble, medical problems, his own death. He was no longer listening to Sister John Frances but imagining the dire days ahead somewhere, and when he refocused he heard her saying, "We have an arrangement with Children's Hospital in Boston where they send specialists down here to work with the kids, evaluate them and so on. They're engaged in long-term research and we've agreed to be part of it. The hospital offers medical care in return and has done a few surgeries—a couple of our kids who are crippled from polio and a hydrocephalic boy. They come down every other week. Sister Julia Weyland can tell you more about that. She's a licensed psychologist and did work with retarded children as part of her doctoral study at Boston College. Do you have Mike's medical records?"

"I do."

"We would need to see those and we would need to spend a little time with him, just us, without you present. Just to observe and to get to know him a little better."

Warren nodded.

"And Mrs. Warren?"

He paused just long enough to betray the difficulty of the subject. "She's no longer with us."

"She is deceased?"

"Yes." He recoiled at the lie, urged himself to take it back and explain, but the seconds were passing. He would make it right later, tell the truth and apologize.

When they were finished, Sister John Frances led them out a set of patio doors that gave on to the backyard. There, a group of older children were gathered around a large puddle that had formed in a shallow ravine at the edge of the woods. Kneeling among them was an elderly priest whose skin was uncommonly bronzed, as if he spent a lot of time outdoors. He appeared oblivious to the wet ground in which the knees of his formal black pants were embedded. One of the children said something that made him laugh and Warren noticed that one of his incisors was missing. He got the impression that the priest was acutely aware of his presence, that he was making an effort not to look in Warren's direction. Sister John Frances led Warren and Mike toward the group. "This is Father Boyle," she said. "He helps out with the children."

The priest glanced up at Warren for no longer than it took to make fleeting eye contact. He looked at Little Mike. "Who is this, then?"

"This is my son, Mike."

"And to what do we owe the pleasure of this young man's presence?"

"Mr. Warren is considering having him attend," said Sister John Frances.

"Ah," said Father Boyle and began speaking with Little Mike. He lacked the cloying earnestness people affected when they talked to the boy. He was direct and inquisitive, considering the boy's comments with an attentiveness that appeared neither false nor overbearing. Warren looked down at the mud stains on the priest's pants and the water on the tops of his shoes. Father Boyle said, "We've been watching these tadpoles for the last two weeks, Mike. Would you like to come see them?"

Mike accompanied him to the edge of the pool and joined the other children there. Father Boyle spoke to them, pointing at the surface of the water. A boy whose nails had been bitten to bloody nubs put his hand up to his mouth and the priest, without looking away from the water, gently caught the boy's hand, placed it by his side, and patted it. As Father Boyle talked about the life cycle of tadpoles, he produced a Life Saver from somewhere on his person and handed it to the boy.

Watching Father Boyle with the children, Sister John Frances seemed to have forgotten that Warren was there. Their conversation awkwardly suspended, he watched her face and could not determine what he saw there: Fondness, perhaps, he wasn't sure. She was an imposing woman, not given, Warren imagined, to easy sentiment.

Father Boyle accompanied the children across the lawn back toward the house. Mike followed, his eyes on the priest. It occurred to Warren that his son seldom encountered men who were kind to him. He watched the children swarm around the priest, who honored them with directness and took the time to be clever with them and seemed genuinely pleased to be in their presence. Even Warren, with the hardened aspect he had acquired over years of police work, was affected by it.

He held the door open for the children as they filed back into the house. "Let's go, kids," he said. "Reading with Sister James."

He paused a moment after the last one and squinted into the woods as if he might have seen something there. Both Warren and Sister John Frances looked in that direction, the nun shading her eyes against the morning sun in the treetops. When they turned to look back at the priest, he had gone into the house.

6

Warren sat in the quiet of his office with the notices and bulletins that he'd taped to the wall gently lifting off the plaster surface in the soft draft that passed through the open windows.

On his desk was a stack of town vehicle maintenance forms that the department mechanic had brought him. The rear wheel bearings on Easy twelve were making noise. The voltage regulator on nine was bad. Thirteen was leaking coolant. Six had a bad tie-rod end. Warren had told the men these things weren't hot rods. The rest of the paperwork was orders for parts and supplies.

Outside he could hear Garrity moving around at his desk in the hallway. Warren was aware that there was an element within the police department that did not like him. He didn't know exactly who they were but he had some ideas and he believed that Garrity was among them. Warren did not believe in fraternizing with the men. He had learned in the Army—the old Army—that it was the most effective way to run a military organization, which is what he considered the police department. There were some new ideas floating around post-Korea, a laxness and what he thought was an abdication of moral responsibility. Warren had tried to let his officers know that a certain kind of behavior was expected of them, not only on duty but in their private lives as well. He was aware that it had not been well received. He had been trying to find a way to let them know that if they did not hold together morally, as a group of men, then the profound responsibility they had accepted as police became something dangerous in their hands.

And Warren knew that this was just the sort of thing that isolated him from people. He believed it was the price of his position but sometimes he wondered if it had to be this way. People found him formal and distant. Ava teased him for it. It pained him to know he was viewed this way, but people depended on him to do what was right. He did not judge. He did not even judge Ava. Once again he found himself mired in the internal dilemma, sure that his attitude was correct while regretting the effect it had.

His parents' Catholicism had bordered on the fanatical. As a child, it had awed and comforted him. As a teenager, it made him feel uneasy. He had turned away from the Mass in the wake of Little Mike and Ava, but he was still deeply affected by the idea that there was a way to live in the world, and it was tied up with his father and after-death images of his father and the world his parents had occupied. In some part of himself, he was waiting for his father to come back and get him. He could see the old gentleman extending his hand out over the years and the disappointments that littered them like so much debris. Warren still believed in a world where things were right and whole and that he and Mike might live in it one day and his father would somehow be present. And when he thought of how his father would have embraced Little Mike and how he would have loved him not in spite of what he was but because of what he was, Warren was filled with a new grief and such a feeling of loss that he was paralyzed until he could work his way out of it again.

He heard Garrity open and close a drawer out at the sergeant's desk. Garrity was obsequious and servile in a way that seemed an intentional parody of servitude. He regretted the day that Jane Myrna brought Little Mike in after he'd wet his pants. Garrity had seen it and Warren suspected he would spread it around the department.

And now, as if summoned by thoughts of him, the sergeant came knocking on the office door, a light rap, rap, rap that was like a wisecrack in itself. Warren looked up and saw his face in the opening, his head slightly bowed in deference, his eyebrows up a little, like a butler in possession of household secrets. "Sir," he said.

Warren waited.

"We got a call from Kalmus Beach. There's a body in the reeds."

Warren grabbed his radio and stood up.

"It's a kid," the sergeant said.

Warren walked quickly down the corridor, trying to raise Ed Jenkins on the radio. He pushed the doors open and walked down the steps to the small lot at the side of the building.

Jenkins's voice came up as Warren was opening the door to his unmarked.

"Have you got a crowd there?" Warren asked.

"Not yet. We're keeping them off."

"This is a kid?"

"Affirmative. A boy. About seven, eight years old."

"Is the coroner there?"

"We've called him."

"Give me about five minutes."

Warren turned down Ocean Street, which was a long, straight run from the center of town to the water, ending at Kalmus Beach. He crossed Main Street and passed the Hyannis Theater, a large gable-roofed structure with a marquee advertising *The Amazing Colossal Man*, and below that, the names of the leads, Glenn Langan and Cathy Downs.

From the intersection with Main Street, the road began to run downhill. There were a few big ramshackle houses with hydrangeas and American flags flying. Then the docks appeared on the left. As Ocean Street approached Kalmus Beach, the land turned completely to marsh, and during low tide, the smell could be overpowering.

As Warren slowed, he looked to his left and saw a cluster of people on the far side of the parking lot where there was a wall of dense brown reeds. A local drunk named Bernard Suggs was standing some distance away from the crowd with Ed Jenkins.

Warren parked and walked over to Jenkins, who turned to Suggs and said, "Stay put, Bernard. Don't go anywhere." The detective went over to the edge of the reeds where a well-worn pathway began. Warren followed.

"We've got a dead kid," Jenkins said. "He's in there about thirty yards in. Looks like he's been strangled. Bernard here found him. He says he was coming in here with a bottle to drink and lay up for a while. And then he comes across this kid laying there."

Warren motioned to one of the patrolmen standing thirty feet away.

"The kid's been sexually molested, looks like," Jenkins said.

When the patrolman reached them, Warren said, "I want you to stay here with this Suggs fellow. Make sure he doesn't go anywhere."

"Yes, sir."

Warren walked past Jenkins and into the reeds. "All right," he said.

The reeds comprised an area of a few acres of a particular species of woody stalk that had expanded into an empire of dense growth. Reaching a height of ten feet and growing as closely as bamboo, they were a formidable mass. The reeds were irresistible to any child who encountered them, the well-established maze of footpaths that ran through them fantastic and foreboding. They doubled back on themselves, split into twos and threes at mysterious junctions, and opened into unexpected clearings where there were sometimes signs of a campfire or a clandestine gathering of some kind. Beer cans and liquor bottles were strewn throughout.

Warren walked in front of Jenkins, their feet making soft, crushing sounds on the ground. The light within the reeds was like that of a greenhouse, silvery and lunar, giving no indication of weather or time of day. "It's up ahead, where the trail heads off to the right," Jenkins said. They came out in a clearing about twelve feet across. A small boy lay there on his back, his arms flung out to the sides. He was naked except for a pair of swim trunks around one ankle and his legs were spread apart in a diamond shape, the soles of the feet nearly touching, the knees far apart. Warren stopped a good distance from the body and looked. Two paths entered the clearing from the opposite side.

"Who's been in here so far?" he asked.

"Me, Bernard, and couple of lifeguards."

"Anybody touch the body?"

"I did, to check the temperature. One of the lifeguards checked for a pulse."

"They didn't move him?"

"They tell me no."

"And he's confirmed DOA, right?" Warren still hadn't taken his eyes off the boy.

"He's dead, lieutenant."

Warren walked over to the body and stood by the feet. The scrotum and the flesh above his genitals had been torn and stood up in several small jagged flaps. Insects were circling above his hairless skin, settling on the little wounds. The clearing was very quiet.

Jenkins said, "He's got those superficial punctures in the genital area, which . . . I don't know what they are."

Warren knelt and leaned over the body. He was aware of his refusal to look at the face. The wounds in the scrotum and pubis looked like bite marks in places and he didn't know whether it was modesty or disbelief that kept him from saying it. He crouched back on his heels and looked the rest of the body over. Someone had grabbed the boy's face forcefully, the neck and wrists, too.

"No evidence on the ground?"

"None that I've seen yet. Everything is just like we found it."

Warren stood up. "Shit." Jenkins looked taken aback by the expletive. "Suggs says he just came in here to drink and stumbled on this?"

"That's right."

"And what do you think?"

"I don't make Bernard for a killer of little boys."

"But you never know."

"Right."

"I want to get a blood sample from him."

Jenkins said, "I don't like to bring this up, lieutenant, but before we spend any time investigating this, we might want to call Elliott Yost. He's probably going to want to give it to the state police."

"We're first responders. We got the call. If he wants the state to take it over . . ." He didn't finish the sentence. "We should give it everything. Then they'll have something to work with when they do take it."

"He'd probably want them here now to do the crime scene."

"Well, they're not here now."

A patrolman stationed out in the parking lot radioed that Detective Dunleavy and the coroner had arrived. Soon, Warren and Jenkins heard them making their way through the reeds. Jenkins said, "I'm going to make sure they can find us."

Jenkins went back up the path. Warren heard voices from out of the reeds as Jenkins met the others and they exchanged information. A minute later, Dunleavy emerged into the clearing, followed by a short, weathered man in his late fifties who wore a white short-sleeved shirt with a tie and a straw fedora.

He carried a bulky black case and had a camera hung around his neck. Dunleavy said little. He stood next to Warren for a moment, looking at the body, then walked around it in a circle, staying close to the wall of reeds that surrounded the clearing, his eyes scanning the ground. Jack Dowd, the coroner, put his case down and wound his camera. Dunleavy circled back around to Warren's side. "Any reports of a missing person?" he asked. "Because this isn't the Gilbride kid."

"Not so far."

The coroner began snapping pictures.

Dunleavy said, "This is bad. This is a bad one."

"What do you make of those cuts?"

"Bites. See that little arc by the left part of the groin? Little dotted lines. Those are teeth marks. They're turning purple now. You should be able to see them real clear in another hour or so."

Dowd knelt down and shot close-ups of the injuries to the boy's genital area. When he was finished he laid his camera on the ground and opened his case. He took out a long, slender needlelike device. Warren knew he was about to push it deep into the boy's midsection so he could read the core body temperature and determine the time of death. Warren did not want to see it. He went back out through the path and when he came out at the edge of the parking lot, there were many more people gathered than before. Ed Jenkins had Bernard Suggs backed up against one of the cruisers, asking him questions. Warren walked over and heard Suggs saying, "I didn't do it, man. I didn't do it. I had nothing to do with this."

"So what were you doing in there, again?"

"I was goin' in there to drink." He pulled a pint of Muscatel out of his pants pocket and showed it to the policeman. "I was just goin' in there to drink, Officer Warren, that's it. Just drink and sleep. That's what I do."

"Put the bottle on the car," Jenkins said. "Turn around and put your hands there on the hood." He started going through

Suggs's pockets. For a moment the man looked like he was about to cry.

"You don't think I did it, do you?"

"Not right now I don't."

Suggs seemed relieved for a moment, and then appeared to be considering the answer further. "But you might think I did it later?"

Jenkins made no response.

"Man, I go out to the airport and sleep, you know that, right? I go out to the airport and get drunk, lay in the woods. I go out behind Buckler's Salvage, I lay up off Mary Dunn Road with those boys up there sometimes, but I *never* . . ."

"Shut up, Bernard."

"I'm just tellin' ya . . ."

"You're all right for now."

"Whoever did that is going to the gas chamber, right?"

"Whoever did that is the reason they made the gas chamber in the first place."

Jenkins finished searching Suggs's pockets and allowed him to turn around. "Let me see your hands."

Suggs reluctantly held them up, long, knobby fingers, weathered, with black dirt worked deep into the cracks in the skin. Jenkins stepped up to look. There were no abrasions or broken nails or anything to suggest he'd been in a struggle. Warren opened the rear door to his cruiser. "Get in. We're going to take a blood sample from you."

Suggs sank slowly into the backseat and drew his feet in after him. Warren turned to Jenkins. "Somebody took that kid into the reeds two or three hours ago. Someone had to have seen him."

"Let's hope."

"I want a check on all known perverts. Check our own list and anything we can get from the state police."

7

The boy was nine-year-old Stanley Lefgren, who lived a half mile from the beach. Warren spent a grueling hour with the family after the discovery of the body. The mother was unable to speak. She remained enclosed in a bedroom with the boy's three siblings. Periodic screams reached Warren where he sat on the porch with the father, who spoke through copious tears as if drugged.

When Warren returned from the Lefgrens', he found a chaotic scene at the police station. The eight-to-four shift had been called in off the street for briefing and reporters loitered on the steps outside. Dunleavy had gone to the morgue to examine the body with the coroner. The hyoid bones in the boy's throat were fractured and he had petechial hemorrhaging in the eyes, confirming strangulation as the cause of death. Officers were checking the whereabouts of a half dozen known local sex offenders and had corroborated alibis for half of them. The records and identification division of the Massachusetts state police was sending down a list of known deviants along with last known addresses.

Three men—one of them quite elderly—were standing in the corridor, each with his back against the wall and each a good ten paces away from the others. They either stared at the floor or gazed at the wall opposite them, but they did not acknowledge one another.

Warren caught Dunleavy coming out of his office. "Who are these guys?" he said. Dunleavy motioned for the lieutenant to accompany him further down the corridor, out of earshot. They stopped by Warren's office door. Dunleavy took a notepad out of his jacket pocket and consulted its pages. "James Frawley. That's the large individual farthest away from us who looks like he's been living outside. Some kids saw him hanging around the pond behind the Hyannis elementary school. They said he was trying to talk to them and they came home and told their parents. One of the mothers called. Frawley's a transient. No job. Stays at a shelter run by the Salvation Army. We've confirmed that with them. He's got a state unemployment card with a name on it but no other ID.

"Edgar Cleve. The guy in the middle. We got a call from someone on Daisy Bluffs Road who said he was wandering around the neighborhood over there. That's not far from the beach. There's a lot of young families there, and lots of kids, too. Anyway, he says he's a courier for a medical lab. I've got Garrity checking on it. The guy says he was there to pick up some specimens or something and it was going to take some time for them to get everything together so he walked over to check on this place he's interested in renting.

"The old guy is Jasper Matsov. One of our patrolmen spotted him sitting in his car in the picnic area at Veterans Beach. He's retired and lives in Falmouth but that's all we know."

Warren glanced at Dunleavy's notes and pointed at Frawley's name. "Bring him in here."

Dunleavy called the man and he left his position by the wall and approached them, scratching the back of his neck. "Go inside and sit down," Dunleavy said, and opened the door to Warren's office. They questioned Frawley, who, while timid, managed nonetheless to emanate a bitter resentment. "What were you doing down at the pond?" Warren asked. "By the elementary school?"

"I was fishing." He moved his head in Dunleavy's direction. "They seen my pole and my bucket."

Warren looked at Dunleavy, who gave a slight nod.

"Why were you trying to talk to the kids?"

"They were just there. All's I did was say hello, that's all."

Frawley claimed he was nowhere near Kalmus Beach, in fact had never been there at all. He spent his time either at the shelter, trying to find work, or looking for food. The conversation was circular, their attempts at exposing incriminating facts about James Frawley thwarted by his readiness to admit them, though the facts—drinking, vagrancy, theft, nonpayment of child support—were not what they were after. His account of his activities and whereabouts described the same dire routine every time they tried to catch him out.

Dunleavy held Frawley's unemployment card in his fingertips and watched him silently. "Is that your real name? James Frawley?"

"Yes, it's my real name."

Dunleavy's eyes went back to the card, then back to Frawley. Warren knew the detective was getting ready to go to work and got up to leave him alone. As he closed the door behind him, he heard the detective say, "Come on. What's your real name?"

Warren opened the door to the office that Jenkins and Dunleavy shared. Jenkins was questioning Edgar Cleve. He was tall and gangly, with large hands like paddles that he held flat on his knees as if they were instruments with which he was unfamiliar. He had big doe-like eyes and high cheekbones. His oversized front teeth and their bony substructure stood out on his face like a separate feature, giving him a slightly simian appearance. It was no wonder, Warren thought, that someone reported him. Jenkins was saying, "Have you ever been arrested before?"

"Mm—no."

"What were you doing on Daisy Bluffs Road?" Warren asked.

"I already told him," Cleve said, motioning to Jenkins. "I was picking up from the oncologists and I was waiting for some

tissue samples. They said it was going to be another twenty minutes so I walked over to look at this place that's for rent."

Jenkins said, "Why didn't you just drive over there?"

"It's real close by the lab. Besides, I'm in the car all day."

Jenkins handed Cleve's driver's license to Warren. "How
long have you been a resident of the state of Massachusetts?"
the detective asked.

"Too long, apparently."

"What's that supposed to mean?"

Cleve lifted one of his big hands in an awkward, waving
motion. "My living situation. It's a problem." He looked at the
detective and then over at Warren as if he expected them to
indulge him in a conversation about his domestic arrangement.
"Anyway. That's why I was over there looking at the rental."

Garrity poked his head in the door and glanced from Jenkins
to Warren. Warren came outside. "I just spoke with Bondurant
Labs," the sergeant said. "They say he works for them and that
the oncology office is on his route."

Down the hall, Warren's office door opened, and James
Frawley came out, followed by Dunleavy. The detective
joined Warren and Garrity. "Frawley's got a story and he's
sticking to it."

"Keep an eye on him," said Warren. "Go down to the
Salvation Army and see what they can tell you about him. Search
the registry of motor vehicle records, corrections, social services,
everything."

"Jenkins talking to the other guy, Cleve?" Dunleavy asked.

"Yes."

"How's he look?"

"About the same as your guy."

Dunleavy said, "You get any hits on any of them yet,
Garrity?"

"Not yet. But it turns out we know Matsov. He's an old
queer from way back."

"What was he doing down at Veterans Beach?" asked Warren.

"He's not saying. But we arrested him a few years ago for lewd conduct over at Hathaway's Pond."

Warren glanced over his shoulder at Matsov. "Tell him to stay the hell away from the beaches. I want fingerprints from all three of them. Photographs, too."

Garrity left them and returned to his desk.

"The beaches are public property," the old man said as he passed.

"Not for you, they're not," the sergeant replied. "Come over here and get your picture taken."

At 7 P.M., Warren and the detectives were still at the station, bleary-eyed, trying to figure out what else they could do. The shifts had changed long ago, and the busy radio traffic, the incessant squelching of keyed handsets, the fuzzy voices delivering clipped messages, the urgent electric conversation that would go on all night until dawn came and the town quieted, reached them from the dispatch room up the hall.

The door opened and the desk sergeant stuck his head in. "Lieutenant? The district attorney's on the phone."

"That's it," said Jenkins. "Pick up your marbles and go home."

"I'll take it in my office," Warren said. This, he supposed, was the call Elliott Yost had put off until the end of the day, the one where he would relieve them of the investigation.

Warren heard Elliott's fussy voice come through the telephone, touching off a rush of anger and resentment. "I heard about the Lefgren boy this afternoon," the prosecutor said. "I would have gotten in touch sooner, but today they found the Gilbride child. He was in a pond in Truro."

"Did he drown?"

"No. He was killed. At least that's the opinion pending an

autopsy, but the medical examiner down there is pretty certain. His arms were bound behind him, so that rules out an accident. Where do things stand over there?"

Warren gave him a rundown of what they had done so far. At the end, he said, "We have notes, names, and addresses for everyone we've interviewed. It will save the state police a lot of work." He tried to keep the bitterness out of his voice.

"That's the thing, lieutenant. Now we've got two murdered kids. I've spoken with Captain Stasiak. The state police are sending two detectives down from Boston for the Gilbride case, but that's all they can send. They just don't have the manpower to spare right now. I want you to continue what you're doing for the moment. I heard the Lefgren boy was sexually molested. Is that true?"

"It is."

"There's a possibility the Gilbride boy was as well. If they're connected, we've got a problem. What I mean is, if we've got some kind of lunatic . . . If the two killings are connected, we're going to have to work it as one case."

"And you'll want us out."

"No. You stay with Lefgren but I'll want you working with the state police. They'll be the lead agency on this. They'll run the wider investigation if it becomes one."

"I'm willing to do that, Elliott, as long as it's reciprocal. Will they work with us?"

"I'll see to it."

Warren was skeptical. He had never found the state police very cooperative in high-profile cases. The new man in Yarmouth, Stasiak, was an unknown.

"Why do they think the Gilbride boy was molested?" he asked.

"His trousers were missing. They could have come off in the water, I suppose, but the way his arms were tied, plus the trousers . . . I don't know. It's speculation right now. What I'd

like you to do is call Stasiak tomorrow, if not sooner, and put
your heads together on this. See if you can determine any connection between the two."

Warren returned to Dunleavy and Jenkins. "They found the
Gilbride kid."

The men looked up at him, said nothing, waiting.

"It looks like a homicide. The coroner thinks it's also a sexual assault."

"Where was he?" Dunleavy asked.

"In a pond in Truro."

"They have a cause of death?"

"No. The autopsy's pending." Warren told them about the
boy's arms being bound and the missing pants.

"Are we off the case?" Jenkins asked.

Warren sat down. "No. We're still on it. If it turns out the
two are connected, the state will take the lead with us in a sup-
porting role."

"This is according to Elliott?" Jenkins asked, surprised.

"Right. He says the state police are sending two detectives
down from up above to deal with Gilbride, but that's all they
can do for the time being. We stay with Lefgren."

"Well I, for one, am not holding my fucking breath," said
Jenkins. "Excuse my French."

Dunleavy said, "Are we meeting with them?"

"Tomorrow. I'm going to call this Stasiak and see what they
have so far. If either of you wind up talking to the press, don't
divulge anything about sexual assault. I'm sure they know
about it but let's keep the details to ourselves. Don't mention
anything about bite marks. That's stuff we want to keep real
close. What time is the autopsy tomorrow?"

"Ten-thirty," said Dunleavy.

"I'm driving over to the state police barracks and I want
one of you with me."

Father Boyle stepped into the foyer of Nazareth Hall. There was a cacophony of voices coming from further in the house somewhere. At the far end of the corridor he saw Sister Julia Weyland walk quickly through and, spotting him, arrest her motion. "Father!" She was young and gangly, with her sleeves rolled up and protruding veins showing in her hands and wrists. She strode toward him like a boy athlete, like a farmhand. "You're going to do catechism?"

"Yes. Whatever you'd like."

"How are you?"

"I'm fine, Sister. Thank you."

"Come this way. The kids are in the yellow room."

He could hear wailing. "Who's that?" he asked.

"Perry Boggs. He's having a terrible time."

They walked down the hallway off of which were a series of classrooms. Crude drawings and attempts at individual letters in cursive form were tacked to a strip of cork that ran along the wall, hanging like sad pennants, declarations of existence more than achievement, banners in a pageant of irretrievable causes. In one of the rooms, a man in a suit was speaking into a Dictaphone. A nun leaned against a nearby desk, jotting in a manila folder. She smiled and waved at Father Boyle as he passed. The man said, ". . . with stereotypic movement disorder and emotional lability."

Up ahead, a pair of nuns was struggling with a boy. There were droplets of blood on the floor and three crumpled tissues. One of the nuns had a smear of blood on her cheek. "Perry, stop. Perry, stop. Perry, stop," she said.

Perry Boggs's screaming was agonized and terrified. Sister John Frances, who was red-faced from the struggle, said, "Let's get him into the lounge." They formed a scrum and shoved their way into a room the nuns used as their personal area. Father Boyle closed the door behind them. He knew from his experiences with Perry that the boy didn't like to be crowded. Now, with four people holding on to his limbs, he was panicking.

Sister John Frances said, "Everybody at once, let go and back away from him." They released Perry's limbs and stepped back. Standing free, he shrieked repeatedly, his eyes closed tightly, his hands convulsed and rigid by his sides. The nuns' eyes were going back and forth between Perry and Sister John Frances. Father Boyle watched them. "What do we do?" asked Sister Julia. "Leave him be?"

"One of us should stay with him," said Sister John Frances. She flexed her meaty fingers and examined a scratch on her hand. "The rest of us should leave."

"I'll stay," said Father Boyle. He knew that this was what was expected of him.

"Thank you, Father," Sister John Frances said. "I'll check back in ten minutes. I have to call his mother."

Perry's methods of self-harm waxed and waned. The latest was tearing at his flesh with his fingernails until he bled. Father Boyle had sat with Perry before while he unwound from tantrums. He had struggled with him as well. The boy was strong for a thirteen-year-old. He didn't speak, was secretive and distrustful, and didn't engender tenderness like the smaller children did.

Father Boyle took a seat on the couch. "Perry. Will you sit down with me?" The shrieking had devolved into a soft moaning and tears flowed down his cheeks. Perry was beginning his descent into the semi-catatonic state that always came after his rages. He shuffled stiffly to the couch and bent at the waist and lowered himself.

Perry Boggs, Father Boyle reflected, might soon be introduced to the world of restraints, locked rooms, and heavy sedatives. The boy's glazed, faraway look seemed to say that he knew it too, and that no god or medicine or good intention was going to stand before it.

Father Boyle slowly put a hand forward and touched Perry's arm. "Why, Perry?" he whispered. "Why, why, why do you hurt yourself? I don't want to see you hurt." Father Boyle knew the boy was unreachable. Uttering the words was just a habit formed by a lifetime of prayer. He lofted them into the air because it seemed appropriate they be put there, perhaps to be received somehow, perhaps to simply hang among the molecules. He didn't even know if what he did was prayer. It was more an offering, an appeal, a general expression of this moment, now, with this doomed thirteen-year-old who was staring down a hellish future in institutions. Father Boyle looked at him and felt a tightness in his throat. Someone had dressed him in checked trousers and oxfords for God's sake.

When one of the nuns came in and said that Perry's mother had come to collect him, Father Boyle went across the hall to the classroom where the children were waiting for what was called his catechism class. He told stories from the Bible in fairytale form, using a large picture book with pages made of thick cardboard, and gave primers on basic Catholic doctrine because this was what the nuns wanted. But what he really tried to do was provide whatever it was they seemed to need most at the moment, a challenge on the best of days. If they were fearful, he calmed them. If they were bored, he amused them. If they were playful, he indulged them. If he was being observed by the nuns, he framed whatever he was doing in such a way that it could plausibly be interpreted as religious education.

Sister Julia had the children sitting patiently at their desks when he entered. She was standing off to the side like an officer presenting a regiment for review. There were children with oversized heads, some with braces on their legs, some with features that looked like they'd been hurried to the finish, smeared while the flesh was still soft. Two were in wheelchairs, their heads lolling, their hands like claws. The Down's children with their owlish expressions. The secret in their faces, the hint of an otherworldly pleasure no one could know. Heavy-lidded toddlers whose jaws hung open, as if they'd never shaken off the sleep of the womb.

He looked out at them and knew immediately that what had happened with Perry Boggs had upset them. They were very still and wide-eyed. Father Boyle said to them, "My friends."

"Children," Sister Julia said, and they rose up in unison. This was their moment, the part they liked the most, when they called out his name and welcomed him into their midst. It made him feel exposed and shabby. It undid him every time. And they called out in distorted voices, slurred and nasal, a compromised singsong of neurological damage: *"Good morning, Father Boyle!"*

8

Warren and Dunleavy got into an unmarked and headed out to Yarmouth to meet Stasiak. The state police barracks was a strictly functional redbrick building composed of a central administrative block with a dormitory wing on either side. Sprinklers were running on the front lawn, where there was a flagpole flying both the American flag and a flag bearing the seal of the state of Massachusetts.

At the front desk, they were met by a sergeant who asked to see their credentials and then led them to Stasiak's office. Stasiak was seated at his desk, waiting. Warren and Dunleavy introduced themselves. The walls were crowded with framed photographs and newspaper and magazine articles. Headlines from the front pages of the *Globe*, the *Herald*, and the *New York Times* announced, "North End Raid Uncovers Hub Mob Link"; "Suffolk DA Delivers Multi-Count Indictment on Boston Syndicate Figures"; "Fed-State Task Force Exposes Attanasio Empire." In photographs, Warren saw someone who looked like Stasiak standing with Senator and Jacqueline Kennedy. There were group photographs with men in state police uniform and with others in civilian clothes who had the look of federal agents—camera shy, reluctant to smile, frozen in the lens in the midst of an unwanted moment of frivolity.

Without offering a greeting, Stasiak said, "What can you tell me about the Lefgren boy?"

Warren said, "We know he was strangled. You'll see in the photographs what look like bite marks in his genital area."

Dunleavy handed the photos over the desk.

Warren described the course of the investigation so far while Stasiak looked quickly through the pictures without expression. He cut Warren off mid-sentence.

"Besides his shorts, was there any physical evidence?"

"Our technicians used a vacuum to see if they could draw any fibers or other material off the boy's skin. We're waiting for an analysis to see what they picked up."

It looked as if a grin were starting to form on Stasiak's face.

"We took a blood sample from the vagrant who found the body."

"Do you have any biological material to compare it to? Material that does not belong to the boy."

Warren looked at him, surprised by the tone of the question, but Stasiak had his head down, writing. "None at this point."

Stasiak questioned them at length about the crime scene, about the Lefgren family, the neighborhood, about lists and information from the work they'd already done.

"What do you know about the Gilbride case?" Dunleavy asked.

Stasiak let out a sigh, as though he were tired of discussing it. "Well, what do you want to know? Badly decomposed body in the water . . . ah . . . I don't know. Cause of death unknown."

Dunleavy and Warren waited. Stasiak stacked the photographs and put them back in the envelope. He looked up at them and said, "That's about it. We're working on it. We'll stay in touch."

"What about the boy's arms being tied behind his back?" said Warren. "Have you spoken with Elliott Yost?"

"Elliott. Yes, indeed. I have spoken with him."

"Elliott and I had a conversation yesterday in which he told me, among other things, that your department and mine are to cooperate. He said specifically that he wanted us to work together to see if there is a connection between the two cases."

"That's a sensible idea. He has lots of sensible ideas, Elliott."

"Elliott told me more about your case than you have so far, captain."

"You're accusing me of being uncooperative?"

"You don't seem too eager to share information with us."

Stasiak rolled his chair back and looked out the window. "Let's see. The boy's family is from Tennessee. They were vacationing here. He wandered off. We find him eight days later in a pond."

"Which one?"

"I don't know. I'll have to get the name for you. And yes, his arms were tied behind his back. I left that out. My apologies."

"How were they tied?" Dunleavy had his pen and notebook out.

"What do you mean, how?"

"With what? What did they use?"

Stasiak rubbed one of his eyelids with an index finger. "With his shirt."

"We'd like to see photos," Dunleavy said.

"Right. I'll get you photos."

"Crime scene, morgue, whatever you have. Do you have interview notes?"

"Not really. We only found the body yesterday."

Warren said, "But you've been investigating the disappearance for a week."

"Let me see what I can find. So, is that it?"

"No," said Warren. "That's not it. We're supposed to be working together on this. But you obviously have no intention of doing so."

Stasiak wheeled back to his desk and put his hands on its surface. He spoke as if finished with diplomatic conversation. "We don't know a goddamn thing about this right now. The kid was in the water. Arms tied. Obviously, that didn't happen by accident, so yeah. Homicide. We interviewed the parents and we don't believe they had anything to do with it. Was he molested? We'll probably never know, since the soft tissue is falling off like he's just spent eight days in a crock pot. That's it. That's all we have. You people have to let us get up to speed and take a fucking breath and you can come back at us later."

Dunleavy and Warren were staring at him from the other side of the desk.

"You can have these back," Stasiak said, sliding the photographs toward them.

"You'll get us your interview notes?" Warren asked.

"When I can get something together, yes. I'll get them to you."

"And pictures."

"Right. Pictures. Is there anything else, gentlemen? Because I have one hell of a lot of work to get done."

Warren said, "I take it you have the photographs here."

Stasiak reached down and opened a desk drawer. He took out a stack of photographs in an opaque envelope and handed them to Dunleavy.

"They can't leave the premises."

"What?" said Dunleavy.

Stasiak repeated the words, a little louder this time.

"Well, it would be helpful if we could take them back and study them."

Stasiak sat there with his arms folded. "I have a meeting with my detectives in ten minutes," he said. "Look all you want, but the pictures stay here."

Warren looked off to the side in exasperation, then turned back and faced Stasiak. When he spoke, there was an edge to his voice, a hard, accusatory quality that transformed the meeting into the confrontation it had been threatening to become. "Do you have any intention whatsoever of assisting us?"

"What did I just tell you?"

Warren shot out of his chair. Dunleavy stood up to intervene. "Gentlemen," he said. "Let's cool down."

"I told you," Stasiak said in slow, deliberate tones, "that once we have a grip on what we've got, we'll be in touch with you. You're out of line, Warren."

Dunleavy glanced at his lieutenant. His face was red and his eyes were wide, a bad sign. He had seldom seen Warren this angry but the occasions when he did were memorable. It was unsettling, the way this man, who was so straight and buttoned-up all the time, could suddenly become uncontrollable. He knew Warren wouldn't listen to anyone if he got to a certain point. He recalled a few incidents where Warren felt he had been undermined by fellow officers, by court officials, by the town. Dunleavy remembered him pacing up and down the corridor of the police station, shouting. The look he'd had on his face was the same one he had right now, glaring at Stasiak.

Dunleavy tossed the Gilbride photographs on the desk. "We'll get copies from Jack Dowd. Let's go, lieutenant." Warren turned away and walked to the door. Stasiak stood on his side of the desk, staring after them.

Outside, Dunleavy said, "He's not our friend. In case you hadn't noticed. He's not going to give us anything and having Elliott mediate isn't going to make it any different because he can always lie his way around concealing information. When the big case breaks and all the glory comes raining down on them, no one will remember they were pricks and they didn't share."

When they got back to the police station, Jenkins was pacing the parking lot, waiting for them. Before they were out of the car, he was heading toward them, tossing his cigarette off to his left. "Wait till you hear this," he said.

"Why aren't you at the autopsy for the Lefgren kid?" said Warren.

"Because I missed it, that's why. It was done at four o'clock this morning. The state police got Jack Dowd out of bed and made him come over to the hospital. They said it was an emergency. They didn't tell anyone, they didn't say shit. They just went in there and did it."

"They did the autopsy?" Warren murmured.

"Yeah. Four o'clock in the morning. Didn't tell a soul. Jack Dowd is madder than hell."

Elliott Yost was contrite, defensive, and confounded all at once. He sat in the conference room next to his office at the courthouse, rapping his knuckles lightly on the table while he listened to Warren tell him what happened. Stasiak's actions shocked him. He didn't think the investigation lost anything because the Barnstable officers weren't involved in the autopsy. He was planning to ease them out gradually anyway, hoping that more state assistance would become available as time went on. The two killings were getting a lot of play up above, and he was in the spotlight. The feelings of Bill Warren and his local constabulary notwithstanding, this was simply too important. The state police were going to run the investigation. But still, Stasiak's surprise autopsy was just an unnecessary provocation.

In the end, he got Warren out of his office with the promise that he would speak not only to Stasiak, but to his superiors in the state police. In fact, Elliott had no intention of doing either. He needed to maintain good relations with Stasiak, not only because he was Elliott's best chance at nailing this case, but because Stasiak was connected. The state trooper had more standing in the state attorney general's office than Elliott did. If a child murderer had to descend on Elliott's jurisdiction, the timing couldn't have been better. Using Stasiak and his seasoned detectives, he was going to make a noise that they would hear across New England.

9

Father Boyle, in his first waking moments, was making a rare return to the years of gentle light. With his face half buried in the pillow and one eye partly open, he recalled that ancient feeling, which was ever more difficult to reconstruct, of time and language having ceased to exist. He recalled the power in the shadows, the mystery around the tabernacle, grave and benevolent at once, the vertiginous sense of God's nearness. What could have accounted for such a condition in a young man of twenty? When did the decline begin? Was there any point in knowing?

Father Boyle got dressed and went downstairs. He wanted to check the notepad they kept by the telephone in the kitchen to see if he had any calls but he could hear Mrs. Gonsalves banging around in there. They were uncomfortable around each other and he did his best to avoid her. There could be any number of fundraising or maintenance and repair items written down on the pad, but Father Keenan always handled those things.

He could be reasonably certain that he would not be asked to preside over any momentous occasions. They wanted Father Keenan's infectious joy at weddings and at funerals they wanted his comforting presence. Father Keenan did not, like many jaded clergymen, view marriage as a flawed and fragile arrangement, nor was he devoted to death for its unerring finality and its impeccable reputation. Marriages pleased him, and he often stood before the congregation rubbing his hands together or clapping them ever so slightly. And to see Father Keenan preside over a funeral was an amazing thing. For the short amount of time the mourners were assembled in the church, he created the feeling that together, they were bigger than death, that if death believed itself victorious, it was sorely mistaken. Father Keenan would say that he knew death, respected it, loved it even, as an adjunct of God. But he also implied that death didn't deserve the credit people gave it. That the secret death didn't want us to know was that somewhere in a world beyond our perception, it had to spit us out. And it had to free the living, too, accidentally bestowing peace and wisdom and compassion on them, unaware that the suffering it inflicted made souls fertile and capable of astounding change.

Father Keenan exuded love and grace and people were drawn to him. He had discovered something, been fed by something that had made on him an indelible taint of the divine. Father Boyle wondered if it had happened slowly over the years. And what was it like as it grew in Father Keenan, as it rose, burning over some horizon in his soul? Did it take place in increments, Father Keenan unaware as he heaved his legs over the side of the bed and hoisted his girth off the mattress to start another day? Or perhaps it had been sudden, the type of epiphany that Father Boyle tended to imagine: a stranger in a hat coming silently up the veranda steps as Father Keenan sat there reading one evening in late June, a man he'd never seen, who looked at him or touched him and then without a word walked back down the steps and disappeared behind the shrubbery.

Father Boyle stood at his window and looked out at the shafts of early morning sunlight on the lawn. He wondered if he would be able to get out to the lower Cape today and do some walking. The incident earlier in the summer—the one he found himself simultaneously reconstructing and trying to forget—was never far from his thoughts.

He had hiked into the woods near the remains of the old Marconi wireless station in Wellfleet, passing the old antenna masts with their concrete moorings scattered across the dunes, abandoned since 1917. He walked farther than usual, into an area he had never been before. Two hours later, he passed through an old-growth forest and emerged in a moor-like landscape high above the sea. He sat down in a sandy meadow to rest before turning back, but he had been sleeping poorly at the rectory and had pushed himself on the hike, and no sooner had he closed his eyes than he fell into a deep slumber.

It was dark when he woke. He could not see a tree in any direction, just boundless night, deep blue and thick. It seemed that a wave of warm air passed over the hollow momentarily. High above, there were flashes in the sky, unaccompanied by any sound, like heat lightning. The underside of the clouds glowed briefly.

At the crest of the hollow in which he knelt, something appeared. He could not have said it was a light. It was more a region of darkness that was a different hue from the rest of the night, and within it, some kind of turbulence, a pale boiling color, changing shape, never taking the form of anything recognizable except for a moment when there was clearly something anthropomorphic there, the vague shape of a head and the uncertain gesture of an arm. The air in the meadow hummed and the temperature changed. Father Boyle was overcome by a sensation he could only know as having some distant antecedent in his early childhood. There was a softening somewhere in him, an inner supplication, a fleeting thought of something or someone he had loved. The interior of his family's bungalow in Sandusky, Ohio, a figure in motion there, his mother, perhaps, a vision that came and evaporated in a single breath as he watched in awe and disbelief the thing that stood out against the night in that forlorn and primitive place. He recalled the way it heated the air, how it changed the way sound behaved. He thought he heard children calling from far-off places in the meadow, and a fizzing in his ears, as of something being ignited.

The night in the meadow was the secret he would share with no one, not even Father Keenan.

10

The shadows cast by the superstructure of the Sagamore Bridge passed through the Oldsmobile's interior in repeating patterns of dark and light and made Frank Semanica think of his time in Walpole state prison, where he pulled a twelve-year hitch for armed robbery in 1947. On the positive side, he didn't get sent to Korea, though he did get stabbed and suffered a botched surgery by a jailhouse doctor who tried to repair a severed intestine. But he was being rewarded now for having kept his mouth shut. He had a great job that wasn't really even a job, and it paid well. He drew in a deep breath and looked down on the Cape Cod Canal and the tiny white sails of pleasure boats going through and the wakes of powerboats, frozen at this distance, one hundred and fifty feet above the water, like furrows on a blue canvas.

He had wanted to drive down in the Thunderbird convertible he'd recently bought, but Grady had told him not to. This four-door Olds was a square John kind of a car, but it drove well and it had a big 303. He got it up to ninety, floating from the right lane to the left and back again. It was a nice machine for an old man's car. He slowed back down to sixty and kept it there. He was carrying a gun and getting stopped was the last thing he needed.

He got off the Mid-Cape Highway at Hyannis and found his way to a side street where abandoned buildings backed up to the defunct railroad, their loading docks sprouting weeds. He pulled into a small lot on the right, where there was a squat, flat-roofed building with Christmas lights in the windows. The Elbow Room was a sinister-looking little tavern whose false stone siding and filthy slit-like casement windows installed well above eye level made it resemble a pillbox. Its disregard for appearances went well beyond simple neglect. There was a willfulness about it, heightened by the irony of the Christmas lights, which were the Elbow Room's joke on itself.

Frank stood in the doorway and waited for his eyes to adjust to the dark. The Everly Brothers were playing faintly and the smell of stale beer and cigarette smoke stirred up a familiar excitement in him. It was 11 A.M. and there was no one in the place. A door behind the bar burst open and a stocky older man appeared carrying a case of beer. His hair was white but greased back in the style a younger man would wear, and where his build might have made him seem formidable at one time, he had mostly gone to paunch and softness and he now looked like a rakish grandfather. "There he is!" the man said.

"What do you say, George?"

"This your first stop?"

"Yeah."

"Look at you. You look like a tourist."

Frank fingered one of the buttons on his shirtfront. "Grady, you know? He wanted . . . you know."

"I know. Everything on the QT. *Everything.*"

"Got me driving this fucking car, too. Embarrassing."

George laughed. "So what's going on up there?"

"Nothing much."

"Any trouble?"

"I don't hear about any. I mean, they're watching, you know?"

"So you drive down here, looking like John Q. from Newton or Lexington or some damn place, that's good."

"Yeah. I don't like it."

"Look at you," George laughed again. "You look like a goddamn insurance guy from Malden."

"Shit."

"Like a regular civilian."

Frank said, "Our good friend been around?"

George made a face. "Our good friend isn't gonna show up here." He seemed surprised Frank had asked the question. "He sends friends of his."

George produced a pair of ledgers and a large vinyl bag with a zipper, the kind banks use, and put them on the bar. "Come on around back," he said.

Frank lifted a hinged section of the bar top, gathered up the ledgers and bag, and followed George into the back area, which was crowded with cases of beer and liquor stacked to the ceiling. George opened the door to an unrefrigerated walk-in. Sections of plywood supported by cinder blocks served as a work surface around its perimeter. There were adding machines, telephones, and four brand-new Philco 20-inch television sets. George knelt and turned the dial on a safe in the corner. Frank sat in one of the chairs and picked up a laminated chart that was a combination table and slide rule manufactured by a concern called American Turf Monthly. Above an artist's rendition of a herd of galloping horses were the words "Rate-O-Matic Speed Rule Handicapper."

"So where's the good beaches around here?" Frank asked.

"Depends what you want."

"Girls in bikinis."

"Go to Craigville. Lots of girls over there."

"I want to get laid down here."

"You can't get laid up there?"

"Sure. But I want to get laid down here. I'm thinking of something like, I don't know, on a beach chair, involving suntan lotion."

George reached into the safe and pulled out two grocery

bags packed with cash. "It's eight hundred for the week. Total's in the ledger." He was trying to get Frank off the subject of sex. Frank sometimes beat up his sex partners and he had cut a couple, too. One, a girl who ran the roulette table at an after-hours club in Revere, was going to press charges until it was pointed out to her that Frank was connected with Grady Pope. Grady gave the girl a settlement and had a session with Frank and that should have been the end of it, but you never knew what the kid was getting up to in his off-hours. He was locked up when he was eighteen and now here it was, twelve years later, and he just didn't know how to be out here in the world. As far as George was concerned, Frank Semanica was a pervert and couldn't be trusted. George didn't think it was a good idea working with Italians. That Stevie Tosca was another one. A master disappearance artist, sure, probably the best. But a sick bastard, from what George heard. It didn't matter to Grady. He wasn't around when the Irish and the Italians were at each other's throats over control of the smuggling rackets during the Depression. Grady was doing a long stretch in Leavenworth when George was a soldier for the Gustins out of South Boston in 1935. They were going after each other in the streets back then with no restraint. By the end of it all, some people were dead and some people were in jail, territories changed and regimes were overturned. The Italians had the North End. The Irish operated unchallenged in South Boston, Charlestown, and Somerville. When Grady reemerged from federal custody in 1945, cooperation was the new business strategy. The fighting had taught everyone a lesson, but for people like George, who'd been through all that, the Italians would always be the other side.

Outside, Frank Semanica opened the trunk of the Oldsmobile and transferred the money into an overnight valise. He tucked the ledgers and the vinyl bag on top and closed the trunk. From one of the windows of the Elbow Room, George watched him drive off. He regretted mentioning

Craigville Beach to him. There were inexpensive vacation cottages and motels there, crowded with kids from up above. He
could imagine Frank Semanica cruising up and down the
beach road, sticking out like a sore thumb in spite of the car
and the John Q. getup, because all you had to do was take a
look at Frank Semanica and you knew he was bad news. The
problem was George could imagine him doing something stupid and getting caught with a suitcase full of cash and a gun in
his possession. He regretted giving him the little paper envelope with the amphetamines in it, which he did as a gesture of
goodwill, because that was the kind of thing George liked to
do. For the ride back, he'd said. So you're not falling asleep
behind the wheel. Now he didn't think it was such a good idea,
Frank Semanica hopped up on speed.

11

Warren and his officers began sorting through the statewide list of sex offenders they had gotten from the state police, trying to account for their whereabouts at the time of the killing and establish any connections to the Cape. Warren took two men off patrol and had them working the phones all day, along with a pair of retired men who agreed to volunteer their time at Chief Holland's request. The registry of motor vehicles donated two employees from their records section to work exclusively with the police. Sequestered in a back room of the registry's offices across town, they fielded requests from the officers, cross-checking information against the state list as needed.

Jenkins and Dunleavy's office had been turned into the command center, such as it was. Inside, it was cramped, warm, and noisy. Several people were speaking on telephones and a technician from the phone company was in there trying to secure the lines out of the way of chair legs and foot traffic. Jenkins and Warren stood outside in the hallway.

"We should save the peepers for last," Jenkins said. "And for the indecent exposures, if we can figure out which ones involved kids, that would be our best bet."

Warren said, "We're going to have to track down where those cases were heard so we can get the records. That's a lot of phone time. Why don't you supervise them until noon, then I'll have Dunleavy take over."

At that moment, Dunleavy turned a corner in the hallway

and came toward them. "Hey," he said. "I swung by the coroner's office on my way in. I had Jack Dowd call the forensic pathologist up at the state police lab in Sudbury. Turns out Jack knows him from the old days."

Jenkins and Warren regarded him with surprise, waiting for him to continue.

"Bernie Suggs is O-positive, for the record. And our guys picked up a few small glass fragments from Stanley Lefgren's hair. They don't know what they are yet but it's very thin glass, like from a lightbulb. There were a few hairs, too, and they say they don't belong to the kid."

"Do they have anything similar off the Gilbride body?" Warren asked.

"Nothing but material from the pond. Anyway, the kid was a mess. They had to keep him in the bag for the autopsy 'cause he was falling apart. Like a stewed chicken."

Warren said, "I wonder if Jack can keep us connected with this guy."

"At least until they shut him down."

"You've got someone on James Frawley?"

"Yes, sir."

"What's he been up to?"

"Sticking close by the Salvation Army shelter on Winter Street."

"What about the place Cleve said he was looking at, the rental?"

"I went over and checked it out. It's like he said. A studio above a garage, currently for rent."

Back in his office, Warren went through the reports taken the previous day. The state police in Maine called about a truck driver who was picked up in Rockport the summer before for soliciting underage girls and did six months in the house of correction up there. He had a north-south route delivering cleaning supplies between Rockport and Boston and might have found his way to the Cape. A drifter named Clyde Pommering was run out of Lee, Massachusetts, for loitering around a carnival that was passing through town, making the parents nervous. According to police there, Pommering claimed to be on his way to Cape Cod. And doctors at a psychiatric hospital in Pittsburgh called about a patient they once had in their care—a man who heard voices that told him to hurt children. He had been discharged months ago but the doctors recalled that he said he might go to live with his parents in New England. Warren was surprised that anyone in Pittsburgh had heard about the murders.

He left the reports with Jenkins and drove toward Kalmus Beach. Sitting in traffic on Main Street, he watched the tourists. A young woman exited a jewelry shop and began walking up the street with her back to him. He was sure it was Jane Myrna. He watched her gain distance, his fingers drumming on the steering wheel, impatient with the traffic. Was that a man walking at her side or was it a coincidence? Had he been waiting for her outside the jewelry shop?

He experienced an unaccountable sinking feeling as she mixed in with the crowd and became indistinct, then turned off down a side street and was gone. When the traffic finally moved, he rolled grimly onward, pronouncing a new discipline to himself. He would have to stop all this business about Jane. There had been dreams lately. She was attractive, handsome even. She wore her dark, straight hair pulled back and clasped at the nape of her neck with a barrette. She was lean, with the wide shoulders of an athlete, and a strong jawline which was particularly striking in profile. She had a frank way of looking at people and her expression often flickered in a fascinating way between a gravity beyond her years and the mischievous look of a teenager.

Jane was a lot like Ava had been, he thought; her hair, her physique. But then he thought that she was nothing at all like Ava, and the fact that he was comparing the two only emphasized how out of line his thoughts were on the subject. Warren had been taken with Jane from the start but he had believed that his favorable impression of her was simply appreciation of a pretty, intelligent young woman who showed compassion for his son. Now there were dreams, and there were some thoughts, too.

When he pulled up to the Lefgren house, there were a state police cruiser and an unmarked car parked on the roadside in front. As Warren was coming up the walkway, the front door opened and Mr. Lefgren came out. He began to speak but emitted only a short, choked sob, a sound that he strangled and aborted so he could try again to form words.

"You put them up to this, didn't you?"

He had left the front door open, and inside, Warren saw Stasiak standing there, in profile, with his hands on his hips. He was speaking to a pair of troopers in uniform and a man in plain clothes. He turned his head to look at Warren. Beyond him, in the living room, Warren could see Mrs. Lefgren sitting on the couch. A man in civilian clothes sat on an ottoman across from her, holding a small white envelope and a pair of scissors.

"How could you do this to us?" said Mr. Lefgren. "When you were here that day . . . *You came to our house . . .* We trusted you."

"Mr. Lefgren . . ."

"You sent these people here." He shoved past Warren and walked to the front gate. Stasiak called out after him, "Mr. Lefgren." Warren could hear children crying inside. Stasiak turned to the troopers. "Go get him."

The officers came out the door and clambered past Warren. Mr. Lefgren was walking up the road in the direction of Kalmus Beach and they headed after him.

Warren addressed Stasiak. "What's going on?"

Stasiak turned away and continued speaking to the plainclothesman.

"I'm talking to you."

Stasiak looked at him. He turned back to his companion and said, "Hold on a minute, Heller." He walked down the steps and stood in front of Warren.

"You and I are going to have problems, aren't we?" he said.

"We already have problems, you and I."

The two kept their eyes on each other's faces, their bodies tensed.

"What are you doing here?" Warren asked.

"We're conducting an investigation. The murder of the Gilbride boy, and I don't need your permission to do it."

"You could have notified me. I spoke with the family two days ago."

"Well, we move awful fast, Warren."

"Why are they so upset?"

"I would imagine because someone choked their kid to death."

"I'm trying to work this case to the best of my ability with whatever I've got at my disposal. That's straight from the district attorney. Until another agency takes it over, we're the lead investigators on this case. That entitles us to certain courtesies from you, one of them being notification of . . . stunts like this."

"Stunts?"

"Like the autopsy. And the evidence you made off with."

Stasiak looked around the yard as though containing himself was taking a monumental effort.

Warren said, "I pull up here and find you guys . . . What are you doing, grilling these people?"

"We're asking questions, Warren, and some of them are hard, yeah."

"Why do you have a technician in there?"

"For hair samples."

"Didn't it occur to you that something like this might concern us?"

"Like I said, we move fast. I can't stop and call up the goddam board of selectmen or the ladies' auxiliary every time I'm going to do something."

"What you're doing has a direct bearing on our case."

"Then why aren't *you* out here taking hair samples, huh? Oh, that's right, you *are* here. A day late and a dollar short. If I have to turn your water on for you, Warren, I'd say that you probably ought to go back to directing traffic."

"Now listen here . . ."

"Where did the hair on the Lefgren kid come from? We need to know that, should the same hairs turn up in some place associated with the Gilbride killing. Should more bodies turn up."

The troopers returned up the road, flanking Mr. Lefgren, holding him by his elbows. He was sobbing openly now, like a child, and a few neighbors were out on their lawns, looking, pretending to perform tasks. An old woman was visible in a house across the street as a ghostly, indistinct figure in a glassed-in porch. Warren watched Stasiak look the man over as he passed. He heard a rumor that the Gilbrides had complained about an interrogation the state police had conducted and that a lawyer from Tennessee had intervened. Warren suspected the same thing was going on here. He thought about the futility of complaining to Elliott about any of it. He was practically in a blind rage and, with difficulty, decided that before he said something to make matters worse, before he actually put his hands on Stasiak, he had better leave.

Stasiak said, "You have that list of sex offenders from our R&I division."

Warren started walking to his car and said nothing.

"I hope you're not chasing down every pansy from here to Pittsfield."

Warren reached the gate in the picket fence and opened it.

"At the risk of hurting your feelings," Stasiak said, "you check parole officers, former parole officers, local tax and real estate records, employment offices, utility companies, court records in the jurisdiction of last known address. In addition to the usual."

Warren turned and glared back at him. Stasiak was watching him with a trace of amusement on his face. "I heard you used to be one of us," he said.

Warren opened the door to his cruiser.

Stasiak said, "That was a different time."

"It sure as hell was."

12

Ed Jenkins and Phil Dunleavy were sitting in an unmarked car in a dirt lot on the east end of Hyannis. They were a block from the ferry terminal that handled freight for Nantucket and Martha's Vineyard, and they could hear the clatter and banging of cargo being moved and the revving of engines as the last ferry of the day was being loaded. It was a quarter past eleven, the night warm and muggy.

They were watching a big seedy-looking duplex across the street. The subject of their interest was thirty-six-year-old Gene Henry, who had served time for taking liberties with the 14-year-old daughter of a woman he was living with in 1949.

Henry had been convicted of engaging in sexual activity with the girl, but there were accusations against him that were not included in the charging documents and were not admissible at trial. The girl had a six-year-old brother, and both she and the mother claimed Henry had molested him, a charge that could not be substantiated. Their statements were documented in the case file, however, and Henry's name was duly flagged.

They had recently discovered that Henry had a connection to the lower Cape—and Truro specifically, where the Gilbride boy's body was found. Rumor had it he often went fishing there and had a girlfriend in the area as well. Since his release from prison, Henry had remained uninvolved with the criminal justice system and was employed as a cook at Mildred's Chowder House where he worked the dinner shift. He was reclusive and slept during the daytime, which is what he had claimed to be doing at the time of the killings, though they hadn't been able to confirm this.

A silhouette appeared in front of a small window. There was a gauzy material hanging from the curtain rod, making the figure look as if it had been drawn with charcoal and then smudged. It stood still for a moment and then moved out of sight. Jenkins said, "That's a terrible thing, that kid out there in the reeds like that."

"Yeah." Dunleavy had his eyes fixed on the window. "I think this is a stretch though, this Gene Henry."

"The lieutenant thinks he's worth a look."

"The lieutenant's never worked a murder, has he?"

"As a lead? I don't know. Maybe with the state police."

"I don't think he had any rank back then," Dunleavy said. "You think they're going to make him chief?"

"Who knows. I hope so."

"I think you're in a minority," said Dunleavy.

"Oh, are you one of those guys who've got a hard-on for him?"

"No. He's all right by me, but I know a lot of guys who don't like him."

"That's 'cause he doesn't pal up with them. He makes them do their jobs. Some of these guys are bums. You know that."

"Well, even the ones who aren't bums aren't crazy about the lieutenant. They liked Marvin."

"Hell, Marvin was more of a politician than a cop," said Jenkins. "A fixer. That's Marvin. Might've been a little dirty, too, as everyone knows. Remember that story about how he might have gotten kickbacks during the airport construction? Marvin and that concrete guy, Langella, or whatever his name was? What they don't like about Warren is he's got integrity. That's why they don't like him."

"You remember that time someone taped a picture of him to the inside of the urinal?"

"Jesus."

"Can you imagine if he'd seen that?"

They were both laughing now.

"But that's the thing," Dunleavy said. "They do that stuff because of the way he is."

"So he's wound a little tight. Come on. He's a good man."

"You met his wife, didn't you?"

"Yeah, once."

"What did she look like? I heard she was good-looking."

"She was. Very good-looking."

"But she was an alkie."

"Yeah. She was that, too."

"Lots of stories about her."

Jenkins didn't say anything. He looked up and down the street.

"I heard stories about her walking down to the package store wearing nothing but a raincoat," Dunleavy said.

"I was here when all that was going on. A lot of those stories are bullshit."

"Some of them must be true, though."

"I don't know."

"You know some good shit, Ed, I know you do. You are not allowed to know good shit without sharing it with me, now come on."

"I'm not getting into the lieutenant's private business, O.K.?"

"We've been into his private business for the past five minutes."

The radio fizzed with static and the shift sergeant's voice came on, droning faintly out of the dash chrome. He was positioning cars around a block of woods off Old Colony Boulevard. Jenkins said, "They're setting up a perimeter."

"Want to go see what it is?"

"We should probably stay here and keep an eye on this guy."

"The only thing this guy is going to do is go to bed. Let's go. We need to get something to eat anyway."

By the time they got to Old Colony Boulevard, patrol officers had a man in custody in an alleyway that ran behind a row of one-story commercial buildings. He was bloodied, his hands cuffed in front of him and his head bowed, dark, stringy hair hanging down over his face. He was bleeding from a head wound and his lips were swollen and split. A group of officers stood around him, including Welke, with whom Jenkins had had words the night Warren choked out the big drunk and disorderly in Barnstable. The shift sergeant turned to the detectives as they approached. "We got a witness says this guy fell out the passenger side of a car going about 40 on Old Colony Boulevard," the shift sergeant said. "We found him hiding in the woods."

A drop of blood formed on the end of the man's nose, another at the tip of his chin, both hanging there simultaneously. "Any ID?" Dunleavy asked.

"Joseph Leapley. He lives in Sagamore. We're calling the name in right now."

Dunleavy spoke to the man. "What happened to you?"

The man was silent, his head bowed.

The sergeant said, "Get a look at his face. He didn't get those cuts from falling out of a car."

Dunleavy, loud and accusing: "Who was driving that car you fell out of?"

The sergeant said, "Who put those cuffs on you?"

Dunleavy turned to the cop. "You didn't cuff him?"

"No. We found him like this."

Jenkins said, "With cuffs on?"

"Yeah. Who put the cuffs on you? You're getting yourself in a shitload of trouble right now."

The man did not speak.

Patrolman Welke said, "What are you, a fucking mute?"

Jenkins turned and eyed Welke. Welke eyed him back. Jenkins said to the sergeant, "Did he have a wallet?"

"Yeah. It's in my car, on the dash."

Jenkins went over and got the wallet. There was no money inside. He found an insurance card, a driver's license, a membership to the Bass River Rod and Gun Club, a picture of a little girl in pigtails, and a slip of paper with a phone number on it. He walked over to the man and said, "Someone handcuffed you. They cut your face and by the looks of it they beat the hell out of you. Instead of going for medical help you go and hide in the woods. What kind of trouble are you in, Mr. Leapley?"

A flashing red light lit the quiet side street as the ambulance turned the corner. The sergeant called out, "Welke. Go with him to the hospital. Get whatever information you can on him. If he gets any visitors, I want to know."

When the ambulance was gone, the alleyway returned to darkness. The only illumination came from the aging street lamps set at infrequent intervals on splintery poles out on the side street. The sergeant took off his cap and scratched his head. "Weird."

Frank Semanica knew he shouldn't have done it. But the guy just sat there and said nothing. When they handcuffed him and started beating him, he didn't beg and he didn't promise. He just got real quiet, like he was going to be brave about it, like he was going to prove something.

They had brought the guy over to Brinkman's Brake & Lube in Dennis. There was no such person as Brinkman, at least not anymore. Grady had a third party lease it and they kept the name that had been on the building for years. He brought down a couple of mechanics he knew from South Boston, guys who could be trusted to keep their mouths shut. They serviced a light volume of cars, enough to make the place look legitimate. Grady ran a booking operation and loaned money out of the rooms upstairs. There was a card game, too, which is how this guy, Joe Leapley, got himself in trouble.

You owe two bills! George McCarthy screaming in his face. *I'll get it,* the guy says. Like he's telling his wife he forgot to pick up the milk. Like this wasn't anything serious and he was going to show them, and that's what really sent Frank Semanica over the deep end. When they were done with him, Frank was supposed to drop him off in Hyannis, but on the way there, he got the idea that this guy was not going to pay, that he was either going to skip town or go to the police, and that's why he was just sitting through the beating and the cutting, waiting it out.

He reached over and opened the door and shoved him out, taking both his hands off the wheel to do it. Frank was so wound up he didn't notice the car behind him and he knew the driver reported it because soon afterward, while he was sitting at an empty intersection, the cop pulled up behind him. The red light went on and he floored it. Then Frank was in that wild desperate place that he hadn't known since prison, where his vision was reduced to a small circle and he had a peppery sensation in the back of his throat, his palms tingling.

The cop pushed that stupid humped-up-looking heap of shit for all it was worth and Frank couldn't get any distance on him. He finally managed to lose him on a long curve by shutting his lights off and running off the road. He hit some rocks and a few small trees and he didn't think it was serious, but now, back out on the Mid-Cape Highway, he noticed that the oil pressure was dropping. He figured he'd damaged the oil pan. He didn't want to risk trying to make it to Boston. They were looking for him and the car was going to break down. Frank took the exit for Sagamore.

He came out on Old King's Highway, within view of the bridge over the canal. There were big drooping trees by the road. He pulled over in front of a mom-and-pop restaurant with picnic tables out front and a phone booth off to the side of the lot. Frank drove the car to the back of the building. The oil gauge dropped to zero and stayed there. There was a narrow passageway between the rear of the building and a wooden stockade fence and he nosed the car in until the front end bumped a row of trash cans. He got out and retrieved his pistol from under the seat and put it in the waist of his jeans. He went out to the phone booth and smashed out the little light in the ceiling so no one could spot him from the road. He waited for his eyes to adjust to the darkness and then he made a phone call.

"Hello?"

"Christy?"

"Yeah?"

"It's Frank."

"What?"

"It's Frank Semanica."

"Oh, Frank."

"Hey, is Ernie there?"

"You woke me up."

"Sorry."

"Frank?"

"Yeah, it's Frank."

"What do you want?"

"Is Ernie there?"

"No."

Christy Fontaine knew damn well that her husband was a thief, a forger, and a former loan shark who had a regular job milking the Massachusetts Bay Transit Authority for a good sum of money for work not performed. So Frank found it galling, to say the least, that Christy thought he was a bad influence from whom her husband needed to be protected.

"Okay. You're not going to tell me where he is."

"I don't know where he is, Frank. It's twelve thirty."

"Well, I need to talk to him. Right now."

"God, Frank. It's the middle of the night."

"Like right fucking now, Christy. *Now.*"

"Don't swear at me."

"I hate to bring this up but your husband owes me. I'm in a fix right now and I need a ride. I need him to come out and get me. He needs to come here now."

"Jesus. Well . . . Where are you?"

"I need to talk to him. If he's there you better put him on the line."

"He's at Arthur's. I'll call him."

"Give him this number." He read the numbers on the white circle at the center of the dial.

"Tell him to let it ring until I answer it. If you have to get dressed and *walk* over to Arthur's, do it."

"What's going on?"

"Nothing."

"Doesn't sound like nothing to me. This better not get Ernie in trouble."

"Ernie's gonna be in trouble if he *doesn't* come out here. Now get in touch with him and tell him to call that number."

Frank hung up the phone, let out a long breath, and began going through his options if Ernie didn't call. Maybe he was where he told Christy he was, and maybe not. Last Frank remembered, he was screwing some hairstylist who lived on the top floor of a triple-decker in Milton.

He walked back over to the Buick. There was a trail of oil on the pavement, tracing the arc he'd made when he pulled in. He looked inside and noticed the blood on the seat on the passenger side. His fingerprints were all over the car. He took off his T-shirt and started wiping down the Buick as he went over names in his head. He needed to think of who else he could call in case Ernie didn't show. He was going to try to keep this from Grady and his people, so they were out. Frank planned to tell them that the Buick was stolen from outside his apartment during the night. They had stolen the car themselves about a year earlier. It was one of a group they kept in a repair shop in Dorchester for general use. They were coming and going constantly, Grady's cars, so Frank was confident this one wouldn't be missed.

Far off toward the road, he heard the telephone ring. Frank ran to the phone booth. He told Ernie where he was and gave him the exit off the Mid-Cape and a description of the restaurant. He didn't say what circumstances brought him there. Ernie told him he was leaving right away.

Frank paced behind the restaurant, out of sight, savoring the relief, then he got back to wiping with a new enthusiasm. When he had cleaned every surface of the car that he might have touched, he went over it again, keeping an ear cocked for Ernie's arrival. Frank had gotten him out of one hell of a lot of hot water when Ernie was putting money on the street in Quincy and Grady got wind of it. He asked Frank if he knew anything about it. Frank said he didn't. Grady decided to send some men over to inform this person that his free ride was over. Someone would be coming by every week to collect thirty percent.

Frank made a quick run to Quincy. He and Ernie had gone to high school together and were part of the same loose street gang when they were teenagers. In his loan-sharking business, Ernie sometimes used Frank for tune-ups, something Grady didn't know about. Frank told Ernie that he was going to get a visit from some of Grady Pope's people—which often meant a trip to the hospital—and that he should shut down immediately. Ernie agreed, and Frank went back to South Boston and told them that the Quincy loan shark was no longer in business, that he'd run into trouble with local law enforcement.

Frank sat back among the trees and watched the road. After nearly two hours, he heard a car approaching and saw headlight beams through the woods. He stayed where he was until he recognized Ernie's Mercury. He came out of the trees and got into the passenger side.

"What's going on?" said Ernie.

"Don't ask questions."

Ernie started to drive off, but Frank said, "Wait." He got out and ran back to the Buick. He opened the hood and reached under the air cleaner until he found the fuel line. He twisted it until it broke free from the carburetor and he felt the cool gasoline running between his fingers. He put his T-shirt under the broken line, and let it soak. Then he stuffed it in the gas tank and lit it. The T-shirt ignited with a *whoof.* He ran back out to the Mercury and said to Ernie, "Go."

They got onto Old King's Highway and passed the great silent abutment of the Sagamore Bridge, going underneath the giant structure, the canal surging past, turbulent and oily-looking in the night. They wound around and soon were up on the bridge. Frank Semanica looked down. Where he had been was all blackness, a particularly deserted section of the canal. Far off, he saw a small orange ball glowing. He watched it get brighter and then blossom into something three times its original size and slowly rise, lighting the treetops around it and churning upward, a roiling, growing mushroom of fire.

13

C hief Holland looked old, propped up in a hospital bed reading a newspaper folded in quarters. His bare feet stuck out from under the blanket, white, with gnarled, yellow toenails. They disappeared beneath the bedclothes when Warren walked into the room. The chief's jowls were somehow accentuated, even while the substance of his face seemed diminished. His white hair, which Warren was used to seeing combed to the side, was standing up in wispy formations around his head.

The relationship between the two was an awkward, stillborn thing, characterized by paternal approval and filial loyalty, but mostly by the uneasiness between two men who were so fundamentally different that each found the other difficult in ways that they could not fully describe. Warren's seriousness and the chief's avuncular, profane ease in a world of men made for an odd tension between them and while there was mutual respect and even a certain affection between the two, they had always found conversation outside the job difficult and one was frequently indecipherable to the other.

Warren perceived that Holland took a liking to him when he joined the force in 1950, a go-getter among a bunch of laggards. Holland appeared grateful to have Warren on hand, praised his enthusiasm, and rewarded his initiative. He was promoted quickly. But when he made lieutenant, and they began working more closely together, it soon became apparent that they weren't entirely compatible.

He knew there were certain things the chief overlooked. Holland played small-town politics and did what was expedient. He had admonished Warren on occasion about his approach to the job. Holland had advised him once to "be realistic," and on another occasion said, "Don't take yourself so damn seriously." These incidents burned anew in his memory as he took a seat beside the chief's bed. "How are you feeling?" Warren said.

"My third goddamn trip to the hospital in three months. I should just move in."

"What's the latest?"

"Damned if I know. Damned if *they* know. I keep getting these heart rhythms or whatever they call them."

"How's Alice?"

The chief waved the question off, then said, "She's beside herself." Holland straightened some of the things on the wheeled tray beside his bed, then made an attempt to smooth the hair against his head. The two started to speak at once. "Go ahead," said the chief.

"No," said Warren. "You go."

"How are things at the station?"

"I guess I've been remiss by not coming in here to give you regular reports."

"You don't have to do that. You're in charge. I believe I'm out of it anyway. Every time I get back on my feet I have more damn problems."

"Maybe it's just going to take some time."

"Oh, hell. What's happening with that murder down at the beach?"

Warren told him about the surprise autopsy, the confrontation with Stasiak, and their meeting with Elliott Yost. The chief seemed to be half-listening, smoothing the newspaper out against his thighs, and it occurred to Warren that he already knew all of it. Suspicion and a sense of persecution began to stir. Perhaps the chief had been calling around for news, but if that were so, why didn't he call Warren, who was in the best position to know things?

The chief showed no concern over the actions of the state police, in fact displayed little interest in the murders. It came as such a surprise to Warren that he wondered for a moment if it were fear of death. He mentioned the disappearance of the Weeks family and Holland looked at him as if he'd suddenly started speaking another language. Warren was going to tell him about the discovery of Joseph Leapley, handcuffed, beaten, and possibly thrown out of a moving car, but didn't bother.

If the chief weren't preoccupied with the possibility of his demise, then he was being tight-lipped for another reason. And the subject of his replacement hadn't come up. Warren had to admit that was the reason for his visit. But he encountered this pudgy old man with whom he was not familiar, reduced and frightened, or cagey and evasive, he wasn't sure which, but he walked out of the hospital wondering if he was being excluded from something, and as he drove away, he felt something solidifying in his stomach: anxiety and gathering anger and a repeating run of scenes in Chief Holland's hospital room that he knew had no basis in fact but which he couldn't help imagining anyway.

In the early evening, Doctor Hawthorne sat on the upper porch of his house in Provincetown drinking gin and tonic, all but invisible in the wisteria and shadow. He was a large, bald man with a classical nose and a broad mouth, his face appealingly masculine, though somewhat compromised now by the effects of age. With him was a colleague, Karl Althaus. They sat in low wicker chairs in the gathering dark, watching a man pace in the yard below.

"Look at him," said Hawthorne. "He is all wilderness."

"Edgar, is it?"

"That is what he prefers at the moment."

"He looks like someone who requires a short leash."

"Twenty milligrams of benzodiazepine in a tumbler of lemonade."

"Oh, Reese, you are awful. Did he ever make any progress on the seropromazine?"

"No."

"You aren't giving him anything at all?"

"Just the occasional 'Mickey,' to borrow a vulgar term. When the situation warrants it."

They watched Edgar Cleve stomp around the yard, examining the weeds, his gaze occasionally drifting over the back of the house, his outsized hands going in and out of his pockets

Hawthorne said, "So what are they working on now, Karl?"

"First trials on an antiseizure prototype. Fenchloravin."

"I assume they're not going to bother with animal testing."

"They're falsifying phase one results as we speak," said Althaus. "Mice, rabbits, even monkeys are only useful to a point. As you well know. Any interest?"

"I'm busy here. And my personal circumstances call for a certain amount of discretion. What are you looking for?"

"Specifically, about a dozen children under the age of twelve with a history of seizures."

Hawthorne put his elbows on the porch rail and peered down through the wisteria as if to get a better angle on Cleve in the yard below.

"It's not really my forte. Children *or* seizures."

"Do think about it," said Althaus.

A bat careened through the dark and Cleve was suddenly alert, his arms rigid by his sides, his face turned upward toward the creature as it passed. He resumed his pacing with an intensified agitation.

"Wilderness and appetite," Hawthorne said, looking down through the screen.

Althaus's cigarette glowed in the dark. "What are you using him for?"

"I'm trying out some ideas."

"Do you think it's wise, keeping him around?"

"He's no risk. In fact he's quite vulnerable."

"He doesn't strike me as someone who is particularly vulnerable. In fact, he looks quite formidable."

"Oh, he's an accomplished manipulator. But that's the worst you could say about him. He craves approval. He wants *my* approval, especially. I'd like him to shed this eventually, for his own sake, but for the moment his desire for approval gives me leverage."

Althaus gulped from his drink, his eyes glassy. "I don't see you dispensing approval very freely."

"That is correct. The trick is convincing him he might get it."

Althaus laughed into his glass. "You awful man."

14

Father Boyle stood in the old sunroom at Nazareth Hall and watched the children playing in the yard. In his car he had a change of clothes, his specimen basket, and his sketchbook. Though he had told Mrs. Gonsalves he would be spending the afternoon helping a parish in Fall River organize a spiritual retreat, he was in fact going to hike into the woods of the outer Cape.

He looked out at the sky. Uncommonly clear and dry. He felt a momentary thrill at the thought of early evening light in the highlands, its burnished tones on the bayberry and dunes, on the broad sea far below. But then he remembered the resolution he'd made to not be out in the woods again at night. Though he told himself he did not want a repeat of the incident in the meadow earlier in the summer, he understood that in fact he wanted it very much. Father Boyle sometimes drove around in the area where he believed it had occurred. He pretended to take meandering hikes when he was actually hoping to recognize some feature in the landscape, to find himself in the very spot where he had had that exceedingly strange experience.

Sitting at a picnic table off to himself was the new child, Michael Warren, who was spending three days at Nazareth Hall on a trial basis. The boy took something out of his pocket just far enough to look at it and quickly put it back. Father Boyle watched him do this several times and glance around at the others. He had examined the file on Michael Warren. The boy was a fairly routine example of mental retardation with some indications of fetal alcohol syndrome. But there was something particularly poignant about him. He was shy and delicate and agreeable; attentive but given to flights of inner retreat during which he was all but oblivious to the world around him.

Father Boyle stepped out of the sunroom and crossed the yard. Mike folded his arms on the picnic table in an attempt at nonchalance. Father Boyle said, "How are you, young man?"

"Fine."

"Why are you sitting here by yourself?"

"'Cause kids make fun of me."

"These kids?"

"At my other school they did. I just like to be with my Dad."

"Why did they make fun of you?"

"I don't understand stuff. I make mistakes."

"Well, that says more about them than it does about you." Father Boyle watched the boy's uncomprehending face. "Mike, these boys who make fun of you, they make mistakes, too. Everybody makes mistakes. Grown-ups make mistakes. Trust me."

Father Boyle was aware of the boy's eyes on him and feigned a casual air. He brushed something off a trouser leg, adjusted the band on his wristwatch. Mike reached into his pocket, took out several small strips of torn white cotton, and laid them out carefully on the table.

"What's this, now?" Father Boyle asked.

"My clothes."

"Clothes?"

"Yeah. I wash them in my washing machine. I have a jar and a pencil and a round thing from a Tonka truck wheel and I made a washing machine. I put the clothes in and I wash them."

Father Boyle took one of the tiny strips in his fingers. "Very nice. You must be using a good detergent."

"Tide. Gets whites whiter."

Father Boyle laughed. "That must be a clever thing, your little washing machine."

"It's a secret. I don't tell anybody."

"I understand." Father Boyle thought about the trip he was about to make to the outer Cape when he was supposed to be at St. George's in Fall River, about the USGS map he had stolen from the library.

Mike carefully gathered up the cloth strips and put them in his pocket. He was shut down and fidgety now, his mind somewhere else.

"The kids here are not going to make fun of you," Father Boyle said. "You're going to be O.K. here. We're glad you've come to be with us."

It was clear that Mike had crossed into some territory where Father Boyle could not follow. The priest got up from the bench. "See you next time, then. Thank you for showing me the laundry."

He was up on the flagstone porch with one hand on the door when he heard the boy say in a small voice, "It's O.K."

Over the years, Warren had developed a ritual of stopping at a package store on Saturday afternoons and buying a pint of whiskey. He kept it in its brown paper bag on the kitchen counter until Mike went to sleep at around nine thirty in the evening. Even then, he didn't open it. He wanted to, but he denied himself, sitting at the kitchen table with the radio monitor on, reading the paper, paying bills, or doing something else to occupy his time. A call could come over the radio, an incident that might require his presence, but that was not why he left the bottle untouched. Warren felt the keen desire for the whiskey and sat at the round Formica table in a contest with it, and this was important. He usually went over the checkbook and redid the sums in the register. He wrote the balance in big numbers on a notepad. It had been steady at about four hundred dollars for a few months.

When he was finished going over his checking account, he went into the kitchen and removed a small, thin book from its place between the refrigerator and the breadbox. Back in April, they had arrested a couple for possession of heroin. They had been staying in a run-down vacation cottage in a copse of pines on the edge of town. The book was lying on a table and he happened to pick it up. It was a collection of poems, or at least what he believed were poems, by writers he had never heard of. He had some dim recollection of a few poems from his high school years, and these didn't look much like what he recalled.

It seemed a curious choice for the wan pair, who looked far too old to be involved with heroin and who seemed sadly resigned to the fact that they would be locked up for a long time. Warren had felt compelled to confiscate the book. He wondered if it somehow defined the couple or the circles in which they traveled, which made the little volume stranger still.

He opened the book to the place he had marked with an extinguished match.

We've been waiting for you
Since Morning, Jack
Why were you so long
Dallying in the sooty room?
This transcendental Brilliance
Is the better part
(Of Nothingness I sing)

He didn't know what any of it meant but it was absorbing in its way, like some weird kind of music. He would discover some passage that caught his eye and he would go back and read it again, asking himself why. Why this part here? It was negative, so much of it, and un-American. But there was some kind of authority in it, a persistent note of sad truth that spoke to him in a way that he was at an absolute loss to describe. He wondered what Jane would make of it.

Jane, he suddenly declared to himself, was thirty-two years old. She was ten years younger than him. Was that a great distance? *A great distance for what,* inquired the chaste inner voice that monitored his sentiments regarding Jane Myrna, the same voice that persuaded him not to pull Jane's record when he was at the registry of motor vehicles checking on a suspicious car that had been spotted around local motels. He had wanted to verify her date of birth. She looked a good deal younger than thirty-two.

At quarter to twelve, he put ice in a tumbler and poured the whiskey. The smell reached his nostrils from the countertop, burning, rich, and smoky. He pulled one of the armchairs up in front of the television and set his drink on an end table. There wasn't much on at this time of night. Most of the channels had gone to blank screens. Sometimes he could pick up Edward R. Murrow's documentary series, *See It Now*, and sometimes he could catch *The Honeymooners*.

As he changed the channels, he caught a glimpse of an actor in a commercial who resembled Joseph Leapley, the man they had found beaten and handcuffed a few nights ago. Warren had gone to see him at the hospital just the day before and was astonished by his resolve. Leapley gave no response to his questions, either looking up at the ceiling or closing his eyes for long periods of time as if waiting for Warren to tire of it and go away. One side of his face was covered with a gauze pad. He had two black eyes and moleskin bandages along one arm. "Is there anything you want to tell me, Mr. Leapley?" Warren asked.

Leapley did not respond.

"Who was driving the Buick?"

It was an interesting case: Felony assault and God only knew what else connected to it. He wondered what secret Leapley was hiding and wished they had more time to put into it but they were on the Lefgren murder full-out and had nothing to spare.

Warren found an obscure station out of Boston that was showing a late movie. On the screen was an establishing shot of a secret experimental laboratory in the desert outside Los Angeles. MPs at the gate in phony Hollywood uniforms. A B actor in a lab coat was having a woodenly earnest discussion with an Air Force general about radioactive isotopes, five-hundred-year half-lives, and arachnids.

Every corner of the house, if he allowed himself to think of it in a certain way, was a nest of sorrows. Sitting alone, late at night, with a fair alcohol high, had for a long time been a bad combination of circumstances for him. But at some point—he didn't know how long after Ava had gone—he realized he could live in the house as if it were a different place. He figured it was due to staying busy with Little Mike and his job. Getting appointed acting chief was a reward in ways he hadn't expected. The department occupied his mind nearly all the time, and he was so busy with Mike and babysitters and domestic chores that he could live in a house full of ghosts and not even see them.

There was a commercial for Burma Shave and he cocked his head a little at the ditty they sang, the men's and women's voices together. Warren had the windows open. The neighborhood was quiet but for the occasional car rolling down Bearse's Way. Mike was fast asleep in his room. If he looked out the window at a certain angle, he could see the end of Henry Sherman's house, where a window was illuminated by the electronic glow of a television set. Outside the window was an overgrown blackberry bush, whose unruly mass was bathed in the pale outer space light. Now it vanished, as the scene on Sherman's television set changed and the light dimmed. When the scene changed again, the foliage was visible once more in the bluish light, and the bush seemed to have lifted its heavy mass, reared itself up in a sluggish display of ill intent. Warren wondered if Sherman was watching the same thing on television.

At the far end of the kitchen he could see moonlight underneath the door to the back hall, which was little more than a utility space built on to the side of the house. When he and Ava first moved in, she suggested building shelves in there, making the most of the little house with a cheeriness that was typical of her at that time. She stocked up on extra things at bargain prices and stacked them in the back hall. She grew vegetables in the yard and canned them, neat rows of tomatoes, beans, and beets with labels bearing her handwriting. He remembered the cranberry sauce and the grape jam in jars with slabs of melted wax forming their lids. This was the danger he faced. The moonlight under the door. The jars of fruit with wax tops. On television a woman in a tight white blouse was following the professor around the laboratory, pleading, concerned. There were going to be giant spiders whether she liked it or not, Warren thought.

15

When the mackerel hit the water, it sent a thin slick of oil across the surface, silvery violet and rose and colors in the cool spectrum, made more visible by the low, overcast sky that was reflected on the creek. A bird concealed in the coarse-looking bushes that grew on the other side let out a long, ugly rasp like a cicada, or a small windup toy releasing its tension through a set of tiny gears. It stopped and delivered a series of three short rasps, then began its long sound again.

The fish sank to the bottom of the creek, where it was visible as a shadow on the bottom. The length of hemp twine that was tied through its mouth and gill led up out of the water and into the hands of a young boy, who stood with an older companion. The older boy sat on an overturned shellfish bucket and held a long-handled net across his knees.

The creek was about twenty feet across and wound through a tall grass marsh. Not far from where the boys stood, a road passed over, beneath which was a concrete culvert with a pair of holes that allowed the water to flow into a much larger marsh on the other side of the road.

The boys watched. Eventually, they saw something move across the bottom in the direction of the fish. "Crab," the younger boy said. The creature grabbed the mackerel with its claws and began tearing at it.

"What's that?" said the older boy, looking up the creek to their right. Something was approaching, floating on the water. The object had caught a clump of seaweed and was pushing it through the water as it made its slow passage toward them. There was something inexorable in its approach, as though its appearance had nothing to do with chance or tide. Its procession down the creek had an aspect of ritual, like it had been intended to reach the boys on a still summer morning. With the few strands of seaweed that hung off of it as though it been garlanded with tasteful restraint, and the flies that accompanied it like a choreographed escort, there was almost something festive about it.

They soon understood that the shape coming toward them was that of a boy, about their age, facedown, one arm bent at a ninety-degree angle and floating off to the side and its fist clenched. His legs were bent, the soles of his feet wrinkled and white, faced up to the sky. He was naked except for a pair of briefs that encircled his thighs just above the knee. The face was down but turned a bit toward them so that they could see the corner of one eye and one side of the mouth, which made a half-formed grimace. The face looked wise and adult in some kind of horrible way. *Look at me now,* it seemed to say. *My mother will wonder what has become of me.*

The boys flew into motion, leaving their net and bucket where they lay. They had to scramble up a steep dirt incline to get on the road, and as they climbed over the wooden guardrail, they saw that the dead boy had reached the culvert and was butting up against the concrete directly beneath them. Then the body dipped a couple of times, tilting its head downward as if it were trying to dive down through the hole. The boys were a good way up the road, yelling at the fronts of houses, when the upper half of the body went completely under and entered the hole, the bare soles of the feet raised upward, and, without a sound, disappeared into the culvert.

The press conference was held at the National Guard armory in Hyannis. Elliott Yost stood before the microphones, sweating in a khaki suit. Dale Stasiak stood next to him with his head tilted back a little, looking out over the crowd of newsmen and spectators. A cumulus cloud of cigarette smoke hung just beneath the fluorescent lights in the ceiling. Media from all over New England were there, including several television stations, whose cameras were now rolling. The twin circles of the reel housings on top of the cameras were visible like islands in a sea of heads.

Elliott Yost introduced himself, then Dale Stasiak, who was standing to his right, then Warren, and the police officials from the other Cape jurisdictions who were standing in a group behind him. He announced that he was speaking on behalf of the Commonwealth Attorney's Office and the Massachusetts state police, which was heading the investigation. At this point, he said, they were of the opinion that the three child killings on Cape Cod were the work of one person or group of persons. He stated that two of the victims had been sexually assaulted, but only did so because this was common knowledge by now. Little, it seemed to Elliott, hadn't been leaked to the public.

Elliott described the three murders and the state of the investigation so far, which was a delicate thing, because there wasn't very much to say. They had no suspects and precious little physical evidence. The investigation at this point consisted of canvassing, records checks, phone calls, and endless interviews, the desperate groping in the dark that was the hallmark of a stalled case. Giving the false impression of progress to an audience that recognized the tactic had him laboring, but Elliott proved adept enough, even if he hunched in on himself a little more than usual and his delivery suggested a grudging participation in the event.

Elliott had met with Lieutenant Warren and his two detectives the day before to let them know the case was now the exclusive domain of the state police. Governor Furcolo had moved state troopers from other parts of the state to work under Stasiak and they now had the resources they needed.

The meeting quickly degenerated into shouting. Yes, he admitted, he was asking them to give the Lefgren case to the state police, files, interview records, and all. He told them they would provide critical support to Captain Stasiak, though in truth, they would likely be used to do footwork and go on long-odds fishing expeditions.

Elliott clammed up and looked down at the dais when the first shouted questioning began. Stasiak leaned in front of the district attorney and spoke into the microphone. "One at a time," he said, and looked at them in a way that could have been threatening but perhaps was just cold and appraising, they weren't sure. They quieted just to look at him and see if he would say anything else, so compelling was his presence.

Reporters ran through the gamut of questions about the killings, then a few versions of the same questions phrased differently. Once the reporters had exhausted their attempts, they turned to the safety of the community and how the public was reacting. Stasiak said that a meeting for Barnstable residents was scheduled in the armory for that evening, which would be followed by similar meetings in other Cape towns. Police would be on hand to answer questions and discuss ways of making sure children were safe. When the press conference appeared to be winding down, a short man to the right of the stage raised his hand and called out, "Captain Stasiak." He wore a winter tweed jacket and kept a bowler on his head even though the temperature inside the armory was uncomfortable even for those in shirtsleeves.

"Over there," Stasiak said, and pointed to the man.

"Yeah. Fred Sibley, *Boston Globe*. What do you say to allegations that you have mistreated the families of the victims?"

The place grew quiet and everyone strained to see who had asked the question. Elliott began to speak, visibly angered, but Stasiak headed him off. "I'll answer him," he said, and stepped in front of the microphone.

"Are you referring to me?" Stasiak asked. "And it's Sibley?"

"Fred Sibley. Yes, sir. *Boston Globe*."

"And you're referring to me, allegations made against me."

"You and your officers, yes, sir."

The television cameras, which had been trained on Elliott and the others on the stage, were now being turned to pick up Sibley. Stasiak said, "There have been no allegations against me or my department, Mr. Sibley. I believe you are misinformed."

"The parents of the first victim, Mr. and Mrs. Gilbride, complained to the board of selectmen about the way they were detained and interrogated. I believe District Attorney Yost was apprised of this."

Elliott moved back to the microphone. "That is simply not true," he said. "I would like very much to know where this information comes from."

Sibley continued as if Elliott hadn't spoken. "The Lefgrens also say they were subjected to a hostile interrogation. They claim they were treated as suspects in the death of their own child." Sibley stood looking back at Stasiak and Elliott with an expectant look on his face, an expression that was nearly a grin. With his hat tilted back on his head and a pen poised above his notepad, he looked like he was enjoying himself a great deal, oblivious to the stares of the police officers in the room.

Stasiak took the space in front of the microphone, displacing Elliott off to the side. Someone in the crowd yelled, "Get him out of here." From the back, by the entrance doors: "Go back to Boston!"

Stasiak said to the crowd, "This is a hard thing. Most of us will never know what it's like to lose a child. I don't begrudge the Lefgrens or the Gilbrides anything they might be feeling at this point. Now, some of you know me and you know where I come from. I'm not delicate about what I do. I'll get the job done, and whoever committed these killings better know that."

Someone in the audience whooped.

"I will step on toes. I will hurt some feelings. I will break some dishware. Hell, I'll turn the whole kitchen upside down if

I have to. I have been very direct with the families in this investigation. I asked some questions that hurt. I had to. Because tomorrow we might pull another little boy out of a creek somewhere. And I don't have the time to think about etiquette. I don't have the luxury, Mr. Sibley, to sit back and complain about the way the engine runs when it has to get us from A to B and it's a matter of life and death."

A good portion of the room erupted in cheers. Pens scribbled furiously and recorders were thrust further toward the stage, over the heads of the packed crowd, like offerings at a religious revival. Fred Sibley broke into a grin. Stasiak said the press conference was over.

The state policemen conferred in a back hallway of the armory, Elliott standing at the edge of the gathering until the officers began to go their separate ways. Then he approached Stasiak and said, "Dale, can I have a word with you?" The other state policemen left the two of them alone.

"That wasn't helpful," said Elliott. "Having that reporter come out with that in front of a room full of people."

"Forget it. Guy's trying to win a journalism prize. He's playing to the wrong crowd anyway."

"What I'm getting at is the Gilbride interrogation . . . We can't have—even the perception of—we don't need to move backwards, is what I'm saying. And if that had been handled differently . . ."

"Why don't you go ahead and tell me what's on your mind, Elliott, because I don't think I'm getting the full picture."

"We can't afford any controversy. We can't alienate the families."

"You weren't there at the barracks when we questioned them, were you?"

"Well, there *was* a complaint. And now here it is coming back to bite us in the middle of a damn press conference with TV and radio and *I'm* up there lying about it."

"The Gilbrides were hysterical. Which I understand. But some of this stuff is just going to be ugly. This is for grown-ups, Elliott. It's a game for grown-ups."

"Do you really think the Gilbrides were involved in their son's death?"

Stasiak seemed to enlarge himself there in the narrow hallway. "Let me tell you something. I did a case out in Worcester in 1954, Felicia Derry. Rich family lived on the West Side. They told me their daughter—three years old—wandered off down the street and got into a van with a man they didn't recognize. They said they saw it from the front yard and ran after her but couldn't get to her in time. We looked all over the state for her. We found her in a cistern in the cellar of her own home. And her skin was black. And it was slipping off her body when we were trying to pull her out of the fucking tank. And her parents did it. Obviously I don't suspect the Gilbrides now because two more bodies have turned up. But back in '54, the Derrys played it all the way to the end like a kidnapping or a disappearance. It doesn't happen all the time but it happens more than you think."

"Look, Dale, I have confidence in you. I respect your methods. But we have to be careful who we alienate. How we're being perceived." He gestured toward the assembly hall they had just left. "The entire world is watching now."

Stasiak's face took on a brief, disgusted expression. "You want to play politics with this thing, give it over to Warren and his boys. I'm sure he'll handle it just as nice and polite as you want him to." He walked away, leaving Elliott standing there alone.

Stasiak walked out to the front of the armory to see how many people were still hanging around. He saw Sibley standing by himself in the lot where the military vehicles were parked, going through his notes. He walked over.

"The *Globe* send you down here to bust my balls, did they?

I thought they were my friends at the *Globe*." To Stasiak's surprise, the reporter didn't even look up from his notebook.

"Oh, they're your friends, captain. They love you."

"Sibley, huh?"

"That's right."

"You look familiar to me. And your name rings a bell."

"I covered the Attanasio trial. You and I actually spoke a few times."

Sergeant Heller walked up and stood beside Stasiak. He began staring at Sibley and did not take his eyes off him. Sibley squinted at him, nodded, and flicked some ashes from his cigarette. "I covered the Grady Pope investigation too," he said.

"Is that right."

"Yes. I'm still on it, in fact. Even though there isn't much to report."

"You staying down here to follow this thing?"

"No. I just came down for the press conference. Good performance, by the way."

"I could say the same thing to you."

Sibley chuckled. "They did make those claims, by the way, the Lefgrens and the Gilbrides."

"Well, with all due respect to the Lefgrens and the Gilbrides, that's a bunch of shit."

"I had to ask."

"You had to showboat."

"I guess you're not going to give me an exclusive, then."

Stasiak laughed, looked at Heller, and said, "You believe this guy?" Heller kept staring at the reporter.

"I think I'll give an exclusive to the *New York Times*," Stasiak said.

"I didn't see the *Times* here."

"They won't screw around with a bullshit press conference. They'll come up later. Do all their research first. Send a crack reporter up here who will come straight to my office and talk to me directly."

The two men were looking at each other, both, it seemed, trying not to smile.

"I guess you are impugning my skills as a journalist."

Stasiak laughed and shook his head. "If you're not going right back up, come over to the VFW this afternoon about three. I'll get you drunk."

Sibley looked uncertain for the first time in their exchange. He searched Stasiak's face for a moment with his mouth frozen in a half-smile. He dropped his cigarette on the pavement and ground it out with his heel. "I'll be seeing you around, maybe," he said without looking up, and walked off down the street.

Heller handed Stasiak a slip of paper. "Make, model, and tag number," he said. "He lives in Jamaica Plain. The address is on the back."

16

Warren made a quick exit from the press conference, returned to the police station, and closed himself in his office, where he smoldered over the district attorney cutting him out of the investigation. On the heels of having the Weeks case taken away, it was particularly aggravating. Elliott, infatuated with Stasiak and his illustrious resume. Bucking like hell to get his office on the map, his name in the papers. Warren thought of his partially completed application to the FBI, wondering whether he should finish it and send it off.

He telephoned the department of public works, which had requested a detail for some roadwork they had scheduled. There was a note to call the owner of one of the new hotels on Ocean Street, who had complained about cars from the ferry to Nantucket and Martha's Vineyard parking in his lot. A teletype from police in Stonington, Connecticut, described a 1948 Hudson they wanted for a hit and run.

He went through some of the papers on his desk. Easy nine had trouble with its drive shaft. Easy four needed a brake job. There was a circular from Titan Distributors—Specializing in Police Equipment Since 1931. Here was the telephone number that had been in Joseph Leapley's wallet the night they found him handcuffed and beaten on Old Colony Boulevard. Warren picked up the telephone and dialed it. "Hello." A flat, nasal inflection, almost a challenge. Some kind of commotion in the background, but Warren couldn't say what.

He hung up the phone, picked up his keys and his radio, and walked out of the office. As he passed the front desk, Garrity said, "You have two calls from the *Providence Journal*. About the murders."

"Refer them to the state police."

Warren drove over to the headquarters of New England Telephone to see the manager, Alvin Leach. Leach was always cooperative. He seemed to consider it a solemn privilege to provide modern communication technology to the people, but there was an air of reproach about him too, as if he believed that the legions of telephone subscribers needed to be watched, that their sins and their schemes and their baser instincts found new ways to express themselves via the telephone, and it was a burden he carried, the dark side of his calling. On the odd occasion when Lieutenant Warren showed up, he closed his office door and sat down at his desk without any preliminary conversation, as if to say, "Let's get at it."

Warren produced a slip of paper and handed it to Leach. "This is a phone number we found in the wallet of an individual we're investigating."

"For the murders?"

"No. It's another matter. We have a reverse directory at the station but I can't find the number there."

Alvin Leach looked at the number. "It's a Hyannis exchange. Let me have a look at the numerical index." He left the room and returned a few minutes later, shaking his head. "I can't find it in our numerical directory. If someone wrote it down wrong, if they transposed a number, that would explain it." He handed the slip of paper back to Warren.

"The problem is," Warren said. "I've called this number, and someone answered it."

Alvin Leach sat down, rubbing the fingers of one hand with those of the other, as if he was trying to get something off them. "There are mistakes in the numerical directory. It's not perfect.

I take it you did not ask who was at the other end of the line, whether it was a business or a residence."

"I don't want to do that just yet."

"Do you mind if I ask what this is about?"

"It's a case we're looking into, Mr. Leach," Warren said. "I really can't say much about it just yet."

"Of course. But this concerns me, because if it's an unassigned number then it could be a bootleg line and then I have to take a look at my technicians."

"Can we find out who's using it?"

"Of course. It will take some time. We'll have to trace it out from the switching center."

"How soon can we get that started?"

"Within the next couple of days. I'll call you when I know something."

Warren gathered the oak two-by-tens on a bench in the saw shed at Cameron's. The shapes drawn on each one represented the ribs of a boat they were building. He opened the back of the band saw and removed the blade, whose teeth were too coarse for oak, and selected a finer-toothed replacement from a nail on the wall. Little Mike didn't like the band saw, either its noise or its appearance, and stayed outside.

He looked at the way the day glared in the door opening and thought of how completely alone he was. His parents had gone to weekly Mass and he had as well until he reached his twenties. He was engrossed in his career, discovering the world, and liberating himself from his parents' cloistered, primitive existence, from their unquestioning belief. His parents' Catholicism had struck him as both ludicrous and arresting. While he dismissed it largely as traditional superstition, he now respected his parents' discipline, their stations of the cross, their rosary, their penance. He still felt a lump in his throat on the odd occasion he found himself alone in a church.

He didn't know what to make of it. Maybe it was grief for the past.

His mother had been like a strange continent to him. She suffered bouts of debilitating depression and sudden storms of fervor during which she spoke rapidly, flew around their small flat, and prepared for something imminent and miraculous in which she had been chosen to play a crucial role. But most of the time she was quiet, reserved, and plodding. Warren felt that she never revealed anything of herself to him except what came out during her sick periods.

His father was a stoic, dignified man of the last century. He had left home at sixteen, sailing out of St. John, New Brunswick, on a clipper ship to Shanghai. He'd traveled around the world until he developed heart trouble and settled in Boston, taking a job with a bank as a custodian. He had never learned to do anything but sail. Warren believed that his father had lived with a great unexpressed disappointment. His new life in the city—a regular job, a wife, a family, monthly rent—was suffocating and rife with unforeseen trouble. This was how Warren imagined it was. Even as a child, Warren perceived a sadness in his father, and while he wished and prayed that it would be lifted, he absorbed some of it into himself.

His father's sense of decorum would not allow him to speak with loose emotion, but his love for his son was fierce. When Warren was small, his father held him in his lap and read to him. They rode the trolley car together to places his father wanted to show him. They went to Haymarket Square, where walking among the produce and the goods and the things hung from ropes overhead was like being at a carnival. The train roared over their heads on the elevated railway, drowning everything else out, and when it passed, the hawkers' voices filled the air again. It smelled like sawdust and fish and cigar smoke and fresh fruit. On the way home on the trolley, his father would sometimes reach over and squeeze his knee and look at him and chuckle, a rare and private thing, as if they had pulled something off, as if it were one of life's greatest joys.

Before his father died he came as close as he ever would to confiding some kind of loss to his son, some disillusionment, some sentiment that was secret and precious. He came to the edge a few times, it seemed, then stepped back. It was 1935, Warren was twenty-one, when he went into his father's room to find him dead. The feeling, seeing him lying there in his pale blue pajamas, changed by death somehow, like a rough likeness of himself, devastated Warren even now in the quiet of the saw shed.

When he got home from the boatyard that evening, he and Mike ate in the little area that served as the dining room. Warren tried to avoid having all their meals in the kitchen, which was their tendency. It helped make the house seem bigger, less desperate, if they used all of its space. Mike was eating, watching him. There was something funny about the way the boy was chewing and looking up at him. The high jaw muscle moved in the side of his head where his hair was shaved close. Warren had to laugh. "Why are you looking at me?" he said.

"Because."

"Oh yeah?"

"Yeah."

"How would you like it if I placed you under arrest?"

"You can't."

"Oh no?"

"Nope."

"Why?"

"Because I'm your son." Little Mike beamed then. It was like a proclamation of victory, that whatever else was true about him, he had this man who sat across the table from him, a man who would always be present. He said, "I am your son," as if it were the source of their happiness, and Warren, his elbows on the table, his hands clasped in front of his face, looked down at the boy, who was completely unaware of the sorrow and regret Warren often felt—the anger—and the fact that his father was deeply unhappy. And Warren loved the boy. He wondered how his own father would have sorted it out. He would have embraced the love and repudiated the rest as so much distraction, unworthy sentiments that had no business trespassing in his heart. Sometimes we are tested, he would have said, and he thought of his father sitting in the hard wooden pew, gazing at the altar, possessed of some kind of equanimity that had never been available to Warren.

After dinner, he decided to walk Mike down to the drugstore and get him a comic book. Though there was no one out, the neighborhood was unquiet somehow. Warren looked up at the wind in the trees. There was a slight freshening in the air that signaled night and perhaps some faraway intention the ocean might have, say, a squall or an inundation of heavy fog. A pickup truck passed and he thought he heard someone yell something out the window. There were three men in it and they turned to look out the back window at him as they went down the road. When Warren and Mike arrived at the drugstore minutes later, the pickup truck was parked outside. The three men were outside it, talking. Warren recognized one of them as David Langella, whose son had bullied Mike and about whom he had called the courthouse for a records check. When Warren glanced at them, Langella made eye contact. Warren held his gaze as he and Mike went inside. Warren watched the back door as Mike looked through the comics. When they came out, Langella began heading toward him, his shoulders held back, arms out a little, the kind of posturing with which Warren was so familiar. Unless Langella were drunk, Warren didn't think he would try anything stupid, but he was prepared all the same, alert to any quick movements. If anything started, he didn't think the two friends would participate. He shot a quick glance their way and they looked worried.

"Have you got some kind of a problem with me?" Langella demanded, his face close to Warren's.

"You'd better back up a little, Mr. Langella, or there will be a problem."

"I want to know why you're calling the courthouse checking on me."

"That's police business."

"I got a right to know why you're checking on me."

"In fact, you don't. If I'm charging you with something you have a right to know. If I detain you for something you have a right to know why. But if I'm looking at records that is official business."

"Then I want to know why you're making me your official business. I know you're checking on me. I haven't done anything. You're harassing me, Officer Warren, and I'm not going to take it. You overstep your bounds and everyone knows it. You think you got a right to get in everybody's business, well, you don't. What did I do that you're checking on me? Answer me that."

"You're frightening my son. Step back."

Langella looked at the boy and then back at Warren. "You're going to tell me why you're looking at my record."

"What I'm going to tell you is to keep your boy away from my son. You tell him not to touch him, not to speak to him, not to even so much as look at him. Your son has been bullying my boy. You're not stupid. You know what the situation is here."

"So that's what this is about."

"My son has enough difficulties as it is."

"Well, you raised him."

"And you're raising a coward."

"*What?*" Langella thrust his chest out and balled his hands into fists. His nose was practically touching Warren's.

"Your son's a coward, Langella. He picks on handicapped children. He's a big boy and he knows how to be mean but he's got no character. I wonder where he got that from."

Langella's body shifted slightly. He moved his right foot back a bit and set it like he was getting ready to do something.

Warren said, "You get any closer to me and I'm going to be putting your face in the pavement."

"Dave," one of the friends called.

"I'm filing a complaint against you," Langella said. "I'm going to the board of selectmen."

Warren looked down at Little Mike. The boy was clutching his comic book, watching the two men. "Let's go, Mike."

As they walked home, Mike was quiet but agitated. He rolled his comic book up, which was unlike him—he would normally be very careful with a new one—and kept looking behind them. Warren could hear him whispering to himself.

"Mike, it's O.K.," Warren said. "That was Matt Langella's father. You know Matt, right?"

"Yeah."

"I told him I wanted Matt to stop bothering you."

"Is he a bad guy, Dad?"

Warren had to think. He knew what Mike's conception of a bad guy was, and Langella didn't really fit. Not yet, anyway. Warren wondered if he would eventually qualify, if he would get liquored up and start something one day, or if he would encourage his son to go after Mike again.

17

That night, as Warren sat at the kitchen table reading the paper, the phone rang.

"Lieutenant Warren, it's Alvin Leach. Am I interrupting anything?"

"No, Mr. Leach. What is it?"

"I'm all but certain that number you asked about goes to a place on Route 28 called the Elbow Room. I had a man trace it out that far but I wanted to contact you before going any further. Finding out for sure is going to mean sending him up the pole out on the street or checking the service box on the side of the building. It will be conspicuous. The number itself is what we call a phantom number. There's nothing in billing, there's no record of a request for service. We have no information on it whatsoever."

Warren knew of the Elbow Room only vaguely. He recognized it from its occasional appearance in the call log—fights, mostly—though he couldn't place its location.

"Unless there's any further step you'd like to take," said Leach, "I need to disconnect the line and issue a citation for unauthorized use."

"I'd appreciate it if you'd hold off. I'll be in touch with you, Mr. Leach."

Warren paced the kitchen. The whiskey sat on the kitchen counter in its brown paper bag but he resolved not to touch it. He was wound up from his confrontation with Langella and he preferred to sit through it on his own, without any ameliorative.

Toward midnight, when the neighborhood quieted and the

only sound was the insects peeping in the weeds, he removed the
little book from its place between the refrigerator and the breadbox and thumbed its pages. It sprung open at a familiar place:

It was a face which darkness could kill
in an instant
a face as easily hurt
by laughter or light
"We think differently at night"
she told me once
lying back languidly
And she would quote Cocteau
"I feel there is an angel in me" she'd say
"whom I am constantly shocking"
Then she would smile and look away
light a cigarette for me, sigh and rise
And stretch her sweet anatomy
let fall a stocking

The author was someone named Lawrence Ferlinghetti.
He'd read that particular poem half a dozen times now. It made
him think of Ava in a way nothing else did, not even the rare
physical remnants of her presence in the house.

He sat there and shook his head. This house could be alive
with Ava if he allowed it but he would not allow it. His responsibility was to make a safe, happy place for the boy. He found
himself looking warily around the darkened living room, ward-
ing Ava off though she'd been gone now for six years.

Warren met Ava in the spring of 1940 when he was a young
state trooper. He was shy and self-conscious around women.
Being relaxed in their presence seemed like an unattainable
quality to him, and he wasn't convinced that simply being himself was something that would interest them in any case.

Ava was a beauty. Her eyes were an uncommonly pale blue.

Against her raven hair and the dark red lipstick she often wore, they made her look exotic, unsettlingly beautiful. She was lively and outgoing and her sense of humor was almost what Warren would have called risqué, though he suspected he probably didn't get out enough. There was an instant physical attraction between them. During dinner she had slipped a hand over his briefly, which thrilled him beyond what he imagined to be normal, which distressed him, and wasn't it awfully forward of her to do that on a first date? She played the awed girl in his presence, asking about his work, but could sometimes change into someone more worldly: irreverent, laughing at everything. Then she could be tender and pensive. It all seemed like play, like she was trying on different versions of herself to see which one would work best on him. Warren watched the display, dazzled.

He couldn't tell if she was someone he should avoid or if he should give in to the incredible pull that was taking him toward her. She was a local girl. She had grown up on the Cape and knew how to fish, sail, shoot, knit, and cook. She seemed to soften as they spent more time together. Suddenly, it wasn't necessary to go out for drinks or dinner. She borrowed a friend's sailboat and showed him how to sail. They hunted pheasant in the marshes in the days before hotels and housing tracts took so much of it away. Ava fixed him dinner and he sat quietly in the kitchen with her and her mother. There was a candle in a mason jar on the table and a summer storm outside. Ava called her mother "Ma" and touched her shoulder when she spoke. Mrs. Kitteridge's eyes glowed in the candlelight as she watched them and told stories about her childhood on the Cape.

They found ways to be together whenever they could. They got married in July 1941 and moved into a tiny cottage one block off Main Street in Hyannis that had mostly been used for summer rentals. It seemed like he had dropped out of his previous life into some paradise for which he'd been randomly chosen. That time seemed enchanted to him now, difficult to recall but for the odd detail that came without his bidding. They floated into his vision, triggered by things that he couldn't anticipate and which often surprised him. He never knew when the happy time with Ava was going to come back, bright and winsome and killing him with regret.

He got called in early 1942. He and Ava left their little cottage, stored all their things at her parents' house, and drove down to Camp Stewart, Georgia. When training was over, his unit boarded a train bound for San Francisco. He said goodbye to Ava. It was like one of them had died. That night, in a cramped berth that smelled of body odor and freshly issued gear, he nearly wept. Ava went back to Hyannis and waited. They wouldn't see each other again for three and a half years.

When Warren came back from the Pacific things were different. He was edgy and disoriented and he got the feeling that she had gotten used to life without him, perhaps had even come to like it. The truth was he had gotten used to living alone himself. He was anxious to go back to work because he didn't know what to do with their time together. But going back to his old job with the state police would have meant living in barracks for six nights out of the week and he couldn't see how that would help matters. So though he had loved the job and was very proud to be a state trooper, he made the painful decision not to go back. He got hired on as a carpenter at Cameron's boatyard, where he worked for a year until the job with the Barnstable police came through.

Domestic life was uneasy, their small talk excruciating. He realized that they could not simply pick up where they had left off. There was something about the whole experience of being away—the entire experience of the war—that he could not stuff down into himself. It all should have had some momentous effect, what, he couldn't say, but after the unforgettable events in those places it seemed his existence should somehow be changed. The bloated dead on Biak, the emaciated prisoners in slimy rags, the long, steamy concrete cellblocks at the military prison in Leyte, it all seemed too significant to simply merge with the rest of the past and disappear in the wake of his passage into his thirties. Now he sat in a frigid squad car on patrol and then went home to Ava and dinner, where she chewed her nails and looked around the room as if trying to find a way out.

The entire time he was overseas, he had his pay sent home. He hoped that when he returned they would have enough for a down payment on a house of their own. When he got back he was stunned to find there was little of it left. The explanation, such as it was, came fitfully over weepy accountings and indignant claims of innocence. He didn't know what it took to run a house, she said. Her mother died while Warren was away and her father immediately took up with someone else and gave her no assistance. The money didn't go very far. They fought bitterly over it. He wondered if she'd been having an affair, or if she'd hidden the money somewhere with the intent of leaving him and collecting it later.

Warren noticed she was drinking more than he recalled. She'd usually had one or two by the time he got home. If he was working a late shift, he'd find her dead asleep and the room had the rich cloying smell of exhaled alcohol. If he mentioned it, she'd get defensive.

They moved into the rental at General Patton Drive and managed to make a life together. It wasn't what it had been before the war, but Ava relaxed and took to the new place. She turned the homely, functional back hall into a pantry and planted a vegetable garden in the backyard. She was clever and resourceful, converting the place into a comfortable, cheery home. She found economical ways to furnish and decorate it, making her own curtains, refinishing a pair of end tables, cutting fresh flowers from the roadside.

During a spell of cold autumn evenings when it got dark early, he thought he perceived a downward turn in her mood. For the first time, he saw a little sarcasm in her humor that carried a sting and it was directed at him. He was alarmed when he called her at one in the afternoon to find her slurring her words. Warren spoke to her about it and she denied drinking.

Their unhappiness was compounded by isolation. Ava always wanted to go out, but Warren, because of his work, didn't feel comfortable being seen at leisure in public. He felt it compromised him somehow. Warren had to maintain authority and respect with the public, and to him that meant he could not be out among them doing the things they did.

Ava's drinking worsened. They fought. She said she would have a drink if she wanted one and it was the first time she ever said "goddamn" to him. "Someone ought to pry you off your cross," she said, with the sheer bitter joy of releasing something that she had always been longing to let go. It whetted her appetite for conflict. Warren didn't know what he was going to find when he came home. He was dazed by how rapidly things were deteriorating and then Ava became pregnant with Mike. Warren ordered her to stop drinking for the sake of the baby but she only made a little more effort at hiding it.

When Mike was born, it was immediately clear that something was wrong. He was premature and underweight and didn't nurse or make a single peep. He looked around him with a strange adult seriousness as if to inquire what he was doing here. He didn't cry when he needed changing and he didn't cry when he was hungry. He was an eerily quiet and somber baby who stared at things as though he were inexpressibly tired of looking at them. They took him up to Boston frequently to see specialists. Warren didn't like subjecting him to all the tests, even though he lay still through each of them with a profound sadness that even affected the nurses.

Warren and Ava ground out another year together. He made lieutenant while the gulf between him and the rest of the force felt like it turned into something permanent and unbridgeable. Mike was about to turn one and he showed not the slightest sign of making a sound or crawling. The house became cluttered and dismal.

Ava disappeared and was gone for four days. One night at about seven thirty, he answered a knock on his door and found Ed Jenkins standing on his front step holding a reeling Ava by the elbow. She looked horrible. Her clothes hung off her, limp, stained, and slept in. Warren brought Ava inside and put her on the couch. He went back out to Jenkins and said, "Where was she?"

"The Westover Motel."

Warren didn't even know the place.

"A cab dropped her off there four days ago. I was over there asking around about some bad checks and the help flagged me down. They were worried about her."

Warren didn't know what to say. He didn't know how he could go on working on the force—in a position of authority— with this kind of scandal in his personal life. He didn't know Jenkins very well, either. His impression of him at the time was that of someone with a very rough edge and a vulgar mouth, a small man with a chip on his shoulder. Warren didn't know whether Jenkins was doing him a favor or just pretending to so he could get a good close look at Warren's domestic catastrophe and report back to everyone else. He thanked Jenkins and they stood awkwardly on the step for a moment. The lilac by the front door was in full bloom and powerfully fragrant and Warren was embarrassed about it for a reason he couldn't fathom. It made everything seem even more humiliating, more painful. Jenkins said, "I'll be going then, sir," and walked off to his car.

Normally, when there was an incident with Ava, Warren knew when it had been spread around the police station. Garrity would peep at him over the previous night's call log as he passed the front desk on his way in. Marvin Holland would give him a weary, appraising look, as if to gauge how he was holding up. Conversations stopped when he passed.

But it seemed like no one knew about what had happened at the Westover Motel. Warren could not bring himself to believe that Jenkins, presented with such a ripe story, could have refrained from telling it.

Shortly afterward, Ava disappeared and did not come back. That was on a Friday, and he spent the weekend looking for her, one hand on Mike to keep him sitting upright in the front seat. He carried the child from motel to motel, with a picture of Ava that he showed to the front desk clerks. When she hadn't turned up by Sunday night, he called Harold Myrna, who was a retired Barnstable District Court magistrate. His daughter Jane had been engaged to a young serviceman who was killed in Korea in '53. She was currently living with her parents and had a job teaching school. Warren heard she sometimes babysat. He told Harold he was in the midst of a domestic crisis and needed someone to watch over Little Mike. Warren had misgivings when he first saw the tentative, dark-eyed girl who was clearly hollowed out from grief, but it was all he could think of.

Mike grew and developed and Warren was overjoyed as he watched him walk and then talk—much later than other children, but it was an incredible gift all the same, like watching a miracle.

He never discovered what became of Ava. If they pulled a body out of a pond, he thought of Ava and remembered her face so he could compare it to the deceased. It was the same with car wrecks involving single females, and the occasional suicide. He felt sure she was going to turn up in some mess, some accident, in a hospital or a morgue, but she was gone.

If Warren was isolated before, it was far worse now. It was painful to be seen in public. He felt exposed at work and besieged behind the walls of the tiny house, which barely seemed enough to shield him and Little Mike from the merciless eyes of the world outside.

18

T his is Dr. John F. Dowd, coroner, town of Barnstable. It is
1037 hours, Wednesday, July 21, 1957. Present are Captain
Dale Stasiak and Detective James Ferrell, Massachusetts
State Police.

*The decedent is a well-developed Caucasian male child. The
body measures fifty-two inches and weighs an estimated sixty
pounds. The decedent is nude except for a pair of underwear,
white, with an elastic waistband. These are located approximately five inches above the knees. There is no staining or any
visible evidence of biological material on the fabric. The underwear is removed, sealed in an envelope, and given to Detective
Ferrell of the Massachusetts State Police.*

Stasiak and Ferrell watched the pathologist examine the boy's
body. His Dictaphone was set up on a white ceramic tray with his
instruments. The child was rigored into a position that suggested
a fetal animal, taken out of its jar for dissection. His knees were
drawn up, presenting his little feet like a pair of ghastly paws.

*The body has been submerged in seawater for an estimated
twenty-four hours. There is a circumferential ligature mark with
associated ligature furrow on the neck. Also, abrasions and petechial
hemorrhages on the neck. There are petechial hemorrhages in the
conjunctival surfaces of the eyes and in the skin of the face.*

The discovery of Larry Crane's body elevated the investigation to a new level entirely. The off-Cape media, sniffing out
the irresistible story line—unspeakable acts in a remote seaside
idyll—had the phones at the district attorney's office, the

Yarmouth barracks, and the local police stations ringing constantly. Reporters started showing up, including some from radio and television, which was a rarity on the Cape.

Stasiak got a call from Lt. Colonel John Fitzgerald, his commanding officer in Boston, who wanted a rundown on the killings and told him that Governor Furcolo would get him whatever resources he needed. He was irritated at Fitzgerald's quizzing. It strayed into areas unrelated to the murders. Nonetheless, he was now fully in charge of the investigation and Elliott Yost was keeping the locals out of the way. But Stasiak needed a seasoned local he could trust for inside knowledge on certain neighborhoods, on individuals, rumors—any number of things.

There is an extensive area of scalp hemorrhage along the right tempoparietal region extending from the orbital ridge all the way to the occipital area. At the superior extension of the hemorrhage is a linear skull fracture which extends from the right occipital forward to the right frontal area across the parietal portion of the skull.

Nine-year-old Larry Crane had been spotted floating in a creek in Eastham by two boys who were crabbing. He had been hunting frogs with some friends in a wooded marsh about a mile away and had wandered away from his companions. Stasiak considered the case, what was known and what was assumed: The person they were looking for was either a longtime Cape resident or someone who had spent a great deal of time familiarizing himself with its waterways. He knew of the ponds in Truro and he knew about the section of reeds at Kalmus Beach. He was familiar with the creek in Eastham and the woods along its course. That covered an extensive area of the Cape. He was either unemployed, worked at night, or had a job with unconventional hours, possibly one that demanded days at a time away followed by successive days off, such as merchant seaman or commercial fisherman. This allowed him to prowl around in his car and find children at times when most people would be at work. All three of the boys had been abducted during weekdays.

It was believed that the Lefgren boy had been surprised in the reeds and that Larry Crane was attacked somewhere close to the creek where his body was dumped. Kevin Gilbride was likely transported to the pond where he was found, since it was too far away from the rented cabin for the boy to travel on his own. The killer arrived at these places—two of them quite isolated—by car, yet somehow managed to remain inconspicuous. In the cases of Lefgren and Crane, he would have to have left the vehicle parked somewhere and gone out wandering around on foot.

Stasiak's detectives were concentrating on finding a common factor among the three locations, working their way through a number of theoretical combinations that might tie them together. The strange car angle was a Pandora's box but they had no choice but to open it. Predictably, they were flooded with calls. Everything looked suspicious to a community in fear. Forensic evidence thus far was practically nonexistent except for four individual hairs and some shards of very thin glass found on the Lefgren boy. Stasiak thought again about finding a local cop he could rely on. The task force had some of the best detectives he knew. They were driven and focused. But it was the periphery of things that concerned him. He needed an awareness of what was going on around him that only a local could provide.

Jack Dowd worked his way down the boy's body, noting a number of small scrapes and contusions, taking their measurements and describing their locations. As he concluded the exterior examination and prepared for the dissection, he spoke in the general direction of the police officers. "Cause of death is asphyxia by strangulation associated with craniocerebral trauma. He was not sodomized but there was an attempt."

"That's the bruising on the buttocks?" Ferrell asked.

"Yes. But there is no semen and no trauma to the anus."

"What about the head injury?"

"Something blunt. It's the kind of injury you see when someone falls from a height or runs into something."

Jack Dowd measured the purple furrow on the boy's neck and commented that it was about the width of common clothesline rope. Stasiak gathered up his hat and jacket and prepared to leave. "Give us a call when you have the report typed up," he said. "We'll send someone over to pick it up."

Jack Dowd did not respond, but continued laying out a set of retractors on his tray. Stasiak supposed he was still angry over them rousting him out of bed to do the autopsy on the Lefgren kid.

Out in his car, Stasiak radioed Heller. "10-81 at Uncle Sam's," he said, and pulled out. He drove a few miles in stop-and-go traffic. The road was crowded with cheap motels, souvenir shops, ice cream places, and seafood stands. Two young boys were sitting at a picnic table outside a place called Dog 'n Suds. Stopped in traffic, Stasiak watched them. They were unaware at first, talking, sipping from straws stuck through the tops of their paper cups. They were small enough that their feet didn't touch the ground beneath the benches on which they sat. One of them swung his legs back and forth, alternating left, right, left, right. They were oblivious to the man in the gray sedan inching slowly towards them as the traffic crawled forward. Stasiak continued staring long after it became clear that they had noticed him and were uncomfortable. Their movements became self-conscious, their free, animated demeanor vanished as they hunched over the table looking cowed and vulnerable. By the time they became so disconcerted that they got up to leave, the road was clear in front of Stasiak and the cars behind him were honking their horns.

Uncle Sam's Motel was a three-story white stucco structure with a fiberglass likeness of Uncle Sam out front. Cars tended to slow and look at it not only because of its size—it was about fourteen feet high—but because it bent at the waist and doffed its top hat, then straightened again and replaced it. The statue did this every thirty seconds or so, depending on the vagaries of its mechanics. Occasionally it got stuck mid-bow, or halfway through replacing its hat. Once it stayed jackknifed at a right angle for most of an entire winter.

Heller was sitting in the lot, facing the road in an unmarked Chevrolet, when Stasiak arrived. He pulled up alongside the sergeant, facing in the opposite direction. "What is the situation, Heller?"

"The situation is good, sir."

Stasiak looked in his rearview mirror and checked the passing cars.

Heller asked, "What do they say about the kid?"

"Strangled and hit in the head."

"Raped?"

"No, but somebody tried."

"You want to take Gene Henry in and have a go at him?"

"Yes. James Frawley, too. See if he's got access to a car. What do you hear from up above?"

"Nothing."

Stasiak looked in his rearview mirror again. "You know I got a call from Fitzgerald the other day?"

"What for?"

"Asking about the homicides. But he was asking about some other things, too."

"Like what?"

"Just about things in general. What's going on down here."

Heller watched the traffic going by on Route 28. Stasiak did the same in his rearview mirror. "We need a friend, Heller."

"What kind of friend?"

"Someone local. Someone in law enforcement."

Heller considered this. "You want me to come up with some possibilities?"

"I'll work on that. I'll be giving you a name or two. I'll want you to do a full check. Background, personnel records, everything."

19

With his sketchbook and specimen basket on the seat beside him, Father Boyle drove along the headlands, among scrub oak, juniper, and squat pines. The wooded areas were sparse and poor, though when his car crested a rise, the vista was breathtaking, stark and exotic at once. The ocean lay flat on the horizon and blended with the sky at the far reaches of vision in pale lenses of pewter and cornflower blue, the hues calling to mind the sentimental iconography of devotional cards, some type of Marian idyll, someone's forever and ever, things that pulled at his heart and in which he was inexpressibly disappointed.

He found it hard to believe that at one time he thought he had been called. To the degree that that later seemed folly, he dove into researching Catholic mania and the early Christian cults. His room was filled with books and articles that would have made people wonder: J. A. Wylie's *The Papacy*, works by Bertrand Russell, Alfred Jules Ayer, and Sigmund Freud. He read heretical texts and crackpot treatises, broadsides from the Masons, the collection of obscure atheist writings from seventeenth-century Europe known as the *Clandestina*.

His arrival on Cape Cod, though occasioned by regrettable events, in many ways seemed like deliverance. It was a beguiling place to him, both its geography and its less tangible aspects. There were tall grass meadows with clumps of wild blackberry, rich and terrestrial as any in the Midwest, rolling hillocks covered with scrub, repeating their forms toward the horizon. Sere dunes and skies like sapphire, and on a certain kind of day, nothing but shades of gray and silver, as the entire place submerged itself in a moist somnolent funk. Rain and fog heralded extended periods of Lenten gloom, like a days-long state funeral. Stand at the edge of that marsh in South Yarmouth—he couldn't think of the name—stand there on a November day and look out over the creek the color of road grime. Look out at the palette of grays and maroons and browns. Sit in the confessional on a dark February afternoon and listen to the people sneak into the church. Hear them settle into the penitent's booth. Listen to the things they say.

On remote stretches of shore, among barnacled boulders, and in still coves, Father Boyle sometimes undressed to his boxer shorts and plunged into the water. Once last summer, he stood up in the middle of some cold and glassy shallows, stricken. He'd seen a little too much of himself in a moment, had observed the sad act of clandestine swimming, and then the sun went under and turned the surface of the water into the moody hues of the insides of empty houses and unslept-in bedrooms. He didn't come out of the rectory for two days.

Sitting at his desk looking through the previous night's call log, Warren saw that at 0211 hours there was a report of breaking glass at an antique shop on West Bay Road in Osterville. The caller was a woman who lived across the street. The log did not indicate any response.

Warren went into the hallway and saw the midnight-to-eight shift sergeant down by the front desk filling out paperwork.

"Sergeant."

"Sir."

"There was a call last night about a break-in on West Bay Road in Osterville."

The sergeant frowned. "I don't recall, sir."

Warren looked at the call log. "0211 hours. The caller reported breaking glass. Said she saw people on the lawn across the street and they ran off when her husband came out on the porch."

"Oh. That was the antique dealers' place." He glanced sideways at Warren. "The queers."

"No one went over there?"

The sergeant stopped writing for a second and looked at Warren. "No, sir. We were, uh . . . We were tied up I think, sir. If I recall."

Warren went into his office and put the call log down. The shop in Osterville was called Antiquitus. It was owned by a pair of homosexuals who had arrived on the Cape sometime during the war. Posing as brothers, they moved into the big Federal-style house. It was a remarkable property, over twenty acres with a century-old orchard, a large barn, and a herring run passing through. It was unusual to see them out anywhere. They lived in the house from May to September and supposedly spent winters in New York City. They dealt in high-end antiques. Jackie Kennedy was said to be a frequent visitor.

It had been unofficial policy under Chief Holland to ignore calls to the place. They had been burglarized a number of times and vandalized as well, and as far as Warren knew, no action was taken. The men themselves didn't even call anymore. If there was an incident, the department usually found out about it through word of mouth. Occasionally a neighbor would call it in.

Warren filed the call log and looked out the window. Eight-to-four was on the road and the station was quiet. Mike had been accepted at Nazareth Hall and had been going there for two weeks now. Jane had asked, "Will you still need me now that he's in school?" He hadn't thought about what it would mean for his arrangement with Jane. "Yes, I need you," he said. He blurted it out, unconcerned with how it might sound until he actually heard it. He needed Jane in his life, and he was just realizing, there, in that moment, all the ways in which this was true. Somehow she raised them up—him, Mike, the sad little house—when they might otherwise plunge into hopelessness. But he didn't know how he could pay the tuition at Nazareth Hall and keep her, too. Her hours would be reduced and she would find work elsewhere.

He sat there for a while longer, thinking about how, if he were formally appointed chief of police, he would be able to pay Jane to be at the house during the day and handle Mike's tuition as well. He considered stopping in to see Marvin Holland, though he didn't particularly want to. It was the promotion, or the possibility of the promotion, that was why he wanted to visit. Warren felt shameful and underhanded. But it had to be done. He would sort it out later, whether it was wrong or not.

Warren found the chief sitting up in bed, going through a pile of mail. The television was on. He spoke to him from the doorway. "You're looking good, chief."

Holland looked up, waved him in, and continued with his mail. Warren entered the room and stood by the bed. "How are you feeling?" he asked.

The chief tossed his head in the direction of the television set. "Turn that damn thing off."

Warren reached up and turned the switch.

Holland stuffed a letter back into an envelope he had torn open. His motions were rough and clumsy. "What's going on?" he asked.

"Not much," said Warren. "I just wanted to stop in and see how you were getting along."

"Oh, I'm all right. They're letting me out next week. I'm supposed to sit down with the doctor so he can tell me what I can and can't do. I probably won't be coming back to work."

There followed a silence which Warren tried to end as quickly as possible so it didn't seem so much like the obvious was hanging between them, but before he could defuse the moment, Holland said, "Listen, Bill, are you having some kind of beef with Dave Langella?"

Caught out, Warren groped for a quick response.

"Did you ask for a records check on him down at the court-house?"

"Yes, sir. I did."

"Why?"

"I wanted to find out a few things about him."

"What for? Has he done something?"

Warren sat down and placed his hat on his knee.

"He's mad as hell, Bill. He went to the selectmen about it."

"With all due respect, sir, who the hell is Dave Langella? I can't run a records check on him?"

"*Why* were you running a check? That's the point."

"He's no good."

"Is that a fact?"

Warren did not respond.

"Has this got something to do with your son?"

"His kid abuses my boy."

"That's personal. *Personal*, Bill. You can't go around using your authority to settle personal issues. We had this discussion the last time you did this. Now, I understand about your son. But you don't use your position to get even, for Chrissakes."

Warren burned inside, furious at the chief's hypocrisy—the chief, who got friends and influential people off the hook, who looked the other way if it was more convenient, who had allegedly used his own position to enrich himself when they improved the municipal airport.

"He approached me when I was out walking with my son. He got aggressive and it came close to assault."

"If he assaults you, lock him up. Break his head for all I care. But this other crap, cut it out."

"Has he got some kind of pull?"

"*I* don't know if he's got some kind of pull. No more per-sonal stuff. That's it."

Warren's heart was pounding, his breath coming heavily. He

tried to disguise it, picking his hat up off his knee and adjusting the dents in its crown. The chief scattered the envelopes around on his bedspread, then collected them all together again. "What else?" he said.

"Not much. Things are pretty quiet. If you don't count the murders."

"A terrible thing. How are the cars running?"

"They're all right," said Warren. "The usual problems."

"You know they're going to be adding a cloverleaf off the highway at the Howard Johnson's?"

"I got a call about it."

Warren waited, going along with the small talk, until he finally said, "I should get back." He walked down the corridors of the hospital miserable with anger. If Holland couldn't see that what Warren had done with Dave Langella was no different from his own dealings with any number of people, then he was blind. And Warren did not believe that the chief was preoccupied and didn't have any interest in the killings. There was a reason he was not discussing it. Didn't Holland trust him?

Warren got in his car and drove down Main Street, through town, into Centerville, quieter, greener, cool and shadowy for long stretches down the road. Osterville's grand old houses appeared, meticulously maintained behind billowing drifts of honeysuckle, meadow rose, and rhododendron, behind sculpted boxwoods and small fields of daylilies, the vegetation like defensive works, the houses like dignified old relics, with crooked windows and canted porches, but glistening with new paint.

The antique dealers' property extended far back from the road. Ava had showed it to him before the war, during the winter. It was unoccupied then. There had been snow on the ground that day. They walked past a big barn in the back with six windows on each side and a large orchard whose trees were gnarled, spidery shapes against the gently rolling white ground. They followed the herring run into the woods, frozen along its edges but rushing and burbling in the center, beautiful, quiet. The air had been harsh in his nostrils but pure and clear and bracing. Ava wore sealskin boots and trudged confidently among the snow-covered rocks at the water's edge, watching the stream with an intent, piercing expression. Warren hadn't been back since.

He pulled into the drive in front of the building. It was a three-story white clapboard house with a slate roof façade in the front, a novelty from the nineteenth century, the kind of house built by people of means who wanted to set themselves apart from the dreary shingled commonality.

He got out of the car, placed his fedora on his head, and bent the brim a little in front. Off in the side yard, two men were watching him. One was squatting in the grass, the other standing nearby holding a rake. Warren approached them. They seemed to freeze, watchful and uncertain. He showed his credentials. "I'm Lieutenant Warren, Barnstable Police." The squatting man went back to what he was doing, picking up pieces of glass and dropping them into a dustpan. James Holbrooke was balding, about sixty, his blond hair infused with silver. He wore white Bermuda shorts, sandals, and a plaid cabana shirt. The man with the rake—Grayson Newsome—looked a bit younger, slight, dark hair shaved military style though most of it was gone. He wore wire-rimmed glasses and a long-sleeved white shirt buttoned all the way up to the top. He had on a pair of paint-stained shorts and PF Flyers.

"O.K.," said Holbrooke. Newsome rushed forward and raked some scattered glass into a pile. Warren said, "I understand you had an incident here last night."

Holbrooke didn't look up when he spoke. "In fact, it was a burglary. And we didn't report it."

"Your neighbor did. Number thirty."

"Eleanor," Newsome said wistfully.

Warren looked at the broken window. It was nearly six feet tall. Its muntins were splintered and he could see the dim cavernous interior of the antique shop. He stepped closer and peered in. There was a set of pocket doors partially open, separating one large room from another. The walls around the pocket doors were packed with objects—hung from hooks and mounted on shelves.

Warren turned back to the men. "Was this the only place they got in?"

Holbrooke dropped another piece of glass into the dustpan and looked up at him. "Yes," he said. "But you needn't bother."

"I need to get a list of the things that were taken, along with a description and their value."

"Honestly, I'd just as soon pick up the glass and get the window repaired and leave it at that. Rather than waste time with a lot of . . ." He waved his fingers in the air instead of using a word.

"This is a burglary," Warren said.

The man turned and appraised the window. "It certainly is."

"You don't want to make a complaint?"

"Mr. . . . Warren, is it? We haven't been treated very well by this community, particularly by the police department, though that might not be your fault."

Warren shifted his feet.

"We've been burglarized many times over the years, and no action has ever been taken. We've lost thousands of dollars' worth of antiques and we never got a single item back. People would probably like it if we left. Maybe it's their way of getting us to leave."

Warren looked over at Newsome and his eyes went to the ground. "Do you know what was taken?" Warren asked.

Newsome said, "A hanging lantern. The Gothic revival one. And a Japanese tea caddy. From what I can see so far."

"I would imagine you have better things to do," Holbrooke said. "Considering recent events."

"There's a state police task force working on the killings," Warren said.

Holbrooke carefully lifted a small shard of glass from the lawn. "I cannot imagine what could possess someone to do a thing like that."

Newsome said, "I feel so sorry for those families."

"If you want to make a complaint," Warren said, "I can get this window dusted for fingerprints right now."

The two men looked at each other. "I don't know," Holbrooke said.

"Maybe they'll find our things," said Newsome.

"Maybe someone will retaliate because we filed a complaint."

Warren said, "If people know there aren't any consequences to breaking into your business, they'll keep doing it."

"Well, that's pretty much the current state of affairs, I would say."

Warren looked down, scratched his cheek.

"Would we have to go to court and everything else if you made an arrest?" asked Holbrooke.

"To describe the stolen items. To testify that your place was burglarized, yes. You didn't see this person?"

"No."

"Then you wouldn't have to identify anyone. I'm recommending you do it."

Holbrooke walked over to Newsome and said something Warren could not hear. He then turned to Warren and said, "Can we discuss it? Grayson and I?"

Warren nodded and walked back over to his car. Jenkins came on the radio, asking for his location. He sat behind the wheel and picked up the mike. "I'm 10-17 on West Bay Road, Osterville."

Jenkins requested he contact him when he was finished, then signed off.

20

J enkins pulled into the parking lot of a shuttered yellow brick building a short distance from a dive called the Elbow Room. He got out of the car and climbed up on the loading dock, from which he had a good view of the place. The lieutenant had traced the number they found in Joseph Leapley's wallet out here. In fact, the manager at New England Telephone had called that very morning to say that he'd had a technician climb the utility pole outside the place at three o'clock in the morning and send a signal through, confirming it.

Jenkins leaned against the wall and smoked a cigarette. Traffic rolled by, east and west. He thought about the murders. He knew the state police were hitting it hard and had gone nationwide with their search but he had been calling around to some of his contacts to see if he could scare something up. So far he'd had no luck. Stasiak had someone watching James Frawley but according to Dunleavy, there was nothing new on him. Gene Henry, the cook from Mildred's Chowder House, was still very much a person of interest, since no one could corroborate his whereabouts at the times of the killings.

Apparently, Dunleavy had made a good impression on someone with the state police. They were always finding things for him to do. Jenkins's days were largely idle. He'd been out here three times now to have a look at the Elbow Room, more because he was tired of sitting in his office than anything else. He'd driven through the parking lot once, but he couldn't be bothered to write down license plates. There was a handful of cars that were always parked by the rear entrance—employees, he supposed. One of them was there now, a blue and white Cadillac.

A Barnstable cruiser went by and he saw its brake lights go on as it went out of sight. A minute later, it came back in the other direction and drove up to the loading dock. "Jesus Christ," Jenkins muttered. Officer Welke got out of the cruiser. For some reason, he and Welke hadn't gotten along from the start. It began at the scene of a domestic dispute, when Jenkins had told the patrolman to go looking for the abusive husband at his sister's place where he was believed to have fled. At the time, a fight had broken out at the Panama Club, but it was under control, with Warren and the shift sergeant on the scene. Welke gave Jenkins a number of reasons why he should go to the Panama Club instead, offering his opinion on the lesser importance of a fat broad getting knocked around by her husband in a lousy neighborhood. They got into it. Jenkins put his hands on Welke, who reached for his nightstick, and they had to be separated by another cop and two ambulance attendants who were there to treat the wife's injuries.

Now, he watched the officer swagger toward him, adjusting his belt, touching the butt of his revolver, his handcuffs. "Is there a problem?" Welke asked.

"Now there is."

"What are you doing? Meeting your boyfriend?"

"Get the fuck out of here, Welke."

Welke looked at him, nodding, as if assuring himself that something he had long believed were in fact true.

"I'm working, Welke. You're interrupting me."

"Yeah? What are you working on?"

"Shit they wouldn't ask you to do in a million years because you can't be trusted."

Welke turned back toward his cruiser. "I'm not going to lose my job over a fight with you."

"No. There's a dozen other reasons they could choose from."
Welke held his middle finger up and drove off.

Jenkins had kept his problem with Welke quiet but now he felt he might have to say something to the lieutenant. He watched Welke's cruiser pull away and seconds later, the blue and white Cadillac materialized at the entrance to the Elbow Room's lot and turned right. Jenkins jumped down from the loading dock and walked to his car. He cut into traffic on Route 28 and followed.

He tailed the Cadillac to Dennis, where it stopped at a service garage called Brinkman's Brake & Lube. It was by itself, with no other buildings around. Jenkins kept going and didn't see another dwelling until he was two miles down the road. He turned around and drove past the service station again. The garage doors were closed. The Cadillac was parked in the back, only the tail end of it visible from the road.

He sat in stop-and-go traffic all the way back to Hyannis, where he stopped at the Ocean Street docks and bought a clam roll from one of the vendors down there. He radioed the lieutenant, who said he was looking into something over in Osterville, but didn't say what. Jenkins requested a call back when he was finished.

The detective sat in his car and smoked. Most of the fishing boats were out and there were a few tourists wandering along the pilings, looking bleakly down into the petroleum sheen on the water below. He looked down the line of boats to find Warren walking toward his car, looking afflicted and severe, like he was getting ready to do something drastic. Jenkins got out and met him by the pilings. "What's going on?" the lieutenant asked, and without taking a breath or waiting for a response, said, "You have a cigarette?"

Jenkins held his pack of Chesterfields out and Warren took one. "What did you want to see me about?"

"Alvin Leach called this morning," said Jenkins. "That

telephone number goes to the Elbow Room. He had one of his guys climb the pole outside and send a signal through at three o'clock this morning."

Warren lit his cigarette and drew on it hard, his eyes wide and going down the row of boats like he was suffering from some kind of possession. Jenkins began to wish he hadn't called him.

"I was just over at the Elbow Room a little while ago," said Jenkins. "There's a two-tone Cadillac that's always parked behind the place. Anyway, I followed it to a service station called Brinkman's Brake & Lube in Dennis."

"Brinkman's."

"Yeah. It's way the hell out in the middle of nowhere. And it didn't look like there was any brake or lube work going on. Anyway, I got the plate number on the Cadillac."

"Run it through the registry of motor vehicles. And see what you can find out about Brinkman's. Have you heard from Dunleavy?

"He's out doing something with the staties."

"Like what?"

"I guess Gene Henry's still on their radar. They got him looking into that, as I understand it."

Warren nodded. "I was just over visiting Marvin."

"How's he doing?"

"They're going to release him pretty soon. I brought up the murders and he didn't have a word to say about it."

Jenkins watched Warren work on his cigarette as he spoke. "He's probably out of sorts," Jenkins said. Warren looked up and down the docks again. Jenkins had seen him worked up like this before. The transformation was so drastic he found himself both compelled to watch and anxious to be clear of him. Each of Warren's movements was explosive, his eyes devouring the scene around him. It was impossible to reconcile this person with the formal, disciplined man he knew. He had seen this side of Warren come out in scuffles or when some suspect was giving him lip. But he also got this way when he felt he'd been crossed. He took things personally, the lieutenant.

"What's going on in Osterville?" Jenkins asked.

"A burglary."

"Where?"

"An antique shop."

"Which one? The homos?"

"Yeah."

Jenkins suppressed his reaction. As far as the department was concerned, the place didn't exist. The two guys who lived there knew it, too. Somehow it figured that the lieutenant, intense and furious, would go over there to check it out. It figured, too, that he would wind up on the wrong end of this one. It was usually kids who broke into the homos' place. Jenkins's boys knew some kids who did it from time to time. He could imagine the mess that was going to fall in the lieutenant's lap when he hauled someone in over this. Warren said, "Any ideas who we ought to look at for that one?"

"No idea."

They went back to their cars. After Warren left, Jenkins sat at a traffic light thinking about the lieutenant. He had unrealistic ideas about human nature and how the world worked. These weren't good qualities in a policeman. On the other hand, he seemed perfectly suited. Naïve, yes, probably, in some ways, but on the right side and willing to go down that way. There were some people who needed a cause—a war, a disease, an idea—and they were only truly themselves when chasing after it. The qualities that made them stand out were the same ones that made them difficult to live with and which sometimes destroyed them. Jenkins reflected that he might have to be careful around the lieutenant, to think very carefully about where he followed him and how far.

21

D r. Hawthorne waited in his study for his ten o'clock appointment. The local paper was on the desk before him, the front page carrying the story about the murdered young boy whose body had been found in a creek in Eastham. Hawthorne read the account, sifting through the lines of newsprint until he was satisfied that, aside from the basic facts, the article contained nothing of interest to him. He raised his eyes at what he thought was the sound of someone downstairs. For a moment he thought it was his patient, but then the house was silent again. Edgar?

Edgar was working on a fishing boat now, which Hawthorne opposed. Keeping company with fishermen. Coarse men. Impulsive. He might start getting ideas.

Hawthorne reached into a drawer and took out his prescription pad. He thumbed through it and reconsidered his earlier suspicion that some of them were missing. Once again, he looked around his study and tried to see if anything was amiss.

Now there was noise downstairs again. *This* was his ten o'clock appointment. Charles Vogel. The halfhearted stealth. The tentative way Mr. Vogel disturbed his surroundings because as much as he wished he could go about unseen, he knew it was not possible, a knowledge that, Hawthorne believed, accounted for at least some of the strangeness of his affect, the combination of mincing about and not giving a damn.

Vogel walked in and quickly took a seat. This was intended, Hawthorne knew, to minimize a full view of him, though what was visible in that brief moment told Hawthorne enough, and that was that Mr. Vogel hadn't made any progress since his last appointment. He wore a short-sleeved jersey with broad vertical red and blue stripes and loose dungarees with the cuffs rolled up to show off a pair of spotless white Chuck Taylors. He wore bangs and had a cowlick in the back, which, Hawthorne suspected, had taken some work to create. Charles Vogel was thirty-eight years old.

"How have you been this week, Charles?" Hawthorne asked. Vogel bridled, stirring in his chair.

"Despite your affinity for 'Charlie,' your formal name is more age appropriate. Which is why I use it. And while I'm on the subject, your wardrobe . . ."

Vogel reddened, his eyes locked on some point beneath the desk.

"You remember the discussion we had last week about clothes," said Hawthorne. "Age appropriate. This is not trivial, Charles. This gets to the heart of why you're here. Do you understand?"

Vogel nodded, mumbling.

Hawthorne watched his patient expectantly, though the man could not come up with a response and appeared to be incapacitated with anger and embarrassment. Hawthorne let the silence draw out, his eyes fixed on Vogel. Finally, he said, "How is your search for employment coming along?"

"Nothing yet. I'm looking."

"Drinking?"

"No, I said I was *looking*. I'm looking for work."

"I heard what you said. I asked if you were drinking."

"No."

Hawthorne subjected him to another prolonged stare, then jotted something down on his notepad. "So tell me about your week. What have you been doing?"

Vogel stammered through a bland litany of his activities. As

Hawthorne listened, he shook his head. Vogel still hadn't learned that this sort of performance, so poorly executed, intended as an offering to keep Hawthorne from pouncing, was just the kind of thing that induced him to pounce. He took hold of the edge of the newspaper on his desk and pulled it toward him. His eyes quickly went over the dateline. "Friday," he said. "What about Friday?"

"What about it?"

"What were you doing?"

Vogel spread his hands. "Same as the other days, pretty much."

"I'd like you to be more specific."

"I don't know. I got up. Looked at the classifieds. Went and filled out a couple of applications, I think . . ."

Hawthorne listened as Vogel's accounting of himself lost steam and ground to a halt. He gave him fifteen long seconds to pick it up again but Vogel merely sat there and foundered in his Woolworth's Junior Style getup. The psychiatrist tilted back in his chair and said, "*Why do you ask about Friday, Dr. Hawthorne? What differentiates Friday from Tuesday? Or Sunday? Why Friday, Dr. Hawthorne?* But you do not ask, Charles. You do not ask."

"I don't know what you mean."

"Hm?"

"I don't have any idea what you're trying to ask me, Dr. Hawthorne. I don't . . . I wasn't supposed to be *here* on Friday, was I? My appointment is always on Wednesday."

Vogel's face was searching, disconcerted. "I mean, I guess you've got some reason for asking me about Friday but I don't know what it is. I feel like I'm supposed to know. Like you'll be upset with me if I don't come up with the right answer."

Hawthorne scrutinized him for a while and said, finally, "That *is* the right answer, Charles."

A half hour later, he watched from the window as Vogel made his way down the street. His gait was stiff and self-conscious but as he gained distance, it became noticeably looser, as if he were transforming mid-stride. In time, his arms swung, his head lolled this way and that, and there was a barely perceptible bounce to his step, as if the person who had walked into Dr. Hawthorne's office thirty minutes earlier had become someone else altogether.

Dunleavy pulled into the lot at the state police barracks and jogged up the walkway to the front doors. Captain Stasiak had asked him to show up for the briefing the state police investigators held every Monday, which had taken him completely by surprise.

Dunleavy showed his badge to the sergeant at the front and was waved down the corridor. At the far end, outside the room where the briefing was held, there were four desks that had been moved out into the hallway, an impromptu workspace for people manning the phones and taking down tips. Standing by the desks was a state police matron, and a uniformed trooper. She was removing brand-new children's clothing from its packaging and laying it out on one of the desks as the trooper watched.

Inside the room, there was a large table where eight men were seated. Captain Stasiak was speaking. "Ferrell, what's— Nice of you to join us, Dimwitty."

Everyone chuckled.

"Where do we stand with the Crane neighborhood, Ferrell?"

The state police detective ran down the latest on his canvassing of the area. "There was a handyman outfit in the neighborhood a couple days before the killing, doing some shingling," he said. "It's a fly-by-night operation. I need to track them down. A single male at 5 Linden Street whose whereabouts aren't real solid. Straight. Got a girlfriend. Works sometimes at Kreigel Produce. Says he spent the previous night with her and stayed part of the day but the time frame is fuzzy. Let's see . . . seven suspicious car sightings. No tags. Makes on some of 'em."

An officer gave an update on the Gilbride murder. The crime scene was remote and detectives hadn't been able to find a single person who had been in the area during the week of the killing. They questioned the members of a small bird-watching society that frequented the location where the Gilbride boy's body was found, and visited bait and tackle shops to ask about who was fishing the ponds in Truro. They were currently working their way through interviews with the agencies that managed inholdings in the vast stretch of land between Orleans and Provincetown—the state department of natural resources and its numerous local counterparts—looking for hikers or campers or anyone else who visited on a regular basis, anyone who stood out for any reason.

"As you all know," said one of the new men who had been sent down from headquarters, "It's ninety-nine percent certain the hairs found on Stanley Lefgren's body are from his mother. They were probably on the clothes the kid was wearing. The lab hasn't come up with anything on the glass found in his hair. They're looking at electrical fuses, different kinds of lightbulbs . . ."

"Have them send it down to the FBI in Washington," said Stasiak. "Where are we with James Frawley?"

The men who had been watching Frawley reported that he wandered extensively: to the woods at the edge of the municipal airfield; to the railroad tracks near the defunct Hyannis station; to the wilderness surrounding a vast salvage yard just outside of town. Recently, Frawley had spotted them, and now wandered no farther than the shade of the locust trees in the front yard of the Salvation Army shelter. Interviews with the staff and residents weren't particularly helpful. Frawley kept to himself. Opinions ranged from the impossibility of him harming children to his being just the type to do such a thing. The policemen had not seen him anywhere near a car.

Stasiak took the cord to the Venetian blinds in his hand and jerked them open. "The list," he said.

An officer consulted the statewide list of sex offenders which he had on the table in front of him. "There are two names that haven't been ruled out."

"Who's got those?"

Dunleavy raised his hand. "I do."

"And?"

"The first guy went to the Vineyard shortly after the Lefgren killing. Supposedly he's still over there but I'm looking into it. He could have come back for Crane. I doubt it, but . . ."

"I don't want to know whether you doubt it, Dunleavy. It's not important to me, your hunches."

Dunleavy looked around the table at the officers, who were suppressing grins, watching him closely.

"Please continue, detective."

"Gene Henry says he's not sure where he was for the Gilbride killing but he says he wasn't in Truro. He was drinking at the Windjammer Lounge for Lefgren *or* he was home asleep. Very iffy. Home for Crane, so he says, but no corroboration. When we—when Barnstable was on the Lefgren investigation, they got information that he had a girlfriend out in Truro and that he liked to go surf casting out there at Longnook Beach. But he says none of that is true and I haven't been able to confirm it. He's really touchy and doesn't want to talk."

"That's a priority," Stasiak said. "Stay with it until he's in or out."

Stasiak's men were looking for ways to connect the three murder scenes, all miles away from one another. Truck drivers, salesmen, commercial fishermen, retirees, and the unemployed, anyone who had an unstructured schedule and freedom of movement was being considered. None of the victims' missing clothing had been found. Stasiak had officers consult with the families and reconstruct what each child was wearing at the time of death, then purchased the items and was having them photographed for distribution.

In the basement of the barracks was a collection of miscellaneous objects they had retrieved from each of the crime scenes: cans, bottles, cigarette packages, a lighter, a small cardboard box for a transistor radio, two fishing lures, six sodden pages of a magazine called *Leg Show,* one PF Flyer shoe, a spent .410 gauge shotgun shell. Anything that had been found in the general vicinity of the crime scenes Stasiak had collected and dusted for latent fingerprints. They had three readable prints, which they had sent off to the state police crime lab to see if they matched anything on file. The items were laid out on the basement floor, in areas chalked off with the victims' names, each numbered, photographed, and indexed.

Stasiak looked out the window and watched a dark blue sedan pull in off the road and park. Sgt. Heller got out, wearing a beige London Fog, his shirt collar open. He looked ill-tempered and weary. Stasiak adjourned the meeting and everyone got up to leave. He called after them, "This guy has a car, gentlemen. He's driving around. He likes the outdoors. He's a local. He's free during the day. Use your heads. Dunleavy, see me in my office."

Stasiak went around to the side entrance and met Heller as he came in. "Where've you been?"

"New Bedford."

"And?"

"Dunleavy's got secrets."

They walked abreast down the hallway. Dunleavy was sitting outside Stasiak's office, waiting. They passed him without a word and went in. Heller closed the door. "He worked for the New Bedford PD before he came here. 1949 to '54. What he likes to tell people is that he came up here because he wanted a nicer environment for his wife and kids. The real story is that when he was working robbery down in New Bedford, he got on to a bunch of guys who were fencing stolen property out of an old textile factory near the wharf. Dunleavy and another cop took payoffs and gave them protection in return. Then he got ambitious and tried to put the squeeze on some guy who was selling pills to the fishermen down there. This guy knew about Dunleavy and the fencing operation. And he'd worked as an informant for the New Bedford narcotics guys in the past, so he had some friends in the department. He saw to it that internal affairs got wind of what Dunleavy was up to. And that was it. He was out of the New Bedford PD. Dunleavy was pretty tight with his CO and I guess he went and talked to him. The CO fixed it so all that stuff disappeared. At least enough so Dunleavy could get the job here. But you can still find it if you go looking hard enough."

Stasiak sat down at his desk. "Does Warren know about this?"

"No."

"Anything else?"

"He's married, got a son and a daughter. I suppose he'd like to send them to an Ivy League college, which he won't be doing on $7,000 a year."

"I want you to spend some time with him."

"What do you want me to do?"

"Evaluate, Heller. Evaluate."

When Heller was gone, Stasiak sat in his office with the door closed, looking around at the photos and news clippings he had had framed and mounted on the walls. There was the famous shot of himself and the US attorney from the photo essay that appeared in *LIFE* in the summer of 1955, when the Attanasio trial was going on. Stasiak was shown in a tight close-up, consulting with the head prosecutor, their foreheads almost touching. The image had something about it of a baroque Old Testament scene. "Last Days of the Dons: A Boston Passion Play" was an intimate portrait of the Attanasios, the prosecutors, and the investigators shot entirely in the shadowy corridors of the Suffolk County Courthouse and the Spartan back offices of the federal building.

His eyes moved over the wall, taking in the headlines and the grainy images of men in trench coats, himself among them—getting out of cars, climbing the steps to the US attorney's office, caught unaware by photographers on the street outside Post Office Square. Freezing nights on surveillance in the North End, showing the inexperienced FBI guys the ropes. The long hours listening to the bugs they'd planted at the Venus Lounge and a warehouse in East Boston. Heller. Fitzgerald. The goddamn Irish. He tapped his cigarette lighter against the top of the desk and called out, "Dunleavy. Come in here."

The detective entered and took a seat. "Get to the bottom of this Gene Henry thing," Stasiak said. "I want some answers from this guy. I want eyewitness corroboration that he was where he said he was. You're supposed to know this shit, Dunleavy. You're local, he's local. That's why I put you on it. Stop in Heller's office and get him. Both of you guys on Henry."

22

Warren walked down the hall to Jenkins's office and found the detective on the telephone. "I'm on the line with the Department of Corrections," he said. "Central records. You know that Cadillac I tailed from the Elbow Room yesterday? It belongs to a guy with a past. Hang on a minute." Jenkins spoke into the receiver. "Yes." He took notes on a yellow legal pad as he listened. "That's everything? O.K. Thanks a lot." He put the phone back in its cradle and faced Warren. "George McCarthy. He was convicted of usury in '50. Bookmaking in '46. Me and Dunleavy have been watching the Elbow Room pretty regular and there are three other vehicles we see out there all the time. I ran their plates, too. Corrections didn't have anything on the owners, but when you consider their addresses—South Boston and Somerville— things get a little interesting. The rackets have always been strong in those neighborhoods."

"So we have a guy who's got a history as a loan shark and an illegal phone line going to a bar where he spends most of his time."

"A bootleg phone line," said Jenkins, "That's usually gambling. And Leapley—handcuffed, beaten, and thrown out of a moving car—that sounds like a bad debt to me."

"Do you suppose there's any connection to the Russell Weeks disappearance?"

Jenkins raised his eyebrows. "That might be a stretch, lieutenant."

"But think about it. Mrs. Weeks was specific about numbers and the amount of interest that accumulated on the loan. And now a guy shows up who's got a history as a loan shark and who's possibly involved in a beating."

"Dunleavy thought Miriam Weeks was full of crap," said Jenkins. "So did the DuPonts' lawyer. And back when Dunleavy and I were looking into this, we never found anybody who'd actually seen Russell Weeks beaten up."

"Well, I'd like to see what else we can find out about McCarthy and the Elbow Room. Let's fill Dunleavy in on what we've got so far. Where is he, by the way?"

"State police called him first thing this morning. Said they needed him over at the barracks."

"This is getting to be a regular thing. What do they have him doing?"

"Making friends in the fishing community."

Warren gave Jenkins a puzzled look.

"They're figuring the killer is someone who keeps unconventional hours, someone who has their days free. So they've got him looking at fishermen."

"I guess it makes sense."

"Could be someone who's unemployed, though."

"Who else keeps unconventional hours?"

"Cops. Wouldn't that be something."

Warren went back to his office, unlocked a desk drawer, and took out the file on Russell Weeks. He picked up the phone and called Alvin Leach at New England Telephone. "Mr. Leach, I'd like to get a look at some phone records. A Russell Weeks of Marstons Mills."

"How far back do you want to go?"

"The last three months."

"Very well, lieutenant. If you want to drive over I should have the records by the time you get here."

A few minutes later, Sergeant Garrity stepped into the doorway. "A call for you, lieutenant. It's a woman. She says it's urgent."

"Send it through."

Warren picked it up and listened for a while. The voice was vague and scratchy, like it was coming from a long distance away over a tenuous connection. He repositioned the receiver against his ear. "And what is your name, please?" he asked, but the woman had hung up.

He went back down the hallway to Jenkins's office. "I just got a call. A female, she wouldn't give her name. She said there's a guy with marijuana in one of the rooms at the East End Lodge."

The East End Lodge was a Victorian-era building that had housed offices for the railroad in its heyday and for an assortment of freight companies and seafood wholesalers. It had been turned into a hotel after the Second World War, the new owners opting to leave its Victorian décor in place, either out of fondness for the period or apathy. The place never did very well as a hotel, becoming a sort of flophouse, and though the management did not allow long-term rentals, it was favored by college kids on break and people of little means, so that it had the air of a derelict refuge where the owners held its guests in contempt.

Jenkins telephoned Warren from the lobby. "Boss, this guy's got a few pounds of Mary Jane on him."

"Pounds?"

"Yes, sir. In his travel bag. But here's the thing. He's a reporter for the *Globe*. He's down here to cover the child killings. His name is Fred Sibley."

"And where is he now?"

"Out somewhere. The manager let us into his room."

"I'll be right over."

Joined by a pair of patrolmen, Warren and Jenkins went up

to the reporter's room on the second floor. Jenkins went over to an open suitcase, pulled out a large plastic bag filled with marijuana, and tossed it on the bed.

Warren said. "Anything on the woman who called?"

"No, sir. But if she asked to speak to you, she's got to be local."

Jenkins handed Warren a laminated card attached to a long chain. The word PRESS was printed on it in large block letters. Below that, it read, "Fred Sibley, *Boston Globe.*"

"I remember this guy from the press conference," Warren said. "After the Crane kid was murdered."

At that moment, they heard raised voices in the hall. "What's going on?" A man, indignant, alarmed. They heard one of the cops say, "You need to come this way, sir."

"What is it? What's going on?"

Fred Sibley appeared in the doorway, his mouth slightly open, looking at Warren and Jenkins. He was pudgy, had fuzzy receding hair and a pasty complexion. In his woolen blazer and heavy corduroys, oxfords, and a sweater vest, he looked like a seedy English professor.

"Are you Fred Sibley?" Warren asked.

"Yes. What is this?"

"You have marijuana in your possession, Mr. Sibley. Quite a lot of it."

"Marijuana? What are you talking about?"

Jenkins produced the plastic bag and held it up. The reporter looked at it, his face frozen in an expression of distress. "It's not mine," he said.

"But it's in your room," said Warren.

"It's not mine. I don't know where it came from."

"Well, the fact that it's in your room is a problem, Mr. Sibley."

"I swear, I don't know how it got here."

"Did you have anyone up here with you today?" Jenkins asked. "A girlfriend, maybe?"

"No. I don't know how this got here, I swear. I got up early this morning and I went out to do interviews. I'm just coming back now. I haven't been in this room since 7 A.M."

Warren said, "You can't expect us to believe that this stuff found its way into your possession by itself."

"I did *not* bring that in here. It's not mine."

"Put your hands behind your back."

"It's not mine! I don't know how it got here!"

"Behind your back, Mr. Sibley. Don't make trouble."

Jenkins handcuffed him and sat him down on the edge of the bed. Sibley looked dazed, staring at the floor. "I've been set up."

"Oh, boy," Jenkins muttered.

"I'm down here on assignment for the *Globe*," Sibley said. "I don't use narcotics."

"All I can tell you is get a good lawyer," Jenkins said.

The lounge at the VFW was crowded early on a Friday evening. The plate glass windows behind the bar were darkened, the blue lights along the runway of the municipal airfield visible as long dotted lines running off into the distance. Denny Nelson was in his element, his hair standing up, his spindly arms poking out of the sleeves of his madras shirt. He walked up and down, ribbing people, filling their glasses, rapping his knuckles on the bar in a tattoo. "Oh yeah?" he called out to someone at the far end. "What do you want, a medal or a chest to pin it on?" A ripple of laughter drifted up the bar.

A man wearing a postal service uniform said, "I don't see how it could get any stranger. Five pounds of marijuana. I'll never read the *Globe* again."

"I never read it anyway," said his neighbor on the adjacent stool.

"Murder and narcotics," said the postman. "That's what

we've got down here now. I hear there's a guy who works at Mildred's Chowder House that they've been questioning about the murders."

"Really?" the man adjacent said. "I didn't hear that. Do you know who?"

"No. My neighbors, though, their kid buses tables there and he says they've been over there a few times to talk to the guy."

Someone two stools down said, "Mildred's Chowder House? Who?"

"I don't know," the postman said.

"They're talking to everybody," a redheaded man said. "State police were down at the trucking company where I work asking about the drivers."

A voice from one of the tables behind them said, "How can this person kidnap three kids and kill 'em without anybody seeing anything? Answer me that."

"He's smart," said a man sitting at the end of the bar.

"He ain't smart. He's just lucky," said the redhead.

"I hope they string him up by his balls," the postman said.

"Oh, they will."

The conversation had drawn in a half-dozen people now, an ever-growing group of commentators.

"What a sick son of a bitch," said the man at the end.

"Stasiak will find him," said the redhead.

"He'd better."

"He did a hell of a job on the Mafia," said the postman. "Did you read about that?"

"Yeah," said the man at the end of the bar. "The Attanasios."

The redhead got up and went to the cigarette machine. "I'm surprised they haven't tried to rub him out."

"Stasiak?" the postman said.

Denny Nelson sauntered up. "They better bring out the big guns if they're going to try that. Big Dale's a war hero."

"What'd he get?" someone asked. "The Silver Star?"

"It was the Navy Cross, I think," said the postman. "Iwo Jima."

Someone further down the bar called, "I heard he took out a tank."

"Killed a bunch of Japs, anyway," someone else said. "But you know what? If he's such a hotshot, why'd they send him down here? Why didn't they keep him up in Boston where there's real crime?"

"Haven't you been paying attention?" said the postman. "Three dead kids. We got crime right here."

"Yeah, but they sent Stasiak down here before all that started."

"It's a promotion," said the redhead.

"Really?"

"You don't get to say where you go," the postman said.

Nelson folded a damp rag and tossed it over his shoulder. "You know what I heard?" he said. "I heard that Bill Warren was madder than hell that the state police took over the investigation. They say he begged the DA to let him take the case."

"That guy's an idiot," said the man at the end of the bar.

"Warren?" asked the postman.

"Yeah."

"There's some people that like him. They say he's decent. A fair guy."

"Some of his own guys don't like him," said a man standing at the bar with a pair of empty glasses. "He'd turn his own mother in, for Christ's sake. He's probably one of those guys who does all the shit he doesn't want anyone else to do."

"Do you know Al Petraglia?" asked the redhead. "He's a Barnstable cop. He told me that him and Warren got into a fight with this great big fella out on Eel River Road. Must've weighed three hundred pounds. Him and one of the summer specials got there first and the guy was crazy drunk. They beat the hell out of him with nightsticks and it didn't even faze him.

Then Warren shows up and frigging head-butts the guy. Then he gets into a wrestling match with him and chokes him out. Petraglia said it was crazy as hell, the whole place destroyed. He said Warren and this big bastard went right through a wall."

"Oh, he's tough," said the postman.

"But I heard he's crazy," said someone else.

"Crazy how?"

"He can't handle power," said a rough-looking older man sitting by himself at a table. "He goes too far with it. Throws his weight around just because he can."

Someone at the bar said, "He got into a beef with Dave Langella over his kid, that retarded kid of his. So he started doing some kind of investigation on him, looking for dirt. That's the kind of thing he does. That's not right."

"Langella isn't someone you want to piss off," said the man at the end of the bar. "His brother-in-law is Earl Mott, the head selectman. Langella filed a complaint."

The conversation drifted off in another direction.

Sitting by himself in a booth against the wall, Alvin Leach drained his Scotch, stubbed out his cigarette, and surveyed the men at the bar. He decided that he would stay away from the VFW lounge after 7 P.M. The place took on a quality he did not like. The communal discussion had broken apart and now there was a din of many small conversations all around him. A hulking man to his right said, "Not for forty-five I can't. Fifty-five, yeah. At least. I got to eat."

"Nellie!" someone shouted. "Whadja say? *Nellie!*"

In the booth behind him, a low voice said, ". . . what happened to my cousin Artie."

Another voice: "I didn't hear."

"He won all that money at the Elbow Room and he kept going back."

"And he lost it all."

"And then some."

Alvin Leach tensed at the words "Elbow Room." He strained to hear but momentarily lost the conversation behind him. The conversation at the bar had swelled, the volume loud and fueled with alcoholic mirth. The congenial quiet of early evening had passed and the night, sharp-edged and ungoverned, was upon them.

"*Douchebag?*" someone farther down the bar yelled. "*Douchebag?* Where'd you get that?"

"Someone ought to wash your mouth out with soap, Nellie."

Denny Nelson was standing directly under one of the spotlights mounted in the ceiling behind the bar. He was grinning widely, apparently satisfied with himself, but his smile was strangely devoid of light. "I wash it out daily with Johnnie Walker," he said. "It doesn't do any good."

The voice came from behind Leach again. "I wouldn't do it, man. My cousin's in a lot of trouble. You see what they did to him?"

"Who's running that place?"

"Some people from up around Boston. What I heard."

Leach paid his bill and got up to leave. He turned to his left and tried to get a look at the men on whom he'd been eavesdropping but the place was getting crowded and there were people walking past, blocking his view. The bar had taken up conversation as one again, everyone shouting to make themselves heard.

"How come he lives in that shitty neighborhood, huh? Don't you think on a lieutenant's pay he could afford something better?"

"The missus drank it all," someone shouted.

"How about the missus?"

A raucous sound went up, hooting, whoops, and whistles. Nelson said, "She used to come around the back of the lounge and I'd give it to her doggie style over the trash cans."

"Yeah, that kid's probably yours, Nellie."

Uproarious laughter drowned out every other sound in the place. Leach tried once more to see the men at the table whose conversation he'd heard, but he could only see one of them, a workman of some kind with rolled-up sleeves and a tanned face, who looked straight back at him, almost as a warning.

23

On Saturday Warren had work at the boatyard—a cat-boat they were building for a surgeon in Brookline. He worked until sunset, keeping Mike occupied with little chores. On the way home, he stopped at the liquor store, then picked up a bucket of fried chicken and went home. He and Mike sat on the back step and ate, even though the oil tank was just a few feet away and they could smell its industrial stink. He thought he should find a picnic table somewhere and some benches so they could eat in the backyard on warm evenings, maybe string up some lightbulbs on a wire between two trees. Some of the neighborhood children showed up, dirty, bare-footed, potbellied kids with fruit-drink-stained T-shirts and runny noses and a musky, uriney smell about them. They gawked unselfconsciously at the chicken and watched Mike with preda-tory eyes. Warren handed each of them a piece and went back inside. He set Mike up at the kitchen table with the remainder of the chicken and found a couple of frankfurters in the refrigera-tor, which smelled a little rich. He boiled them and dipped them in a jar of mustard and had them with a bottle of Knickerbocker.

On the kitchen table were scraps of paper from something Jane and Mike had been doing. Amid Mike's crayon pictures and his awkward scrawling, he saw her neat, rounded hand-writing. Warren swept the paper aside and tossed an old news-paper on top so it was out of sight. When he got home from work on Friday afternoon, he'd found the two of them in the backyard. To his surprise, Jane was in the lower branches of a pine at the edge of the woods. She had both legs wrapped around a branch and was knotting a rope, her hair hanging in her face. She had on calf-length dungarees. He saw the high arches of her bare feet, the dirty soles, her painted toenails. She looked down at him and grinned tightly, concentrating on the rope. He said, "Jane. Don't fall."

"You'll catch me, I hope."

He nodded and stammered. "What are you doing?"

Mike said, "She's making a Tarzan rope for me, Dad."

He looked down at the boy, who was dressed in an old section of faux leopard skin, something that had belonged to Ava. Jane had fashioned it into a costume, pinning it over one of Mike's shoulders like a prehistoric shift. Warren didn't even know that it had been in the house.

Jane sat up and put her hands on her hips, her thighs gripping the branch, her ankles crossed beneath it. The low angle of the late afternoon sun revealed lines at the corners of her mouth. "We watched Tarzan on TV today," she said, climbing back down. Warren stepped forward to help, but then froze where he was. Jane dropped the last four feet to the ground, landing squarely on her feet, knees bent, arms straight out, like a gymnast. She gave a tug on the rope and looked at Mike. "That ought to hold you and six monkeys."

"Are we going to find some monkeys?"

"That's a job for tomorrow. Maybe your dad can help us with that. I'll bet he knows where he can find a few." She gave Warren a quick look as she said this, playful, sly, he couldn't tell. He felt hopelessly old in her presence. He watched as she slipped into her flip-flops. "Where did you learn to tie knots?" Warren asked.

"Ted showed me. My fiancé. We used to sail."

Inside the house, she gestured toward a framed photograph standing on the dining room table and said, "I hope you don't mind. We found that this afternoon while we were looking for a Tarzan suit."

Ava was staring into the camera. She was wearing a woolen coat, her hands in a muffler. It was the winter of 1948, some outing they'd taken, Warren no longer remembered where. Ava already looked worn-out by then, like she knew what was coming.

Now he was angry. Jane had unthinkingly pushed the past at him, this unwanted artifact of a time he wanted to forget. And what did Mike think of this? Was Warren now going to have to answer questions about his mother, answers the boy couldn't even begin to understand? Was all that bad history now going to have another run at them—this time with the boy in its sights—thanks to Jane's interference? And where on earth had she found the picture in the first place?

She said, "I notice you don't have any pictures of Mrs. Warren around."

"We've put it behind us."

Jane seemed to read his discomfort. "I shouldn't have," she said. "But it was just such a beautiful day and there was sun coming in the windows and there was this picture buried in a box in the utility room and it seemed so sad. We put it in the sun there on the table."

Warren's anger evaporated as suddenly as it had risen. He saw her again with her legs wrapped around the tree branch like a tomboy. Now here she was saying these things. She had no idea, the effect she had.

After dinner, he put Mike in the tub and sat out on the front step with the little book, smoking and watching the evening deepen.

What happened to Robinson
Who used to stagger down Eighth Street
Dizzy with solitary gin?
Where is Masters, who crouched in
His law office for ruinous decades?

A car came out of the neighborhood, moving slowly down General Patton Drive. It nearly came to a stop when it was abreast of Warren. The driver turned to look at him, his face opaque, featureless except for dark curls on the forehead and an upper lip that seemed enlarged somehow. The brake lights flashed for a second and Warren thought the driver was going to speak, but he only looked out his window, his head perfectly still, staring. Warren was about to ask him what he wanted when he drove on, turning right on Bearse's Way.

Years ago, Warren had fastened a holster to the underside of his bed, driving screws through the leather into the wooden slats of the box spring. It was positioned so that, from a prone position in bed, he could drop his hand down and reach the handle of the .38 revolver he kept there. Once Mike was able to go exploring around the house, Warren removed the pistol but the holster was still there. He went into his bedroom closet and reached to the rear of the shelf and felt for the revolver, wrapped in an old T-shirt dampened with Hoppe's oil. There was a box of fifty rounds next to the gun. He opened the cylinder and spun it. He snapped it shut, checked the action, and opened the cylinder again, inserting the rounds into their places.

Warren slipped the loaded revolver into the holster under the bed and went to check on Little Mike in the bathtub. "Are your feet starting to shrivel up yet?"

"Not yet."

"You clean?"

"I guess so."

"The water's brown. You must be clean."

"Can you read me a comic book? Green Lantern?"

"Did I get you a Green Lantern?"

"Yeah. Remember?"

"O.K. Out. Let's dry off, now."

The telephone rang. Warren tossed Mike a towel and went into the kitchen to get it. Alvin Leach was on the other end.

"I'm sorry to call at this hour, lieutenant. But I wanted to let you know that I pulled those records you asked about. Russell and Miriam Weeks. And I thought you might want to know that the number you asked about—the number we traced to the Elbow Room—is there."

"In their records?"

"Yes. Someone called that number several times." Before Warren could respond, Alvin Leach continued. "And last night I was at the VFW and I heard some fellows talking."

Warren, pacing the tiny kitchen as he listened to what Leach had overheard, could feel the excitement of a quickening chase. "There's a good chance I'm going to want to tap that line," he said to Leach.

"Very good. I'll wait for your call."

Outside, a car went by, its headlights making shapes on the wall behind the television set, revealing the spidery dead branches in the high pines as it made its hushed passage down General Patton Drive. Warren watched it turn right and disappear among the little cottages. He couldn't say if it was the car he'd seen earlier.

24

Father Boyle turned off the road somewhere in the vicinity of Truro and wound his way down a narrow blacktop lane through the woods. On his left appeared a cluster of dilapidated cottages set back off the road, vacant, by the looks of them, their shingles so stained with verdigris it looked like they had become part of the woods. He slowed to look at them but suddenly saw a heavy, crew-cut man standing knee-high in a sea of ferns in front of the cottage nearest the road. The sight of him, standing there as if he knew someone was going to drive by, was disturbing.

He drove until the pavement ended in a grove of ghostly cedars and got out of the car. As he bent to get his sketchbook and specimen basket out of the back, he experienced shooting pains in his chest and stood erect until they passed. Sweating and jumpy, he made his way into the brush. The terrain headed upward, the tall conifers continuing up the slope like grave sentinels in the gloaming. In time, he found himself in an old-growth forest where the light was sanctuarial. Father Boyle registered the brief rush of excitement. He had passed through just such a place on that late afternoon in May, not long before falling asleep in a hollow on the moor and waking to that extraordinary experience.

Among some stones near a downed, rotted tree trunk was a discarded bottle. Predictably, he found himself thinking about his time at St. Sebastian's in Erie, Pennsylvania. Though he had begun drinking a few years earlier, it intensified at St. Sebastian's. He was mortified at the turn events had taken, astonished, in an anaesthetized kind of way, at the rapid fall of something that had been so central to his life and his conception of who he was. Even now, years afterward, it was frightening to recall how rapidly he descended.

He had had a grand mal seizure on the kitchen floor of the rectory and was sent to Talbot House in the country outside Baltimore, a place where the Church sent its troubled priests to either dry out or undergo psychoanalysis. There, he sweated and trembled his way through the hours. They started him on Phenobarbital to ease his tremors and Librium to quell his sense of impending panic and he spent his days adrift on a wide sea of dreams in a pharmacological twilight.

When he was finally well again, he was sent to Our Lady of Good Counsel in Belmont, Massachusetts. Some seemed intrigued by the troubled new arrival who spoke cryptically and kept to himself. It was something that was in the air at the time. There was some rearrangement in the culture, or in Catholic culture anyway, that attributed romance to experiences such as his. At Our Lady of Good Counsel, they put him on medications, which calmed his mind, though they produced a certain torpor he found disagreeable. He felt glib and flat, like someone he himself would avoid. Father Boyle stopped taking the medication and began to feel better. But by then, he had earned the pastor's trust and was rewarded with the honor of saying Easter Mass.

It was personal experience that prompted him to say during his sermon, "If you let the garbage get high enough, you're going to have rats." The words did not sound particularly priestly and it was a conservative congregation. He couldn't remember what prompted him to speak so familiarly but he did remember the final week of Lent that year he had felt peculiar, light of body, uncharacteristically voluble. He thought he might have caught a touch of the flu.

He heard himself saying, "You, John Jones, and your infidelities. You, Mary Brown, and your peccadilloes, whatever they may be." Before the Mass, Father Boyle had had the idea to talk about how people often search for God where he is not. He had been trying to say that one should find God—or at least go looking for him—in *agape*, in acts of selflessness, that we are too often taken with form and ritual—"tokens, talismans, and trinkets," he called them, with an ill-advised gesture to the sanctuary around him. He had been trying to say that a life of virtue demands discomfort.

But he had mumbled something, too, about his own sinfulness, his unworthiness to say the things he had just said, and stopped just short of an apology to the congregation. He was lost. His thoughts flooded in on a tide of uncertain inspiration and eddied in a pool, mingling with one another so that he was unable to assemble anything coherent with them. Then, when he became aware that there was no rescuing himself and he had gone on too long, he made one last thrust at resolution. "Why do you come here?" he asked them. "When you look up here, what do you see? A man with soft hands and a cowardly heart. You bring your hope, your fears—your ambition, some of you—and you expect . . . What?" Father Boyle stopped himself, turned to his co-celebrants, the monsignor and the bishop (who had come out for the special occasion), who were gaping at him, and finished with a pathetic pair of sentences that were the equivalent of slamming a lid down on an erupting blender.

In the wake of what was to become known as the Easter Sermon, Father Boyle was ostracized and under watch. But he was strangely unperturbed. Certain hours of the day seemed heralded by angels and his ears sang. He began to think that his past troubles had been intended for his purification, that they were, as St. John of the Cross had written, "the light that wounds and yet illumines." He was changing, changing in ways that were intriguing in some ways and disturbing in others. There were more sermons. He did not recall them very well. He was called before the bishop. There had been complaints, even requests to have Father Boyle moved to another parish. He left Our Lady of Good Counsel in the early summer of 1954. Things had ended so badly there, he didn't like to think about it.

Finally, he was packed off to Cape Cod, which he found peaceful and accommodating, where his thoughts settled down and he was able to function without the medication. He immersed himself in working with the sick and the suffering, which he did with a Spartan intensity, a grim resolution that had something of spite in it, and perhaps a kind of self-hatred.

Father Boyle walked until he could perceive light between the trees, as though a large open space might lie beyond. He passed out of the old-growth forest and entered a wide region of dune and meadow that was a considerable height above the ocean. He tottered on his feet as a knot of pain worked through his chest, then passed. He surveyed the tattered-looking hummocks around him, now unsure whether this was the place. He thought it was peculiar that he had been unable to find it, which lent to the overall unreality surrounding the incident.

He recalled that night. How all the insects fell silent and the outdoors took on the feeling of a close, stifling room. Father Boyle had had the sensation of surreptitious fingers on his skin, of a weight settling down over the rolling grassland, and felt that if he spoke, the sound would echo like a word uttered in an empty church, so strange had the outdoors become.

What was he doing out here? If he admitted he was looking for something, then didn't he also have to admit that he believed in it?

He thought he heard someone laugh far off in the brush. Though it was only 2 P.M., the sky was getting dark, with purple and gray clouds converging overhead. He thought of the big man standing in the ferns and experienced a crawling sensation on his scalp. How strange it was, the man with his air of authority and menace, planted there in what looked like dress pants and a T-shirt.

Father Boyle retraced his steps, moving more quickly than he meant to, his chest aching. He kept thinking he heard movement behind him, as if someone were tracking him through the woods, but every time he stopped to listen it was quiet. For a while he was convinced that he was lost and he headed blindly west until he could hear a car rolling down a distant road in the quiet. There was a whispering in his left ear and he began to trot toward the road. He burst out of the woods a half mile from his car and ran the entire way, losing his sketchbook and his specimen basket. He yanked the car door open and fumbled with the key in the ignition. He locked the doors and stepped on the gas. In the rearview mirror, the road was empty.

25

George McCarthy entered the Elbow Room through a locked side door. He went into the back area, grabbed the big wooden handle on the walk-in door, and yanked it open. Four men were seated at the plywood counter around its perimeter. A teletype was churning out lengths of paper—sports lines from Las Vegas. Four televisions were on, their volume down, one showing the news, another *Death Valley Days*, the other two tuned to a horse race at Suffolk Downs. Two of the men were on the phone, the other two checking columns of figures in a ledger. One of the men on the phone held the receiver away to his right and spoke. "What's going on, George?"

"You guys get off the phone for a minute."

Everyone stopped what they were doing and turned in their chairs.

"The cops might be sniffing around. I think they been over here sneaking around the parking lot. I don't know what it's about yet but everyone's got to be careful. Pay attention to who's around you. *Don't* be stupid with the phones."

"Anybody know who they are?" one of the men asked.

"Barnstable cops. It's usually a little guy. Some detective, I don't know his name. Thinks he's a tough guy, what I heard. Lieutenant Warren is the one in charge. I want to know if you spot any of these guys."

Someone said, "Are our phones O.K.?"

"As far as I know. But we're gonna need a phone guy down here. I gotta go call Grady. Stevie, come with me."

Steve Tosca, who had been hovering at the edge of the room, followed him out.

"I want you to make sure they're careful in there," McCarthy said.

"I will. This is going to get fixed, though, right?"

"I hope so."

"Is Frank Semanica coming down today? We got a lot of checks to go up."

"Yeah, he's coming. But this will be the last time, if I have anything to say about it. I got a feeling he fucked up that Leapley thing."

"Leapley was a mule, though, George. He had it coming."

"Yeah, but you notice how we bring Frankie in to do a tune-up and all of a sudden we got trouble? We've tuned up a few guys since we been down here, right? Not once did we have trouble. Now we do."

"Leapley going along with the program?"

"We paid him a visit at the hospital. He knows enough to keep his mouth shut. That Warren's been dogging him, though. Frankie overdid it. Cutting him in the face. We don't need that."

"He's lucky he ain't floating in a creek somewhere. That's how it works."

"I know how it works, Stevie. I'm gonna tell Grady I don't want Frank down here no more."

"We got to balance our books on the Wednesday night fight. Asher versus Jefferson. Everybody thinks Asher's a dog. We gotta do a layoff."

"How far are we out?"

"Three hundred. Something like that. Is the Cock n' Bull still up and running?"

"In Brighton? I'm not sure. I'll ask Grady."

McCarthy checked his watch and then called a number in South Boston. Grady Pope came on the line, terse and unreadable.

"We might have some trouble down here," McCarthy said. "The cops are nosing around. One of our guys says they tailed him last night."

"You talk to our good friend?"

"Yeah."

"Tell him I want it fixed," said Pope.

"I told him that."

"Tell him again. These are local cops?"

"Yeah."

"Who?"

"Barnstable."

"You got any names?"

"Someone named Warren. William Warren. You know him?"

"No. And this is all from the Leapley thing?"

"That's right. And I don't think we should be using Frank Semanica anymore."

"Why?"

"I think he fucked up. He overdid it. He didn't use his head."

Pope was quiet for a moment. "Did this guy talk to the cops?"

"Leapley? No. They're working on him, though."

"You make sure he stays zipped tight, George. Make sure he understands what this is. As for Frankie, I'll talk to him. Everyone else is being watched. Frankie they don't know. He just got out of prison and he wasn't around when everything went to hell. We had him running that poker game in Braintree and they never got their nose into that, so they don't even know who he is. That's why he's useful. Are the phones O.K.?"

"I don't know," McCarthy said. "We need to get a phone guy down here to check it out. Oh, yeah. Is the Cock n' Bull still up?"

"Yes and no. They're operating out of a basement in Arlington."

"Jesus."

"Yeah. It's that bad."

"We're gonna take it on the nose in the Asher-Jefferson fight. The action's out of whack."

"I'll make a phone call and get back to you. How much you need to lay off?"

"About three hundred."

"O.K. Make sure everyone's being careful. I'll get someone down to check the phones. Talk to our good friend. Do it right now. Tell him I don't like what's going on and he needs to get on it. What's this Barnstable cop's name?"

"Warren. William Warren."

On Monday morning, as Warren was driving through town in his unmarked, the dispatcher's voice came up on the radio. "KCA374 to Easy seven."

"Easy seven."

"Request to stop by Wentzel and Livingston auction house and make contact with one Irving Wentzel."

Warren acknowledged and turned in the direction of the Mid-Cape Highway. A few days earlier, he had taken photographs of the items that had been stolen from the antique shop in Osterville to Wentzel and Livingston auction house. It had happened in the past that thieves who found themselves in possession of an object they believed to be valuable took it to Irving Wentzel to be appraised or auctioned off. Wentzel was a stickler for provenance and knew when something was suspicious, which discouraged people from trying to use him as a fence, but from time to time Warren got a call from him about someone who had brought something by his auction house and had left him with an uneasy feeling.

Warren found Wentzel seated at his desk. "Good morning, Mr. Wentzel," he said.

"Lieutenant. How are you, sir?"

Wentzel stood and they shook hands.

"You wanted to see me?"

"Yes." Wentzel moved a few papers around on his desk and came up with the photographs Warren had given him. "A boy came in here this morning with this lantern. He wanted to know what I'd give him for it. I told him that's not how we acquire our inventory, by people just walking in off the street. This is not a flea market. At any rate, the boy I know. Stephen Nicholas."

"The selectman's son?"

"Yes. He's . . . I don't know. He thinks he's a gangster or something."

"You're sure it was him?"

"He went to high school with my daughter. She'll tell you. She was here when he came in."

"And you're sure that's what he showed you?" Warren pointed at the photograph.

"I'm sure. There aren't many of these around anymore. At least in this part of the country. It's not valuable but it is rare."

Warren pinched the bridge of his nose.

"It's never simple, is it?" said Wentzel.

"Not lately."

Warren drove out to Selectman Nicholas's home. Mrs. Nicholas answered the door, prim and immaculate in a light cotton print dress and a rose chiffon scarf with matching shoes and earrings. She had the look of someone who was accustomed to being in charge and who expected treachery and incompetence. When he stated his business, she told him that her son was not at home, that she was insulted by Warren's accusation, and that Selectman Nicholas would see him in his office within the hour.

When Warren came through the front doors of the station, Sgt. Garrity looked up at him like a spooked domestic whose boss had just gone on a tirade. "Selectman Nicholas is here," he said quietly. Warren found the selectman in his office, looking at one of the duty rosters that was taped to the wall. He turned immediately to Warren when he entered. "Did you speak disrespectfully to Mrs. Nicholas?"

Warren shut the door behind him. "I did not," he said. "I explained to her . . ."

"That's not what she told me. Why are you asking about Stephen and a burglary? Why didn't you come to my offices and speak with me?"

"It's your son I need to speak with. No one else."

"Well, let me tell you something, Warren. You're not speaking with my son. You'll speak to me."

"That won't do."

"It will have to do."

"It was your son who was identified as the person who tried to sell stolen property to Irving Wentzel at his auction house."

"Irving Wentzel."

"Maybe your son got it from someone else, but I need to know who."

"What burglary are you talking about? Where?"

"Antiquitus. On West Bay Road in Osterville."

Nicholas shouted, "Are you kidding me? That place is always getting broken into."

"Well, that's going to stop."

"Do you have any idea what you're doing here? These are two perverts who run a junk shop. Who don't hide the fact that they're perverts and do nothing but bring more of their kind up here from New York. And I don't know if you've noticed but a number of children have been murdered, lieutenant, and their killer is still out there walking around."

"The state police are working on that."

"But you're not."

"Everything else doesn't stop, Mr. Nicholas. What if it was your place that got broken into?"

"Drop it right now. This doesn't even rise to the level of vandalism. I'm telling you to drop it right now."

"You don't have that authority."

"This is my family you're talking about here. This is my name. Irving Wentzel is a sneaky little Jew who doesn't know a goddamn thing if he can't find it in his account book. He's wrong."

"He identified your son without any trouble. His daughter was there when your son came in. She went to school with him."

"Who the hell do you think you are?"

"I'm the acting chief of police, Mr. Nicholas."

"That's right. Acting. And not for long, if I have anything to say about it, which I do."

"This is a burglary, Mr. Nicholas, and I'm going to treat it like a burglary. I don't care who did it."

"Don't you try to strong-arm me. You're in over your head."

"It's your son who's in over his head. We have fingerprints from the crime scene."

"Crime scene? Are you serious? Those two fags out there? Crime scene, my ass."

"I need to fingerprint your son."

"You can go to hell."

That evening he sat staring at the television set, watching images from the news. There was footage of a caravan of U.S. military trucks driving through a Japanese seaport, the American occupation headquarters in that country having been recently closed down. Negroes in Tuskegee, Alabama, were boycotting local stores, and there were pictures of radar dishes revolving slowly against the sky in some tundra, part of a new system of radar stations designed to detect Soviet bombers approaching North America, something called the Distant Early Warning Line.

Warren wasn't interested but he didn't know what else to do with himself. He realized he was angry all the time now. In the odd moments when he wasn't angry, he felt heavy and weary, like his limbs were made of lead. He looked at his watch. It had taken some doing, but he had arranged for a state police technician to meet Jenkins at the New England Telephone switching center with an induction device and a recorder. They were probably there at that very moment. Toward 11 P.M. he was ready to go outside and radio Jenkins with his handheld when the detective called.

"Lieutenant?"

"Yes."

"You're not going to believe this but it looks like someone disconnected the line to the Elbow Room. I'll take your silence to mean shock and outrage."

"How many people knew we were going to do this?"

"Well, there was you, me, Dunleavy, Alvin Leach. The state police technician was clueless. We called him out of the blue."

"Whoever it was, they did it on short notice because I didn't even say the word 'wiretap' until about eleven o'clock Friday night."

"Any way someone could have known enough to pull the wires before that?"

"I don't know. Alvin Leach made some inquiries before he started tracing the line."

"What kind of inquiries?"

"He checked the billing department. He checked the records over at the switching center to see if he could find out who hooked up the lines. He asked around inside the company."

"So anyone who knew he was doing that could have been the one."

"I suppose so. But the timing is one hell of a coincidence."

"Someone knows what we're doing," Jenkins said. "And they don't want us doing it. They're gambling. They're running an illegal gaming operation out of the Elbow Room. They've probably got money on the street, too. Bunch of guys from Boston trying out the water down here. But I found someone who will go in there for us."

"Who?"

"Wilson Hayes. I worked with him in the Providence PD. He was a hot shit back in my days as a patrolman. A lot of guts, and very smooth."

"Can he be here tomorrow?"

"I'll find out."

"They actually went into the switching center and pulled the lines."

"And they did it quick, too. We've got ourselves a caper, lieutenant."

26

Warren struggled to find what it was that made Wilson Hayes seem somehow immaterial. Sitting across from him and Jenkins in a booth at a diner, Hayes's eyes flitted here and there, in some moments amused, in others nervous and uncertain, and in yet others hard and cold. Jenkins said that Hayes had once told him he was from Oklahoma, though at other times he had claimed other places of origin. He was a bullshit artist, Jenkins said, which suited him for the kind of work he'd done for the Providence PD and the side jobs he did as a private investigator, though he didn't need the money—he was head of corporate security for Gillette. Warren watched him and noticed that he was reluctant to make eye contact. He had misgivings.

Jenkins had explained what they believed was going on, and their suspicion that the Elbow Room was at the center of it.

"They Irish?" Hayes asked.

"Some of them."

"The FBI was on the Irish pretty hard not that long ago. Right after the Attanasio thing."

"And what happened?"

Wilson Hayes shrugged. His eyes made a quick tour of the diner, light and dancing. "They had an investigation going and they shut it down or something. I don't know. Wouldn't surprise me if the Justice Department ran out of money. You know how much that Attanasio investigation cost?"

Jenkins said, "A lot of the people we've connected to the

Elbow Room are from the Boston area. I wonder if they're associated with the Irish."

"George McCarthy is. It's either that or he's gone off on his own."

Jenkins lit a cigarette. "What do you know about McCarthy?"

"He might work for Grady Pope. I say *might*. McCarthy's an old-time gangster. He's been around a long time. There's some association there or was at one time."

Warren reacted visibly to the name Grady Pope. Hayes shot his eyes in his direction.

"Let's not get worked up yet," said Hayes. "People like McCarthy are likely to pop up anywhere there's illegal money. Doesn't mean Grady Pope's moved down here, too."

Warren asked, "Are any of the other names we gave you familiar?"

"No. But let me get in there and see if I recognize any faces."

Wilson Hayes left the diner and drove off in the direction of Hyannis. He would be staying in a motel that he'd cased out ahead of time and whose name he had given only to Jenkins. He said he would call with a number where he could be reached.

Warren and Jenkins walked to their car. As Warren got ready to put it in gear, Jenkins said, "There's something you should know about Wilson." Warren just looked straight ahead through the windshield, waiting.

"He does black bag jobs for Fran Kasdan." Jenkins watched him for a reaction. "Kasdan owns the Gillette Company."

"I know who he is. What else?"

"He does things for other companies too."

"What kind of things?"

"Union busting, mostly. He's been known to cross the line from time to time, though, work for the unions."

"Coercion?"

"Persuasion."

"Coercion."

Jenkins threw his hands up. "Whatever word you want to use. It's not pretty, I'll give you that."

"Has he ever been charged with anything? Any connection with known criminals?"

"Not unless you consider Fran Kasdan a criminal. He's got some principles. But you remember that thing where the CEO of Borg-Thurman Corp. was caught with a Chinese prostitute in a motel off the Mass Turnpike?"

Warren had to think for a moment but he recalled the photographs in the newspaper, the disheveled executive, wide-eyed and pallid as the police led him into the Watertown station, a bed, sheet falling from his bare bony shoulders. Warren also recalled the Chinese girl, who could be seen flanked by cops a short distance behind, her hair looking like a fright wig, her mouth a tiny oval as she said something to the photographer. There were rumors she wasn't even sixteen. "Yeah, I remember."

"That was Wilson Hayes."

"Jesus."

"The CEO was bent on moving the electronics production down to Havana or some damn place. The union was against it and they couldn't change his mind."

Warren thought of how devious it was, the choice of a Chinese hooker at the peak of the Red Scare, and thought of the glittering, dishonest eyes of the man he had just met. He thrust a thumb in the direction Hayes had driven. "That guy?"

"What, you don't think he's capable?"

"No. I'm sure he's capable . . ."

"He's on our side, lieutenant."

"I suppose that's a good thing."

"It's a good thing. Let's go."

Doctor Hawthorne and his guests sat around the dining room table and finished the last of the red wine he had served with baked striped bass, asparagus, and new potatoes. From the open kitchen windows they could hear the revelers on Commercial Street and smell the occasional briny draft off Provincetown Harbor.

The guests were two photographers, a painter, and a playwright. As was his habit, he had invited no one from the medical profession. The sole exception was Karl Althaus, who had come down from Boston to discuss research currently under way at Luxor Laboratories, the pharmaceutical firm for which he worked. Hawthorne had agreed to help them with their latest project, Fenchloravin, an experimental antiseizure prototype.

Hawthorne was a peculiar host, seeming to prefer to remain apart from the conversation, the evening less a spontaneous gathering than an event he had staged so he could observe the participants. His dinners were known in the Provincetown artists' community and were considered an experience one should have at least once (few people were invited twice). It was not only the novelty of spending an evening under the doctor's gaze, at once probing and detached, but the fact that he was a psychiatrist, of all things, who talked about Shiva and Byron and occasionally invited his patients, who enlivened the evening with their furtive movements, their nonsequiturs and fits of staring. A local writer had said it was like finding oneself in a scene from Edgar Allan Poe.

Toward the end of the night, Edgar appeared. It wasn't clear whether he had been in the house all along or if he had come in from outside. He hovered around the entrance to the kitchen as the guests were preparing to leave. At one point, Hawthorne looked over to find him engaged in conversation with Karl Althaus. He made his way in their direction, but Edgar drifted away before Hawthorne was halfway across the dining room.

That night, Hawthorne sat in the tiny room that served as his study, up later than usual because Edgar kept moving around the house. Hawthorne heard the back door open and thought he'd gone out, but then he was back in the house again; in the kitchen, the bathroom, the front parlor. Hawthorne went downstairs to find him sitting at the kitchen table in the dark. "What is it, Edgar?" he asked.

"Nothing. I can't sleep."

"Did my guests disturb you?"

"No."

"I noticed you talking to Karl Althaus."

Edgar averted his eyes. He slowly rubbed his palms together, watching their motion. He said nothing.

"What did you discuss?" Hawthorne asked.

Edgar looked around the kitchen.

"Hm?"

"Fishing," said Edgar.

"There probably isn't a subject that interests Karl Althaus less than fishing. Not even *I* am less interested in fishing than Karl Althaus."

Cleve sat there looking at the floor.

"I advise against any more of this in the future," Hawthorne said. He took a quick look around the kitchen, scanning the countertops, the sink, the dish towel hanging from the oven door. Before going back upstairs, he removed his car keys from the hook on the wall and put them in his pocket.

27

Warren went in the front doors of the town hall and stopped at the reception desk. He'd debated whether to show up in uniform for his meeting with Earl Mott, the head selectman, but in the end decided against it. He was concerned now about looking foolish for his pursuit of the burglary at Antiquitus, and he thought appearing in uniform would just make it worse. Mott was waiting for him, his elbows on the desk, touching the tips of his fingers together in a repetitive motion. "Close the door please, lieutenant," he said.

Mott was portly, in his mid-sixties. He had the face of an old teamster, pockmarked, blunt, void of nuance. He wore a blazer with a broad light blue plaid pattern and a white tie. He was cut of the same mold as Marvin Holland; in fact, the two were friends. Warren had heard he was crafty and treacherous but had never had the opportunity to discover whether this was true.

Mott hocked something up out of his throat and swallowed it. "What's going on with the Nicholas kid and this burglary? I want it done with."

Warren explained the situation.

"Why did you go out there in the first place?" Mott asked.

"Where?"

"To Osterville."

There was a silence as the two men looked at each other, Mott squinting, smiling almost, as if waiting for someone to explain a punch line he'd missed.

"We got a call. It was a burglary."

"Oh, Christ." Mott wheeled around in his chair and struggled to open the window, which he accomplished after some effort. "You've been a cop down here how long?"

Before Warren could speak, Mott waved off his last remark as if intending to start over. "Look," he said, "with all respect to the uniform, et cetera, et cetera. You need to learn how to pick your battles. These fellas out on . . . Where are they?"

"West Bay Road."

"Right. That's not a battle. That's not even a goddam tick on the radar. So I hear about you going out there for fingerprints and going after Donny Nicholas's kid over this—what—do you have a feud going with Donny Nicholas?"

"No."

"Well, what the hell are you thinking, then? People are talking about this, you know. And they want something done. You're not going to charge Donny's kid with burglary. You're not doing it."

"I've got no plans to charge him. I just want to fingerprint him and interview him."

Mott raised his voice: "You're not getting this, are you, Warren? Did you hear anything I said in the last twenty seconds? This thing ends now. Right now. Drop it." He looked directly into Warren's eyes. "You're a good officer and we don't want to lose you," he said, and waited for the implication to sink in. "We're good to our people, you know that. Now, I know you've got your challenge there with your son, and . . . your situation. I know all that. Raises are coming up in January. Merit increases. We get more tax revenue, good things are going to happen. And that means you, too. Because we're a family and we take care of our family. So if one of them strays a little, we correct him, we don't cut him off. We bring him back into the family. And we play by house rules. Now, just give Selectman Nicholas a friendly visit—he's just down the hall—and apologize and we'll let the whole thing blow by and get on to better things."

"This is wrong."

Mott chuckled. "Wrong. There's nothing wrong."

"Nobody knows what wrong is anymore."

"And you do. What are you, a damn saint?" Mott's voice had dropped its conciliatory, fatherly tone and gone harsh in an instant. "Are you going to let this go?"

These people, Warren thought, Mott, Nicholas, and the rest of them. They were arrogant and vindictive. He considered the act: Simple burglary. Theft. The attempted sale of stolen property. If it had happened to anyone else, they'd have a court date by now. He thought of the antique dealers' defenselessness among a people who prized civility and lawful behavior. They stole from no one and kept to themselves but they lived in a community that had turned against them. It amounted to a kind of tyranny, a collective cruelty that he had seen directed at weak children and people of little means. His own father would never have tolerated it. A procession of things passed through Warren's mind in that moment, Nicholas, the burglary, Chief Holland, the Elbow Room, Stasiak, even the killings. He didn't know why. He reconsidered. Maybe he wasn't thinking straight. "I'll go down to Selectman Nicholas's office on my way out," he said.

Mott nodded his big head. "Good."

"I want his kid in my office by noon tomorrow."

When Warren got to the station, Jenkins intercepted him outside his office. "What the hell happened?" he said. Warren brushed past him. "Mott just called here ranting like a goddamn lunatic. The chief called too. He wants you to come over to the hospital right now. Both of 'em's madder than hell."

"I'm bringing Stephen Nicholas in here tomorrow."

"Whoa. Hold on."

"He tried to sell stolen property. He was in possession of stolen property. He's had more than a fair chance to come in and straighten this out, if he's innocent, but he hasn't done it, has he?

Instead, I get hauled over the coals by Earl Mott. I get threatened by Donald Nicholas, who thinks the rules don't apply to him or his kid. He's got more authority than the law, Donny Nicholas. And we're supposed to roll over and say, O.K., we'll let you make the rules. You and all your friends with money and connections. You go to the front of the line. You do whatever the hell you want and it's just too goddamn bad for everybody else."

Jenkins said, "Can I make a suggestion?"

The lieutenant paced, gritting his teeth, his eyes wide.

"Sir, leave it alone. You're going to lose your shirt over this and for what? Some knickknacks taken off a couple of queer antique dealers?"

Warren sat down behind his desk and started opening and closing drawers. He was breathing as if his lungs couldn't take in enough air. He folded his hands on his desk and looked at Jenkins. "Stephen Nicholas. Here in this office by noon tomorrow or I arrest him on suspicion of burglary."

Warren slowed as he passed the newspaper stand in the lobby of the hospital. The killings were a constant staple now, the headlines orchestrating the tempo of hysteria: "Who Is Killing Cape Cod's Children?" "Evil Visits a Seaside Resort." Less imaginative editors went with the predictable trouble-in-paradise angle, which was a stretch because the victims were from working-class families and the murders committed in such unremarkable settings as to add to their squalor. Dunleavy had told him that a reporter from the *New York Times* had settled into a suite at the Sheraton and the murders got national television exposure recently on CBS's nightly "Douglas Edwards with the News."

Captain Stasiak was seldom available for comment. People griped about the secrecy of the investigation. An editorial in the *Standard Times* asked why the FBI hadn't been called in. This prompted Elliott Yost to respond in a radio interview that the investigation was proceeding in good order, and that they had the finest detectives in the region on the case. The task force had gelled and was operating smoothly and would not benefit from the "administrative disruption" the introduction of a federal agency might cause. Stories of Dale Stasiak's heroics at Iwo Jima had multiplied and circulated everywhere, augmented by tales of audacious raids in search of the child killer.

People recounted his involvement with the FBI's campaign against the Mafia in Boston—rumors and outright fabrication given equal standing with fact. Light gray two-door Fords got a second look because everyone knew Stasiak drove one, and was that him flying down the highway early yesterday evening at sunset, headed down Cape at about eighty? Someone said that Stasiak had the state police mechanics install a specially designed engine in his car, a secret Ford prototype that was supposed to be faster than a drag racer. He carried a .45, the same one he killed a slew of Japanese with in 1945. Stasiak was a judo expert, could break your neck with a flick of his wrist. They said he knew Jack Kennedy personally and went sailing with the senator and Jackie.

Warren found Chief Holland's hospital room empty. He stood in the doorway, looking at what appeared to be the signs of a recent departure: the drawers of the small bureau open and empty, a tray with remnants of breakfast and a crushed cardboard orange juice container, the bed unmade, its sheets trailing off the mattress onto the floor. A nurse approached from behind. He turned to face her. "Chief Holland's been discharged," she said. "Are you with the police?"

"Yes."

"Hold on a minute. I have something for you."

The nurse went out and came back a few seconds later holding a gray felt fedora. "You left this here last night."

"That's not mine."

"You're not Officer Dunleavy?"

"No."

"Oh. Well, the night shift told me Officer Dunleavy left it when he was visiting. Can you give it to him?"

Warren was momentarily paralyzed. He looked about the room and was shaken back to the moment by the awful intimacy of Chief Holland's slightly yellowed bedsheets and the feel of Dunleavy's hat in his hands.

28

The Japanese tea caddy sat on Warren's desk, its clumsy newspaper wrapping partially undone. On the floor, leaning against the desk, was the lantern, similarly wrapped but encircled twice in masking tape. Outside, the hallway was noisy with the eight-to-four shift coming upstairs from the locker room and going out to their cars. He went out and headed down to Garrity's desk, the men parting to make way for him. "These antiques in my office, where did they come from?"

"A lady dropped them off this morning. Before you got here."

"Did you get her name?"

"Uh . . ."

Warren reached for the visitor log. "Selectman Nicholas's secretary, huh?" Warren knew by Garrity's false ponderous movements, by his look of mild befuddlement, that he would have protected Nicholas, but it was too late.

Warren put the antiques in his car and drove out to Osterville. When he pulled up in front of the shop, Grayson Newsome was out retrieving the mail. He was engrossed in reading the envelopes and when he saw Warren's car pull in he gave an uncertain wave. Warren got out of the vehicle and went around to the trunk. "Mr. Newsome," he said.

·"Good morning, lieutenant."

"I have something I'd like you to look at."

Grayson went over to the cruiser. Warren opened the trunk lid. When he saw the antiques he clapped one hand on to his mouth and the other on to Warren's shoulder. "You got them. You found them."

"These are the items?"

"Yes, they are. I can't believe it. I have to get James. Hold on, I'll be right back."

Grayson ran back to the house. Warren heard him calling James Holbrooke's name inside. Soon they both came out, walking quickly, James wiping his hands on a dishrag. He was looking at Warren as he came toward him, shaking his head. Grayson led him to the open trunk and pointed inside.

"God," said James. "I don't know what to say."

"Thank you so much," said Grayson.

"How did you find them?" James asked.

"Someone brought them by Wentzel and Livingston and tried to sell them. Irving Wentzel reported it."

"Who was it?"

Warren was wrestling with whether to press things with the Nicholas boy, now that the antiques had been returned. "That's a little sketchy right now. I'm working on it."

"Irving Wentzel must know."

"He does," Warren admitted. "I'm trying to fingerprint and question that individual right now but he's, uh, he's got some influence."

"And you won't tell us who it is?"

"It's an ongoing investigation. But if you give Mr. Wentzel a call, I don't think he'll be shy about letting you know."

Grayson and James digested this information quietly. They looked at the objects in the trunk, still wrapped in newspaper. "This has never happened to us before," James said. "The police." He gestured toward the trunk. "Someone actually helping us. We don't know how to thank you."

Grayson said, "Lieutenant Warren, I don't know why you did this, but I can assure you I will never forget it. The antiques themselves aren't that important. It's the principle." He looked at Warren, both pleased and perplexed, it seemed, as if seeing him for the first time. James reached in and lifted the lantern out. "If there is anything *we* can do for *you*, I hope you'll let us know. I know they're going to be appointing a new chief of police soon and I certainly hope it's you."

As he left Antiquitus, Warren decided to drive out to Marstons Mills and check on the Weeks place. As Warren pulled up to the house, he saw a pickup truck with New Hampshire plates in the driveway and a skinny man loading things into the back. He seemed prematurely aged, his clothes oil-stained. He wore a baseball cap and a baggy denim jacket that gave off a strong petroleum smell. Warren pulled up in his unmarked and got out. "I'm with the Barnstable police," he said. "Are you a relative?"

"This is my brother's place. Russell Weeks."

"Do you have any idea where he is?"

"I sure don't. I just found out the bank's gonna foreclose on the house. I thought I'd come by and take out some stuff before they do. If Russell ain't gonna use it, I will. Is he in trouble?"

"The state police are trying to find him. He's been reported as a missing person."

"I didn't know."

"How did you find out about the foreclosure?"

"Friend of mine gave me a call. He lives in Mashpee and he knew Russell and me. He said Russell skipped town and left the house empty."

"What kind of relationship do you have with your brother? If you don't mind me asking."

Weeks shrugged. "We don't socialize. Hell, I haven't seen him in something like seven, eight years. My brother's a pain in the ass. Contrary. He's good to her. What's her name. Miriam. But he's always bitching about something. He's a great one to start a fight and then walk off and leave you to straighten out the mess."

"So you have no idea where he might have gone?"

"No idea."

"Have the state police contacted you?"

"No."

"Would your brother call you if he was in trouble?"

"Oh, I don't know. I think he'd have to be in one hell of a lot of trouble to call me. We're not on the best of terms."

"I think your brother might have borrowed money from some disreputable people."

"Well, that's his problem. We talked about that a long time ago. 'Course, you can't tell him anything."

"He's done this in the past?"

"Gambling, borrowing money, hanging around with shady people, yeah. She got him straight pretty much, but he's hard-headed."

"I'd like you to call me if you hear from him. Here's my number."

"He's more likely to call you than he is me."

"Just take my number. I need to talk to him. And let him know he's not in trouble of any kind. I need to ask him about the people he borrowed money from."

It was Wilson Hayes's fourth visit to the Elbow Room. He sat at the bar watching the first race at Suffolk Downs, not paying much attention to what was going on around him because he'd seen enough. Hayes knew what this place was. It was just like places he'd seen in New Bedford, Fall River, South Boston, Charlestown. The patrons of the Elbow Room were, on the whole, rough men. But what he noticed most about them was their docility. They shouted and swore and blustered. They glowered at newcomers or stared hard from beneath the brims of baseball caps or small-brim fedoras. Behind the posturing, Wilson Hayes could tell that they were afraid and he had been around enough of these kinds of places to understand why.

What he wanted to do was get into the back area and see what was there. He had to get back up to Boston soon and he wanted to wrap this up. By the looks of things, he didn't know if he'd be a witness for the state if this turned into a gambling prosecution and went to trial. There was too much going on here. Too much activity, too many people, too much money. It had the feel of a mob operation.

Wilson Hayes was suddenly aware of people around him. He looked to his right to see a squat man with silver hair standing by his elbow looking at him. Directly behind him were a couple of big kids in their twenties. "Come on, sport," said the older man. "You're done."

"What?"

The man took him gently by the elbow. "You're done. Let's go."

Wilson Hayes got off his bar stool. One of the kids leaned into him, breathing on his face. "What did I do?" Wilson asked.

They escorted him outside.

"Get the hell out of here," the man with the silver hair said. "Don't come back."

Late that night, a group of men stood around George McCarthy in the parking lot of the Elbow Room. "Nobody works until I say so," McCarthy said. "Answer your phones so they don't think we been pinched. Just tell them we're closed for the time being."

Someone asked, "Was this the guy the cops were sending? This Wilson Hayes?"

"He fit the description we got," said McCarthy. "Anyone know how many times he was here?"

"The fellas say maybe four or five times."

One of them said, "Is he a cop?"

"We don't know what he is," McCarthy said. "That fucking Warren. Christ. Like he doesn't have better things to do."

"What's our good friend say about him?"

"Warren?" McCarthy lit a cigarette and tossed the match aside. "He's weak."

Steve Tosca's voice came out of the darkness, "Speaking of our good friend, none of this shit is supposed to be happening. Isn't he getting paid to do a job?"

"What do you want me to do Stevie, call him up? Pay him a visit?"

"Well, ain't he talking to Grady? Ain't he talking to anybody?"

"I'll be talking to Grady in the morning. He's gonna shit when he hears this."

"Maybe this Warren can be convinced to back off," one of the men said.

McCarthy shook his head. "It won't work. He ain't like that."

"Well, what about something else?" Tosca said.

"He's a cop, Stevie. This may be East Nowhere but he's still a cop. You know better. You think we got trouble now."

"Some of them will play along if you get them in the right spot. He's got a kid, don't he?"

"Yeah," said McCarthy. "I sent guys by his house a few times."

"We ought to set his fucking house on fire."

"I'll talk to Grady tomorrow," said McCarthy. "Everybody just calm down and keep your mouths shut."

They left the parking lot in a line of four cars. When they were gone, Wilson Hayes emerged from the woods. He carried a few pieces from his lock picking set and a Luger shoved into his pants at the small of his back. He inserted his tension wrench into the deadbolt lock on the side door and applied twisting pressure. Then he pushed the pick in and forced it upward against the key pins inside. After some wiggling, the bolt turned. Then he turned his attention to the knob. He pulled the door open slowly and stepped inside.

Warren, Jenkins, Dunleavy, and Wilson Hayes sat in a car at a beach in Yarmouth, the wind blowing rain sideways across the parking lot, the bay churned into a turbulent plain of white-caps. Hayes described his visits to the Elbow Room and what he'd discovered in the back room. It was, he said, a major book-making operation. If he had to put a number on it, he'd say it was a hundred thousand a year operation, or at least in that ballpark. Patrons watched sporting events on the bar's several televisions. Betting slips found their way to the back, where the wire was and where they set the line, kept their books, and generally ran the business. They kept the music up just enough so you couldn't hear the phones ringing back there, but he had used the toilet and could hear them through the wall.

The seat he chose afforded him a view of the side door, and he noticed that the men who came and went often carried bags or satchels and in them, he suspected, was money and betting slips. They had collection men coming in with payments from the losers and slips from the other locations they ran.

Jenkins had mentioned that tailing the people associated with the Elbow Room revealed a few other locations believed to be connected to the bar—a place in Dennis called Brinkman's, a dive in Orleans called the Bilge, and a private home in Harwich—and Hayes figured these were satellite locations, part of the franchise, where guys in Chatham or Brewster or wherever could get some action on a race or a fight or a ball game. What was coming in the side door of the Elbow Room, he surmised, was business from those places. They had done a good job building a bettor clientele. They could probably cover costs just with the action in the bar alone.

They were probably loaning money, too. Hayes didn't have anything solid but would be surprised if it wasn't happening. Occasionally, individuals were called out and were ushered into the back. When they returned, they looked either pale and dazed or revved up and jumpy. These, he suspected, were either men who were receiving counseling on their debts or hopeful loan applicants.

"Any indication whether this is tied in with organized crime?" Warren asked.

"I'd say yes. There's too much going on here for it to be an independent thing. Too much activity, too many people, too much money. It has the feel of a mob operation."

Hayes had sketched them a rough layout of the interior of the Elbow Room and a list of the items they would find inside the converted walk-in: A teletype machine connected to Continental Wire Service, five telephones, four television sets, bettor lists, line sheets, racing forms, five illegal firearms, and a large safe in the corner.

"If you're going to hit the place," said Wilson Hayes, "you better do it soon. It wouldn't surprise me if they got rid of everything already. Or moved it all somewhere else."

"We'll do it tonight," said Warren.

Warren met Jenkins and Dunleavy at a vacant textile factory alongside the railroad tracks a half mile from the Elbow Room. He had picked eight men from the midnight-to-eight shift and called them to the location. The cops were bewildered when they saw the lieutenant standing there in uniform, the detectives beside him in casual street clothes and shoulder holsters.

When all the officers had arrived, Warren briefed them on what they were about to do. He told them that the Elbow Room was a bookmaking operation with possible ties to organized crime. He gave them a list of the items they were looking for. Two men would take up position behind the Elbow Room with Jenkins. The shift sergeant would cover the side door with a shotgun. Everyone else was going in the front door. The patrons would be gone but they expected to catch the bookies, bar employees, runners, collection men, and anyone else who was hanging around after hours. They left the factory in a convoy and drove the short distance up the road to the Elbow Room. When they turned into the lot, the building was completely dark and there was not a single car in sight. Warren was stricken by a sudden, uncomfortable feeling in his chest and his palms started sweating. "There's no one here," he said

"Let's go anyway," said Dunleavy.

"Something's wrong."

The shift sergeant parked his cruiser out by the side door and got down on one knee behind it, leveling his shotgun on the trunk. Jenkins and two patrolmen went around back to cover that side. Warren and Dunleavy hauled a length of six-by-six out of the trunk of one of the cruisers and used it as a battering ram against the front door. On the fifth blow, the metal door tore free of its dead bolt and the knob's locking mechanism sheared off. The officers rushed with guns drawn into total darkness and an empty building. Warren led the way into the back and opened the walk-in refrigerator. There was nothing inside but the plywood counters. There were phone jacks in the walls and ashtrays full of cigarette butts, but no evidence of what Wilson Hayes had described. Dunleavy went through the drawers of the desk in the storeroom. "There's nothing here," he said. "Orders. Receipts. Catalogues. Check register."

"They've got someone in the department," said Warren. "Someone must have told them."

Jenkins came through the swinging doors. "What the hell happened? Where is everything?"

Warren said, "How well do you know Wilson Hayes, Jenkins?"

"What are you talking about?"

"Someone tipped them off," Dunleavy said.

"Well, it wasn't Wilson."

"How do you know?"

"Because I know. Before you start throwing accusations around . . ."

Warren said, "The only people who knew about this were us three and Wilson Hayes."

"Wilson would never get in bed with these people."

"Seems he has no trouble getting in bed with some others who aren't much better," Warren said.

"Lieutenant, I'm telling you, Wilson Hayes did not tip these guys off." Jenkins's voice was defiant and he took a step toward Warren.

"I'm not convinced," the lieutenant shouted back.

Officers were gathering around the other side of the swinging doors.

"Boys," Dunleavy said, "let's not do this in here."

"Pack it up," Warren said.

Once they were outside, a car pulled into the lot and a man in a porkpie hat got out carrying a camera and approached Warren. "Hey!" Warren shouted at one of the uniforms, "No one in this area. I want this guy out of here." The man raised his camera and a flash went off. Warren covered his eyes, swore, and advanced fast on the photographer. "Get out of here! This area is off-limits!" The flash went off again. Warren grabbed the photographer by the front of his shirt. Two officers came up behind him. "Sir," they said, "lieutenant." Warren pulled the man toward him. "How did you find out about this?" he yelled.

"Easy, easy." The man was frightened, his face contorted. "I got a phone call."

"From who?"

"I don't know."

At this, Warren flung him to the ground. Jenkins suddenly had him by the arms from behind. "Calm down, sir. Calm down."

"I want to know how this son of a bitch knew! You answer me!"

Several officers got in between Warren and the photographer.

"It was anonymous," the man shouted back. "It was an anonymous phone call to the offices of the Cape Cod *Standard Times*, that's all."

Dunleavy spoke to Warren. "We'll talk to him. We'll see what's going on. Lieutenant, you have to calm down."

"Don't you tell me to calm down!" He jerked his head toward the building. "Someone leaked this. Someone tipped them off. And how the hell does this son of a bitch know to show up?"

"We don't know anybody leaked anything yet. Let's take it slow."

Dunleavy walked over to where Jenkins was standing over the photographer, who was sitting on the ground. Jenkins said, "You better tell me who called you and I don't mean maybe."

Dunleavy nudged the man with his shoe. "Give me your driver's license."

"I don't know who called me," the man responded. "A man called and said there was a police raid going on at the Elbow Room. I said, 'Right now?' and he said, 'Yeah, right now.' And that was it."

"You ought to know better than to just walk up on a police operation like this," Jenkins said.

"Your lieutenant ought to know better than to put his hands on me."

Dunleavy said, "Ed, come here."

The two walked a short distance away from the photographer and stopped.

"We need to get the lieutenant out of here," said Dunleavy.

"Right."

Dunleavy pointed to the photographer. "If that guy's boss starts making phone calls this is going to get messy."

"Well, I don't see any way around it. It's gonna happen anyway."

"Just get him out of here."

"Wilson didn't tip this off."

"It had to have been."

"No. I know him."

"You'll never get me to believe that, Ed. I know he's your friend, but you guys fucked this one up."

"What do you mean, *you guys?* Huh? What do you mean by that? You were involved too, Phil."

"Hayes was your deal, though."

"Fuck you, Phil. Who the hell are you? I don't see you putting much into this, traipsing around with the goddamn state police and fucking around with that goddamn Stasiak."

"Like this is real police work and that's not. You're as crazy as Warren is."

"This is what we got. This is a bookie operation with an assault, a possible abduction, and who knows what else wrapped up in it."

"And we got three murdered kids."

"Yeah, I'd love to work on that case, Phil, but I wasn't invited. I'm just trying to earn a paycheck. Don't stand there and tell me that this isn't worth our time."

"That's not what I'm saying. My point is Hayes tipped this thing off. If that hurts your feelings, maybe you need to get a new set."

"I'm not talking to you anymore, Dunleavy. I'm about to say something both of us will regret."

"See if you can get Warren to go home. I'll answer phones at the station. Because they'll be ringing."

29

Marvin Holland's retirement dinner and testimonial was the last place Warren wanted to be. It was a Saturday night and he had a hard time finding someone to watch Little Mike. Jane Myrna had plans and he wound up calling one of the neighbors, who sent her cousin over, someone Mike did not know, which caused the boy a fair amount of anxiety. Warren sat at a bank of tables near the podium, where the selectmen all got up to say a few words about what a decent, upstanding man Marvin was. Earl Mott, Donald Nicholas, and a few others made remarks to the effect of Marvin having wisdom and an intuitive sense of what was right, the clear implication being that these qualities were sorely missed at the moment.

Warren sat with Jenkins and Dunleavy to his right. He was still working over the discovery that Dunleavy had visited Marvin in the hospital, wondering how many times he had done so and what it could mean. But now there was something else, too. Two days earlier, in the hellish aftermath of the raid on the Elbow Room, he had driven out to the Weeks place again to find it still unoccupied, the grass knee-high, a notice from the post office advising them to come down and get their ever-growing pile of mail. On the way back to Hyannis, Warren spotted a gray car parked among some trees, sitting perpendicular to the road. It looked like an unmarked and Warren checked it out as he passed. Phil Dunleavy was behind the wheel looking directly back at him.

Warren turned to look at him now, and in doing so, caught a glimpse of Captain Stasiak sitting with Elliott Yost and some town officials. Up at the front of the room on a raised platform, Marvin sat with the board of selectmen. Off to the side, on a small stage surrounded by gold curtains, was a band led by a Dean Martin impersonator with bags under his eyes.

Warren was trying to gauge the right moment to step out, not that an early departure would have damaged his standing any further. He had heard plenty about the raid on the Elbow Room: the formal complaint from the managing editor of the *Standard Times*, the meeting with the bewildered selectmen who, while they seemed inclined to give him the benefit of the doubt, couldn't understand why he took such action based on information that turned out to be false. They didn't know about Wilson Hayes. He'd have to tell them by the end of the month when he reported the department's expenditures. In the current climate he couldn't bring himself to tell them that he'd spent three hundred dollars—two weekends' worth of extra traffic details—on a questionable ex-cop who took advantage of him. There would be consequences but he would handle them later.

The photograph of him in the *Standard Times* was almost worse than the raid itself. His cap had somehow gotten tilted back and his mouth was open as he yelled at the photographer. His eyes glowed with the light from the flashbulb and his teeth showed. He looked demented.

He turned to Jenkins. "I'm going to make my exit."

"I'll be right behind you."

Warren walked toward the doors, threading his way through the tables. People looked at him but said nothing. Mrs. Holland was standing by the bar speaking with two other women and she gave him a brief, withering look. As he entered the lobby, he ran into Stasiak, who was coming out of the men's room. He was buttoning his suit jacket and looking at Warren like he was about to laugh. "Hey," he said. "I need your guy Jenkins."

"Are you asking me or telling me?"

"I'm telling you. Three dead kids, Warren."

"I need him at the moment."

"Putting him to good use, are you? Raiding empty bars and whatnot?"

Warren felt the hot flush of anger and for a second he saw himself striking Stasiak in the face. Even though the book-making and moneylending operation was now likely shut down and its members either off-Cape or lying low, he held out hope that he could pull off something miraculous and show them all he was right. Warren was hoping he could count on Wilson Hayes to at least sit down with him and the district attorney so he could get support for an investigation, but if Hayes had in fact betrayed them, then that avenue was closed as well. Short of new witnesses coming forward, it came down to finding Russell Weeks or discovering what had become of him.

"I need Jenkins for the task force," Stasiak said. "If you don't want to make him available, you can take it up with the district attorney."

"I have him working on a case. A missing person we're trying to locate."

"A kid?"

"No. A guy named Russell Weeks."

"Russell Weeks? What the hell are you doing with him? You have no business with that."

"He might be tied into a gambling and extortion racket. He and his wife and daughter disappeared . . ."

Stasiak waved him off. "We located them some time ago down in Florida."

"Florida?"

"He had some debts he was trying to get away from. There's nothing mysterious about it, Warren. They've been moving around from motel to motel down there."

"That's interesting, because I spoke to his brother the other day. Fred Weeks."

Stasiak looked around the lobby and adjusted his belt buckle. "Fred Weeks."

"Yes. Did you know about him?" Warren asked.

"Of course. We interviewed him."

"Well he's unaware you located his brother. In fact, he says he's never been contacted by the state police."

"He's a drunk. We talked to him. He's half out of his mind. Spent some time locked up in Bridgewater."

Stasiak suddenly seemed slightly off balance. Warren waited a moment longer and watched him but he betrayed nothing. Warren said, "Well, since you located Russell Weeks, maybe you can tell me where he is because I'd like to talk to him."

"You're wasting your time. Weeks is a six-time loser. Biggest thing he ever did was write some bad checks. You're headed down another blind alley. Not that that's going to stop you. But it would be good if you didn't take Detective Jenkins along with you. I want him at the Yarmouth barracks at eight o'clock tomorrow morning."

"Don't tell me what to do with my own people."

Stasiak laughed. "Warren, you're a little fish in a little pond. You'd be a little fish in any pond."

"What did you say?"

"You heard me."

"I ought to knock you on your ass right here."

"Stop pretending. You don't have it in you."

Warren could hear his heart pounding in his ears. Suddenly, Jenkins was there at his side. "Jenkins?" said Stasiak.

"That's right."

"I need to talk to you."

"Yeah? Am I authorized to speak with Captain Stasiak, lieutenant?"

"Depends what it's about."

Stasiak addressed Jenkins: "I want to bring you on to the

task force. I need you to be at the barracks tomorrow morning. 0800 hours."

"Forget it," said the lieutenant. Then, moving slightly closer to Stasiak, "If you don't like it, take it up with Elliott Yost."

Warren went outside. He stood by the front doors of the hotel and when he tried to light a cigarette he noticed his hands were shaking.

The following morning, with Jenkins sitting in one of the chairs against the wall in Warren's office, the lieutenant raged about the failed raid, about the total lack of support he'd gotten from the town, about Chief Holland, about Earl Mott, the *Standard Times*, his inability to get anywhere with any of it. "And you're not working with Stasiak," he said to Jenkins. "You're not working with the state police. Dunleavy's already with them practically full-time. I've got one detective. How am I supposed to run a department?"

He knew Jenkins would rather be working on the child killings and he knew it was unfair to use him as a token in a turf battle with Stasiak. The detective had worked doggedly for him on an investigation that had never gotten any legs and was now lying flat on its face, unlikely to rise again. And still, Jenkins would not complain. Warren stopped in the middle of the room and looked at the detective. "What would you like to do?" he asked.

"Sir?"

"What would you rather do?"

"Whatever you say. I don't have an opinion."

"I've never told you how much I appreciate how you've worked with me on this."

Jenkins shrugged.

Warren went over to his desk and sat down. He took a pile of papers off his desk, opened a lower drawer, dumped them in, and kicked it shut. "Go on over to the barracks and see Stasiak. Help them out with the investigation. It's more important than this."

Jenkins looked at Warren. "Are you sure?"

"Yes. I'll call Elliott before he calls me and starts giving me hell."

Warren reached Elliott Yost at his office. Before he could say anything, the district attorney said, "I've already heard from Dale Stasiak. He needs extra people. Why are you not cooperating?"

"I already sent Detective Jenkins over."

"You did?"

"He's on his way over now."

"O.K." Elliott sounded unhappy and fatigued.

"I wanted to ask you a question about the Weeks case," said Warren.

"The Weekses have turned up in Florida."

"Do you know where in Florida?"

"Dale said they were moving around. Call him if you want to know more."

"Did he happen to say where this information comes from?"

"Local law enforcement. Are you checking his work, lieutenant? Why?"

"Do you know when they were located?"

"Lieutenant . . . I just got the call from Captain Stasiak this morning so I assume within the last couple of days. Is there something else happening with this? Do you have information?"

"I talked to Stasiak last night and he said they located the Weekses some time ago. I wonder why you're only finding out now."

Warren heard the district attorney let out a sigh. The line was silent for a moment. "Well, I don't know what that means. But they're in Florida and unless they come back up here and file a complaint about whatever it was that was done to them, we're finished with it. We have considerably bigger fish to fry at the moment. In case you hadn't noticed."

30

F ather Keenan was in the study, paying bills and catching up on paperwork. Mrs. Gonsalves had had to nag him to get on top of these things, which he didn't like to do. Now he couldn't find the recent bank statement she'd given him. He was about to call out her name when she appeared in the doorway. "There's a phone call for you."

"Where is the bank statement?"

"I just gave it to you."

"I know you did. Now I can't find it. What's the phone call?"

"The archdiocese."

Father Keenan looked at her and saw that she was watching him. He knew this was about Father Boyle, about whom Mrs. Gonsalves had firm opinions. He took the call in the parlor. The voice on the other end triggered a feeling of chagrin.

"This is Monsignor Van der Lohse. I'm calling about Father Boyle."

"Yes, monsignor. I'm terribly sorry I didn't give you my report last month. I hope you'll forgive me."

"It's important that you keep me apprised, Father. There is a protocol and we have to follow it."

"I understand."

"How is Father Boyle?"

"He's very good." The words came out too quickly, unconvincingly cheery.

"What's he doing?"

"Let's see. He says Mass once a day. Twice on Sundays.

He spends a lot of time at the hospital. He's quite devoted to the sick."

"Have there been any complaints?"

"No. Not a one."

"How is his medication?"

"As far as I know he's taking it."

"As far as you know?"

Father Keenan opened the door a crack and looked down the hallway. Mrs. Gonsalves was just disappearing back through the kitchen door. "I should keep closer tabs on it, Monsignor," he said, watching the kitchen. "But he seems fine to me."

"Does he have contact with children?"

Father Keenan closed his eyes and paced the parlor. "He does. A bit. He helps out at our little school down here for retarded children."

Van der Lohse was silent on the other end of the line.

"But I'm convinced there's nothing to be concerned about. They love him there. And he has hobbies which he very much enjoys."

"So his mental state seems stable to you?"

"Yes—well, he's a depressive, as you know. What can I say? Depressively stable."

"The last thing we want is a call from down there saying that something's happened."

"I understand."

"I'm going to write this up as satisfactory, but you need to call me at the beginning of every month. We're having this conversation two weeks late."

"I'm sorry, monsignor. I'll call you on the first of August for his next report."

Stasiak sped down the Mid-Cape Highway, the only car on the road. It was an oppressive, misty evening, the smell of skunk strong in the air. His cruiser dipped into hollows, where the air was cooler by five degrees, and when it rose back out, it was noticeably warmer and he could feel the clammy night on his skin.

He'd been sitting in his office a few minutes earlier going over leads when one of the sergeants came in with a report of a suspicious car that had been seen parked in an alleyway behind a convenience store in Brewster, a place frequented by kids. The license plate came back registered to a medical lab called Bondurant. A call to the lab revealed that the car was normally driven by one of their couriers, one Edgar Cleve, but that he was not on duty at the time the car was reported. The name was vaguely familiar to Stasiak, who went over the case file and dug out the reports compiled by the Barnstable police during their involvement in the Lefgren investigation. On the day of the murder, they had pulled in the vagrant Frawley, who turned out to be a waste of time, an old poof looking for some action at a public beach, and Cleve. Employees at the medical lab were able to tell Stasiak that Cleve had part-time work on a fishing boat out of Provincetown known as the *Darius*.

Stasiak turned off on a remote road that ran through an open landscape dotted with low dunes and isolated stands of cedar. He found Heller's Chevrolet parked at a turnoff and pulled up alongside. "What do you hear?" said Stasiak.

"Nothing."

"You talk to anybody up above?"

"No, sir."

"Nothing from Fitzgerald?"

"No, sir."

"How's it going with Jenkins?"

"I'm keeping him busy."

"Make sure he stays that way. What've you got him doing?"

"Chasing dead ends. But he doesn't like it. He isn't stupid."

"That's why we need to keep him out of the picture."

Stasiak put his cruiser in gear. "We need to make a trip out to Provincetown."

"Do we have something?"

"I'll tell you when we get there."

A half hour later they were at the waterfront in Provincetown, walking between the boats, two men in expensive suits amid the rusting steel and cables and shellfish rakes. The *Darius* was tied up alongside a dragger about halfway down the length of the wharf. Stasiak and Heller walked the length of the vessel, looking it over. A man came out of the pilothouse and glanced at them, then leaned on the gunnel with his elbows. They saw motion toward the stern, a rope flung out onto the deck from behind twin cable drums. They walked to the rear of the boat and saw a thin man of about thirty squatting with a length of rope, his hands moving quickly, fashioning it into an elaborate knot. Suddenly aware of their presence he looked up at them with wide eyes. "How you doing?" Stasiak said.

Cleve gave a slight nod. Stasiak looked at the rope in Cleve's hands, two identical loops, formed and cinched off with a fluidity and precision that recalled cursive script. "You're pretty good at that," said Stasiak.

The captain called down from his place at the gunnel. "All my guys are pretty good at that."

Stasiak looked up at him and then back at Cleve. "Are you Edgar Cleve?" The man nodded.

"The guy's just trying to make a living," the captain said. "Why don't you leave him alone?"

Stasiak removed his sunglasses and faced the man. "Why don't you go back to shucking clams, admiral?" He turned back to Cleve. "Come down here, Mr. Cleve. You've come to our attention one time too many."

They escorted him to the entrance of a nearby warehouse. "Any idea why we came out here to see you?" Stasiak said.

Cleve shook his head.

"What were you doing at the Kwik Mart in Brewster yesterday?"

"Nothing."

"Driving around doing nothing."

Cleve shrugged.

"Sitting in the alleyway behind the Kwik Mart doing nothing. I know one thing you were doing."

Cleve looked at Stasiak expectantly.

"You were violating section 622 of the Massachusetts General Code. Unauthorized use of a motor vehicle. Care to say anything about that? No? O.K. You used to work at Bondurant Medical Labs. Did you catch the past tense, Cleve? *Used to* because as of this morning, you're fired. You were using one of their lab cars to . . . well, we don't know what, do we? But you were using one of their lab cars without permission. You weren't on the clock, Mr. Cleve."

"I don't have a car."

"Most people find a way to get one legally."

Cleve looked past the two policemen, down the long line of buildings that backed up to the harbor. Among the people strolling along the waterfront, Cleve spotted someone who bore a striking resemblance to Dr. Hawthorne.

"Are there any priors on you?" Stasiak asked.

"No. I've never been in trouble of any kind."

"I understand you lived in New York before you came here but the registry of motor vehicles down there has no record of you. Didn't you have a driver's license in New York?"

"No. I didn't need one. I lived in the city."

Cleve looked back toward the piers and saw that the man he'd noticed was indeed Dr. Hawthorne. He was walking in that languid way he had, looking over the little establishments like a tourist, but his eyes kept going out to the water, checking the boats. Hawthorne was headed in their direction but he hadn't seen them yet. He was frowning now, his hands in his pockets, looking at the *Darius*.

"You ever serve in the military?" Stasiak asked.

"No."

"Did you go to college?"

"No."

So you're a bit of a mystery, huh, Mr. Cleve. This is not a good time to be a bit of a mystery. And you still haven't answered the sixty-four-thousand-dollar question. What where you doing in Brewster?"

"I was just . . . getting out. Sometimes I have to. It's my living situation . . ."

"I'm not interested in your living situation."

"You would be if . . ." Cleve had sneaked a look past Stasiak at Hawthorne, who now gazing straight back at him, his look intense and severe. Cleve wiped away the film of sweat that had suddenly formed on his upper lip.

"If what?" said Stasiak.

"Nothing."

Stasiak looked to Heller, and with a movement of the head that was nearly imperceptible, launched the sergeant into motion. Heller took Cleve by the front of his shirt and pulled him into the empty warehouse. Stasiak remained outside, watching the docks. Just inside the doorway, Heller slammed Cleve against the raw wooden wall. "What about your living situation?"

Cleve muttered and looked away.

Heller jabbed two fingers into his collarbone. "What about your living situation?"

"It's nothing, really. Just, personal. It's nothing you . . ."

Heller slammed the heel of his hand into Cleve's chest, driving him back against the wall. "We didn't come out here to play games with you, understand? We're running all over the goddamn state working a murder investigation. There ain't enough hours in the day for us to do what we have to do. So I don't appreciate making the trip all the way out here to Queertown so some shitbird like yourself can play cute. Now what is it about your living situation you think we should know?"

Cleve shook his head. Heller grabbed his wrist with one hand and bent his fingers back with the other.

"Pot!" Cleve gasped. "Marijuana. The guys I live with."

"Where?"

Supplied with an address and two fictitious names, Stasiak and Heller left a sweating Edgar Cleve standing just inside the doorway of the darkened warehouse. He waited for some time and was preparing to peer around the frame of the door when he heard shoes on the pavement, nice shoes, the kind that would make a clicking sound walking down the street but here produced a thin crunching grind on the bits of broken shell and grit covering the ground.

"Edgar." Hawthorne's voice. "Edgar, come out here."

Cleve rushed into the oily-smelling depths of the structure, feeling his way around heaps of discarded rope, empty crates, and pieces of heavy equipment in various stages of disassembly. A row of tall, clouded windows gave on to an alleyway, one of which was open a few inches. He forced the sash up enough to squeeze his body through, dropped into the alleyway, and disappeared into the crowds on Commercial Street.

That evening around dusk, Cleve sat with the captain of the *Darius* in the vessel's galley. Each had a thick ceramic mug in front of him containing a small amount of bourbon. "I got turned around in some neighborhood over in Brewster," Cleve was saying. "Someone wrote the license number down and reported it. That's why they showed up here, to ask me about it."

"They're out here at least once a week, seems like. I hear they're always prowling around Barnstable Harbor, too, crawling all over the guys down there. That one with the dark glasses, the big one. I don't like him." The boat creaked in the gentle swell made by a pleasure boat leaving the harbor. "You know that doctor you're renting from came around not long after they left."

Cleve pursed his lips and looked out the porthole. There was only the vague shape of the pilings to which they were tied, looming like phantoms in the deepening night. "He comes by the boat a lot," the captain said.

"I know he does."

"Well, what's he doing? *Checking* on you?"

"I don't know."

"Has this guy got something on you?"

"No. But you could say that *I've* got something on *him*."

"Yeah, like what? I won't tell anyone."

Edgar looked up and quickly took in the tiny enclosure in which they sat. His eyes glittered. "I'm holding on to that for the time being."

The captain watched him, turning his cup around in circles on the battered surface of the table. "Whatever you say. But I tell you what. If I see him here again, I'm going to set him straight. Me and a couple of the guys get hold of him, he won't be back."

"No. Don't do that."

"Then move out, Edgar. Jesus Christ. Find a new place to live."

Edgar wrapped his hands around his cup, looked down into its contents, and nodded.

"In the meantime you can bunk here. I'm staying with that waitress from the Lobster Pot. Use my rack. Or put a mattress down in the hold, I don't care."

The captain got up and put his cup in a strainer on the counter. "I'm going. If you're staying here, make sure all the equipment is off up top." He started out of the passageway then stopped. "You've got to watch out for yourself, Edgar."

31

Ed Jenkins crossed the packed dirt lot at Barnstable Harbor, skirting the water-filled potholes, on his way to the harbormaster's office. Working with the state police on the child murders was challenging, but not in the way he'd anticipated. They kept him busy. Check this address. Pull this file. Go talk to a Mrs. So-and-so, who saw something suspicious the other night. Go to the registry of motor vehicles for this reason and that reason. They had him chase down some apparently phony information Edgar Cleve had given them about a couple of guys in possession of marijuana at a house in East Dennis. It took an entire day of footwork to discover the guys didn't exist. The only upside to that little excursion was that Heller was furious.

Now, the state police had him compiling a record of commercial fishermen who leased slips at the various town docks. What they were going to do with this information, Captain Stasiak wouldn't say.

At his first weekly briefing at the barracks in Yarmouth, with all the detectives on the task force present, he and Stasiak had clashed. He challenged some of Stasiak's ideas, such as compiling a list of fishermen who rented docks in the town of Barnstable but not in Chatham or Orleans or anyplace else. He raised the point that this approach didn't even take into consideration the fact that each boat had a crew of six, on average, which could change weekly. Some guys loaned the slips out to other fishermen to whom they owed favors, and Jenkins happened to know that some falsified their paperwork because they were dodging creditors or tax officials. Stasiak stopped everything and said a few things to Jenkins, he no longer remembered what, except there was some reference to keeping his ass in his chair and his mouth shut and something about the extent of information that he, Jenkins, *didn't* know.

But Jenkins didn't particularly feel like keeping quiet. The captain slammed his palm down on the conference table so that they all flinched. "Heller," was all he said. The next thing Jenkins knew, this big son of a bitch was standing behind him, telling him to get out of his chair. "I don't need this shit," Jenkins said, and followed Heller out into the hallway. There were uniformed troopers and some volunteers manning the phone lines there, so Heller led him into an adjacent office and closed the door. The state policeman put the tip of his nose practically against Jenkins's, though he had to lean down considerably to do it. "You are insubordinate, Jenkins," Heller said.

"What the hell kind of operation are you guys running here, Heller? A guy can't ask questions?"

"You don't rate asking questions. Sit down, shut up, and do as you're told. We're not amateurs here."

"Neither am I."

"You're nobody and you're lucky to be here. If you want to go back to that Podunk department, go right ahead."

"Maybe I will. I don't even know what the hell I'm doing here in the first place."

"Captain Stasiak obviously felt you could contribute to the investigation. You should be honored."

"Well, Captain Stasiak doesn't do a whole lot for me, sergeant, you know what I mean? I think Captain Stasiak is riding a lot of hype from the Attanasio case. I haven't seen anything from Captain Stasiak that impresses me all that much. Aside from his clothes. You impress me even less. Big fuckin' farm boy without two brain cells to rub together."

The next thing Jenkins knew, his feet were suddenly no longer touching the ground and he was listening to a long, slow tear working its way through an armpit seam in his jacket. Heller had two fistfuls of material, his eyes just inches away from Jenkins's. "Get in your car," he said quietly. "And get the fuck out of here. You're finished."

As it turned out, they gave him his assignments through Dunleavy. He joked with the clerks at the registry of motor vehicles that he ought to have his own desk with as much time as he was spending there. Jenkins didn't believe the investigation had any focus. He'd heard that Edgar Cleve had been spotted in Brewster, hanging around a corner grocery, attracting the attention of the neighbors. Stasiak had grilled him about it and hadn't really come up with anything. And as far as Jenkins knew, nobody was talking about Gene Henry anymore. He wasn't sure, because no one—not even Dunleavy—would tell him anything.

Warren had gone to check with his officers at the scene of an accident just before noon, and when he returned to the station, he found Stasiak standing in the front hallway at Garrity's desk. Stasiak turned as Warren came through the front doors. "Well, look who it is," he said. "The district attorney tells me you were on the phone with him." He paused and watched Warren. "About Russell Weeks."

"I spoke with him, yes."

"Why did you do that?"

"I wanted to know if he was aware you'd found the Weeksees in Florida. It turns out he'd just found out, which is strange, since you told me you located them some time ago."

Stasiak stared at him. Warren couldn't stop himself. "I get the idea there's something you're not playing straight about this."

"Is that the idea you get?"

"That's right."

"Well, I've got an idea for you, and you'd damn well better get it through your head."

"I'm done talking to you, Stasiak."

The state policeman looked at Warren, appraised him from his forehead all the way to his patent leather uniform shoes. "You know what I think the problem is?" he said. "We just need to get to know each other better." He put an arm around Warren's shoulders. "Let's go outside for a minute, Warren," he said, steering the lieutenant toward the door.

"I'm not going anywhere with you."

"Come on." Stasiak's arm clamped Warren in, an amazing force. Just one arm and Warren felt he would have to struggle in order to break free of it. "What are you doing?"

"Come on outside for a sec, talk in private."

Stasiak shoved the door open and propelled Warren out. Warren turned on him. "What in hell do you think you're doing? Don't you ever put your hands on me."

Stasiak looked around the street in all directions and then turned to Warren. "Stay the fuck out of state police business," he said. "Are you accusing me of lying? Huh? You think for some reason I'd make up a story about locating the Weekses? For what? I got a bunch of murders on my hands, you shitstain. And you call the fucking district attorney to tell him you think there's something suspicious about the Russell Weeks thing?" Stasiak looked around the street once again, then drove his fist into Warren's solar plexus. The wind left his lungs and he rocked back against the chainlink fence. Warren was about to fall to the ground when he felt another hard blow, this one high on his jawbone just below his left ear. A white streak shot past his eyes and he went down. Stasiak took him by one of his arms and, with shocking ease, hoisted him upright and propped him against the fence. Stasiak hit him in the side, just below his rib cage, then again in his solar plexus, a lightning-fast combination that brought Warren to his knees, his forehead on the ground. "Now you know me a little better, Warren. But, believe me, you don't want to know me any better than this."

*

Sitting on the edge of his bed, his jaw and rib cage still smarting from Stasiak's blows, Warren stared out the window but his eyes were unseeing. They had appointed Dunleavy chief of police over him. He was too stunned for anger.

The day before, he had been sitting in his office, the door closed, trying to absorb what Stasiak had done to him, trying to figure out what to do next. Warren remained sequestered there until four-thirty in the afternoon. He called Jane and asked her if she would pick up Mike from Nazareth Hall and stay with him until he got back. He didn't know how late he would be. He could not face his son, knowing what had happened. It was humiliating to the point of devastation, the idea of coming home and greeting the boy and knowing that a mere three hours earlier, he had been laid out on the ground outside the police station, one hand gripping the chain-link fence, unable to breathe.

Somehow, Stasiak knew that Warren would never tell a soul about the assault. If he had come out on top, Warren would have reported Stasiak's actions. But as it was, the incident would go with Warren to his grave, both because he was ashamed and because it was a question of honor: He was not going to appeal to any outside force to intervene for him. Somehow, Stasiak understood this, which made it safe for him to strike Warren with closed fists.

He had had disagreements both in his police career and in the military—some of them sharp—but never had anyone so much as suggested violence. Stasiak's attack over Warren's interest in the Russell Weeks affair had him wondering just what it was he was dealing with. Stasiak was a bad cop, that was clear now, but it was possible that he was also mentally unstable.

At four-thirty, his phone rang. It was Donald Nicholas, who informed him that the board of selectmen had made a decision for the chief's position: Phil Dunleavy. Nicholas was obviously gloating, thoroughly enjoying being the one to make the phone call. "Earl Mott is going to ask you to stay on as lieutenant. I'm going to recommend against it. Just so you know."

Jenkins came in as Warren was preparing to go over to the town hall and give his resignation. "I just heard," he said. "I can't believe it. Phil? I mean, he's a smart guy but you're already doing the job."

Warren said nothing. He unloaded his service revolver, dumped the bullets on the desk, and threw his badge and credentials down with them.

"Boss, you better say something 'cause you're worrying me. What are you doing?"

"Going over to town hall."

"For what?"

"To resign."

"Oh, come on."

Warren got up and headed for the door. Jenkins blocked his way. "Don't do it."

"Move, Jenkins."

"You're cutting your nose off to spite your face."

"What do you expect me to do? Just accept it? They want me out. You know who gave me the call? Donny Nicholas. He probably begged Mott to let him be the one to do it. He told me he was going to recommend against me staying on as lieutenant, which I'd never do anyway. This whole goddamn place is corrupt. They want things run the way Marvin ran them. A rigged system. If you're nobody or you're on the outside, like those antique dealers, watch out, because they're going to roll right over you."

"I hate to say I told you so, but I warned you'd pay for that."

Warren hurled the duty roster across the room. "And I'd do it again!" he shouted. "That's not the only thing I'm paying for and you know it! I tried to take care of my son. Did I use my position to do that? Yes, and maybe I was wrong, but that boy has no defenses whatsoever and they wouldn't leave him alone.

You'd probably do the same thing if you had a kid like Mike. He's my son. I have to protect him."

"Which you can't do very well if you're unemployed. Maybe you need to take a few days and think about it."

"Marvin Holland. That thing with the airport, those rumors about him using his influence to steer the contract to Dave Langella's concrete business. What about that? People were talking about Marvin getting a cut and Earl Mott getting a cut. And then the thing ran over budget. We had to cut overtime and run fewer cars per shift. Why? So Marvin and Earl could get paid? If I was ever involved in anything like that—if my name had even been *mentioned* in connection with anything like that—I'd have been finished. I've tried to do what's best in this job. I've tried to do what's right but apparently that's not what they want. What they want is a political appointee disguised as a police chief. I can't do that. I don't know how."

Warren took a breath and looked around his office. "Take my weapon, will you? Stow it or put it in property or whatever you want to do. The other stuff, throw it away."

"You need to think about this, lieutenant. You're making a mistake."

"You know, the least Dunleavy could have done is tell me he was interested in the job, too. He didn't have to go sneaking around."

"Maybe it's as big a surprise to him as it is to us."

"No. He was spending time at the hospital visiting Marvin in the evenings."

"Huh?"

Warren looked over his desk one last time, then headed to the door. Jenkins still stood there, digesting what Warren had just said. Warren looked at him and for a second felt a surge of emotion. "Would you please get out of the doorway so I can go do what I have to do?"

32

After his resignation, Warren had a week's worth of work helping out at Cameron's as an assistant to the shop mechanic. He had one more paycheck coming from the town, and that would be it. He would have to withdraw some of his savings to make Mike's next tuition payment. Perhaps the most difficult thing was that he'd had to let Jane go and he missed her. He was often tempted to call her up and ask her what she thought about this, or what she suggested he do about that, or how would she go about such-and-such. Her absence enhanced his melancholy. A few days after his resignation, he had gone to pick Little Mike up after school, and the nuns asked him how he was getting along. Sister Julia told him that there were some projects they needed to have done, and asked him if he wouldn't mind looking at them.

Grayson Newsome and James Holbrooke from Antiquitus called him, offering him their condolences. They asked him to come out to Osterville to look at some things they wanted done around the property because they had heard he was a carpenter. There were a number of stunning acts of kindness in the wake of his leaving the department. By far the most touching was Jane offering to watch Mike three times a week on credit. She would keep track of the time and Warren could pay her when he had the money. No rush. Mike needed her, she said.

The *Standard Times* had called him repeatedly for comment on his resignation but he declined. He also got a call from Fred Sibley, who had been convicted of narcotics possession and got five years in state prison at Walpole. The call was made on his behalf by a prison officer who asked if Warren would accept it, which he did not. The *Globe* ran a surprisingly straightforward article documenting the downfall of one of its most talented reporters. "Squandered Promise: A Reporter's Tragic Descent Into Drug Addiction," divulged that Sibley had a history of drug use, in fact was sent away for three months in 1955 until he could get straight. He redeemed himself during the Attanasio trial but then came the debacle on Cape Cod.

Warren did a lot of thinking about the failed raid on the Elbow Room, the tipped-off wiretaps, and the child murders. He ate little and did not sleep. He stewed in anger over Dunleavy's subterfuge and Stasiak's assault on him at the police station. To ease the pain of those events, he dwelt on other things, trying to solve the problems in his head.

Phil Dunleavy knew about both the raid and the wiretap, and though Warren now knew that the detective couldn't be trusted, he couldn't go so far as accusing him of being the leak. Wilson Hayes was convincing when they met him at the diner, but then his stock-in-trade was to be convincing, so that didn't count for much. Warren could see him double crossing them on the raid but Hayes had not known about the wiretap.

On a sultry Sunday afternoon, the two priests sat on the veranda behind the rectory. The morning Masses were done and the church was quiet. It was unusual for Father Keenan to have no place to be on a Sunday, and Father Boyle was grateful for his presence and the peaceful moment with him on the porch, a warm breeze stirring the curtains in the open windows. Mrs. Gonsalves had prepared a pork loin on Friday, which sat heating in the oven. They would have a rare meal together if nothing interrupted.

"Let me ask you," Father Keenan said. "You visit the hospital several times a week. You visit the elderly. You work with the retarded. The works you perform are some of the more demanding in ministry. If you're jaded with religious life, you could make a much easier time of it. Do baptisms, weddings. Just say Masses. Socialize. But you choose not to. I wonder why."

"There are only two of us. If I didn't do it, it would all fall on you. So many sufferers, so little time." Father Boyle grinned briefly, exposing his missing tooth.

"My question to you, Terrence, is whether your devotion to the suffering and the rejected does not contradict your statement that you have no faith."

"These days, Father, I operate on instinct. This is all I know. I try not to think too much about things. I visit the sick and I sit with the dying because I must. I make no claims to sainthood—you know I don't, but doing for others is the only thing that keeps me . . . If I didn't do this, I'm afraid I would break apart in a thousand pieces."

"It validates you?"

"I suppose so," said Father Boyle. "I happen to be someone who requires validation with a very big stamp, something that makes a loud thump when it hits the paper. Some would say it's perverse. Perhaps I could be accused of seeking out misery."

Father Boyle was looking at the screen door and he thought he saw Mrs. Gonsalves move like a shadow on the other side, wiping her hands with a dishrag, but he knew that she was off today. He began to feel a little light and dreamy and he looked hard through the screen to see what it was that had drifted past. Father Keenan said, "You've been staying out late at night and I've been wondering where you go."

"I've been taking walks in the woods."

"Really. Where?"

"Down Cape. Brewster, Truro, Wellfleet."

"Way down there? Why?"

"Wonderful things to draw. And there are places out there . . ." he let the sentence trail off. "Once I would have sworn

I heard the seraphim, had I been so inclined." He let out a little chuckle, which sounded false in his ears.

"You *are* inclined, Terrence. That's what concerns me. And Lucy says she's noticed things."

"Oh, she has, has she?"

"I'm thinking of events at Belmont, Terrence. There was a place like that in Belmont, if you recall."

"Oh, it's nothing like that."

"Terrence, I think it would be a good idea if we got a doctor here to see you."

"No doctors, Father. No medication. I don't like it."

33

That's a bad fuckin' stink, man. What is that?"

"You aren't used to stink by now?"

"That isn't regular stink."

"A dead dog, probably."

The two men rode in the cab of a backhoe, navigating the bottom of a long mesa of compacted trash at the town dump. The seagulls had concentrated at one spot, forming a gray and white mass, their cries loud and frantic. One of the men took a .22 rifle out of a scabbard that was affixed to the side of the cab. They carried the weapon for sport, to shoot rats they occasionally saw burrowing through the mountains of trash.

"Roy hears that thing go off, he'll shit his pants," said the driver.

"He can't hear anything way the hell back here. Look out. I'm gonna clear 'em out."

Three cracks rang out in succession. The seagulls lifted off in a storm of flapping wings, stray feathers drifting down over the trash. The driver put the backhoe in gear, and moved forward, lowering the shovel. The place where the birds had congregated was a nearly vertical wall of refuse, formed when a portion of the mound sheared away of its own weight and rolled downhill some twenty-five yards. From among the cardboard and paper and cans and grime and broken glass, a whitish object was visible, unmistakably a hand. Five slender fingers extended from out of a shapeless mass of brown. A short distance from that, located in such a way that it could have been connected to the hand, was a crumpled face, its eyes closed tightly, its features distorted, like that of a mummy discovered in some far-flung peat bog or tun-dra, like something from *National Geographic.* The two men got down and stepped over the garbage for a better look.

"Oh my God."

"We better get Roy."

Jenkins was in his office compiling a list of suspicious car sightings he was supposed to check out when his phone rang.

"Barnstable Police, Detective Jenkins."

"Hey, Eddie, it's Roy Campo over at the dump."

"Yeah, hey, Roy, how's it going?"

"Will you come over here and take a look at something? Some of my fellas over here were up on the backhoe and they found something. I thought maybe it's a dead animal but now I don't know. There's clothes and stuff."

"Is it a body?"

"Hell, I don't know. I hope to hell not."

Jenkins got in his car and drove to the dump. Roy and two of his workers were in the shed at the entrance. They were awed quiet, stunned, it seemed. Roy, normally unpleasant and vulgar, actually appeared thoughtful. "Eddie, my guys here found some-thing I think you ought to look at."

"O.K. Where is it?"

Roy turned to his workers. "You guys take him out there."

They walked to the backhoe. The driver got behind the con-trols. "You can just stand up here," he said to Jenkins. "Hold on to the cabin frame like that."

Jenkins stepped up on the slimy surface of the machine and hung on. His stomach momentarily lurched with the smell of the place. They rolled down a dirt road with mounds of garbage on either side and then turned off of it to roll over a broad, flat ridge of packed-down refuse, then down its side until they were near the edge of some woods. Suddenly, the driver turned the engine off. "It's right there," he said, pointing. Jenkins tried to find places to step where he wouldn't sink or get anything on his shoes or trouser cuffs but it was hopeless. He peered at the wall of garbage but had to get closer to see. The smell was, without a doubt, that of a decomposing corpse. "There's two," he called out.

"Huh?"

"There's two bodies. One's a kid."

He turned around and trudged back toward the machine. "All right. Shit. We're gonna need some way of getting them out of there. Can you get the shovel in just underneath them and lift them out?"

The man sat with his hands draped over the controls, a doubtful expression on his face.

"Come on, man. They're not gonna jump out at you. Stink is the worst thing you have to worry about. Just get them in the shovel and take them down there and put them down on the ground. Then you're done."

He did as directed, dumping a shovel full of garbage on a stretch of flat ground at the edge of the woods. A soaking cloth tarpaulin flopped open with a clank of cans and a slopping, wet sound and a femur appeared, partially wrapped in mud-colored fabric, its tibia still attached and trailing off at an angle. Jenkins had to turn away and heave once. He walked toward the trees and took several deep breaths. Viewing the pile from a distance, he saw another tarpaulin, this one tied at its top with a length of clothesline rope. He called out to the man on the bulldozer. "Take me back up to the shed, will you? I have to use the telephone."

Warren was sitting at his kitchen table, redoing the sums in his checkbook for the third time, when the phone rang.

"Lieutenant? It's Jenkins. What are you doing?"

"I'm waiting on some work to come through."

"Listen, I'm at the dump right now. We found two bodies."

Warren was silent.

"An adult and a juvenile. They're in pieces and they're tied up in tarps. You there?"

"Yes, I'm here. You better call Dunleavy."

"I will. But I just want to keep it under wraps for a little while."

"Why?"

"Because from what I've seen so far, it looks like a woman and a little girl. And you know what I'm thinking? Miriam Weeks and the kid. If that's true, it's a long way from Florida, if you know what I mean."

"Again, I'd call your superior."

"Lieutenant, I don't know about Phil anymore. I'd like to put Stasiak in a corner on this. I think Phil would try to help him stay out of one."

"Are you saying you think Stasiak is involved?"

"No. But I think his arrogance has come back to bite him in the ass. I think he made the whole Florida thing up. I think he can't stand having an unsolved case on his resume. He probably figured the Weekses had disappeared into the woodwork and everyone would forget about them. Once he realized you were snooping around he lied to get you to back off. It would have worked except now we have this."

"You haven't ID'd the bodies yet."

"That's right, but now he's on record as saying the Weekses were found in Florida. So if these bodies are them, he's going to be in a hell of a fix trying to explain this."

"Unless he can convince people that they found their way back to Massachusetts and into those tarps in the meantime."

"Nobody's going to buy that. They're going to want to review his inquiries down there, who he called, who he talked to, the whole thing. If it's the Weekses, it's gonna be too good to be true. I plan to call the district attorney as soon as I find out because I want to see Stasiak try to explain himself. I might see that the *Standard Times* gets a call, too, really give his ass a jolt when he sees it in the paper. And this would put the Elbow Room investigation in a completely different light, too."

"You need to get them ID'd, Ed. And you need to call Dunleavy. Don't give them anything to hang you with."

"Yeah, yeah. I'll do all that eventually. I have to call Jack Dowd."

"O.K. Call me when you know more."

Jenkins hung up the phone and turned to Roy Campo. "Roy, you think you can keep quiet about this for a day or so?"

"What do you mean, do I think I can? Of course I can keep quiet. You think I want everyone to know they're dumping bodies out here? Goddamn, how the hell did something like this wind up out here, anyhow?"

Jenkins dialed the coroner's office.

"Jack."

"Yes?"

"This is Ed Jenkins."

"Hello, detective."

"Jack, we have a couple of bodies out here at the dump."

"What?"

"A couple of bodies. A woman and a girl. We think."

"At the dump?"

"At the dump."

"Holy Jesus."

"Yeah, that's what I said. Now, what we'd like to do is keep this quiet. We want to get them on ice while we try to find dental records and we don't want the whole goddamn town going crazy over it."

"All right."

"You're gonna need . . . I don't know . . . Bags or something."

"What condition are they in?"

"Bad. We got pieces. I won't lie to you, Jack, it's a hell of a mess."

"Can I get a vehicle in there?"

"You can get part of the way. We can take them out to you in the shovel of the backhoe."

"O.K. You want pictures?"

"Yeah, I guess we better take pictures."

Jenkins visited the old woman who lived next door to the Weekses. Through a broad line of questioning that would not arouse her suspicion, he got from her the name of the Weekses' dentist and Jenkins paid him a visit at his practice in Centerville. He retrieved the records and brought them to Jack Dowd's office. There was a small lavatory adjacent to the morgue, where he found Dowd leaning over the sink, scrubbing his hands. He planted a thumb over one nostril and blew mucus into the sink, then moved his thumb to the other side and repeated. Suddenly aware of Jenkins standing in the doorway he straightened up. "Sorry," he said, and took a towel off the rack. He looked a little stunned. "Are those the dental records?"

"Yes."

"These people were cut apart."

"Mm-hm."

"There are tool marks on the cartilage and bone. I'd ask you what's going on but I know you won't tell me."

"You'll find out, Jack."

"Give them here. I'll call you within the hour. Unless you want to wait around."

"Not really. So it's a woman and a girl?"

"Yes. I'm going to say thirty-five and eleven, respectively. Thereabouts. Strangled and dismembered."

"I'll come back in an hour."

As Jenkins walked out to his car, he noticed a red and black Studebaker rolling slowly through the lot, the driver glancing in his direction. Jenkins went to a diner on Main Street and took a seat where he could watch the door. He had a cup of coffee and read the paper and then went back over to the hospital. As he approached the building, he spotted the Studebaker behind him again. When Jenkins turned into the lot, the car continued on. He found Jack Dowd sitting at his desk filling out forms. "Miriam and Doreen Weeks," he said.

"*Goddamn,*" Jenkins said. "*Goddamn.*"

"This is good news?"

"Yes—well, not for the Weekses, but yeah, it's good news. Jack, thank you." Jenkins shook the coroner's hand. "I need to go see the DA."

On his way to the Barnstable courthouse, he watched for anyone who might be following him but he saw nothing suspicious. He parked down the street in front of a restaurant and walked to the courthouse, surveying his surroundings. He climbed the granite steps and signed in at the desk that guarded the suite of offices belonging to the district attorney. Elliott Yost was in a meeting with two men from his staff.

"Tell him it's important," Jenkins told the secretary.

"He's requested that he not be disturbed."

"Oh, he'll be disturbed all right."

"I beg your pardon?"

"Tell him to come out, honey. This is more important than his meeting."

She flopped her hands on her desk in an exasperated gesture and poked her head into Elliott's office. She came back, shaking her head. "You'll have to come back later." Jenkins walked around her desk and went for Elliott's office door.

"Hey!" she said. "You can't go in there!"

Elliott and his two colleagues stared at Jenkins when he swung the door open. "I'm sorry to interrupt, Elliott, but we need to talk."

"I'm in a meeting!" Elliott said. "Vera!"

"Elliott, we need to talk."

"You can't just walk in here, detective."

"I know."

"*Damn* it. You people." Elliott grabbed his jacket up off the back of his chair and followed Jenkins out. They went into the conference room next door. Elliott was furious.

"What is it?"

"The Weekses have been located."

"I *know* that."

"At the town dump. Wrapped up in tarps. Cut in pieces." Jenkins told him about the discovery.

"I don't understand," Elliott said.

"I don't either. Stasiak said he found them in Florida."

"I know what Stasiak said."

"I believe this is connected to a gambling and extortion racket that's being operated out of the Elbow Room. I know you've got the child murders and everything but someone needs to investigate this."

"I know, I know. I can't do it all at once."

"So let me take this case."

"I've got the state police on it."

"Elliott, I hate to point out the obvious . . ."

The district attorney held up a hand to silence him. "I know. I don't know what Dale did or didn't do. It's a hell of a mix-up, I know that."

"I'm not doing much with the task force. Frankly, they're wasting my time. I could chase this down. Warren and I put together all the intelligence."

"Let me talk to Dale."

Roy Campo was sitting in the shack at the dump trying to get a small television set to work when Jenkins drove up. "Roy, where are your guys?"

"Out back somewheres."

"Call them in, will you?"

Ten minutes later, the two men rolled up in the backhoe. Jenkins told them that they were free to talk about the discovery of the bodies. He said a reporter from the *Standard Times* would be over soon and they could tell him everything they knew. From there, Jenkins found a payphone and called the *Standard Times*.

"Cape Cod *Standard Times*, news desk."

"Two bodies were discovered at the Barnstable town dump this morning. They were identified as Miriam and Doreen Weeks. They were dismembered. The guys at the dump will give you the information. If you don't believe me, call the district attorney's office. Want his number?"

"Wait, wait, wait, wait. Who am I speaking to?"

"SPring five, three-two-five-oh. Got it?"

"Hold on, fella. Who . . ."

"Got it?"

"Yeah, three two . . ."

"Five-oh. Elliott Yost. When you get to the dump, talk to Roy Campo."

Jenkins hung up and drove to Warren's house. There was a black car parked on the side of the road a short distance down the street with a man behind the wheel. Jenkins watched it as he walked across Warren's yard. As he knocked on the door, the car pulled away, the driver looking away from Jenkins as he passed so that his face was not visible. Warren opened the door a crack. Jenkins noticed he had the chain lock fastened on the inside.

"I got some news."

Warren undid the chain and let Jenkins in.

"Those bodies at the dump are the Weekses. Jack Dowd checked the dental records this morning."

"Damn."

"I told Elliott."

"What did he say?"

"It knocked him on his ass. He doesn't know which way is up."

"They have to go after the gambling thing now."

"I don't see how they can't," said Jenkins. "If we can tie this to the Elbow Room, boy, we can put the hammer down."

"We don't have the kind of evidence it's going to take. They can string a lot of the dots together but there's nothing substantial. And Elliott needs to know they might have somebody inside the department. What does he plan to do?"

"Talk to Stasiak."

"Does *he* know about the bodies?"

"Not yet, but he will soon. I know this is probably way out of line but I think it's awful funny—*awful* funny—that Stasiak told you those people were found in Florida."

"Be careful what you say, Ed. Not to me but to others."

"Well, I'm only stating the facts. We know that Stasiak claimed the Weekses were found in Florida some time ago. We know he lied about interviewing the brother. We know that he never called Elliott Yost to tell him, but he sure was in a hurry to do it right after telling you. And then there's the fact that he basically threatened you—did he threaten you?'

"To say the least."

"O.K., threatened you to stay away from the Weeks case."

"Do me a favor," said Warren, "and let me know before you do anything with this, will you? You're treading on thin ice."

"O.K. Hey, is someone following you?"

Warren looked at Jenkins. He paused for a moment. "Why do you ask?"

"Because there was a guy in a black car parked outside. He left as soon as I pulled up."

Warren's expression darkened. His eyes went to the window.

Jenkins said, "I think someone's following me. In fact, I'm sure of it."

"Who? Someone connected to McCarthy and the rest of them?"

"That's my guess. I'll send a squad car by your place every few hours."

"Thanks."

"I'll call you later."

34

J enkins made anonymous phone calls to the *Boston Globe* and the *Herald Traveler*, telling them about the discovery at the dump. He also told them that a state police officer, Captain Dale Stasiak, had told the district attorney for the Cape and Islands that he had located the Weekses in Florida some time ago and suggested they look into the amount of time that elapsed between the state police locating the family and their informing the district attorney. He finished with the explosive revelation that the deaths were possibly connected to a gambling and extortion ring that had once been investigated by local police.

The discovery of the Weekses' bodies threw the region into yet a higher pitch of lamentation and paranoia. The conspiracy-minded had a field day connecting the Weekses to the dead children. There was talk of death cults, UFOs, zombies. There were renewed calls for FBI involvement, strenuously rejected by the state police, less so by Elliott Yost, who was feeling so much pressure that respect and liberation from the doldrums of a backwater district were no longer important. Now, he didn't view the case so much as his ticket to higher places but as something he had to survive.

The *Globe* ran an editorial that raised questions about the capabilities of the state police. At a time when the public was depending on its law enforcement agencies to be at their absolute best, it did not inspire confidence to have two people the state police thought they had located turn up in a garbage dump right under their noses.

Warren and Jenkins met with Elliott Yost at the courthouse. Around the time of the raid on the Elbow Room, Warren had delivered a dossier including all the information they had gathered. At the time, Elliott had been impassive. Now they sat in the quiet of his office. The attorney's eyes were watery and his face strained.

"Who was the confidential informant?" he asked.

"A guy named Wilson Hayes," Jenkins answered.

"This is someone you turned?"

"No. He's a former colleague of mine. He went in there and observed. We worked a couple of gaming cases together when we were both with the Providence PD. He knows what he's talking about. He'll confirm there's gambling going on—and most likely moneylending too—and there's a bunch of guys from up above who might be connected to Grady Pope. George McCarthy is apparently an old associate of Pope's. And McCarthy's down here now, running the Elbow Room."

Jenkins told him about how Leapley had been badly beaten, their surveillance of the Elbow Room, the compromised wiretap, and the hearsay evidence they had developed. "Wilson Hayes told us they had a full-service bookmaking operation going in there. They had a sports wire, phones, the whole thing. We went in there and everything had been cleared out. We think Hayes was telling the truth, and we think someone in the department tipped them off that the raid was coming.

"So as far as the Weekses go, we know from the phone records the husband had been calling the Elbow Room. He called the illegal line and we figure it was about borrowing money. He got behind, they threatened him. The missus starts yacking to the DuPonts, you get involved, and then they all disappear. It got out of hand. He wasn't paying and they had to shut her up. The kid, well, she just happened to be there."

Elliott put his head in his hand. "God," he said.

"There's no way you can get more resources on it?" Warren asked. "Jenkins, for example?"

"I can't possibly. How can I?"

"Just tell the state police you want me on it," Jenkins said. "I know a whole lot more about this than they do."

"Have you considered the possibility that Russell Weeks is responsible for the murder of his wife and daughter?"

"I doubt it," said Warren.

"Well, it's a scenario Captain Stasiak raised."

Jenkins and Warren looked at each other. "Captain Stasiak," Warren said, "probably isn't aware of the information we've gathered."

Jenkins said, "This isn't nickel poker at the Elks Club, Elliott. This is serious. Wilson Hayes told us he figured the whole operation is probably taking in a hundred thousand a year. These guys are bad bastards. And someone in the department or someone somewhere giving information to the subject of an investigation, I would think that would get somebody's attention."

"That's a very serious allegation," Elliott said. "That would need to be looked at very hard." He folded his arms on his desk, hunched his shoulders, and looked around the room, bleary-eyed. "You've informed Chief Dunleavy of your findings, I assume, detective?"

Jenkins nodded and looked out the window.

"I want to concentrate on the Weeks murders," Elliott said. "Not any intrigue about informants or whatever else. If there's something to all that we'll take it on later. This isn't an illegal gaming investigation and I don't want it to become one. That is relevant only insofar as it relates to the Weeks killings. You work for Chief Dunleavy and the town of Barnstable, detective. And the Weeks murders are a state police case. I'm going to recommend they assign you to it. But ultimately, I will concur with any action your superiors want to take. I'll speak with Chief Dunleavy as soon as I can."

35

S eptember was uncommonly warm that year. There were reports of lights in the night sky over the lower Cape. People went out to high, lonely places and sat on the hoods of cars, hoping to see a UFO. Late afternoons were humid and steamy, the air leaden yet filled with an ambient electricity, like the kind that preceded a severe thunderstorm, though none ever came. Father Keenan noticed it and looked out the tiny bathroom window of the rectory as he splashed water on his face in the morning and thought about his friend, Father Boyle. Patrons of the Elbow Room looked around the parking lot as they came out in the dark hours of early dawn, remarking absently that the weather felt strange. Ed Jenkins, sitting in traffic on Main Street in Hyannis, watched the tourists amble along the sidewalk with a vulnerable, slightly disconcerted look. One of the men counting money in the kitchen behind the Bilge in Orleans looked up and said, "Open that window. It's hot in here." Another said, "Leave it closed. It's going to rain like hell."

In the first week of September, along a lonely stretch of beach in Truro, Warren lay concealed in the brush that grew among the dunes and watched Dale Stasiak pull up to a public phone booth in the beach parking lot. Warren lay with his back against a rise in the sandy soil, his legs stretched out in front of him, and looked through a spotter's scope that he had once used to examine targets on the police firing range.

He watched with the exquisite anxiety of the birder who has discovered a very rare specimen, thrilled at the good fortune of having stumbled upon it at all and fearful that the thing would fly off to the inaccessible places where it concealed itself, never to be seen again. Tailing Stasiak had been nearly impossible. He reversed direction, changed speeds, parked unexpectedly to observe his surroundings, even switched cars. Warren had lost count of the number of times Stasiak had shaken him completely. Nearly every time he had tried to follow him, Warren was either outmaneuvered or duped outright. He would have given up if he had a job to go to, but work at Cameron's was sporadic. He finished a number of jobs at Nazareth Hall, which he traded as tuition payments for Mike's continued attendance. He never got back to James Holbrooke and Grayson Newsome at Antiquitus about the work there because he felt uncomfortable about it. Now they were gone on an extended vacation to Europe and he didn't know when they'd be back. Much of his savings were gone. He needed to look at his balance before he wrote any more checks but was avoiding it.

With a surplus of idle time on his hands, Dale Stasiak became an unhealthy preoccupation.

Watching him now through the scope, Warren was amazed at his good luck. He had lost Stasiak in this vicinity a number of times and finally, guessing that the beach was where he had been headed, decided to stake out the parking lot.

There was a boarded-up bathhouse and a small playground beside it, the seesaws and rocking horses empty, the swings moving slightly in a breeze. He watched Stasiak get out of his car and circle the bathhouse, disappear from sight briefly, and reemerge on the other side. He stood by a phone booth and looked at the empty playground.

After some time, Stasiak entered the phone booth and pulled the door shut behind him. Through the glass, which was streaked with bird droppings, Warren could see him talking. He saw Stasiak's head rotate slowly around, checking his surroundings, as if he sensed the presence of someone else. Stasiak looked down at the floor of the phone booth for a moment, then raised his gaze in Warren's direction. In the round aperture of the spotter's scope, it seemed as if Stasiak were staring directly at him.

Seated perfectly still in the confessional, Father Boyle listened to the sounds outside in the church. It was nearing five o'clock on a Saturday afternoon. He had heard a half dozen confessions, similar litanies of minor sins, some from voices he recognized, all no different from those he'd heard the previous week. Outside, he could hear the occasional creaking pew, the odd cough, and once in a while a snatch of whispering.

At five till five, the adjacent booth opened. He heard someone kneel on the small padded ledge below the screened window. Instead of beginning with the ritual words of confession, the penitent simply knelt there quietly. "Go ahead," Father Boyle whispered. When there was no sound from the other side, he said, "Are you there?"

"Yes."

It was a man's voice. The scent of tobacco and sweat drifted through the wicker, acrid and primal, suggestive of some extremity of circumstances the priest could only guess at.

"Go on. How long has it been since your last confession?"

"I have never been to confession."

"You are Catholic?"

"No. But I need to tell something."

"I empathize with you, friend. I'm humbled you came to me. But the sacrament of penance . . ."

"I know something terrible."

"I see."

Father Boyle strained to see through the wicker. In the tiny interstices of black, there was nothing. He could hear the man rustling in the dark on the other side. There was a long pause during which it appeared he would not speak at all.

"Perhaps this is not the time for you to speak," Father Boyle said.

"It's past time."

Another silence passed.

"I myself am guilty of things that would surprise you," Father Boyle said. "Does that put you more at ease?"

"My name is . . ."

"I don't want to know your name."

"I want you to know it. In case something happens to me."

"This is all very dramatic, but in the scheme of things, how serious can this be?"

"Very serious."

"I've been a priest for more than forty years. I've heard just about every wrong a human being can commit."

"I doubt it."

Father Boyle waited. He could hear people shuffling in for the five o'clock Mass. Whispered conversation in the entrance foyer. The man said, "There's something happening and I need to stop it."

"Are you talking about a crime?"

Light flooded the adjacent compartment as the man opened the door and let himself out. Father Boyle sat there, fighting the temptation to follow. He counted to twenty—time enough for the penitent to get out of the church. When he emerged from his booth, the heavy front doors of the church were open, the afternoon ablaze outside. Just before they swung shut, he saw the black form of a tall, thin, long-limbed man hurrying out.

Late afternoon settled thick and damp over General Patton Drive. Crows sat in the dead branches of the pines in the back-yard and looked silently down on Warren as he smoked on the back step. He had no work and had been roaming the house look-ing for something to do, as if this were the only thing that stood between him and some terrible fall. He ran for the telephone when he heard it ringing on the kitchen wall. It was Jenkins.

"Hey," he said. "Did you see today's *Globe*?"

"No."

"They killed Wilson Hayes."

Jenkins showed up ten minutes later. It had been a long time since two grown people had sat at the kitchen table. It seemed incredibly cramped.

Wilson Hayes was discovered sitting behind the wheel of his car at the parking lot of the Gillette Company's headquarters. Employees arriving for work noticed the shattered driver's side window. Hayes had been shot once in the side of the head by someone, police surmised, who knew his schedule and was waiting for him.

"I know Wilson was asking questions up in Boston about George McCarthy and the other names we gave him," Jenkins said. "He was asking around about Grady Pope, too. I never believed that he screwed us on the Elbow Room."

"Then who?" Warren asked. "The phone guy Alvin Leach used to trace the lines? Dunleavy?"

"Shit. The more I see, the less I'd put it past him. How'd you know Phil was visiting the chief at the hospital?"

"I found out from the nurses. He usually showed up at eight o'clock at night."

"I never thought he would've done something like that. I didn't even know he and Marvin were close."

"I didn't either. Dunleavy is ambitious. I guess there's nothing wrong with that, but he went behind my back and he robbed me of an appointment I should have gotten. God only knows what he said to Holland."

A car with no muffler rattled slowly up the street.

"I just can't believe they killed Wilson."

They walked back out to Jenkins's unmarked. "Listen," the detective said, "I've got something for you." He reached into his car and felt around under the front seat. He came up with a small box. Warren opened it and found a .45 automatic inside.

"Where'd you get this?"

"I figured it would be a good idea if you kept it in your car."

"Tell me you didn't take this from the property room."

"I didn't take it from the property room. O.K.?"

Warren looked around the street, removed the weapon from the box, and examined it. "Is this the gun they used in the holdup at the Sunoco on Phinney's Lane last Halloween?"

"No. Come on."

"Yes, it is. Ed, this is illegal."

"At this stage of the game, lieutenant, I think we need to stop playing by the rules."

On the highway heading down Cape, Stasiak watched the other vehicles on the road. He doubled back twice, then continued, checking to see if any of the cars that had been behind him before were still there. On the northern edge of Truro, there was a series of dirt roads that led into the woods. There was an old house on the right, completely overgrown, its single dormer melting into the structure itself, its weight too much for the water-damaged roof. The front porch sagged dramatically, the ground around it covered by a black, algae-filled lake from which frogs chirped and grunted. On the left there was an illegal trash dump just inside the woods, and shortly after that, a sandy road that led to a group of dilapidated cottages. Stasiak pulled his car around to the back of one of them and parked it by a pair of propane tanks. Fugitive smells rose in the air and spoke in the secret language he shared with them: The dregs of discarded bottles, sodden clothing, coniferous decay. He went in the back door and walked through a small, bare kitchen, its linoleum floor blistering, the sink full of unwashed dishes. She was sitting up on the edge of the bed, her hair unkempt, her head bobbing slightly. Stasiak took off his sunglasses. The scents from outside had found their way into the cottage through the screens in the windows. He could smell them here, in her room, and he felt the excitement stirring. No one knew about her, about this place or what went on here. Sometimes it stayed in his mind for days afterward.

He looked around the bedroom for signs of any visitors. "You haven't had any guests, have you?" he said.

The woman shook her head.

Stasiak checked the bathroom and the tiny front room, looking in ashtrays, picking up stray items of clothing to see whether there was anything that did not belong to her. He returned to the bedroom and stood over her. "You got any liquor in the house?" he asked.

She did not respond.

"Not likely, huh?"

He took a small package out of his wallet and tossed it on her bed, then went out to the telephone in the front room to make some phone calls.

Stasiak called her Mitzy. He didn't know what her real name was. In fact, the woman carried no type of identification whatsoever. He had met her one day while driving through the area during the Gilbride investigation. Stasiak discovered her walking down the road in a tan raincoat and a kerchief, a bottle in a brown bag in her arms. He initially stopped to question her but when he saw that she was inebriated, he drove her to her place and they had sex. He left her some money and spent some time scouting the area. The cottages were extremely isolated.

Stasiak kept an eye on the place, driving by at odd hours to see what she was up to. There was never so much as a car on the road and at night the cottages were dark masses in the woods, the only light a dim outline around one of her drawn shades.

He finished his phone calls and went back into the bedroom. She was lying on the bed with her eyes closed, the needle and tourniquet beside her. He knew by now that there wasn't any risk of her running off and telling anyone about his visits. She was drunk all the time. And now she had acquired a taste for heroin and Stasiak was the only way she could get it.

Whenever he left, he went out to the box on the side of the house where the telephone line came in and pulled out the jack. She wouldn't be able to figure out how to get the phone working again. When Stasiak came to the cottage, he opened the box, reconnected the jack so he could use the telephone, then disconnected it again before he left.

He stood in the front room and peered out through the curtains over a sea of ferns toward the road. He looked in on her one more time, found her unconscious, and drove off.

When the sound of Stasiak's car faded into the late morning quiet, the woman got up on one elbow and retrieved the heroin from a small dish where she had poured it and which she had concealed behind the lamp on the floor. She lit a candle and prepared the drug, drawing it up into the syringe once it started to liquefy and bubble. He always talked on the phone afterward, sometimes for as long as an hour. She never injected the drug until he left. She pretended to, and lay on the bed feigning unconsciousness while she listened to what he was saying.

When she was in school, she had a good head for figures and could memorize well. In spite of all she'd done to herself—or allowed others to do—she could still remember things if she really tried. She had a feeling she was heading toward death and there was some relief in it, though she sometimes thought she should try to do something about it all; what, she couldn't begin to say. She cast around in her mind for the thing she would do, however small, the one good thing in all this impossible mess of wrong and ugliness, but then, as the point of the needle sank into her skin and she pushed her thumb down on the plunger, she decided it didn't matter anymore, whether she ever committed a good act again. She felt the sun rising inside, and once again she was trying to think of some small good thing, but then she lay back on the bed and was gone.

36

J enkins made it a habit to stop by the state police barracks
early in the morning so he wouldn't run into Stasiak,
Heller, or any of the cadre of goons they kept around them.
He also got there early because he got to the tip sheets before
anyone else. As Jenkins expected, he did not get assigned to the
Weeks case. Dunleavy put him off repeatedly and now was acting as if he were wary of approaching Stasiak about it again.

The tip sheets were the bottom of the barrel for anyone
working on the task force, and they usually comprised an eter-
nity of partial plate numbers, vague hunches, dead ends.
However, they were sorted through daily and if there happened
to be anything promising, one of the state police detectives took
it. If Jenkins waited till midmorning to check the tip sheets, he
found that anything remotely intriguing would be gone. So he
arrived at the barracks well before seven and rifled through the
pile for the best ones. Most of the time there was nothing, but
since he'd been doing this, he had amassed quite a lot of information and he just had to hope that he would discover one particular vehicle that had been spotted in all the wrong places.

Jenkins walked down the empty main corridor of the barracks, eyed Stasiak's office door, and went to the rear of the
building where a state police matron was seated by the silent
phones. "Good morning, Margaret," he said.

"Good morning, Jenkins."

"Anything good come in last night?"

She huffed out a laugh. Jenkins began going through the

sheets. "Come on," she said. "I don't want you fishing through all that stuff. Just take some off the top and get out. Jenkins, I'm serious."

"I know. But I get all the shit work on this case and I want something halfway decent to look at. Is that too much to ask?"

"You're going to get us in trouble. We're missing some tip sheets, you know."

"You're not missing any tip sheets."

"Yes we are."

"You're just overtired, Margaret. What's this? 'Man walking on golf course at the Sea Pines,' O.K., I'll take that."

Jenkins drove around to the rear of the barracks on his way out, passing a chain-link enclosure where there were a few state police cruisers parked. At the edge of the lot, near the fringe of the woods, he spotted a light gray unmarked. Stasiak was standing by the open trunk. In his hands was what Jenkins first believed to be a tarpaulin but turned out to be a much thinner material, like that of a bedsheet. Stasiak had his back to the road. Jenkins watched him, anticipating the point when Stasiak would notice his approach. When the policeman's head began to turn in his direction, Jenkins looked away and drove past, but in those final seconds, he got a look at the sheet Stasiak was holding and saw that it was stained a reddish brown.

He got on Route 28 and headed back to Hyannis, his eyes on the rearview mirror. It said something, he supposed, that he fully expected Stasiak's car to materialize in the road behind him.

Over the weekend, Fred Sibley called Warren for the third time and he finally agreed to speak with the reporter. "There are some things I need to talk to you about," he said. "There are some things you need to know."

Warren called Jane Myrna. She answered the phone, her voice clear and fine. "Oh, *hello*, Mr. Warren." She sounded genuinely thrilled to hear from him.

"Listen, I was wondering if you could possibly come over this morning to watch Mike. I have to run up to Walpole on business. Don't worry if you can't. I know it's short notice."

"No," she said. "I'd be glad to. Do you know how long you'll be? We were going to go out to Sandy Neck about three if the weather clears up."

"Oh, I should be back long before that."

She arrived soon afterward. White lamb's wool sweater, tight in the arms. Lavender skirt. Sandals. He tried to pull himself together. "Thanks for coming over on such short notice," he said, and made a hasty departure.

He arrived in Walpole early and drove into town to kill a half hour. He found a small bookstore in an old townhouse, a tall, narrow structure, all its rooms filled with books. There was no one there but a young man who sat behind a desk near the fireplace reading the newspaper. Warren climbed the creaky staircase three stories to the top. On the landing was a poster of a Negro saxophone player who went by the name John Coltrane. On a display rack he spotted a small yellow volume. He picked it up and looked at the cover. *Pictures of the Gone World*, by Lawrence Ferlinghetti. Warren felt an excitement that he could not account for. He supposed it was just the coincidence of the thing.

He paged through the book and found that peculiar poem that had so transfixed him. It was called, simply, "Number 8." His eye ran down the lines. *We think differently at night, she told me once . . .* He was intrigued and embarrassed, flummoxed somehow, standing there in the cramped top floor of the old townhouse. He went downstairs and put the book on the counter. The young man at the register looked at it and then glanced at Warren, took in his charcoal suit, white shirt, and dark blue tie, and made a kind of weary smirk.

When Warren arrived at the state prison, he found Fred Sibley waiting for him in a booth with a reinforced glass partition. "You know what I heard about you, Warren?" he said.

"Nothing would surprise me at this point, Mr. Sibley."

"I heard you were the proverbial honest cop. I was told you were decent and honest and upstanding and all the rest of it and that it's made trouble for you."

"I can vouch for the trouble. I don't know about the rest of it."

"I'm innocent. They never produced this so-called informant who claimed I had pot in my room and that is because there was no such person. There was no pot in my room. They brought it with them when they came to toss the place."

"A woman called my office to report it. She asked to speak to me directly."

"Sure. They used you as the patsy. Who knows who she was?"

"Mr. Sibley, you have a history of drug use . . ."

"Yes, for a certain period in 1955, but I quit. I got off the stuff and I never went back to it."

"Do your former employers at the *Globe* think you're innocent?"

"No, and that's the whole idea, isn't it? You really know how to keep a stiff upper lip, Warren, but I know I've got your interest."

"Is that so?"

"Yes. I need an ally and I know you don't trust Stasiak."

"How do you know that?"

"I'm a reporter."

"Who told you I don't trust him?"

"A detective named Phil Dunleavy, in so many words. A Sergeant Garrity. Word gets out. Hard feelings follow Stasiak around. I knew it wouldn't take much looking to find out who he had problems with. Word has it you went to the district attorney about him."

Warren sat silently for a moment. He was surprised at how busy the reporter had been in the short amount of time he was on the Cape. "It's true," he said. "But I'm out of it now. I have a handicapped child to take care of. I have to find work."

"You may be off the police force but you're still connected. I know things about Stasiak. I know things you want to know. And yes, I'm claiming he had that pot planted in my motel room so he could get rid of me."

"You would have to sell this to Elliott Yost. Or someone."

"I was hoping you could help me do that."

"What do you know about Dale Stasiak?"

"Sometime during the coverage of the Attanasio trial, I got curious about him. Everyone was curious about him. He's got this charisma. My editor got the idea to do a side piece on him. Well, we knew he was a war hero of some kind. He won the Navy Cross at Iwo Jima. I knew he grew up in Charlestown. They love him there, even if he's only half Irish. Not much good comes out of Charlestown, so this is a big thing for them.

"The popular belief about Dale Stasiak is that his parents sent him off to the Marine Corps to keep him from falling in with street thugs in Charlestown. That's not the way it happened. Stasiak was not only already a street thug, he was an accomplished street thug. And he was feared. At sixteen. Even grown men were afraid of him. He worked for a gangster named Bob Gormley running betting slips across town and driving his collectors around. Gormley liked him. He used him as muscle. Stasiak was beating people up when other kids his age were studying geometry. What happened was, back in 1940, Stasiak was among a group of guys who tried to hijack a truck full of liquor on Route 1 outside Neponset. It turned out it was a sting and they all got caught. Since he was underage and it was his first offense, the judge gave him the choice of the Marines or reform school. He joined the Marines and his record was expunged.

"Anyway, when Stasiak came back from the war, he joined the state police but he never let go of his Charlestown connections.

I've been told he had all kinds of little rackets going. Selling information, graft, doctoring records."

"Who told you this?"

"Wouldn't the DA like to know. I'm not telling, Warren. People have told me things, and they're people that anyone investigating Stasiak—if they happened to be investigating him—would love to talk to. But I'm not telling you who they are until I see some payment in kind."

"Fair enough. Go ahead."

"Everyone talks about Stasiak and the Attanasio investigation. But what people don't know is what happened afterward, and that is at least as significant as Attanasio, if not more so."

"What happened afterward?"

"After the whole Mafia thing transpired, the Attanasio indictments, the trial, the conviction, the *Globe* special series, I followed up on what the FBI was going to do next. Well, whatever they were doing, it was super-secret. Nobody was talking, and I mean *nobody*. But I had a contact at the federal building in Boston, a mid-level attorney who worked for Justice, and he told me the FBI got a warrant to bug a place in Charlestown, a plumbing supply warehouse. I did some asking around and in no time I knew the FBI was chasing after Grady Pope. In the meantime, I'd done this puff piece on Stasiak and I had all the background on him which, of course, I never put into the article, and I'm just sitting on this stuff because it's so explosive."

"You never went to anybody with this?"

"What was I going to do? Shit on a local icon? Me, who's got an embarrassing history of drug use that I'm trying to keep secret? No one knew the paper had to send me off for the cure and I wanted to keep it that way. And just between you and me, it wasn't just marijuana. I'd got started on opium as well, and it took me to parts of the city that I'd never meant to go. That's how I found out a lot of these things. Some stuff about Stasiak I found out through the people I used to buy narcotics from.

The drug dealers in certain parts of Boston have to pay Pope in order to operate, and he's not cheap. Of course, I started hearing later that Stasiak was getting paid to protect Pope's operations. People were scared to death of them both, but some of them couldn't resist telling a few tales. And yes, you heard correctly. Dale Stasiak providing protection for Grady Pope. 'Our good friend.' That's what they call him.

"Then I found out that the FBI's investigation into the Irish mob is suddenly over, an investigation that I couldn't get the slightest tip on because it was so secret. But there was a lot of recrimination in the aftermath of that thing and some people were talking. They had some eavesdropping or surveillance exposed, is what I hear, and the FBI thought someone inside the investigation betrayed them. Suddenly, Stasiak gets sent down to the Cape, which more than a few people thought was strange. Maybe the state police just transfer people like that. I don't know. But I heard the feds didn't trust him and the staties just wanted to get him out of sight. Somehow, somewhere, word got out that I'd been asking questions. When I showed up in Hyannis to cover the child murders, I had ulterior motives. I was pursuing Stasiak. By then, they knew it. Now, here I am. I should have been smarter.

"He's complicated, Stasiak. He's not just a bad guy. He's a bad guy with an asterisk. I know it sounds strange to hear it, but I'm convinced he has a very strong sense of right and wrong. Yes, he's a thug—probably a psychopath. But somewhere in all that is the man he might have been. I understand, being a drug addict. I guess that's something Stasiak and I have in common: That little voice that's always telling you it will be O.K. to go ahead and do something you know you shouldn't. Always that pull from the past.

"Anyway, I heard there was a meeting—all high-level cops—where the feds basically accused Stasiak and some others of being in bed with Grady Pope. There's a lot of bad blood. But in the end they had to drop the investigation. If they could be persuaded to pick it up again—if you want to send some FBI people in here to talk to me—I can tell them who to talk to in Boston, Charlestown, Somerville, Medford. These people are bookies, drug peddlers, loan sharks, pimps. You put the right kind of heat on them, they'll play ball. They've all got something to hide. I can help you with that, too."

Warren sat there, thinking.

"Listen," Sibley said. "Do they have something going on Stasiak?"

"We're looking into some things."

"What things?"

"I'll be back, Mr. Sibley."

37

W arren and Jenkins sat in the living room of the house on General Patton Drive. It was mid-morning, the neighborhood still. Jenkins, in a suit and tie, had one arm draped over the back of the sofa and drummed his fingers on his knee. Warren was in work clothes and sat hunched forward, staring absently across the room and out the kitchen window. He had just told Jenkins about his visit with Fred Sibley.

"So what do we do?" Jenkins asked.

"I don't know."

"Do you think he's telling the truth?"

"Yes. The only problem is the truth is connected to a deal we don't have the authority to make. No one is investigating Stasiak for anything and no one is going to. Sibley's out of luck."

Jenkins's face suddenly took on a quizzical look. "What's this?" he said. Warren turned and looked out the front windows. Two Barnstable patrol cars had pulled up in front of the house. He saw Welke get out, then Petraglia and a handful of others. Jenkins and Warren got up and went out the front door. Petraglia led the group across the patchy grass and up to the front step. In his hands he held an envelope. Welke hung back by the cars. "Sir," Petraglia said. Warren was embarrassed by his appearance, a ratty old T-shirt and paint-spattered khakis, home in the middle of a weekday because he was out of work, the neighborhood dumpy and neglected. Warren watched the policemen approach. For one terrifying moment he thought something might have happened to Mike and that they had come to tell him. But Petraglia cleared his throat and held the envelope forward while the others looked down at the ground. "Sir, some of the men and myself took up a collection and, uh . . . Because we knew you were short on work and you might need some cash. And we—the fellas and myself—we put together a little something to maybe tide you over."

Warren thought he heard Jenkins mutter, "Jesus *Christ*" and glanced his way to find him trying to stifle the surprised expression on his face. It was with great consternation that Warren realized tears were coming to his eyes. The constriction in his throat was such that he feared his voice would break if he tried to speak. He was mortified but profoundly moved, looking down at the envelope, unable to speak or look at them. "You can't say no, lieutenant," one of the cops said. "That's the deal." He tried to croak out a "thank you" but only a noise escaped, which he tried to conceal as a cough. "Thank you," he said, finally. "Thank you. I can't tell you what this means to me."

They made awkward small talk with him, discussing their patrols and what had been happening around town. Jenkins walked over to Welke, who was standing back by the cars with his thumbs hooked into his utility belt. "You in on this too, tough guy?"

"Yeah. So?"

Jenkins watched the men gathered around Warren. He shook his head. "You disappoint me, Welke."

"Is that right?"

"You're ruining my picture of you as a complete asshole."

"Jenkins, there's some things I gotta ask you."

"Yeah, like what?"

"There's some things going on—I think—that you and the lieutenant know about and I think I know about them too. I'm no genius but I can put two and two together as well as anybody."

"What are you talking about, Welke?"

"In early July I arrested a guy who'd broken into a sheet

metal shop in Cotuit. He was trying to steal copper out of there. I get him handcuffed and I get him outside my patrol car and I'm going through his pockets and I find these slips of paper. And I says, 'What's this?' and he says, 'Betting slips,' and he starts telling me about places where there's gambling going on. Anyway, he named a few places and one of them was the Elbow Room. He told me he heard there were cops involved and I just figured he was full of shit so I brought him in and booked him and that was the end of that, but I made it a habit to drive by the Elbow Room every now and again. Now, I got a brother-in-law who tells me there's gambling at a place called the Bilge in Orleans and he says he heard they have some kind of protection. He said the rumor is they've got some cops on their payroll. I went into the property room and pulled out the stuff belonging to the guy I arrested in Cotuit and the betting slips weren't there. Not only that, but the inventory I did when I booked him wasn't there either. And then I came up on you that day you were over at that abandoned gas supply place across from the Elbow Room. You remember that?"

"Yeah."

"I started paying real close attention then."

"Why didn't you come to us with this?"

"Because I know I'm on the outs with you and I figured the lieutenant didn't like me very much. I've said some stuff about him and I figured it got back to him somehow. I don't know. I just kept it all to myself. But then there was the raid and the papers have been talking about that whole Weeks thing and how it might be connected to some rackets down here. How'd they find out about that?"

"Beats me."

"I'll bet. I know you're watching, Jenkins, because I seen you parked near the Bilge and I seen you at a house in Harwich, too."

"You followed me?"

"A couple of times, yeah. After I started working midnight-to-eight I started noticing things. I've seen guys at the station late at night. City guys. Badasses. You know the type. I came in once at about three in the morning to book a drunk-and-disorderly and I saw one of them standing behind some cars back by the radio tower. I went over to see what the hell was up and there's Dunleavy sitting in a car talking to the guy. Three o'clock in the morning. Dunleavy acted real shifty and the guy stepped away like he didn't want to be seen. I got a damn good look at him, though. The next night, Dunleavy's at the station again and he comes up and tells me the guy was plainclothes state police working on the murders. That made sense to me but then I was parked down the street from that house in Harwich one day—same place I seen you parked—and a guy pulls up and goes into the house. And you know who it was? The guy that was with Dunleavy. The same guy. Sometimes I see the light on in Dunleavy's office and the door closed and I can see him moving around in there. What the hell he's doing at the station at that hour I don't know. I figured I'd talk to him about some of the things I was hearing. I always got along good with Phil and I just wanted to see what he'd do. But all of a sudden he doesn't have any time for me. There's something going on. I know it and I think you and the lieutenant know it. How about you tell me what it is?"

The men started walking slowly back to their cars, leaving Warren standing on his step, looking at the envelope in his hands. Jenkins said, "Have you talked to anyone else about this?"

"No."

Jenkins reached into his inside jacket pocket and took out his cigarettes. He lit one and snapped his Zippo shut. Welke said, "I'm just trying to do the right thing."

"Me too, Welke. Me too."

The patrolman watched Jenkins, waiting for an answer, but he just nodded to the others as they passed. Welke stood there, staring at the detective, silently demanding a response. Jenkins finally looked at him. He squinted through smoke, his eyes hard and assessing. "Sit tight," he said. "I'll be in touch."

Stroke, narcolepsy, hypotonia, idiopathic aphasia, the usual variety of head injury. Dr. Hawthorne leafed through the Cape Cod Hospital's admittance records for neurological cases for the past five years. The managing staff at the small hospital—the only one on Cape Cod—was eager to accommodate the doctor from Boston who was engaged in research for an article in the *New England Journal of Medicine*. Since the war, the small facility had seen an influx of money, equipment, and expertise and was making the transition from the rural triage station it had always been. Its directors were anxious for both visibility and a connection to the research community.

But an hour and a half into his search, Dr. Hawthorne had only come up with one seizure case, and that a twenty-two-year-old hypoglycemic male. He looked at the two boxes full of buff folders. It was unlikely he was going to find the test population Althaus wanted here. As a psychiatrist, Hawthorne was uneasy about this latest project with Luxor Laboratories. All of the others had involved drugs intended to address disorders of thinking and behavior. It would be difficult for him to explain his involvement in a neurological issue. The prototype antiseizure medication that Luxor was testing—Fenchloravin—was not entirely a secret. Another firm had developed something similar using the same basic compounds. It was unknown where they were with their trials but Althaus was confident that Luxor had the advantage thanks to the services of Dr. Hawthorne.

He spent another half hour going through the files and eventually came upon a case of a thirteen-year-old boy admitted for evaluation after a seizure. The unfortunately named Perry Boggs was mentally retarded, with a history of self-injurious behavior. Extensive skin lesions were noted by the examining physician. At the bottom of the admitting form was the signature of one Father Terrence Boyle. Hawthorne paged through the documents and discovered a second admitting form—a different date, a separate incident—and again the signature of Terrence Boyle. Further examination revealed that Boyle was from St. Clement parish in Hyannis.

Hawthorne carefully aligned the edges of the papers before him. A retarded boy. A priest. Possibly a fruitful avenue of inquiry.

38

J enkins spent the better part of the morning at the registry of motor vehicles checking license numbers Dunleavy had given him. When he was finished, he headed back to the station to see if he had any messages: Gladys, asking him if he would pick up the dry cleaning on the way home. Heller with the name and address of some people in Barnstable who probably had some kind of half-assed information for him. His dentist, reminding him of his appointment next week. And a message from Pete Gabbert, the cop who had been his partner when he was a patrolman in Providence, and who was now the detective in charge of the robbery branch down there. They still spoke often and even managed to get in a couple of fishing trips together every summer.

Jenkins called his old partner. "Pete, it's Jenkins."

"Hi, Ed."

"We going fishing?"

"You're not doing any fishing. Not for the foreseeable future. Hell of a thing you got going up there."

"That's a fact."

"That's why I called, as it turns out. I don't know if this is anything at all, but I think you need to know about it."

Gabbert told him that back in the summer of 1954, Providence cops were contacted by a woman named Sally Vogel. Her brother Charlie had gotten out of prison two months earlier after serving time for driving drunk and causing a serious crash. She was putting him up until he could get back on his feet, but

Charlie had certain predilections she felt the police should know about—namely an attraction to young boys. Sally Vogel reluctantly agreed to take him in temporarily but her brother soon reminded her of why no one had had any contact with him over the years. Charlie was borrowing her car and hanging around places where there were children: Playgrounds, schoolyards, bus stops. There were things he brought into the house that made her feel uncomfortable.

"Our vice guys started watching him," Gabbert said. "And one day they tailed him to this athletic field where some elementary school kids were out having gym class. Now, I'm just reading from the report here in front of me, but this Vogel was dressed like a goddamn kid, apparently. Let's see . . . *kid's one-piece jumper*—I don't even know what the hell that is—aah . . . Here we go. *White short-sleeve shirt, Buster Browns.* He even had a kid's haircut for Christ's sake. Well, you get the idea. Pretty goddamn weird. Anyhow, our guys told him to screw and that if they ever saw him around any kids again, they'd lock him up for good. Right after that, he left town. But then the sister finds this pornography he'd been hiding and it sounds like it was pretty serious stuff. Again, just what I'm seeing in the report from '54. It showed children . . . Kids tied up . . . Pretty bad, it sounds like. We would have charged him but his sister got rid of it all and we didn't have anything to pin on him."

"Did you go hunting this down on your own?"

"No, we just got a call from his sister this morning. Like everyone else, she's been following the murders up there. Charlie Vogel is on the Cape. He's been there since April."

Jenkins paced around his office, wondering whether to call Dunleavy, but decided against it. He allowed himself a little fantasy as he gathered his radio and keys, an extra pack of cigarettes out of his desk drawer: The state police in shock that he'd broken the case, Elliott Yost chagrined, speechless. He hustled down the hallway on his way out to his unmarked. Charlie

Vogel might be just another of a half dozen losers they'd looked at already: Henry, Frawley, Cleve, all the rest of them. On the other hand, it had some promise. He'd been on the Cape since April. Kids. Pornography. Jenkins slapped his keys against his thigh as he strode toward the double doors. "Hot shit."

From behind him, he heard a voice, echoing in the corridor: "What is it?" He turned to see the big orb of Garrity's head peering around the enclosure of the sergeant's desk. "Something up?'

Jenkins half-turned, slowing his pace. "No. It's nothing."

Jenkins found Charlie Vogel on the second floor of a dark, two-story duplex in Cotuit. Vogel answered the door, a man of average height and build who, though clearly approaching forty, had an unwholesome youthfulness about him. His skin was milky and nearly translucent, his hair soft and limp. Vogel's appearance seemed to present some kind of visual trick and Jenkins eyed him there in the doorway, trying to figure out what it was. "I'm Detective Ed Jenkins," he said. "Barnstable police. Mind if I come in?"

Vogel stepped back and allowed Jenkins to enter. He looked around the place. It was mostly bare, with partially unpacked bags on the floor, a mattress with rumpled sheets, and containers of takeout food scattered around. On a round table a newspaper was open to the classifieds section. "What's the problem?" Vogel asked.

"Are you Charlie Vogel?"

"Yes. What's this about?"

"I'm investigating the child killings."

"Well, what do you want with me? I don't know anything about that."

"How long have you been living here?"

"About a week and a half."

"And where were you before this?"

"In Illinois."

Jenkins paced the apartment, looking around, Vogel watching him. Jenkins said, "See, already we have a problem, Charlie."

"What?"

"You weren't in Illinois. You were down in Providence."

"This is harassment. I want to know why you're here talking to me."

"You have a thing for little kids, Charlie. Right?"

"No. Where'd you hear that?" Vogel's face was suddenly crimson.

"You got picked up in Providence for prowling around playgrounds, dressed up like a little kid, right?"

"No."

"You would have got picked up for child pornography, too, if you hadn't left Providence and come up here to lay low. Or whatever it is you're doing."

"That's not true. None of that is true."

Among the clutter on the kitchen counter, Jenkins saw an appointment card from the office of a Dr. Reese Hawthorne of Provincetown. "Yeah, it is. That's why I'm here. I heard you got a thing for kids and I want to know where you were on the seventeenth of July. That was a Thursday."

"This is bullshit!"

"In fact, I've got a list of dates here. I'd like you to tell me where you were and what you were doing on each of them."

Jenkins questioned him for a half hour. While the hostile but compliant Charlie Vogel tried—largely without success—to reconstruct the days in question, Jenkins's eyes roamed the flat, searching its clutter and disarray for anything incriminating, glancing at Vogel's fingers, hands, and arms to see if he could spot any signs of violence.

"I want to know who told you I was queer for kids," Vogel said indignantly.

"Never mind who told me. You're not to leave the Cape,

understand? We're watching you, Charlie. I'm coming back, and you need to do better than this on your whereabouts."

Before leaving, Jenkins slipped the business card on the kitchen counter into his pocket.

Watching the stunted woods of Truro flow past, Warren rolled his window down a crack and threw his cigarette butt out. The soil on the verge of the highway was beginning to show sandy patches as they neared Provincetown, the trees interrupted more frequently by barren places and marshy swales where the grass was starting to go brown with autumn. Over the tops of the tired-looking pines, now a silvery shade of grayish green, he saw the white monolith of the Truro Drive-In, its plastic sign out front blank except for some letters that spelled out, simply, "Closed. Thanks."

Warren had no work today, the third day in a row. So when Jenkins called and asked him to come along to check out the doctor whose card he had found in Charlie Vogel's apartment, he said yes without a thought. He would be back in plenty of time to get Mike at school, which put him in mind of money: How little of it there was, how he was again at a financial crisis. They were letting Mike stay at Nazareth Hall under the pretense that Warren was actually doing something useful for them in return. He'd finished the majority of the work there weeks ago. He'd gotten in touch with Grayson and James at Antiquitus but they were reconsidering the improvements they had originally planned and the project had been put on hold. Warren hoped it would work out, but he knew he couldn't go on like this. He felt encroaching despair, sitting silently beside Jenkins, who seemed unusually bitter and withdrawn. He glanced over at the detective. The murders and his situation in the police department were wearing on him. He was always cleanly shaven, but now he had two days' growth.

The glittering surface of Provincetown Harbor appeared on

the left. They went down a causeway where there was barely anything on either side of the blacktop but a thin margin of sand, water on both sides, and signs warning of blowing sand during high winds. The town itself appeared, nestled in the curve of the shore, rooftops, steeples, and masts intermingled in a sudden visual cacophony, surprising after long miles of desolation and dreary country. Jenkins steered the car down Howland Street and put it in a public lot.

They found Dr. Hawthorne's address on Daggett Lane, two blocks off Commercial Street. It was a two-story structure with weathered white clapboard and gingerbread millwork around the porch. The door opened and they faced a large man in his late fifties, bald, tanned, with the fringe of gray-blond hair that remained on the sides of his head cut short. He looked well-relaxed, louche, even, with a hint of amusement in his face, as if he found something humorous about the sight of the two men on his step. He wore tight, magenta-colored European swim trunks which were visible as the sash on his robe worked loose and exposed his shiny golden belly and the region below it. To Warren's mortification, Hawthorne caught him looking and tried to make eye contact with him.

"You have identification, I assume?" the doctor said.

Jenkins showed his badge. "Mind if we come in?"

The doctor did not say anything, but walked back into the house and left the door open. Warren and Jenkins stepped inside. It was not what they expected for the residence of a doctor. The house looked much lived-in and indifferently cared for, cluttered, heedlessly bohemian. Hawthorne said, "What is your business, please?"

"We're here to ask you some questions about an individual named Charles Vogel," said Warren.

"Charles Vogel." The doctor repeated the name as if trying out the sound of it.

"We understand he's a patient of yours."

The doctor hesitated. He drew the robe back over his girth and cinched the cord lightly. "Yes. What's the nature of your interest?"

"We'd just like to ask you a few questions about him."

"I can't answer any questions about Mr. Vogel. Doctor-patient confidentiality."

Warren said, "We're looking into the murders, Dr. Hawthorne, the murders of the children on the Cape this summer."

Hawthorne grimaced. "The murders. Yes."

"What can you tell us about Vogel?"

"Very little, I'm afraid, that wouldn't breach his confidence."

Jenkins stepped forward, startling Warren. "That's not how it works," he snarled. "We're talking about the murder of three children. Strangled. Raped. You don't get to say, 'No thanks, I'll pass.' Who the fuck do you think you are?"

The doctor was completely unperturbed. "What is your name again?"

"Jenkins."

"Ah." Hawthorne nodded once, then addressed himself to Warren. "Charles Vogel is of no interest to you. He's a standard depressive with a drinking problem. Nothing sinister. Very routine, in fact."

Warren looked over at the bookshelves and saw a volume entitled *Crime and the Sexual Psychopath*, by Dr. J. P. De River. He scanned the spines. It was a mix of art books and medical material, with a good dose of fiction thrown in. There was *Moby-Dick*, the *Bhagavad Gita*, and a book of Man Ray's photographs. On a wall was a framed portrait of what looked like a nineteenth-century military personage. Napoleon, perhaps, or Nelson. It was hard to tell because the figure's head was obscured by scribbles, hard, frenzied strokes with orange, black, and red crayon, the painting defaced in such a way that it was almost stylized. Its eyes had been crudely gouged out, leaving ragged holes through which the surface of the wall could be seen. An aggressive scrawl in heavy black paint in the corner read, "Clyde." Warren's eyes went over the bookshelf again. He saw what looked like a professional journal: *Endocrinology and Sexual Deviance*, edited by Dr. Reese Hawthorne, and nearby, a heavy three-ring binder: Clinical Trials Protocol, Bridgewater State Hospital.

Jenkins and the doctor were engaged in some petty sparring. Hawthorne was smart and unflustered, giving Warren the impression that he had probably conducted much more difficult interviews, had played far cleverer games, than either of them. He maintained a neutral demeanor while delivering stinging sarcasm and insinuation that was so drily expressed it seemed harmless and outrageous at the same time. Jenkins was up to his neck and sinking fast.

"What is your specialty, Dr. Hawthorne?" Warren asked.

Hawthorne turned to him, his face blank. "I am a psychiatrist."

"I know, but do you specialize in any particular form of psychiatry?"

"No."

"We've developed information that Charles Vogel has an interest in children, and . . ."

"*Developed information.* What does that mean?"

"It's information we have. It's something we've been told."

"So it's gossip?"

Warren saw Jenkins gather himself, as though ready to launch into a tirade. He held his hand out to steady him. "Maybe it is. It might be just gossip. That's why we're here. He was on the Cape for most of the murders and we're just trying to find out if he's capable of something like this. Surely, you can help us out with that."

"An interest in children, you say."

"That's right."

"If someone told you he had an interest in children, that could mean anything, no?"

"Why are you unwilling to cooperate with us?"

"I am not, in fact, being uncooperative. You came in here with certain expectations. Namely, that I would be uncooperative. I would venture to say that recent events find you out of your depth and prone to hostility and suspicion. Unfortunately, any answer I give you, you will interpret as uncooperative. No matter what I say, you and the hominid here will interpret it as evasive, slick 'smart-assery,' as a colleague of mine used to say."

"All that aside," Warren said, "we heard Charlie Vogel has a sexual interest in kids."

"If so, he's never shared that with me. That much I can tell you. I won't go into my discussions with Mr. Vogel. I can't. But they wouldn't interest you. He suffers from the human condition. Nothing that would raise eyebrows. In fact, he misses most of his appointments. I haven't seen him in two weeks."

"You got a private practice here in P-town, do you?" Jenkins asked.

"I see patients here, yes."

"How many people live in this house?"

"Am *I* the subject of this investigation?"

"Is it just you living here?"

Hawthorne stared back at Jenkins. He looked as if he might be starting to get angry. "Yes."

"No one else?"

"No."

Walking back up Daggett Lane, Jenkins unleashed a storm of profanity. Warren let him go, thinking about the books he'd seen on Hawthorne's shelves. He knew who Dr. Joseph De River was. He worked as a consultant with the Los Angeles police department and was hired on to take charge of their sex offense bureau, the only psychiatrist in the United States to serve in such a capacity. De River was considered the top specialist in sexual deviance and made a name for himself during the Black Dahlia investigation.

"Did you happen to notice the books he had on his shelf?" he asked as they got into the car.

"No. I was too busy trying to keep from grabbing that fat bastard by his throat and choking the shit out of him."

"Books on sexual deviance. Medical books. Professional books. He had something in there from Bridgewater Hospital for the Insane."

Jenkins's expression changed, lost its wild look and became sharp and suspicious. "Is that so?" he said as he turned the key in the ignition and squinted out through the windshield.

"Things keep getting curiouser and curiouser," Warren said.

"What?"

"It's from a book I read to Little Mike once. Let's go back and see if we can find Vogel."

39

M rs. Boggs brought Perry out on to the porch by his arm. He took odd, high steps, his brow furrowed, his expression distressed and uncomprehending. "Here we are, Father," she said. They all walked down the steps together and across the lawn to Father Boyle's car.

The Boggses had found a place for their son at a residential program for retarded children off-Cape. He could come home on weekends, but his parents did not know what they would do with him if the new arrangement didn't work out. They did not want to send him to a state institution but they were dying beneath the weight of his presence. Father Boyle had offered to take Perry to the outer Cape, perhaps up to the high grassy areas where he could see the ocean. He thought Mr. and Mrs. Boggs would enjoy the few hours' relief.

Mrs. Boggs was extraordinarily careworn and pale. Even her hair, which was once blonde, had gone colorless.

"How is he getting along at the new place?" Father Boyle asked.

"We're not sure it's going to work, Father. He's hurting himself there, too. It's worse, I think. Maybe we shouldn't have sent him away." Tears appeared in her eyes and rolled down her cheeks. She removed her glasses and reached into the sleeve of her dress for a tissue. "Are his shoes all right?" she asked.

Father Boyle looked down at the boy's feet. He had on a new pair of sneakers, brilliant white. "They'll be fine, Mrs. Boggs. We're just going to walk on easy paths. Maybe I can convince him to take them off and put his bare feet in the ocean. What do you think about that, Perry?"

"Well, have fun." Mrs. Boggs wiped her cheeks.

"We might be a bit late. After dinner sometime."

"That's fine. Goodbye, hon. You be good for Father Boyle. Just bring him back if he acts up, Father."

"I'm sure we'll be O.K. We'll see you later tonight, Mrs. Boggs."

An hour later, Father Boyle pulled to the side of a gravel road deep in the woods down Cape. He got out of the car, went around the front, and opened the door for the boy. Father Boyle looked around, taking in his surroundings. There was, he thought, an unreality about late summer, an unhealthy, sulfury quality to the light. There were rustlings and unattractive noises in the trees; the leaves had turned a silvery shade of green, full of strange chlorophyll. He took Perry by the arm. "Come along," he said. "This way."

Warren paced off the late hours in the little house on General Patton Drive. His habit now was to stay up and keep himself occupied in any way he could and to do this until his eyes began to close. Lying in bed and waiting for sleep, the night seemed eternal.

Somewhere toward midnight, he was aware of a shadow beneath the light outside the front door. He waited for a knock but none came. He reached up on top of the refrigerator and took down the .38 snub nose he'd been keeping there. He unlocked the door and pulled it open, keeping the gun concealed down by his leg. Standing on the step was a man, about mid-thirties, well-dressed in a dark suit and gray tie. "William Warren?" the man asked.

"Who are you?"

"Special Agent Robert Baldesaro. FBI."

"I need to see your credentials."

"If you're carrying a weapon, Mr. Warren, put it away."

"Show me an ID."

The man reached into his coat and took out a black leather wallet. He flipped it open to show a badge and a photograph. Warren scrutinized it in the porch light. His eyes scanned the street but it was empty. He couldn't see where the man had parked his car. "What do you want?"

"I'd like to get in off this porch. Or have you turn out that light. It's important that I'm not seen here."

Warren shut off the light. He stepped back and pushed the door open. The agent's eyes went to the pistol. "Are you expecting trouble?" he asked.

Warren didn't answer. Baldesaro handed him the wallet. "Here, if you want to take a closer look."

Warren took it from him and examined it. "What do you want?" he said.

"We need you to stay away from Dale Stasiak. We know you're watching him. I'm telling you to stop."

"Why?"

"I'm going to share some confidences with you, Mr. Warren. Others in my organization think it's a mistake, but since I'm in charge, it's my choice. I hope I'm not wrong."

Warren locked the front door and motioned toward the living room. "Have a seat."

"We have Captain Stasiak under surveillance. We've been down here since late July tailing him. As far as we know, he's unaware of it, but with your involvement, you risk tipping him off. That's why we need you to stop what you're doing."

"What's your interest in Stasiak? "

"I'll get to that. First I need to impress on you how important it is that you do as I say. There'll be repercussions if you don't."

"Now, hold on."

"Listen to me, Mr. Warren. This is very serious. I need your word."

Warren walked slowly back to the kitchen. He put the pistol back up on top of the refrigerator. He turned and looked Baldesaro over. "You have it."

"We're trying to put together what's going on down here. I believe you know things we want to know."

"Does this involve the murders?"

"No."

"Do you have people following me?"

"Yes. And you have others following you as well, as you may have noticed." Baldesaro glanced around the house. "Are you in the middle of anything? I know you have a son."

"No. He's in bed."

"You must be familiar with the Attanasio case. Dale Stasiak was a big part of it, as everyone knows. It never would have gotten off the ground without him. He's a local, he grew up around these people and he had a whole network of informants that we never would have developed on our own. There were times when the Department of Justice was going to pull the plug on the investigation because it was taking too long and it wasn't going anywhere. Stasiak pulled off a couple of last-minute miracles. He was a hero to us. Of course, he was a few other things, too, as we found out later. We had a lot of momentum going after Attanasio. So we decided to go after Grady Pope and the Irish but we couldn't get a thing going. I assume you know who Grady Pope is."

"I do."

"Well, everything we tried to do—we tried bugs, wiretaps, everything—it failed. They were on to us every time. We couldn't figure it out. So we started investigating some of our own. We didn't want to suspect Stasiak but there were a limited number of people on the Pope investigation, far fewer than we had on Attanasio and that was intentional. We've figured out that Stasiak and another state trooper—Sergeant Heller—were behind our investigation going south. They were among a very few who had privileged information and we've documented their contact with Grady Pope's people. It may go higher up the chain in the state police, but we don't know.

"So we had a big meeting—all high-level state and federal guys—and basically accused Stasiak of corruption. John Fitzgerald, the head of the state police, said he'd look into it, but it never went anywhere. The whole thing turned into one hell of a mess.

"The US attorney thinks—and I agree with him—that there are factions in local politics who don't want us bothering Grady Pope. Jack Kennedy's stayed out of it. He's big on organized crime, but for some reason, we can't get his attention on this.

"So they wound up transferring Stasiak down here. That raised eyebrows. They tried to pass it off as a promotion, but it's not a promotion. It was intended to get him out of sight.

"We suspect that what he's doing down here is what he'd started up in Boston. He's running interference for Grady Pope's gambling and extortion enterprises. He makes sure no one gets in the way and everything operates smoothly. The murdered kids—that's just a fluke. Perfect timing. Everyone is so caught up in that, they're not paying attention to anything else. We're going to want to talk to you at length about the Elbow Room. We're aware of your investigation."

"Do you know any of the people associated with the place?"

"George McCarthy we know. Steven Tosca. But that's it. When Stasiak turned up down here, so did a lot of guys from the Boston area. But they were mostly people we had no knowledge of. That was intentional, I'm sure. Stasiak knew he might be watched, so he made sure everyone who came down here to start the operation was someone we'd never had in our sights. But everything you're seeing with the Elbow Room and the other places, that's the way they operate up in Boston. Stasiak makes sure the local police stay out of it. He probably provides muscle when they need it. And now we're possibly talking about a hell of a lot more than gambling and extortion. We're talking about murder."

"You're aware of the Weekses."

"Yes. And we'll talk about that." Baldesaro looked at his watch. "It's time for me to go. Can I use your phone?"

"It's on the wall in the kitchen."

The agent called a number and spoke into the phone. "I'm ready," was all he said. He went to a window and looked out. "We'd like to do a formal debriefing with some other agents present. We'll be in contact with you."

A car rolled slowly down General Patton Drive and flashed its lights once. Baldesaro put his hand on the doorknob. "Listen," he said. "I have to say this. You seem like a decent man but if you turn around and screw us on this, we'll ruin you."

"Don't threaten me, Agent Baldesaro. It's uncalled for and I don't like it."

"I'm just letting you know how much of a risk we're taking bringing you into this."

"You either trust me or you don't."

"We're trusting you."

"Then I won't let you down."

When Mrs. Gonsalves saw the man in a suit and trench coat coming up the steps to the back porch, she was suddenly filled with uncertainty about what she'd done. For all her meddling, for all her snooping around, she really didn't want to be in the middle of this. Mrs. Gonsalves kept trying to tell Father Keenan about Father Boyle, that he was not a good priest, that he shouldn't be at St. Clement's. He had secrets. She didn't know what they were, but she knew there were secrets. Where did he go all the time? Father Boyle was gone entire nights now—*entire nights*—and no explanation of where he'd been.

In truth she doubted, when she called the state police, that they'd actually show up. Now the man was showing her a black wallet with a badge and a photograph inside. "I'm Detective James Ferrell, Massachusetts state police," he said. She looked around the kitchen, her eyes wide, her hands smoothing the fabric of her apron.

"Are you Mrs. Gonsalves?"

Father Keenan must have heard the unfamiliar voice in the house because he soon appeared in the kitchen doorway. "How can I be of assistance?"

Ferrell said, "I understand a Father Terrence Boyle resides here."

"Yes, but he's not here at the moment. What is this in reference to?"

"Is there someplace we can talk?"

Father Keenan led the way into the parlor. Ferrell asked about Father Boyle's habits, his movements, his mental state, his past. Father Keenan was torn over how much he should divulge. Some confidences were sacred, especially those between penitent and confessor, and he had served as Father Boyle's confessor a number of times. And so he gave safe responses to Detective Ferrell's questions. He omitted things and was troubled not only by this but by Father Boyle's long absences, his secretive behavior.

Ferrell produced a sketchbook and specimen basket and put them on the coffee table between them. "These were found by a Boy Scout troop out in Truro, just off a fire road that goes to Head of the Meadow Beach. Father Boyle's name is written in the book."

Father Keenan examined the sketchbook.

"Can you confirm that's his?"

"Yes."

"And the basket here?"

"Yes.

"How often does he go down to the lower Cape?" Ferrell asked.

"I don't know. He is a great admirer of nature. I know he goes all about, drawing, collecting specimens. But I can't say for sure."

"Is he someone who might hurt a child?"

"Never. Never." Suddenly Father Keenan was fighting to maintain composure, suppressing the guilt and the fear and the uncertainty he felt until the detective was gone. Father Keenan then bid a curt goodbye to Mrs. Gonsalves, who watched him back his car out of the driveway. She busied herself around the house, distracted, trying to decide what to do. Suddenly there was a knock on the back door. Detective Ferrell was standing on the veranda. He smiled at her through the screen. "So do you want to talk?" he said.

40

U nder a low gray sky the color of ash Warren and Jenkins drove west, passing the yellowing foliage, the woods suddenly bare in places, wet black branches showing like emerging skeletons. They drove past the buttoned-up marinas, seafood takeouts, and bicycle rentals of Wareham; Buzzards Bay's tragic-looking main drag, three blocks long, bleak and colorless; and an hour outside of Hyannis, they arrived before the oppressive redbrick mass of Bridgewater State Hospital for the Criminally Insane.

Jenkins had gone back to interrogate Charlie Vogel, who did no better corroborating his whereabouts the second time than he had the first. Shortly afterward, he cleared out of his apartment. Jenkins watched the building for two days with no sign of him. He was now in the awkward position of telling Dunleavy that he had an emergency on his hands, the result of an investigation that was done entirely in secret. They had to find Vogel but Jenkins hadn't been able to bring himself to reveal his existence.

They had as many questions now about Dr. Reese Hawthorne as they did about Charlie Vogel. If Hawthorne was a specialist in sexual disorders, why had he concealed it? Why, knowing they were pursuing a child murderer, had Hawthorne not mentioned the fact that he was a specialist in this type of behavior? "We've had how many shrinks come out of the woodwork to offer their help with this," Jenkins said. "People from as far away as California. And here's this guy right in our midst—a specialist in sexual psychosis—and he doesn't even come forward."

Warren and Jenkins had discovered other things about Dr. Hawthorne as well. He was a faculty member of Columbia University and had served on the staff at Bellevue Hospital. Through an extended string of contacts Warren had through his tenure with the Barnstable police, he located a detective in the New York police department's twenty-third precinct who was willing to do some footwork. He discovered that in 1954, Hawthorne was the subject of a professional review at Bellevue. Shortly afterward, the editor of *Endocrinology and Sexual Deviance* found his way to Boston and set up a private practice on Beacon Hill. He published several papers—*Cultural Relativism and Sexual Practice, Causal Postulates of Sexuopathology, Fetishism and Sexual Imprinting, Basal Frontotemporal Profile of Five Sex Offenders*—and joined the staff of Bridgewater State Hospital for the Criminally Insane. The New York detective suspected that both Bellevue and Columbia University were stonewalling him on the subject of Dr. Hawthorne, but he couldn't prove it.

They signed in at the reception desk and took the elevator to the fourth floor, where they found Dr. John Fulton, head of psychiatry.

"We're here to ask you about a doctor on your staff," Warren said. "Reese Hawthorne."

"He's no longer on staff."

"Can you tell me why?"

"He went on to other work. What is this about?"

"It's related to the child murders on the Cape," said Warren. "But that's as specific as I can get with you."

"Dr. Hawthorne was here for two years or so. But I can't release any information without his consent. We have regulations on that sort of thing. Protocols we have to follow as a state institution."

Jenkins said, "If we have to go and get a subpoena and come back here with it, I've got no problem with that."

Fulton stared at them, his elbows on his desk, his shoulders hunched forward. "You're asking me to divulge confidential information."

"Not talking to us is not really an option, doctor," Jenkins said.

"We're not interested in making trouble for you," Warren said. "We only want to know a few things about Hawthorne."

"But a *subpoena*? Is there a way around this?"

Jenkins said, "Sure. Tell us about Dr. Hawthorne."

"Dr. Hawthorne . . . became a problem."

"A problem how?"

"There was a degree of unprofessionalism in his methods."

"Can you be specific?"

"Gentlemen, I'm afraid . . ."

"We need the context." Warren said. "All of it."

Fulton removed his glasses, folded them, and set them off to the side. "We started running a study in the fall of '55. We were looking at a population of adult men who exhibited deviant sexual preferences. Paraphilia is what we call it. That's a universe of sexual behavior that includes bondage, sadism, masochism, bestiality, various fetishes . . . The paraphilic continuum. Paraphiles by definition are not necessarily pedophiles, but the reverse is true. Pedophilia falls under the general class of behaviors we call paraphilia. It was a risky thing to undertake, so we were kind of . . . circumspect when we did it."

"What was the big secret?" Jenkins asked.

"This isn't like polio or tuberculosis, detective. The sympathy factor is zero with these disorders. That's why we tried to keep a very low profile with this study. There was public money involved and I don't think the public would have been too pleased to find out how it was being spent."

"What they don't know won't hurt them?"

"What they don't know *will* hurt them, as you're seeing for yourself with this case. It's important work, as unpleasant as it may be. Everyone wants to lock these men up and forget about them. That's not a solution. We need to understand it. We need to see if a rapist, for example, is made by some biochemical component or lack thereof, if there is any physiological commonality among men who molest children, if the solution lies in a particular psychoanalytic approach.

"Anyway, we didn't announce the study. We didn't publish anything in the journals. We partnered with the VA in Brockton. We supplied some of the test population from our patients here and the VA supplied the rest. Others came from private practices with which some of the doctors are associated.

"At any rate, the study was discovered by the local representative here to the State House. We had a situation where taxpayer money was being used to conduct a study that most people would find . . . unnecessary. Repulsive, even. Given the highly emotional reaction people have—rightly—to things like rape and molestation, the study would have been difficult to defend. But we believed in it. We still do. But our local representative somehow got wind of the project, and he told us to shut it down immediately. He was afraid he'd be politically damaged if people found out about what we were doing. This institution is a political albatross that he hasn't been able to get rid of because the state needs it and no other jurisdiction wants it. Every few years the surrounding towns start a petition to have it moved or closed down. We've always been told that our representative receives certain favors for not raising a fuss about it in the State House. So he's found himself defending this place to his own constituents. Now, if it was discovered that we were using their tax dollars to study a bunch of sex criminals . . . It would look like he wasn't paying attention to what was going on in his own backyard.

"So he ordered us to dispose of all information related to the study, data, notes, recordings. He said he didn't ever want it getting out, and he threatened consequences, for me in particular. So to have you come in here threatening to subpoena records—if this winds up in court, everything will be a matter of public record. We just can't afford to let it get out."

Warren said, "Are you familiar with an individual named Charles Vogel?"

"Yes, but only superficially. I do know that he took part in the study and was one of our pedophiles. He was brought in by Dr. Hawthorne."

"What can you tell us about Dr. Hawthorne?"

"He came from the faculty at Columbia University and had a practice in New York. He was very good. Arrogant—he created problems—but a good psychiatrist. He invigorated the research, I have to say. But I felt—as did others—that he had a certain unhealthy attitude toward the patients. He seemed fascinated by them. I would even go so far as to say infatuated. But more troubling than that was the fact that patients in Dr. Hawthorne's group tended to become ill. Always in the same way. Pain in the kidney area, extraordinary fatigue, discoloration in the eyes. One of them had to be hospitalized. The rest of us discussed whether it was something Hawthorne was doing. We couldn't prove anything but we were watching him closely.

"Then we discovered that he was interacting with one of the study subjects outside the hospital, helping him out, finding him jobs, and so forth. I dismissed him then. By that time, our local representative had intervened and we were in trouble. Dr. Hawthorne threatened to expose the study if we went to the state board of medical licensure with any complaints about him."

"Do you know if there were any sanctions against him in New York, any reprimands?"

"No. And I don't want to know. I can only imagine what that would add to the scandal if word of the study ever got out."

"Did you know he's got a practice in Provincetown?" Warren asked.

"I haven't followed his movements since he left. What led you to him?"

"Charles Vogel. He's a suspect. He was living on the Cape but it looks like he left in a hurry. Do you have any idea where we might find him?"

"No."

"Do you still have a list of the people who took part in the study?" asked Jenkins.

"Yes. But I just hope we'll all be discreet about this."

When Warren got home that afternoon, he found Mike and Jane sitting on the floor at the coffee table in the living room doing rubbings of fallen leaves with crayons. A few strands of Jane's hair had come out of her headband and fell in her eyes. She swept them back with her hand as she held her work up and assessed it. Warren was aware that he was staring. "I'll get your money," he said.

He went into his bedroom and counted the cash in the white envelope in the drawer of his nightstand. He experienced a moment of panic when he thought he might not have enough. He counted it out and still had a dollar left. Why were his hands trembling? He put the extra dollar in with Jane's pay, then took a breath and walked out of his bedroom. Jane's clavicle. Is that what they called it? The way the skin was copper and shiny in the depression around Jane's clavicle.

She was gathering up her purse and sweater when he got out to the living room. "Mr. Warren," she said, "they're having a house and garden tour on Martha's Vineyard this weekend and I've got two free tickets. It includes the ferry ride over. You can come if you want to. We could bring Mike."

She was looking directly at him—a different look from her usual candid regard, and somewhere behind this new subtlety in her face, she seemed to be enjoying his discomfiture. Was she mocking him?

He sorted through excuses in his head. He stammered and made a mess of it. Jane graciously came to his rescue. "It's O.K.

I've got a girlfriend I think will go with me. I just thought it would be good for you to get out. Mike, too." She tousled the boy's hair. "See you, kid."

When she was gone, Warren slumped into the sofa with the Ferlinghetti book. There it was again. Something about himself that kept people at a distance. He thought of Jenkins and Marvin Holland, who were so easy with others, so spontaneous. More honest. Was that it? It was an upsetting thought. There were ideas he had grown up with—decorum, a careful examination of one's intentions—and he couldn't shake them. His formality, what others might call rigidness, was it something that originated in some flawed aspect of himself? He had always thought that it was just who he was, the imprint life had made on him, but he wished he could be different.

Jane still called him Mr. Warren. Would he have them go to Martha's Vineyard, looking at the houses and gardens with her calling him Mr. Warren the entire time?

He sat there watching his son, making some adjustment to the crude washing machine he had fabricated out of a mason jar, a pencil, and the wheel of a Tonka truck.

"Mike." He sometimes asked the boy questions that were actually intended for himself. Warren did this to hear the questions, to take their measure, and, he suspected, out of loneliness. "Mike, am I a rigid sort of person?"

Mike looked up from his makeshift contraption, looked into his father's face trying to guess what the expected response might be.

"Yes!"

Warren laughed softly and Mike went back to his tinkering. "Is that thing working all right?"

"It has a gremlin in it."

"A *gremlin*?"

"Yup."

"Where'd you pick up that word?"

"Father Boyle."

"Come up here."

Mike climbed on to the couch and moved in close beside him. "What are we going to do, Dad?"

"I sure don't know."

The telephone rang. Warren went into the kitchen and picked it up. There was silence on the other end but he could hear voices in the background. He thought he could hear the caller breathing. "Who is this?" he demanded.

"It's me."

41

Stasiak, Heller, and Ferrell sat in a closed office at the state police barracks. On a desk sat Father Boyle's sketchbook and specimen basket. "When the priest was posted in Belmont, Mass," said Ferrell, "he took a kid from the hospital in the middle of the night—a kid with cancer—and drove him out to a marsh somewhere. He was working as a chaplain and spent a lot of time on the pediatric ward. So everybody's looking all over the place for this kid. Total panic. Then the next day, some duck hunters came upon him in the marsh. He had the kid wrapped in a blanket, laid out at the foot of a tree. They didn't arrest him. The parish confined him to the rectory and the police questioned him there. The Church paid a settlement to the family for not raising a stink about it. There weren't any charges. They did agree to ship him out of Belmont, though. I'm hearing rumors about a suicide attempt but I haven't nailed that down yet."

Stasiak said, "Did he molest the kid?"

"No one knows."

"What'd the kid say?"

"The kid couldn't speak. He had cancer in his esophagus or something. He was in bad shape. He died about a year later."

"So no one knows what happened?"

"No one but Boyle."

"What did you get from the Portagee woman? The house-keeper."

"She says he goes out for long periods of time," Ferrell said.

"He comes back with debris on his clothes: Thorns, bristles, and whatnot. They found the canvas pack and the sketchpad about a half mile from the pond where the Gilbride kid was found, so he's been out there. He frequents the area.

"Otherwise, he stays locked in his room a lot of the time, like he's hiding something. She tells me he's got contact with kids at a school for the retarded, a place called Nazareth Hall."

Stasiak said, "See if you can get access to his medical file. See if it includes his blood type. Stay on him and follow him wherever he goes. This guy is very active right now and I want to stay on him while he's feeling nice and free. I don't want to spook him. Put a man on the church and have him watch it round the clock. First chance we get, we're going in."

On a Saturday afternoon, an undercover state police officer watching the rectory at St. Clement picked up the handset on his radio and notified Stasiak that Father Keenan had left the premises and the house was unoccupied. Boyle had left a half hour earlier and was now being followed down the Mid-Cape Highway in the direction of Provincetown. Keenan's car remained in the drive until half past noon, when he came out dressed in civilian clothes and drove off. As soon as they got the call, Stasiak and his men descended on the church. They walked four abreast toward the house, searching the windows for any signs of life. Stasiak used a bump key to unlock the back door. They entered the kitchen. "Top to bottom, boys," said Stasiak. "And don't leave a thing out of place."

The search turned up signs that the priest, as the housekeeper claimed, was spending a significant amount of time out in the woods. The detail that followed him down Cape watched him get off the highway and park his car in a secluded area off South Pamet Road in Truro. But Stasiak did not find the damning evidence he had hoped for—forensic material or some trophy from one of the child victims—and was impatient for progress.

Shortly after they searched the rectory, investigators got a call from a Mrs. Caroline Boggs, who claimed that Father Boyle had taken their retarded son out for the day and kept him out until nearly 10 P.M., and that when he brought the boy back he was soaking wet and filthy, his clothes ruined, the boy traumatized. The priest claimed they had gotten lost, but Mrs. Boggs was furious. She kept the incident to herself until she heard rumors that the police were considering the priest as a suspect—rumors that had to have originated, Stasiak figured, with the Portagee woman.

He went to Mrs. Boggs's house to interview her. The kid was beyond hope, a walking abortion. He couldn't have told Stasiak what time of day it was let alone whether the priest had done anything to him. He told the mother to get the kid examined by a doctor to see whether he'd been molested, but she was hedging. She claimed the boy wouldn't stand for it but Stasiak believed she didn't want to know.

Ava's face was appalling, ravaged and swollen. One of her eyes wandered, or both, Warren couldn't tell. She was underweight, bony shoulders poking through a cheap raincoat. There seemed to be some kind of palsy in her face, judging by the heavy, sluggish look to the right of her upper lip. He would never have recognized her if she hadn't said she would be wearing a light blue scarf on her head. She had aged twenty years.

Sitting across from her, he was nervous, grieving, and angry all at the same time. His palms sweated and his mouth was dry. The bar wasn't exactly a dive. The clientele looked like fairly respectable working-class people. It looked to Warren like the kind of place that got rough after a certain hour. It was probably something between what Ava was used to and the kind of place that wouldn't let her in.

Her voice was hoarse and chilling, like it was coming from somewhere else in the room, beneath the table or someplace behind his elbow. "I suppose you want to know what I've been up to all this time," she said.

He simply looked down at his folded hands and shook his head.

"Did you bring something to write with?"

Though Warren could not fathom what her slurred request for him to bring a pad and pen had been about, he had complied all the same. "Yes."

"You know Dale Stasiak."

"Yes."

"Write this down."

Stunned to be in Ava's presence, shocked by the extent of her decline, and beset by the storm of his own emotions, he put his pen to the notepad and listened.

She said, "George McCarthy, Steve Tosca, a man named Grady. Do you know these names?"

"Yes. How do you know them?"

"You just need to know that I know them, that's all. I have heard Dale Stasiak talking on the telephone. I know he's involved with gambling and some other things. I know he's crooked. They killed a man named Wilson Hayes. They killed a man named Russell Weeks and something bad might have happened to his family, too."

"Slow down. How do you know these things?"

"I know them. O.K.? I just know them."

"You've been in close enough proximity to Dale Stasiak that you could hear him talking on a telephone?"

Ava nodded.

Warren's mind was reeling, trying to understand how such a thing could be. He struggled with the possibilities, speechless, and she must have known because her low, scratchy voice continued, telling him things of such a shocking nature—to divert his questions, he suspected—that he had trouble keeping up. So incredulous was he that she had an association with Stasiak that he kept having to ask her to repeat things and finally decided that however it had come about, he did not want to know.

In a disconnected narrative, Ava divulged everything she knew: Stasiak's frequent conversations with a man named Grady, their talk of betting slips and bookies, of money owed, who was in trouble and needed to be dealt with. She mentioned the Elbow Room, Brinkman's, and a private residence on Depot Road in Harwich. "Russell Weeks owed them money," she said. "I don't know how much, but Stasiak talked about it a lot. He talked about finding him, how important it was to find him. They have beaten people up. People have disappeared."

Ava said there was a lot of talk about Weeks's wife and child, hushed talk that she never got all of except that Stasiak and the others were very interested in them.

"Money," she said. "They're always talking about money. And betting slips. And checks. They send checks to a place in Boston called Wayson's. I don't know what it is but they're always talking about it. Dale calls them all the time. Frank Semanica is a name I hear a lot. I don't know who he is but they talk about him. I think he's a messenger or something."

Warren stopped a passing waiter and ordered ginger ale on ice for them both. Ava lifted the glass to her lips, her hands shaking so that the liquid spilled and she had to put it down. She closed her eyes and said, with great effort, it seemed, "Most of the gambling is at the Elbow Room, I think."

He got the waiter's attention and called him back to the table. He handed him Ava's drink. "Would you put some Scotch in that?"

When the drink came, she appeared transformed with relief, though miserable and ashamed as well. "Fred Sibley," she said, finally. "Do you know him?"

"Yes."

"They arrested him for marijuana."

"*I* arrested him for marijuana."

"He's innocent. That stuff wasn't his. They put it in his room. They had me call and report him."

"Who told you to do that?"

"Dale Stasiak. When I called, I asked for you. I wanted to hear your voice."

Warren turned to a new page in his notepad, looked at her, and then looked back down.

"You have to be careful," she said. "They're going to do something to you."

"Stasiak said this?"

"Yes."

"Where is the phone that he uses?"

"I don't want to say."

"Why?"

"Because. It's my business."

They sat in silence, Ava looking into her drink and Warren staring out the windows to their right, into the bright afternoon outside.

"So how is he?" Ava asked.

Her mouth moved, her lips shifting to the left and bunching out for a moment, the only change he had seen in the rigid, masklike quality of her face. It was impossible to tell what it signified though it had the look of a word she was unable to pronounce or something she found extremely difficult to say.

"Our son."

Warren tapped the edge of his notepad on the table and looked around at the backs of the patrons at the bar. "Listen, I *have* to know how to contact you," he said.

"I'll contact you."

"There are some people I want you to talk to. You'll have to tell them all the things you just told me. And you're going to have to tell them how you wound up close to Stasiak. The nature of your relationship with him."

"I'll meet them here. Or wherever they want as long as I can get there. I don't have a car."

"How did you get here?"

"I hitchhiked."

"Can I drive you home?"

"No," she said, and he thought he caught her voice breaking. She got out from behind the table unsteadily and got to her feet. Warren did not want to look at her now that more of her was visible. "Where are you staying?" he asked, his eyes on his notepad. When she didn't respond right away, he looked up to find her gone.

42

The swing set in the yard behind Nazareth Hall had gotten a little more complicated than Warren had intended. He had gone for a more ambitious design than most homemade affairs, using a plan he'd seen in *Popular Mechanics*. And he was having difficulty concentrating, unsettled as he was following his meeting with Ava. He recalled how her voice had sounded, the eerie way it seemed to come from somewhere else, like some trick of ventriloquism.

In the time after Ava's disappearance he had sometimes been approached by people sympathetic enough to come up and talk to him. During the war, they said, Ava could sometimes be seen at the Mill Hill Club, at the Panama Lounge, or Oliver's on the Cove, usually in the company of various men. When everyone was trying to get by under rationing, Ava always had plenty of everything.

In the early years Warren felt nothing but rage. But in time he discovered that thoughts of Ava often felt very much like a visit from his father. The girl was young. She was lonely. And like all of us, she had weaknesses. Under the light his father cast from the beyond, Warren felt obliged to forgive Ava. As time went by he found that he was uneasy living in judgment of her. It crowded his life and consumed too much of him. She had betrayed him. She had betrayed her own child. But if there was one thing he had learned in twenty years of police work it was that it was possible to understand why people did the things they did.

He had set a pair of planks on some sawhorses to use as a

work surface and was sorting through his drill bits when he remembered that he had to install a new switch on his drill because the thing had been giving him trouble. As he was looking through his toolbox for the new switch, the children came out for their ten o'clock recess, each carrying a half-pint container of milk with a straw. They came down the back porch steps tentatively, watching Warren. Father Boyle came out and put a hand on a little girl's head, saying something to her in passing. He watched Warren arrange his things on the bench, distracted and self-conscious. Suddenly, Warren said, "Somewhere along the line I heard that people like this—retarded people—are incapable of sin."

Father Boyle did not respond.

"I was told they're guaranteed a place in heaven. Do you think that's true?"

"I don't know. Why does God allow them to endure cruelty in life? You would think they would have nothing but mercy after death."

"I keep thinking that they'll come up with something. Medical, scientific, or something. Some kind of operation or a drug. I don't know. Maybe it would take a miracle."

"He's the miracle."

"Who?"

"Your boy. He's guileless. He's full of love. The miracle is your boy."

Warren grabbed his drill and began taking a screwdriver to the handle. "God's will," he said, a hint of sarcasm in his voice.

Father Boyle said, "His mother . . ."

"He doesn't have a mother."

"She is deceased?"

Warren looked at the priest. "Yes."

"I'm sorry."

Father Boyle watched Warren disassemble the drill. He looked at the partially built swing set and the lumber lying in neat piles. "How do you know how to do this? I know nothing of these things."

"When I was a kid I took a job on a framing crew up in Boston. It was during the Depression. I lied about my ability but they kept me on and I learned."

Father Boyle walked over to the partially constructed braces for the swing set and looked down in the holes filled with concrete. After a few minutes he came back to the workbench. "I don't pretend to know about God's will," he said. "An honest man should refrain from speaking about it, other than to say it is unknowable."

"But you're a priest. Aren't you supposed to know these things?"

"A common misconception, Mr. Warren. What is wrong with your drill?"

"The switch is bad. I've had this since 1946. Sometimes the switch just goes."

"Are you finding enough work?"

"No. I could use a lot more."

Father Boyle said, "I only heard about your resignation a few days ago."

Warren nodded. He was tired of talking about it.

"I'm surprised, frankly, that they didn't choose you," Father Boyle said. "I don't know the other man but I do know that you are highly regarded."

Father Boyle watched him separate the small pieces of the drill on the plywood, his hands quick and sure but his face troubled.

"How are you adjusting to things, then?" Father Boyle asked.

"I don't know. I'm just trying to figure it out as I go."

"Mike is aware of the change."

Warren didn't know how to take this. Was the priest assuming a knowledge of the boy superior to that of his own father? Was it a reprimand?

"He's quite perceptive," Father Boyle said. "The sisters will let you know, of course, if there's anything to be concerned about, but for now he seems to be just feeling things out." Father Boyle looked at the boy and laughed. "He's quite a little gentleman."

At Nazareth Hall, Sister John Frances sat at her desk checking her appointment calendar when one of the other nuns appeared in her doorway. "He's coming to the door," she said.

"Ah," said Sister John Frances with some relief. It appeared that the man who had been sitting in a parked car in the shade of the maples across the street while the children were at recess was, in fact, her ten o'clock appointment. Soon, the doorway to her office was occupied by a large, bald man in a tan suit, white shirt, and lavender tie. "You must be Doctor Hawthorne," she said. "Please sit down."

Hawthorne explained that he was in the early stages of a research project and wanted to compile profiles of a number of mentally retarded children with a history of seizures.

"Is your research funded?"

"I've a grant application pending with the Luxor Foundation."

"Hm. I haven't heard of it. But that's not really surprising. Our doctors tell us that research labs are springing up like mushrooms all around Boston. I understand they've even built one in a meadow out in Lexington. A big white laboratory out in the middle of a field. It's remarkable. President Eisenhower and Congress love the NIH, which is wonderful. They say this will be called the 'pharmaceutical century.'"

Dr. Hawthorne gave a thin smile. "One of the conditions of getting institutional backing is having a study population identified, which is why I'm here." His eyes went to the file drawers behind the nun's desk, where the records on the children were kept. "You can contact Dr. Karl Althaus at the Luxor Foundation. He's handling my grant application."

"Very good. You'll want to speak to our doctors. They've done work on this very subject. They come down from Children's Hospital twice a week. I can give you their names and phone numbers."

Hawthorne seemed to show no interest in this. "There are two things I would need, actually, for my research. One would be an opportunity to examine the children's medical information. The other would be to set aside some time to observe them."

"The files, I'm afraid, are confidential. As far as observing the children, that would best be done in the presence of our doctors, and they won't be coming down again until next week. I'll get in touch with them and see about you meeting with them. How's that?"

Hawthorne was in the act of assuring her that he had worked out this type of arrangement with other institutions in the past, but the woman had risen from her seat and was summoning someone from out in the hallway. A young woman appeared in the door. "Sister Julia, would you show Dr. Hawthorne around the school?"

As they walked down the corridor, Hawthorne said, "Can you tell me, Sister, how many children in your care suffer seizures?"

Sister Julia considered this. "Probably half a dozen. That's kids that have them regularly. There are others where it's episodic and we don't necessarily see it while they're here but they do have them."

In one of the classrooms, an elderly nun was showing a child in leg braces how to make change, a scattering of coins on the table between them. The old nun had cataracts and was hard of hearing; she strained to lift her face toward Hawthorne as she said, "We pray to St. Jude for all the children."

Children came out into the hallway as Sister Julia led Hawthorne along. They swarmed around her and touched her arms. They took her by the hands and said her name. Hawthorne watched her as she greeted them. She bent and took the face of a tiny Downs girl in both her hands. She engaged in a brief pantomime of roughhousing with one of the boys. When the children had passed and they were alone in the corridor, Hawthorne said, "The therapeutic role of sentiment. I don't see that much in the journals."

She turned to him. "There is nothing sentimental about what we do here. These children have no hope for a normal life. We know that the best we can expect for them is likely very little. And if all they can ever enjoy is very little than we will make sure they get no less than that."

Hawthorne stepped back slightly and looked at her, his eyebrows arched.

"We're not dupes, Dr. Hawthorne, is what I'm saying. We know what's what as far as these children go."

Hawthorne regarded her with such candid assessment that the young sister shifted on her feet. "What is your age, if I may ask?"

"I'm twenty-six."

"You are a young woman. No husband, no domestic riches, no home or children of your own? I would say that the lesser sex is missing out on a rare specimen, if you'll excuse my frankness. Such passion and charisma."

"I chose this life because I'm happy in it. There's a lot more possibility in it for me than in those things you just mentioned."

"One day places like this will be run by people like yourself. You'll bring your dedication, your sense of *possibility* to the work. It will be a new day."

"I think we've got a pretty good handle on it right now, Dr. Hawthorne."

"It is admirable, what you're doing here. St. Jude and secrecy aside."

"*Secrecy?*"

"Maybe that's too strong a word. I, too, have great faith in what is possible, especially in this day and age. But I encountered some reluctance with your colleague, Sister John Frances. I'm only asking for a chance to look through your files."

"We're like any institution, doctor. We've got rules."

"Which I'm asking no one to break. This is what I'm proposing in my study: A weekly session of observation for eight or so of your children at a place convenient to the parents. And very likely, intervention. Preference, in fact, for any kind of new treatment that shows promise and with which my funding institution is involved. *That's* the possibility you're talking about. If I haven't misread you. If the young firebrand isn't, in fact, what she'd have me believe."

When Dr. Hawthorne had gone, Sister Julia began preparing for her reading class. Sister John Frances found her in the front hallway where the workbooks were stored in wooden crates along the wall. "How was the doctor?"

The younger woman shrugged.

"He wanted access to the files," said Sister John Frances. "To the kids, too. I suggested he consult with our doctors from Children's Hospital but he didn't seem terribly interested in that. Professional jealousy, I suppose."

Sister Julia said, "Why was he sitting in his car like that?"

"He must have gotten here early."

"Anyone with an ounce of common sense should know not to do something like that right now." Sister Julia picked up an armload of workbooks from a wooden crate in the front hallway and started off toward her classroom. Sister John Frances thought she looked uncharacteristically gloomy and preoccupied. She would have to ask her young friend if everything was all right.

Back in his car, Hawthorne looked at the old house. It was not isolated and yet it had some quality of isolation about it. There was no activity on the street, the houses still and silent behind barricades of privet, boxwood, and rhododendron. He looked at his watch. There was little traffic on the street this time of day. In his rearview mirror, he watched the road, long and straight, narrowing with distance and disappearing into the shadows of the big arching maples. A panel truck slowly emerged from a side street, crossed the road, and vanished on the other side. Hawthorne read the sign affixed to its side: "Taggert & Sons." His hand froze at the ignition switch as he recognized the name: The remodeling outfit Edgar was currently working with. But hadn't he said they were doing a job in Brewster?

A coincidence that the truck would turn up in the same neighborhood. For a moment he considered following after it but then decided that a coincidence was all it was.

43

The Sea Mist backed up onto a brackish swamp that stunk at low tide. Agent Baldesaro led Warren to a bare room on the ground floor of the run-down motel where a group of agents was gathered, their eyes impassive and unreadable. He wondered if Baldesaro was the only one of them who thought it was a good idea to include him.

"Besides what I've told you," Baldesaro began, "what do you know about Dale Stasiak?"

"Aside from the fact that he's unstable, not a whole lot that I could prove. His methods are unconventional, to say the least." Warren gave an account of his interactions with the state trooper. One of the agents got a map out and spread it across the table. Warren saw that it was heavily annotated with different colored markers. There was a circle around the location of Stasiak's house and another around the state police barracks in Yarmouth. Various routes were drawn out and dozens of points marked and dated.

Baldesaro asked, "Where have you seen him?"

Warren pointed out the places on the map where he had tailed Stasiak and lost him.

"Do you have any indication whether or not he's figured out you were following him?"

"I don't know. But he must know that someone is, because he uses evasive tactics when he drives."

"That's because of what he was involved in up in Boston," Baldesaro said. "He expects to be watched. Now, why were you watching the Elbow Room?"

Warren related the story. Baldesaro scribbled notes as he spoke. When Warren got to the part about recruiting Wilson Hayes, the agent stopped him. "Wilson Hayes?" he said.

"Yes. Did you know him?"

"We know he was shot outside the Gillette Company's headquarters. That's the guy you sent into the Elbow Room?"

"Yes."

"I'd say maybe Hayes screwed you," Baldesaro said. "But the fact that he wound up dead tells me different."

"Hayes could have double-crossed him *and* wound up dead," one of the agents said.

Warren said, "As I understand it, he went back up to Boston and started asking about some of the guys we connected to the Elbow Room and the other places. His opinion was that this is being operated by the Irish mob."

Baldesaro turned to one of his men. "Find out who's running the Hayes murder investigation. See where they are with it."

The agent got up and left the room. Baldesaro quizzed Warren on Hayes's report on the Elbow Room and what he'd seen inside. "Are you aware of Brinkman's Brake & Lube?" he asked.

"Yes."

"What about a place in Chatham called the Bilge?"

"We know about it. There's a house in Harwich we were watching."

"Depot Road."

"That's correct."

"What do you know about Detective Dunleavy?"

"He went behind my back and got himself appointed chief over me. He's no good if you ask me. I believe he was following me around there, at the end. Is *he* involved in this?"

"We've seen him, Stasiak, and Heller together a fair amount."

Warren asked, "Do you know of a man named Fred Sibley? Reporter for the *Boston Globe*?"

"Yes," said Baldesaro. "We know him from the Attanasio case and we know he's conveniently locked up at Walpole."

"I visited him not long ago."

"Really. What brought that about?"

"He kept calling me. I never took his calls. Then one day I decided to talk to him and he told me he knew things about Stasiak. He wants to trade the information for help with his case."

"What did he tell you about Stasiak?"

"He substantiated a lot of the things you've told me only he has specifics, which he's not giving up. And I think he knows the names of a lot of people you should be talking to."

"Sibley's a hophead."

"Maybe. He says he was set up."

"Interesting. He became a security risk during the Grady Pope investigation. We figured he knew there was more to it than us chasing Pope. He's smart. We didn't even know he'd shown up down here until we found out about the drug arrest at the East End Lodge. If you hadn't locked him up, we would have found a way to take him out of the picture. He was going to compromise us with his nosing around."

"He believes the state police planted the marijuana in his room for the same reason," Warren said. "I think he's been on to Stasiak longer than you have."

"Have you ever seen Stasiak or Heller at the Elbow Room?"

"No."

"Have you ever seen either of them at any of the other locations we've discussed?"

"No."

"Have you seen either of them with any of the people we've mentioned here?"

"No."

"Let's talk about the Weeks case."

Warren recounted the tale, from the first call from the

DuPonts' attorney to the morning he got the call from Jenkins at the town dump.

"You say Russell Weeks's brother claims he was never contacted by the state police."

"That's right."

"But Stasiak claims to have spoken to him."

"He claimed that, yes."

"You've confirmed Russell Weeks called one of the illegal lines at the Elbow Room."

"Yes."

"And Stasiak warned you to stay away from the Weeks investigation."

"In the strongest terms." Warren looked around the room at the radio equipment, the cameras and lenses in their black cases, at the men in shirtsleeves leaning forward in their chairs, watching him. He shook his head slowly. "Why would a man . . . Stasiak has the career I wish *I* had. How do you explain it?"

"It's not our job to explain it," Baldesaro said. Then, as if reconsidering, he indicated the annotated map on the table. "What you're seeing here . . . What we know, apparently, it's not the entire truth. Stasiak has—*had*—good qualities. He was fair to the people in Charlestown. He took care of them, in his way. Whatever that took. Some of the things he did I didn't have a problem with. And when he worked with us on the Attanasio case, our guys loved him. He was really good with the new agents who were trying to learn their jobs. But this . . ." Baldesaro put a finger on the map. "This is the truth that matters the most right now. And we're here to do something about it."

He went through his notes page by page. Finally, he stood, looked at the other agents, and said, "Does anyone have anything else?"

"Actually," said Warren, "I do. I was married at one time.

My wife was . . . is . . . an alcoholic. She walked out a few years ago. But she called me out of the blue the night before last. She wanted to meet with me. So I did. And she . . . I don't know how to put this. She knows Dale Stasiak."

Baldesaro sat down.

"She's been around him and she knows a lot about him. She knows things that could put him away."

"How the hell can that be?

"I don't know. I don't want to know. It's embarrassing—the implications."

Over the next half hour, the agents watched him intently as he spoke. Baldesaro said, "The place she mentioned in Boston . . ." He consulted his notes. "Wayson's. She said they send checks up there?"

"That's right."

Baldesaro addressed his agents. "One of you get in touch with the Boston office and have someone go check it out. See if we can get tax records, business license, all the rest of it. Make sure it's not done through official channels or it will get back to them that we're poking around. Have Agent Coates do it. He's good with that stuff." He turned back to Warren. "Now, I want to back up a minute and go over something." Baldesaro read from his notes. "She told you that Stasiak said you might be a problem?"

"He said that Jenkins and I had been talking to the DA and that it could be a problem."

"Where was the place where you met her?"

"In Eastham. A place called Sonny's."

"And she left no phone number, no address, nothing?"

"No."

"We have to find her. It's critical. If she contacts you again tell her we'll pick her up wherever she is. What's her maiden name?"

"Kittredge. Ava Kittredge."

Baldesaro spoke to the room. "Check utility company records

for one Ava Kittredge. Check under Ava Warren, too. Then check town records in Eastham, Truro, Wellfleet, Chatham, see if we can get a last address or at least some trace of where she may have been. You never know. We might get lucky. Warren, we need to get you home. You need to be by your telephone in case she calls."

44

Two days after Dr. Hawthorne's visit to Nazareth Hall, Sister John Frances was walking down the back hallway leading to the kitchen when she heard a sound. She stopped at the foot of the stairs leading to the nuns' living area. The weather had been strange all day, brilliant sunshine and tropical humidity alternating with angry purple cloud masses and a leaden breeze that threatened a downpour but gave way to blazing sunshine again. There was something aggressive about the weather, even in its fairer moments.

Now, as she stood still in the hallway, the house darkened once more as a new disturbance formed in the sky and she heard a rattling sound emanating from the kitchen. She retraced her steps and looked in to find an unnaturally long-limbed man trying to open the patio doors. She did not enter the kitchen but peered around the edge of the doorway and watched him twist and shake the doorknob. Sister John Frances walked quickly through the silent house. The children were having their after-lunch nap, their heads resting on pillows on their desks. She found Sister Julia and motioned to her. "Come," she said.

They found the man still at the door, his back to them now, looking out over the yard and the children's toys scattered about. They opened a window and spoke to him through the screen, startling him. "Can we help you?" said Sister John Frances.

He gaped back at her. "Um, yes. I need to see whoever is in charge here."

"What do you want?"

"It's about Dr. Hawthorne."

The two women exchanged a look.

"Reese Hawthorne. He was here a couple of days ago."

"What about him?" asked Sister John Frances. "And why were you trying this door a few moments ago? We have a front door, you know. And a doorbell."

"I don't want to be seen."

"By whom?"

"By Dr. Hawthorne."

"Dr. Hawthorne isn't here. What's this about?"

"I'm working in the area. Shingling a house on Sea Street. I'm on my lunch break. I wanted to come by and warn you about Dr. Hawthorne."

The two nuns watched him through the screen.

"He's not who he says he is."

"What on earth do you mean?" said Sister John Frances.

"I don't know what he told you his business was. But I guarantee you he didn't tell the truth."

"How do you know this?"

"I make it my business to know what Hawthorne is up to."

"Well, suppose you tell us why he was here, then."

He rearranged his limbs, a strange effect, as if they had only a rudimentary connection to his torso. His hair stood up in spiky formations, though it hadn't rained, and he was wet with per-spiration. "He wants to spend time with the kids, doesn't he?"

Sister John Frances said, "Who are you?"

"Don't have anything to do with him. That's all I came here to say."

They noticed that his hands were trembling and beads of sweat stood out on his upper lip.

Sister Julia said, "I'm calling the police."

The sounds of the children starting their afternoon classes reached them from down the hallway. Michael Warren appeared in the kitchen. "Sister Julia," he said. "It's time for reading."

The man looked through the patio doors at Mike. His Adam's apple rose and fell and he seemed unable to compose an answer. Without taking his eyes off the boy, he said, "I need to go."

The boy had been shoved into the rotted out center of a large hollow stump, his legs and buttocks protruding, garish white in the gloomy wood, his pale flesh almost luminous against the dead brown-black of the tree. Stasiak stood there alone, the woods silent all around him. Behind him, two troopers came crashing through the woods in their high boots and utility belts. Stasiak turned to them as they arrived. "What's the situation?" he said.

One of the troopers said, "There's a hell of a mob up there."

"Keep them back. I want them far away from here when we take this body out, understand?"

"Yes, sir."

Jack Dowd came down the slope in his straw fedora and white short-sleeved shirt. He carried his camera around his neck and a large black bag by his side. Dowd froze in the pathway when he saw the legs sticking straight up out of the hollowed out stump. He gathered himself and continued on.

Stasiak said, "There's five stab wounds in the right rib cage. There's a cut in his neck near his right ear but it doesn't look fatal."

Dowd walked over and began examining the body. "I can't imagine the kind of impulse that's driving this," he said as he peered into the trunk and tried to get a look at the boy's face. "We live in strange times."

Stasiak said nothing.

"I'm going to make way for your forensic people," said Dowd. "I can't see much, the way he's positioned in this tree. I'll take the body temperature and examine him further once the body's out." The pathologist picked his case up off the ground. "Oh. I'm ready to discuss the Weeks autopsies whenever you get the chance."

Jack Dowd moved around the small laboratory that served as his work space at the rear of Cape Cod Hospital. He opened the door to the morgue and looked in on the body of the latest victim. Remarkably violent, compared to the others.

He jumped when he heard two dull thuds on the door. He opened it to find Ed Jenkins and Bill Warren standing outside. Jenkins edged into the opening before speaking, his hat down low over his eyes. "Hey, Jack. What do you know?"

"Have you heard?"

"Yeah. That's why I came over. They know who he is?"

"Randall Stamper. Eight years old. From Sandwich." Dowd closed the door behind them. "I could get in trouble for letting you in here. I suppose you want to see the body."

"Yeah," said Jenkins.

"Let me show you something," said Dowd. He went to a refrigerated chest adjacent to the morgue and came out with a small metal box. Inside was an empty blood vial that contained a tiny shred of cotton mesh. "I found this attached to the small of the boy's back. It's going up to the state police lab for analysis but I ran a little test on it myself just a while ago. The fabric is saturated with amyl nitrite."

Dowd removed it with a set of tweezers and held it under a high-intensity light so they could see it. "Amyl nitrite is an inhalant," he said. "It's chemically related to nitroglycerin. I know it as isopropyl nitrite. It's used for angina. Heart ailments. But it has other purposes as well." He reached into the box and produced another vial. "They also picked up these tiny slivers of glass that are identical to the ones found on the Lefgren body. The FBI lab said they thought the fragments from Lefgren came from some kind of small lightbulb. These here look like the same type of glass except they have traces of amyl nitrite on them. My opinion is they're from capsules."

He crossed the room, opened a cabinet, and searched until he produced a handful of capsules encased in cotton mesh.

"Here. Like this." They looked into Dowd's outstretched hand. Jenkins said, "We raided a place in Providence once, a queer bar where we found a bunch of these. They use them for sexual purposes."

"What?" said Warren.

"It's—I don't know, lieutenant—it's supposed to be like getting an extra kick. Like a shot of whiskey or something."

"Amies," said Jack Dowd.

"Huh?"

"Poppers."

Jenkins turned to the pathologist. "How do you know this, Jack? You must get around more than I thought."

"I've been in this job for thirty-seven years. You see all kinds of things."

Dr. Hawthorne looked at them through lowered eyelids as they stood on the porch of the house on Daggett Lane. "We just wanted to ask you a few more questions," Warren said.

"I understand there is a trend where the courts are becoming less tolerant of the police intruding on private citizens," said Hawthorne. "I wonder what happened to that."

At the far end of the porch there was a table, and on it was a cigar box filled with stubs of crayons, scattered pieces of construction paper, and open copies of *LIFE* and *Redbook* whose pages were scribbled on and crumpled, as if done by a child having a tantrum. Some of the magazines had been cut with no apparent object except for cutting. Jenkins looked over at the table. Hawthorne followed his gaze and stiffened. "What do you want now?" he said.

"We've discovered some discrepancies in some of the things you've told us," said Warren.

"Is that so?"

"Charlie Vogel did come to you about his attraction to children."

"That's not a discrepancy. That is called protecting a patient's privacy."

"But you felt free to tell us he was depressed and had a drinking problem."

"Not quite the same thing, is it?"

"It turns out you've done a lot of work in that field. Sexual deviance."

"I didn't murder the little children, Officer Warren. Mr. Vogel didn't either. And there is no crime in my not presenting you with a full CV. If there is, I would like you to direct me to the statute."

"Why did you conceal the fact that you're a specialist in sex disorders?"

"It causes discomfort."

"For who?" said Jenkins. "You?"

"No, others."

Warren said, "Knowing we came here to ask about the murders—sex murders—you didn't think to mention it."

"You didn't come here asking for advice, you came asking about Charles Vogel. And now, for some reason, you're here asking about me. Are you under the impression that *I* know something about these murders? I can't think of a bigger waste of time."

"While we're on the subject," said Warren, "who do you suppose this guy is, doctor, if you had to make an educated guess? He's a loner, single, right?"

"Not necessarily. Married men carry a Pandora's box of frustrations. You'd be surprised the things they get up to, married men." He glanced at Jenkins's wedding band, then looked at Jenkins and smiled.

Warren said, "I understand you were the subject of a review when you worked at Bellevue Hospital. Do you mind if I ask what that was about?"

"What mystery are you chasing here? Why are you in my home?"

Jenkins said, "Care to answer the question?"

"My background is no concern of yours."

Warren said, "We understand there was a review and then you left New York not long afterward."

"I left New York for a better situation in Boston. And there are many different kinds of reviews: Performance, tender of position, application for research, ward management, et cetera, et cetera. But I doubt you're aware of that."

Jenkins said, "I think you're full of shit."

"Those cheap tactics are not going to work with me. You are impotent here, Mr. Jenkins, and you fail to realize it. You should grasp the concept of impotence. It has a strong phallic association." He turned to Warren. "And you, so solemn and regal. You look very much like Tyrone Power. Has anyone ever told you that?"

Jenkins glanced again at the crayons, the X-ACTO knife, and mangled paper on the table. "You got kids?"

"Let's please get to the point of all this. I do have the right to ask you to leave my home, which I am about to do, so cut to the chase."

"We understand you used to work at Bridgewater State Hospital."

Hawthorne folded his arms and raised his chin a little.

"Can you tell us why you left?"

"I decided to devote my time to my private practice. Why are you rooting through my employment history?"

"You aroused interest," said Warren.

"In what way?"

"In the things you chose not to say."

"Look. I'm under no obligation to give you every last detail about myself and I resent the implications you're making. If I have to retain the services of my attorney to stop this harassment, I will do so."

Jenkins said, "You live here in P-town year-round?"

"This is my summerhouse. I have an apartment on Beacon Hill."

"A summerhouse," Jenkins said. "A place on Beacon Hill. Must be nice."

"It is nice, Mr. Jenkins, very nice. It's every bit as nice as you imagine it to be. Now, we're done here. Goodbye. And if you come here again, I'll call my attorney."

Hawthorne closed the screen door and latched it. Jenkins and Warren walked back to their car. Neither said anything, each stealing looks back at the house. "Asshole," Jenkins muttered.

As they drove away from Provincetown, Warren said, "What do you make of those capsules Jack Dowd showed us?"

"Maybe our killer's got heart trouble," Jenkins said. "Maybe it's something else."

"Like what?"

"Well, I know they're used for sexual purposes, but in this case, maybe it's the act of killing that's the thrill. He pops one as he's killing the kid. It's not for the sex. Or it's mixed up with the sex. One or the other. What's your sense of this Hawthorne character?"

"Hard to say. But I'm thinking you should turn it over to Stasiak. They can put more resources on it."

Jenkins shook his head. "I'm not doing that. Then they'll know I've been freelancing on this thing. They wouldn't give me the time of day anyway. I'd never get an appointment with Phil or whatever I have to do nowadays to speak to him."

45

F ather Boyle looked out over the countryside, a low savanna studded with ragged shrubs and scrubby wooded islands that stood in the open like primitive fortresses. It was nearly dark, the final traces of pink disappearing rapidly from the western horizon. He walked in the direction of the Atlantic.

Once again, he reflected on how odd it was that he could not find the site of the experience he had out here in early summer. He had replayed the events of that night again and again in his mind in the subsequent weeks: The sudden appearance of the light, its materializing right before him at the edge of the hollow in the meadow—there was never a question of whether or not he had actually seen it.

All the details of that night were forced into the background by one particular thing, and that was the feeling that came over him as the thing perched at the edge of the hollow. It was an extraordinary peace, a sudden sense of well-being, not only in the moment, lying there in the grass, but in his past and in his future as well, all in order and right and blessed, a sense of himself moving smoothly over the continuum of his own life, as though over a silken surface, and finding everything satisfactory, absent regret or fear, only a gladness with which he turned his face to the light and tried to recognize the figure moving within its bright, glowing center. The experience was so intense and profound, he had to ask himself the question: Was it something of the Divine he had beheld?

Low ridges descended into small plains, which were dotted with shallow depressions like craters filled with grass. Wild blackberry and raspberry bushes grew on the slopes in thickets. Somewhere in himself, he felt a quickening, a sense of recognition. It was here. He had found it.

Parked a short distance from General Patton Drive, Steve Tosca watched Warren come out of his house and get into his car. He followed him as far as a newly constructed Howard Johnson's by a cloverleaf on the Mid-Cape Highway. Tosca pulled over by a row of phone booths and watched through a small pair of binoculars as Warren parked and then got into the passenger side of a light-colored sedan. The car circled the lot, passing near Tosca, who got a look at the driver and, as the sedan was waiting to enter the highway, wrote down the license number.

Twenty minutes later, he was walking into the kitchen of the Depot Road house where George McCarthy was meeting with some of the others. "Hey," he said. "I just seen Warren get into a car with someone up at the Howard Johnson's on the highway."

"That doesn't tell me a lot, Stevie."

"With a cop, George. He's with some kind of cop. And he isn't local."

McCarthy turned in his chair.

"And I think I seen that car parked outside Warren's house before. I wrote down the license number."

No one said anything. The kitchen was quiet for a full ten seconds. "Give it here," McCarthy said, finally.

At the Black Rose, a pub beneath an elevated section of the partially completed Central Artery in Boston, Grady Pope stood by a window peering out the drawn blinds, his narrowed eyes sweeping across the empty street, peering into the dim entrances to alleyways, scrutinizing the steel trestles one after the other as they proceeded down Atlantic Avenue and curved out of sight.

He was alone except for the man who managed the place for him. It was a small bar, for drinkers only, and only certain types of drinkers, because its location in the shadows beneath the noisy highway project was both off-putting and little known.

Pope heard the phone ring in the storage room where the man was stocking booze. "It's for you, Grady," he said.

Grady walked over and picked it up. It was Stasiak. "We've got a problem down here," he said.

"What."

"Warren's meeting with the FBI."

Stasiak waited for Pope to respond, but there was nothing.

"He was seen getting into a car with one of them. We got the license number. The car is registered to the U.S. attorney's office in Boston. We have to do something. Now."

"I figured it was going to come around to this sooner or later."

"This guy *disappears*. I'm going to do this one personally."

"No, you're not."

"What?"

"I'm gonna have Frank Semanica do it."

"What?"

"Just listen to me. I've been having problems with Frank. He told me that this Buick Special we used to have got stolen from out front of his apartment in Quincy. But I find out he was down there on a run earlier this summer and he had the goddamn cops chasing after him for something he did. He set the car on fire up by the canal and the cops down there got the VIN number and started asking questions up here. I just found out about it last week. And there's trouble over some weird sex shit he pulled with some girl up here. He's got to go."

"And this is who you want to go after Warren? My ass is on the line too, you know."

"I'm going to have him kill Warren and then you'll take him out. It'll look like you came to the rescue just a little too late.

George says Frankie's been doing a lot of speed lately. That's another thing. We're going to work it so George gives him a bunch of bennies and then we'll send him over to Warren's house late at night. You'll be set up somewhere near there and when you see Frank coming out of the house, you go in and take care of him. You say you spotted a wanted car sitting outside Warren's house. When you went to check it out, Frank came out and pulled a gun. When they do the autopsy they'll find out he was all hopped up on speed and we'll make sure he has a trunk load of stolen goods. It will look like a burglary gone bad. Some out-of-control bastard from Boston."

"You know Warren's got a kid, right?"

"With any luck he can finger Frank as the guy who shot his Daddy. Knowing Frankie, he'll probably kill the kid, too. We get rid of Warren, we get rid of Frankie, Frankie takes the rap, you come off looking like the cavalry. They already think your shit's ice cream down there anyhow. What about the DA down there? Is he going to be a problem?"

"No. He's under control. He'll do whatever I tell him."

"All right. And quit worrying about Frankie," he said. "I've been doing this a long time."

"So have I."

"Not on my level, you haven't. Play it like I say and we'll be fine."

Stasiak hung up the phone and looked around the tiny cottage. He wouldn't be back here again. The last time, he was finishing a phone call to Pope when he turned around to find Mitzi retreating unsteadily from the doorway, hurrying to get back into bed. He followed her into the bedroom. "Not as sleepy as we pretend to be, are we?" he said. She had hidden the dose of heroin he had given her beneath her pillow. He made her cook it up and inject it, then waited while she nodded off. He prepared a second dose and stuck the needle into her arm, which roused her sharply. "No, no, no, no," she said. Mitzi's mouth gaped open and she closed her eyes. She rolled over on her side, away from Stasiak. He readied a third and gave it to her.

That was two days ago. The place was starting to smell bad. Stasiak wiped down every surface in the cottage he might have touched. He looked in on Mitzi and he saw the lividity in her legs and a brown stain on the bedding. He didn't know what she'd been up to but he didn't like it. For good measure, he wiped the entire cottage down again.

The house on Daggett Lane was quiet, the windows open on an Indian summer midmorning. Edgar Cleve stood alone in Dr. Hawthorne's office. He looked around at the sunlight in the screens and listened for any sound in the house. Reassured by the silence, he approached the doctor's desk. The drawers were locked. Cleve saw the binder that had to do with Hawthorne's dealings with Karl Althaus and Luxor Laboratories. Partially concealed beneath it was a prescription pad. When Cleve reached for it, he saw the newspapers, four individual front page sections of the *Cape Cod Standard Times*, folded in quarters, their edges neatly aligned: *Third Child Death Stuns Community*; *Hyannis Victim Strangled, Coroner Says*; *Truro Boy, 9, Slain*. Affixed to them with a paper clip was a piece of Dr. Hawthorne's personal stationery on which he'd written numbers. Cleve held it up to his face. It looked like a list of dates and beside each, illegible notations, which he struggled to read until a distant movement that he perceived through one of the screens halted his effort. Looking down Daggett Lane from the second-story window, he saw Doctor Hawthorne walking back from the direction of Commercial Street, a newspaper under his arm.

Cleve hurried to his place on the porch, where he pretended to work with his magazines. He listened to Dr. Hawthorne enter the house and go upstairs to his office. A few moments later, Cleve heard him come back down. He thought he heard the back door open and close. A long period of silence followed. Cleve crept quietly back inside, entered the kitchen, and was startled to find the doctor standing there. "What's the matter?" said Cleve.

"Have you been in my office?"

"No."

"There are thirty-five slips on that prescription pad upstairs. I'll know if any are missing, Clyde."

"How many times do I have to tell you? I don't want you to call me that."

"Look, I've indulged you more than is reasonable. The reason we're doing this business with the names is because you made some unwise choices."

"What about the choices *you've* made?"

"You are here, spending the summer in Provincetown and not in other, much more *dire* surroundings, on account of me and a certain amount of trust I have placed in you. Now if you're going to say trusting you was a bad choice, maybe you have a point."

"I haven't done anything."

"I am uncomfortable, Clyde. Uncomfortable with what's going on here. Do you know we had a couple of visitors here the other day? Authorities. *Police.*"

"They weren't here for me."

"They were not, as it turns out. But who's to say they won't be back?"

"Why would they?"

"A good question. I don't suppose you'd hazard an answer."

Cleve reached for the hook where the car keys had hung but they were gone.

"No more car," said Hawthorne. "The car is revoked permanently."

Cleve reddened. "You know what I'm going to do? I'm going to tell everyone about you. I'm going to tell everyone about what you've been doing."

"And what does that mean?"

"What do you suppose it means? That's what *you'd* say to *me*. Well, now the shoe's on the other foot. What do *you* suppose it means? You and children. You and all kinds of other things I know about."

"Sit down, Clyde."

"Don't call me that."

"Sit down. You're out of control."

Cleve said, "I know what benzodiazepam tastes like, even if you crush it up."

Hawthorne opened a drawer and reached in.

"The needle is gone," said Cleve. "I found out where you were keeping it."

"Is this the voice of liberation, Clyde?"

"I said don't call me that."

"There is nothing quite so feeble as a feeble rebellion."

Cleve turned and bolted, flinging the door to the farthest extent of its arc so that it hit the wall and left a scattering of broken glass on the floor. Hawthorne watched his ungainly form round the bushes in front of the house, out of sight, and then reappear in the backyard, where he planted one hand on the points of the six-foot stockade fence and then cleared it in a motion that seemed nearly superhuman. Hawthorne gazed at the spot where Cleve had stood. It was time, he decided, to search the house.

46

B ring your car around back, Frankie."
Night was picking up pace at the Elbow Room. At 10 P.M. the place was getting noisy and crowded. The televisions were tuned to the Colts-Steelers game, the tables were full, and the bar was crowded three deep in the chaotic traffic of drinks and betting slips. Frank Semanica was already showing the signs of the speed George McCarthy had given him. He had grown quiet but more volatile. The bouncers had had to tell him twice already to keep his hands off the customers. When Semanica went out to get his car, McCarthy and one of the bouncers went into the back. The door to the walk-in was open, the telephones ringing with late action on the game. Outside the back door was an assortment of items, a vase, a crystal bowl, a set of golf clubs, a new Admiral record player still in its box. They had been stolen in a series of quick burglaries over the last two nights.

McCarthy looked at the stolen property. Each item had been carefully wiped. "Fucking Frankie."

"How many did you give him?" asked the bouncer.

"Four."

"He musta took them all. He's fucked up."

Semanica pulled around to the back of the building. "Grady wants this stuff," said McCarthy. "Take it up to Boston."

"Golf clubs? Grady's playing golf now? Motherfucker."

McCarthy stared at him. "Whoa, Frankie. Whoa." He stepped back inside, calling over his shoulder to Semanica, "Go ahead and load it up." He took a nine-millimeter pistol out of the safe and wiped it down with a rag, then went back outside and handed it to Semanica. "Are you ready for this, Frankie?"

"Of course I'm ready. What do you think?"

"Remember he's got a kid in the house. If he doesn't see you, leave him be. If he does, do him, too."

Parked within view of Warren's house, Dale Stasiak looked at his watch. Semanica should be showing up any minute now. But Warren's car was not in the driveway. There was a female in the house. He had seen her shadow behind the drawn shades. He raised his binoculars. There she was, peering out from around the edge of one of the shades. He pulled out and turned on to General Patton Drive. She answered on the first knock. Stasiak could see the heavy chain on the door pulled taut. "Good evening," he said, holding up his credentials. "I'm with the state police. Is Mr. Warren home?"

"No. He was supposed to be back an hour ago. Is something wrong?"

"No. I'm here to see him on police business. Do you know where he is?"

"Cameron's boatyard. They had a late job to do there. I don't know why he isn't back yet."

"Cameron's. Where is that?"

"Osterville."

"O.K. Thanks."

Back on the road, Stasiak radioed Heller. "State zero nine to five seven."

"Five seven."

"We're stand down on detail one. Stand down. Copy?"

"Copy. Stand down."

Under the floodlights at Cameron's, the hoist finally came to life. Warren gave a thumbs-up to the mechanic, who stood at the controls. Suspended over the open engine bay of a fishing boat was a six-cylinder diesel engine. The boat belonged to longtime clients of Len Cameron who had brought it in to replace bad crankshaft bearings and the rear main seal. Len had promised them he would have it ready in two to three days but the parts had to be back-ordered and the vessel had sat for more than a week and now the owners were missing the crucial fall season. Warren had been sitting at home when he got an unexpected call late in the day, asking if he could come over for a few hours to help get the engine installed and running.

Everything went well until they were ready to lower the engine into place. The hoist rolled out over the fishing boat on its twin I beams and suddenly stopped. It was an electrical problem but locating it had taken them well into the night.

Now, they lowered the engine down and worked to get it into position. Standing in the hold of the fishing boat, Warren suddenly realized he had forgotten to call Jane to tell her he would be late. If she had been trying to reach him, he never would have heard the phone out here. "Hold on for a minute," he called out to the mechanic. "I have to call my babysitter."

He ran to the phone in the dry dock bay. "Jane, I'm sorry," he said. "We ran into a problem here and I completely forgot to call. Is everything O.K.?"

"Yes. I was just getting a little worried, that's all."

"I apologize. I'll be home in about a half hour. We just have to finish up. Is Mike in bed?"

"No. He wants to wait up for you."

"Would you put him on?"

He told Mike to do as Jane said and get in bed. He would come into his room and see him when he got in. "O.K.," he said. "Dad, Jane wants to talk to you."

Jane came back on the line. "Mr. Warren, a state policeman was here looking for you."

"Did he leave a name?"

"No."

"Did he say what it was about?"

"No. He just said it was police business."

Warren worked his way around the engine, tightening the bolts that held it in place, wondering who had visited his house and why. His mind fabricated ominous scenarios, which pre-occupied him to the point where he had torqued down all of the bolts and started going around a second time before he realized what he was doing.

Jane Myrna read Mike a story, put him to bed, and went back out to the living room. She thought she heard a car pull into the driveway. Pushing back the shade, she was relieved to see a car there but then saw that it was not Warren's. She closed the door, then turned to find a man standing in the kitchen, the back door open to the night. She fought the impulse to scream, holding a hand over her mouth. The man had long hair and wore a denim jacket with the cuffs rolled up. He looked dirty and crazy. Jane tried to sneak a hand to the front doorknob, but he was across the room in an instant and planted his hand on the door. In his other hand, he held a gun.

"Where's Warren?" he whispered.

"I don't know."

"You better tell me, honey, because I am *not* fucking around."

"I don't know where he is."

He brought a hand up and grabbed her breast. She closed her eyes tightly. He massaged it and squeezed hard. Jane let out a cry. Semanica lifted her skirt and looked at her panties. He hooked a finger in the waistband and pulled them down for a look.

"Please," she cried.

He wheeled her around and grabbed her by the arm, twisting it behind her back. "You're coming with me," he said, and pushed her out the door. "Who else is in the house?"

"No one."

"No kid?"

"Mr. Warren took him with him. They went out to visit someone."

"Out kinda late, aren't they?" He shoved her into the car. "You're going to tell me where Warren is and I don't mean maybe. Stay down on the floor. Don't look at me. *Don't look at me!*"

Dale Stasiak sat in his car, concealed off a dirt road a short distance from his rented house in Wellfleet. Whoever was following him, they knew what they were doing. And they had resources. He counted at least three cars involved in the relay technique they were using. He first spotted them near the shuttered Hyannis rail depot where he had met Heller and told him to intercept Warren at Cameron's boatyard in Osterville. Stasiak then headed down Cape, leading his followers far enough away that they could not interfere with Heller.

He needed to contact Heller and let him know that something was up, tell him to get to a telephone. Stasiak figured it was likely they were monitoring the state police net but he and Heller used codes that no one would understand. He radioed Heller but got no response.

He watched the wind stir the grassy wastes outside his windshield. The chronology of the child murders unrolled before him. He didn't need files or notes or photos. Gilbride, Lefgren, Crane, Stamper. He could see the details of their deaths in his mind's eye—reed, sand, seaweed, pale flesh, splayed young limbs, the cloudy gel of an eyeball—like they were the grammar of a language he'd been born speaking.

Stasiak remained in his car, concealed amid the low dunes and beach grass, and waited for word that Warren had been taken care of. In the meantime he thought about the killings, the entire string of events playing out in his head like a mathematical equation, the one variable being the priest and how he could be made to fit, how the numbers could be worked so the priest stood alone, distinct, on the opposite side of the equals sign.

Father Boyle made the long journey back to his car, making careful mental notes on the terrain, placing a boulder in the path here, shoving a stick into the ground there so he could find the route again. He sped back in the direction of Hyannis on the darkened, deserted highway. When he pulled up in front of Warren's house, he sat for a moment and tried to collect himself. He got out of the car and looked in the front windows. The view allowed him to see through the kitchen to the back door, which hung wide open, the night a solid mass of black in its frame. "Hello?" he called out. "Mr. Warren?" He walked through the kitchen and into the small dining area. Michael Warren was standing in the hallway to his right, holding a blanket. "Well, hello," Father Boyle said to him.

"Where's my dad?"

"I don't know."

"Where's Jane?"

"I need you to come with me, Mike." Sweat was pouring off the old priest's face. He realized he was frightening the boy. "I'm not going to hurt you." He put his hand out and moved toward Mike. "I want you to come with me."

Father Boyle headed for the Mid-Cape Highway and punched the accelerator when the road opened up before him. He looked over at Little Mike, who was cowering against the door, his blanket held to his chin. Father Boyle put a hand on his knee. "I'm sorry," he said. "I'm scaring you, I know. It's going to be all right."

Henry Sherman sat in what he liked to call his TV chair, his head turned so he could see over his shoulder out the window toward Bill Warren's place. Three cars had pulled up there in the last hour or so. It was busier over there now than it ever was when Warren was head of the police department. Sherman knew Warren wasn't home and he wondered if that babysitter was up to something, though it would have surprised him because he knew she was a nice kid. Sherman did wonder about the boy who went around the back of the house about half an hour ago, though. He guessed it was the babysitter's boyfriend. And the last car, just a little while ago, the old fellow standing on Warren's front step. He wondered if something had happened over there.

Driving down a mostly deserted Route 28, Frank Semanica looked down at Jane Myrna crouched down on the floor on the passenger side. He had pulled over a short distance from Warren's house and tied her hands with the cord from the stolen lamp in the trunk. He found a rag to stuff in her mouth and used the cord from the record player to secure the rag in place. Now, stopped at a red light, he ran his hand down her bare leg and listened to her pained whimpering, which aroused him fiercely.

He drove toward Yarmouth, checking the motels as he went by, most of them closed for the season. The few that were still open were too well lit and close to the road. Just before the Yarmouth line, there was an extinguished neon sign made up of a set of letters arranged in a jaunty, irregular arch to form the word "Kismet." As he pulled off the road, the sign came alive briefly, sluggishly, the gas in its tubes momentarily energized, glowing dully and going out again. At the far end of a drive flanked by untended hedges, he could see a dim light in the rental office.

The woman behind the desk looked up at him, mildly surprised. She was wearing a pair of bifocals that she pushed up on her nose. "You open?" he asked.

"Not supposed to be. We closed yesterday, officially." She turned around and took a key off the board. "But if you want a room I'll rent it to you. How many?"

"Just me."

"For how long?"

"Just tonight."

He found Jane twisted around on the floor of the car, her legs up on the seat, her face on the carpet. Semanica yanked her head up by the hair. "Don't you try any shit like that again," he said. "You kick my windows, I'll cut you from your cunt to your chin."

Warren said good night to the mechanic and backed his car out of its space in front of the hangar. He hadn't gone a quarter mile when a car pulled out in front of him and blocked the road. Warren stopped and put his car in reverse. When he turned to look out his back window, another car pulled out of the woods and blocked the road behind him. Two men emerged from the first car with guns drawn and another two were getting out of the second. The .45 Jenkins had given him was locked in a closet at home. He never anticipated that he would be caught out at 11 o'clock at night on the lonely road to Cameron's.

Warren got out of the car. As the men converged on him he recognized the state police sergeant, Heller. "What's the problem?"

"Let me see your hands," said Heller.

"What's this about?"

Heller holstered his revolver but didn't say anything. Warren was aware of the others milling around him. Heller drifted out of his vision, somewhere behind him. "What do you people want?" Warren asked.

Heller produced a length of wire, flung it over Warren's head, crossed the ends and yanked them tight. Warren arched his back and kicked his legs as the wire cut into his flesh. Heller pulled with all his might.

Headlights appeared at a bend in the road. Steve Tosca yelled out, "Someone's coming." Heller released his grip on the wire and let Warren fall to the ground. He lay there white and still. "Let's get him out of here," Heller said, and one of the men came over to help him carry Warren's body to the car. "Stevie," Heller called, "go out and stop that car."

The mechanic from Cameron's boatyard rolled up on them suddenly. Steve Tosca leaned into the driver's window. "Accident," he said. "You have to go back the other way."

"Anyone hurt?"

"Shaken up, that's all."

The mechanic pointed. "That's Bill Warren's car. I know him."

Tosca put his hand on the roof of the mechanic's car and leaned in close. "You should take off."

In Wellfleet, Father Boyle pulled over at a Dairy Queen that was getting ready to close down for the night. Shaky and sweating, he looked at Little Mike, who seemed tiny and frozen in the seat beside him. "How would you like an ice cream?" Father Boyle asked.

"Are we going to find my dad?"

Inside it was brightly lit, with colorful posters of floats, ice-cream cones, and sundaes mounted on the plate glass windows. It was ethereally quiet and smelled so good and wholesome that Father Boyle felt choked up. He looked down at Mike in his ill-fitting pajamas and the blanket he had taken with him. He wiped sweat off his forehead, then realized a droplet of it had appeared on the end of his nose. A young girl with a pixie haircut slid a napkin across the counter toward him and looked at Mike. "What would you like?" she asked. There must have been something about his appearance, he thought, or perhaps he had made some kind of strange utterance of which he was unaware, because the three customers in the place were looking at him and the girl behind the counter had now been joined by the manager.

"You've never done speed, have you? I can tell just by look-ing at you you've never done speed." Frank Semanica had tied Jane's hands to an overhead beam that ran the length of the motel room. She stood there, weeping quietly. He walked over to the bureau and emptied the contents of his pockets on its surface. "You're a fucking whore." He sorted through the coins and bills and found a small white envelope that he tore in two, looking inside both halves and throwing them on the floor. He sat on the edge of the bed. "Shit," he said. "I don't have a goddamn thing."

He picked up the telephone and called the Elbow Room. One of the men in the back answered. "What do you want, Frankie? We're tallying up."

"Put George on."

"I don't know where George is."

"Well, you better find him." Semanica's voice was rising with anger.

"Frankie, it's tally time. We're busy."

"I need to talk to George."

"We got trouble?"

"You will if I don't talk to George."

"Do we need to lock up, or what? 'Cause if the cops come in right now, we got our pants down."

"Put George on right now."

A moment later, McCarthy came on the line. "What hap-pened with Warren?"

"He wasn't home."

"Where are you now?"

"A motel in Yarmouth somewhere. Hey, listen." Semanica's voice lowered to a confidential, almost embarrassed tone. "You got any more speed there?"

McCarthy paused for a while. "Yeah, Frankie. I can get you some. What hotel?"

"The Kismet."

"O.K. I'll be over. Wait for me there."

47

J enkins sat in front of the television listening to the late news. He went to the telephone and called Warren but there was no answer. He tried again a few minutes later, but the phone just rang. It was unusual. He supposed it could be phone trouble, but Jenkins felt uneasy about it.

The lights were on in Warren's house when Jenkins drove up. He knocked on the front door but there was no answer. He looked in the windows but didn't see anyone there. Jenkins tried the door and discovered it was slightly ajar. He went in, calling out Warren's name. He looked in the two bedrooms but found nothing amiss. Mike's bed was unmade and looked to have been slept in. He looked through the kitchen and then went to the back door. A hook that locked the screen door to a small eyebolt in the door trim was lying on the floor. Jenkins looked at the door itself. There were gouge marks where someone had inserted a tool of some kind and pried the hook out. On the floor by the front door Jenkins found a barrette with hair in it. More hair, he felt, than one ought to see in a barrette that had simply fallen out or been dropped. He picked it up and put it in his pocket, then went out on the front step. He looked around the silent street. As he was about to get in his car, there was a voice behind him. He put his hand on the butt of his pistol and turned.

"Are you looking for Bill Warren?"

It was an old guy in work pants and slippers and a heavy sweater thrown over his shoulders.

"Who are you?"

"Henry Sherman. I live across the street. Who are you?"

"Barnstable police."

"Is everything all right?"

"I don't know. Have you seen Warren?"

"No, but it sure has been busy over here."

"How do you mean?"

"You're the fourth car to pull up to this house in—I don't know—a little over an hour."

"Did you see the others?"

"Didn't see the first one 'cause I thought it was Warren and I didn't pay much attention. Then right after that one left, there was another one. There was a young fella went around the back of the house. It was a green Pontiac. Two-tone. I think it might have been the babysitter's boyfriend."

"Did you get a look at him?"

"Not really. Just a young guy from what I could see. Then just before you came, there was an old guy who I saw standing on the front step."

"An old guy?"

"Yeah. I didn't want to get in Warren's business, but then you came up and I seen you going through the house. I figured something was up. I didn't know you were a cop. You think something's wrong?"

"I'm just trying to find him, that's all. You say the guy who went around the back of the house was in a two-tone green car?"

"A Pontiac, yes, sir. That's why I noticed it, 'cause it was snazzy."

Jenkins got on the road and drove toward the center of town. He recalled tailing a two-tone green Pontiac out of the Elbow Room and chasing it around Harwich for the better part of an hour earlier in the summer. Jenkins drove through Hyannis, down deserted streets, the branches on the trees still and heavy, looking exhausted by the recent season. He drove down 132, over the railroad tracks, turned left at the textile factory, and pulled into the lot at the Elbow Room. At midnight, the place was packed. He rolled slowly past the cars, looking for the Pontiac, but didn't see it. Jenkins parked at the outer edge of the lot, practically in the woods, in a place from which he could see both the back and side doors.

Bobby Nevins met the cars at the Starlight. His step van was parked behind one of the cottages, out of sight. In the back seat of one of the cars was Warren, the ex-Barnstable cop, handcuffed and either unconscious or dead. Heller got out of the lead car. "Get him upstairs," he said. They took him under the armpits and by the ankles and climbed the two flights to the apartment above the laundry room. Bobby followed with the tools and the oilcloth. As they struggled through the darkened kitchen, he said, "Is he dead?"

"Makes no difference," Tosca answered. "He will be soon."

They carried him through to the bathroom and laid him down in the tub. Tosca said, "Cut his clothes off, Bobby," and went out into the apartment where Heller and the others were talking. "You guys go back to the Elbow Room," Heller said. "See if Frank showed up there. If he didn't, give Grady a call and let him know he's probably on his way back up. He can take care of it there. One of you take Warren's car up to Boston and see that it gets cut up. Any personal shit he's got in there, get rid of it."

Heller followed them outside and down the stairs. He watched them drive off, then sat in his cruiser and radioed Stasiak. "State five seven to State zero nine."

"State zero nine."

"Detail one is 10-24."

From his observation point in the parking lot of the Elbow Room, Jenkins saw the side door open and a figure emerge. He was too far away to recognize, but Jenkins watched him climb into the blue Cadillac that was registered to George McCarthy.

The detective started his engine and headed out in pursuit. On Route 28, the Cadillac suddenly pulled off at a darkened motel sign that he could not make out, a series of letters up high on a pair of poles. Jenkins shut his lights off before making the turn. There was a long drive that led toward the motel: twin ruts filled with white gravel, a strip of weeds growing up in the center. The woman in the rental office looked up as his car passed by. The long, single-story motel extended out along the edge of a dirt parking lot, with the woods pressed up close to the back of the place. Only one room was lit, and parked out front were the car he'd just been following and the green Pontiac.

Jenkins drove back to the rental office and went inside. The woman watched him apprehensively. He produced his badge. "Barnstable police."

"I knew it."

"The room with the lights on back there. Who's in there?"

She looked at the register. "Frank Sinclair."

"What's he look like?"

"Like a hoodlum. Greasy. Kind of nervous."

Jenkins looked at the register. "Frank Sinclair, huh?" He spoke into his portable radio, calling Officer Welke's call sign. "Easy nine, 10-95 at the following number." He read the telephone number over the air. Welke confirmed, and a few minutes later the phone rang.

"Welke, you know a place on 28 called the Kismet?"

"No."

"About a mile over the Yarmouth line. Right-hand side if you're eastbound. It's off the road a ways down a gravel drive."

"O.K. What do you need?"

"I need you to get out here right now."

Before Welke could respond, there was a gunshot from the one occupied room.

Frank Semanica opened the door just a crack and peered out.

McCarthy didn't like the way he looked. His eyes were crazy and he was half undressed. "What the hell, Frankie," he said.

"You bring it?"

"Yeah. How about letting me in?"

"I got a girl in here."

"We need to talk."

"Why?"

McCarthy had the gun in a holster at the small of his back, concealed under an oversized cabana shirt. "What happened with Warren?"

"He wasn't there."

"You're in trouble, Frank."

He watched Semanica's face contort with indignation. "What do you mean I'm in trouble?"

"With Grady."

"Wait a fuckin' minute." McCarthy knew it would work. He watched him undo the chain on the door. McCarthy stepped into the room and saw the girl hanging by her wrists from the beam overhead, naked. McCarthy noted the cigarette burns on her arms and buttocks. She was shivering and had urinated on the carpet. "Who's the girl?"

"She was at Warren's house. She's going to tell me where he is."

"Where's the kid?"

"He wasn't there. He's with Warren. What do you mean Grady's mad at me?"

"Don't you think maybe if Warren's not there, you don't go in the house, Frankie? Now we got this." He gestured toward the girl.

"She's going to tell me where Warren is."

"And then what?"

"I'll take care of that. Don't you worry. You got what I asked you about?"

"Yeah." McCarthy took a vial of capsules out of his pocket

and handed them to Semanica. "This is a fuckin' mess. What about the lady in the rental office?"

"She didn't see anything."

McCarthy watched Semanica sit down on the edge of the bed and start opening the pill bottle. "Why is Grady mad at me?" he said.

McCarthy slipped the revolver out of its holster and shot Semanica once, hitting him under the right arm. He dropped the pills, looked upward, wincing, and toppled sideways on the mattress and then onto the floor. From behind, McCarthy heard the girl make a pleading noise. He pointed the gun at her, aligning the sights at a point just below her ear. At that second, there was a loud pounding on the door, two hard blows that shook the room. McCarthy moved the barrel a foot to the left and fired two shots through the door.

When Jenkins heard the gunshot, he sprinted across the parking lot, his revolver out. He stopped in front of the room and delivered two hard kicks to the door. Two shots rang out from inside and his face and left arm were stung with flying splinters. He stepped to the side and planted himself against the wall. In the rental office, the telephone rang. The night manager picked it up and in a shaky voice, said, "Kismet, this is Elaine."

"This is Officer Welke with the Barnstable police department. I was just talking to a Detective Jenkins. Is he there?"

"Yes. And you better hurry. There's been gunshots."

Father Boyle left the Dairy Queen and drove north until he was among the towering conifers, his headlights illuminating the ferns and underbrush. He was driving fast, practically ecstatic with the release of giving himself over to instinct.

He glanced over at Mike as they plunged into a dip in the road and the undercarriage scraped the pavement, the boy cowering in the seat beside him. The road took two sharp turns in the shape of an S. Father Boyle barely made the first and lost control on the second, plunging into a shallow ravine, the car coming to a stop with two wheels off the ground, the passenger side buried into an embankment.

Father Boyle looked around. He undid the latch on his door and forced it open with his foot. "You won't be able to get out your side, Mike," he said. "You'll have to come out this way."

Mike was trembling, crying silently, every now and then a whimper escaping his lips. "I want my dad."

Father Boyle took him gently by the wrist and guided him across the seat. "I'm sorry," he said. "I'm so very sorry."

"Where are we going?" Mike asked in a tremulous voice. Father Boyle did not answer but took him by the hand and led him into the forest.

Mike began sobbing. They walked into the thick cover, mounting an incline that Father Boyle knew eventually leveled off, then thinned out to the moors over the Atlantic.

Warren was wading through thick atmosphere. He didn't know if he was sleeping or stranded somewhere in the tentative world between slumber and wakefulness. He thought he saw his father—just in front of him but somehow far away, unreachable. He was in a field of tall golden grass in a summer shirt, suspenders, and a straw boater. The old man smiled—an expression that was rare in Warren's recollection of him—and motioned. Warren didn't know what it meant, was lost in the bright haze of the vision, awash in the aura the past had brought with it, flowing around the moment like a fragrance, like the fine, pleasant turbulence of its passing. Warren could see a boy. Who was he? He felt Little Mike's hand in his, heard his voice say, "I will be all right." Warren looked around him, or did so in a dream, but he could not see his son.

48

In the room at the Kismet, George McCarthy drew the blinds back just enough to look out at the parking lot. He didn't see anyone. He looked at Semanica lying on the floor. He was gurgling and trying to spit blood out of his mouth but he seemed to lack the strength to do it. He opened the door and rushed out to his car, looking around, his gun out in front of him. From a doorway to his left, there was a loud crack. He heard the round buzz about three feet in front of him. He crouched and sprinted. Another shot blew up a hail of dirt and gravel at his heel. A third blasted the lens on one of his headlights and sent the chrome trim ring sailing off into the darkness. McCarthy turned, let off his three remaining rounds, and ran back to the room, slamming the door behind him. He picked up the phone and called the Elbow Room.

"This is George. We got trouble."

"What?"

"I'm in a motel down 28 and there's guns involved."

Welke sped down 28, looking for the motel. Over the past few days, Jenkins had told him what he knew about organized crime on the Cape. He even raised the possibility that the state police captain, Stasiak, could be involved. Since Jenkins had gone out of his way to keep their communication off the police network, Welke assumed that whatever he was up to, it was related. But now, with the report of gunfire, he wondered whether to call the entire shift in. Then Jenkins's voice came up on the radio, mumbling and veiled, conveying a strange alarm: "Easy seventeen to Easy nine, 10-18."

Welke responded, "Easy nine en route, code two."

Catching Jenkins's use of the 10-18 code—which meant "urgent"—dispatch came up on the radio: "KCA374 to Easy seventeen. Please advise on your status."

Welke listened to see if Jenkins would respond. He did not. The dispatcher radioed Welke. "Easy nine. Status?"

Welke hesitated, unsure of whether to answer, and just as he was getting ready to pick up the handset and report that Jenkins might be in trouble, he spotted the entrance to a ratty-looking motor court called the Kismet.

Jenkins stood behind his vehicle, reloading his revolver and watching the door to the motel room, when two cars appeared. They stopped and half a dozen men piled out. He radioed Welke with a 10-18 code. The Barnstable dispatcher wanted to know what was going on and Jenkins, who had decided it was no longer wise to keep everything under wraps, lifted the radio to his mouth, ready to respond, when one of the men strode forward with a raised pistol. Jenkins put down the radio, raised his own weapon, and shouted, "Police," but his voice was drowned out by an eruption of popping sounds accompanied by flashes. He was sprayed by a shower of glass from his car windows and heard the heavy metallic clang of a round striking the sheet metal. Jenkins was armed with his police issue .38 revolver, but had also brought a Browning nine-millimeter automatic, which he now stuffed into his rear pocket, then bolted toward the building. He hurled himself shoulder first at the picture window of one of the rooms, the heavy shards falling all around him as he landed on the floor with his feet sticking out through the opening. Outside, he could hear them yelling, running footsteps coming toward him. He looked around the darkened room and dashed toward a door on the right. He tore it open and was looking into an adjacent room.

He went through and barricaded the door with the dresser. Then he opened the outside door a crack, got down on the floor, and peered out. They were out in the open, all of them carrying guns, their attention on the broken window. He could hear them moving around in the room next door, overturning the beds, frames and all. Jenkins heard someone say, "He's in here." The door moved against the dresser. He threw the dead bolt on the exterior door and secured the chain, then he got down behind one of the beds, holstered his revolver, and drew the automatic.

They began throwing their weight against the door. The dresser wasn't much of an obstacle. Now they were kicking in the exterior door, too. Jenkins saw a head appear over the top of the dresser. He pointed the muzzle of the automatic at the dresser, calculating where the person's midsection would be. The weapon kicked back in his hand and he heard a yell, the head dropping out of sight. The door to the outside broke free of its dead bolt. A last kick snapped the chain and the door flew open. No one appeared in the entrance. Suddenly, there was an eruption of gunfire outside. Jenkins, crouched behind the bed in the dark with his pistol trained alternately on one door and then the other, inched his way down the wall toward the exterior door and looked outside. He saw three men behind the green Pontiac. Facing them, about ten yards away, was a Barnstable police cruiser.

Jenkins rushed outside just in time to see one of the Pontiac's windows exploding. Out in the open parking lot now, he ran at a crouch until he reached the other side and dove into a row of bushes that were growing along the edge of a drainage ditch. He was shin-deep in water but out of sight. Jenkins got down in a prone position beneath the branches. He saw Welke, barricaded behind his cruiser, firing at the men behind the Pontiac. Jenkins selected one of them and aligned his sights. He let a round go and they all ducked. At the same instant, a picture window in one of the rooms shattered and fell out of its frame in a cascade of glass. He took aim again and fired. They stayed down, no longer shooting, and suddenly, realizing they had been outflanked, ran all together into one of the rooms.

Working his way toward Welke, Jenkins slipped and fell in the water. He heard a bullet zip past him, clipping the branches and leaving a fading howling sound in the air. He called out at the top of his lungs, "It's Jenkins! I'm coming out. To your right. In the bushes."

Father Boyle led Mike through the tall grass. He searched the undulating landscape around him, looking for the large sunken meadow. They were on high ground, within view of the great dark Atlantic, both of them panting from the effort. It seemed to Father Boyle as if he had been wandering most of the night when he kicked one of the large round rocks he'd earlier placed as a marker. Then there was a stick, shoved into the soft sand of a hillock, positioned so it would be visible from the path. Father Boyle emerged at the edge of the hollow. He descended through the brush and seated Mike on a flat rock that was there at the bottom, where the ground leveled out. He circled the boy and summoned his resolve.

The FBI agents were crowded into the small suite at the Sea Mist. They had called Warren's home repeatedly but got no answer. They tried the boatyard but he was not there. Two agents drove to General Patton Drive and found the lights on, the front door unlocked, and the rear door wide open. The house was deserted. One of the agents came in from the adjacent room where they were monitoring local police radio traffic.

"Has he called yet?" Baldesaro asked.

"No."

"Anything from the wife?"

"No, but there's been shots fired at a motel in Hyannis. The Barnstable police are involved. Sounds like a gunfight because they've called for support."

Warren looked through his eyelashes. There was the boy again. He looked troubled, doomed. Warren's throat burned and he needed to clear it or swallow but he suppressed it and shut his eyes tight against the pain.

He listened but he could not hear them. He sat up and looked over the side of the tub. On the floor was an assortment of knives, cleavers, and various kinds of clippers. Warren leaned over the edge, lowered his cuffed hands to the floor, and picked up a carving knife. He tried to get up and heard a door open. Voices in the kitchen. He lay back down and slipped the knife under his shirt, concealing its handle in his fist. The boy came in again and sat on the edge of the tub. He untied Warren's shoes and removed them, placing them outside the bathroom door. Warren watched him through barely open eyes. He took a pair of surgical scissors and made a motion to reach for the hem of Warren's T-shirt when something worked free in Warren's throat, something trickling down—blood, he imagined—that caused him to make a slight sound. The boy froze. Steve Tosca walked in. He kicked at the pile of tools on the floor. "Where's the clippers, Bobby?"

"They're right there."

"Not those. The curved ones. The curved clippers for the cartilage. Ha-ha. You don't like that, Bobby, do you? Are you all right? You look fucked up."

"I'm O.K."

"Go out to the truck and get them."

Tosca sat on the toilet and sorted through the tools. The boy knew. The boy saw him move and still he said nothing. Tosca came up with something in his hand. Warren could not see what it was. He was going to have to make two motions, one to draw the knife out of his shirt, and the second to thrust. He tried to see through his eyelashes what Tosca was doing—he was leaning over him now—and thought frantically for a way to reduce everything to one quick motion. But Tosca then touched something to his throat and it pinched and then stung, and Warren realized that he was going to cut him. He jerked the knife out from under his shirt and blinked his eyes open. Tosca's eyes went wide and he planted a hand on Warren's left shoulder, pinning him down in the tub. Warren thrust upward and hit him in the side, driving the point of the big knife through Tosca's shirt somewhere beneath his arm. Tosca dropped what he had in his hand and backed away from the tub. Warren thrashed around, trying to get up. Tosca reached down for one of the tools on the floor. Warren rushed at him, holding the knife with both hands, but tripped on the tub edge and sprawled out on the floor. Tosca moved to the side for maneuvering room. He coughed once and a bloody spray flecked the toilet tank with small red droplets. He grabbed Warren's handcuffs with one hand and put the other around his throat and squeezed. They struggled silently for a few seconds. Tosca tried to knee him in the groin but missed. Warren jerked his hands free and thrust at Tosca, slicing his fingers. Tosca punched him in the face and his vision went white for a moment but he used his body to pin Tosca to the wall in the small space between the sink and the toilet. In the struggle, Tosca coughed again, spraying Warren's face with blood. He yelled, *"Heller!"* but it was more of a rasp. He held Warren's wrists with both his hands, trying to keep the knife away. Warren wrenched his hands free and swung the blade point first at him, piercing his diaphragm. Warren felt Tosca's grip go slack. He swung the knife again. Tosca had begun to slump and the knife plunged into his upper chest just below the throat. Warren eased him to the floor. He lay on his face, blood flowing out across the tile. Bobby appeared in the doorway with what looked like a pair of bolt cutters and gaped at Warren. Neither of them spoke. Bobby shifted the cutters from one hand to the other. He looked over his shoulder. "Don't yell," Warren said. "Don't make a sound. I'm not going to hurt you. Just undo these handcuffs."

The boy swallowed. He looked past Warren at the body of Steve Tosca, whose face looked flattened against the bloody tile.

"It's not too late to get out of this, son. Do what I tell you. Unlock the handcuffs."

With trembling hands, Bobby Nevins detached the key chain from Steve Tosca's belt loop. Warren stood over him, the knife still in his hands. Bobby sorted through the keys until he found the right one. He looked at Warren as if he was having second thoughts. "Don't try anything," Warren said. "Because I am madder than hell right now."

Bobby unlocked the handcuffs. Warren was aware of blood running down his front. "Did he have a handgun?"

Bobby didn't answer.

"Come on. Answer me."

"He usually has one. I don't know where it is."

"Stand right there. Stay quiet." Warren went out into the living area and looked around. Then he checked the kitchen. There was a pile of oilcloth on the floor and on the counter a .38. He opened the cylinder and checked it. Heavy footsteps sounded on the stairs. Warren retreated back into the living area, out of sight. Heller came in and Warren stepped into view. He watched the policeman register the sight before him. Heller's eyes moved rapidly—for a fraction of a second they were everywhere at once. There was almost a smile on his face but it was not a smile. It was some kind of slight distortion, his thoroughly private reaction to the massively bloodied Warren standing before him pointing a pistol.

Heller forced out a dismissive sound. "Put it away. You're not even capable."

"You have *no idea*."

"Steve!"

"Steve can't help you now."

"Put that gun down, Warren."

"Give me your car keys."

"No. Put that thing down, Warren."

Heller reached around for his weapon.

"Don't, Heller."

"What are you going to do? Shoot me?"

Heller, in a confident, relaxed fashion, began unholstering his pistol. Warren shot him once in the groin, the noise incredible in the small apartment. In his peripheral vision, he saw Bobby practically squat in response to the sound. Heller fell on the floor. He got up on one elbow, his eyes closed. "Goddamn you. Goddamn you." He still held his gun. Warren pointed the revolver at Heller's chest. "Slide the gun over here." Heller checked his wound. Blood was pooling on the floor around his left leg and buttock. Warren closed one eye and sighted. "It doesn't make any difference to me whether you walk out of here or not, Heller. I'll kill you like it was nothing."

Heller tossed the gun toward him. His head lolled back and he looked at the ceiling.

Warren took the weapon and went through the pockets of Heller's jacket until he found the keys to his cruiser. Heller began writhing, the shock beginning to wear off and the pain starting. "Come on!" he shouted. "Finish it! Let's see what you're made of, Warren."

"That would be doing you a favor. I want to be there when you have to answer for what you are."

Warren opened the door and stepped out, looking back toward Bobby Nevins and nodding once.

49

With the radio turned up nearly full volume at the Sea Mist, the agents listened to the Barnstable police net. An officer at the Kismet had called in the license numbers and descriptions of a '53 Cadillac and a '57 Pontiac at the scene. Baldesaro pointed to one of his agents and said, "Get the list." They searched the list they kept of cars and plate numbers associated with the Elbow Room. One of the agents said, "The Cadillac belongs to George McCarthy. The Pontiac is unknown."

Baldesaro turned to his second-in-command. "Come with me for a minute."

The agent followed him outside and stood in the courtyard.

"What do you think?" Baldesaro said.

"I think Jenkins got ahead of himself. He got ahead of us anyway."

"I think we have to move. We have to do the raids right now."

"It's going to have to be very fast. They're going to shut everything down and cover their tracks. They're probably doing it right now."

"We need to get started on an affidavit immediately."

The agent looked at his watch. "It's one o'clock in the morning."

"I'm going to call the US attorney. Make sure somebody stays by the telephone in case Warren or his ex calls. And send someone back over to his house to see if he's shown up. You get started on the affidavit. I'll get ahold of the US attorney and tell him what's happening. Then we'll get everybody together and tell them we're doing it now."

Jenkins found Welke crouched behind his cruiser. Steam rose from around its hood and its windows were smashed. Welke gawked at him. "Where were you?"

"In the motel. They had me trapped in one of the rooms."

"Who are these guys?"

"They're from the Elbow Room."

"The Elbow Room?" Welke echoed, mystified.

"Is backup coming?" Jenkins asked.

"Should be any second."

Welke said, "I've only got a few rounds left." His hands trembled as he spoke. "And one of them's got a shotgun. Every time I get up to shoot, he lets rip with that thing."

They trained their weapons on the door the men had run through and watched for movement. "Where the hell is our help?" Jenkins said. Welke took his radio and spoke into it: "Easy nine to KCA374 . . ."

"KCA374. ETA five minutes, Easy nine. Code 18 all units. Code 18. Kismet Motor Lodge, 5200 block of Route 28."

The parking lot was quiet. They turned toward Route 28 and listened for sirens but heard nothing. "How the hell did all this happen?" Welke asked.

Jenkins started to speak but then just shook his head. "I think they've done something to Warren," he said. Welke turned to him and opened his mouth, but the word never got out. From one of the motel rooms, a group of men came charging out. Jenkins said, "They're going to rush us."

The first man out fired a shotgun. Welke and Jenkins ducked behind the cruiser as the pellets raked the car's body and sprayed them with broken glass. When they stood to fire, the group had reduced the distance between them by half and was coming on fast. The shotgun went off again, dropping the two policemen to the ground. Air rushed out of the car's tires and Jenkins smelled gasoline. He shouted at Welke to run and got up to lead the way. The roaring apparition in front of him—a dark vehicle, blurred in motion, sucking air through its grille and bearing down on them like some kind of fierce animal—shifted the moment firmly into the surreal, despair and joy and fatigue converging to dream-like effect. Four state police cruisers skidded to a halt, one behind the other, the searchlight on the lead car illuminating the parking lot so that the walls of the motel served as a backdrop for the distorted shadows of the men who had been charging toward them and who were now mere feet away. Jenkins heard the state policemen exit their cars, shouting.

The man with the shotgun was hit in the throat and fell with the weapon across his chest. Another was hit in the upper torso and fell a few feet away. The others managed to retreat back inside the motel. A state police sergeant approached Jenkins and Welke. "How many are there?"

"I don't know. I'd say five, six."

The sergeant organized a room-to-room search of the motel. Jenkins pushed open the door to the single lit room, the one he had first approached. He saw a naked young woman suspended by her wrists from a beam that ran the length of the room. A man was lying on the floor in his underwear, his right side glistening with blood. Walking around so he could see the girl's face, he recognized her. Jenkins looked around the room. On the dresser was some loose change, a few bills, a pack of cigarettes, and a buck knife. He cut the cord holding her wrists and caught her as she fell. He tore the bedspread off the bed and wrapped her in it, holding her against him. Welke appeared in the doorway. "What's this?" he said.

"She's Warren's babysitter."

"What the hell is she doing here?"

"I don't know. Tell one of the staties we got a gunshot victim here."

Welke spoke to Jane Myrna. "Who did this to you?"

She began crying, silently at first, then in long moans. She struggled against Jenkins's touch. He let go of her and let her cry, patting her lightly on the back to reassure her. "Sshh," he said. "Sshh. Sshh. Honey. You know me. Ed Jenkins."

Welke crouched down before her. "Who did this to you?"

Jenkins said, "Put her in an ambulance. Have one of our guys stay with her."

Welke led Jane out into the parking lot. Jenkins stood in the room's entrance and surveyed the scene outside. The Barnstable police had arrived in force, their cars backed up the narrow drive. There was a small crowd around the two bodies lying in the courtyard. Flashing lights lit the sky from the motel all the way back to Route 28.

Warren drove out of the Starlight in Heller's unmarked and sped to General Patton Drive. The house was open, all the lights on. He looked at Mike's comic books scattered on the sofa. The house had an eerie, hostile air, all the lights burning bright, like it had been waiting all these years to rise up against him and had finally done so. He was still dripping blood from somewhere. There were splashes of it on the floor.

Warren ran to his bedroom, retrieved the .45 Jenkins had given him, pocketed four full clips, stuffed Tosca's revolver in his waist, and headed back out. Henry Sherman came running out of the dark and, jolted by Warren's condition, stopped abruptly. "Jesus. What happened?"

"Henry, have you seen Mike?"

"No. What happened?"

"I'm all right. Henry, I need to find Mike."

"I don't know where he is. There's been an awful lot of people over here, though."

"Who was here?"

"Well, let's see. A young guy in a two-tone green Pontiac. An old guy in a brown car. And then there was . . ."

"Hold on, hold on. Here at the house?"

"Yes."

"They came *in* the house?"

"I'm not sure, Bill. I wasn't watching real close but a bunch of cars have pulled up here in the last hour and a half or so."

Warren stood there, trying to make sense of it. He saw Sherman's eyes go to the pistol he had stuck into the waist of his pants in plain view. "You said an old guy in a brown car?"

"An old guy, yup. In a tan car. Looked tan, anyway."

The priest from Nazareth Hall drove a tan car. A '53 Ford.

"Did you see him go in the house?" Warren asked. "Did you see him leave?"

"I seen him standing on the front step, Bill, that's all. I think you need a doctor."

Warren headed for Heller's unmarked. He burned rubber in reverse out of the driveway and gunned it toward downtown. He roared down empty streets on his way to the police station, planning to have the dispatcher put out an all points bulletin on Mike and Jane. A voice came out of the radio, calling, "State zero-nine to state five-seven." It repeated like a metronome as he squealed around corners and shot through red lights at empty intersections, never getting a response. As he approached the station, the state police dispatcher called for a unit to check out a report of a suspicious male at the Dairy Queen in Wellfleet. He skidded to a halt in the parking lot and was ready to jump out when he heard, "The individual is described as a white male, approximately sixty, sixty-five years of age. He's in the company of a minor. Male, blond, about seven years old. Red pajamas."

Warren tore out of the parking lot and pointed the car in the direction of the Mid-Cape Highway. The voice kept coming over the radio: "State zero-nine to state five-seven." As the speedometer hit one hundred and ten, Warren's eyes went to the temperature gauge and then the fuel. Above the instrument cluster was a small plaque that read, "STATE 5-7." They were trying to reach Heller.

Stasiak was behind this. They tried to kill him. They were going to dismember him in the bathtub in that motor court. He'd probably driven past the place a hundred times on patrol. Occasionally, they chased kids and vagrants out of there. He had no idea they were using it. Warren thought of Heller wrapping that wire around his neck and trying to strangle him. He'd damn near done it. He was shaking now, crazy with adrenaline, panicked, anguished for Mike. The speaker buzzed in the dash: "State zero-nine to state five-seven." Warren knew the voice. It had been nagging at him since it first started coming over the radio. "Five-seven, what is your location?"

It was Stasiak. It was Stasiak looking for Heller. Warren picked up the mike. He wasn't thinking, blind with rage. "This is state five-seven. I'm northbound on the Mid-Cape Highway, approaching Old County Road."

The radio went silent. Let him come, Warren thought. He glanced at the two handguns he had laid out on the seat beside him. The skin around his left eye began to feel hot and tight, the place where Steve Tosca punched him, probably swelling. Warren took the exit for Wellfleet in a long, sweeping curve, the road flanked by tall weeds, the woods and isolated buildings flying past. The Dairy Queen was brightly lit, its red and white sign visible from a good way off. The place was empty except for the manager and one waitress. They started at the sight of him. The manager said, "I'll call an ambulance."

"Don't touch the phone."

"Have you been in an accident?"

"No. There was a man in here with a little boy. The boy was wearing red pajamas."

They nodded. "We called the state police," said the manager. "Was the boy all right?"

"I don't know. He looked like he'd been crying."

"What were they doing here?"

"The old guy was trying to buy some ice cream for the kid but he was upset and he didn't want any."

"Which way did they go when they left?"

"They turned left out of the parking lot. They were in a light brown car."

Warren headed back out. He was desperate, helpless, with no idea where to look for his son. He decided to find a place to pull over and call in an all points bulletin. He'd get the Barnstable dispatcher to do it. He drove down the road in the dark, consumed by a torment he had never known, thinking that if it went on much longer, he couldn't bear it. He realized that if anything happened to his son, he would not go on.

Stasiak roared down the Mid-Cape Highway, watching for the Old County Road exit. Whoever was driving Heller's car, it wasn't Heller. He didn't know whether it was fatigue or his imagination, but the voice sounded like Warren's. He exited the highway and listened for an update on the shooting at the motel in Hyannis. Then he called Heller again on the radio and listened hard to the voice that came back through the speaker. Something was not right.

He drove in the direction of the Dairy Queen and confirmed the report with the dispatcher: An elderly man and a little boy in a light brown 1953 Ford. The priest from Hyannis. It would be too lucky, Stasiak thought. Up ahead, the round red and white sign came into view, glowing in the night.

After speaking with the manager at the Dairy Queen, he got back on the road. He radioed Heller's call sign again but got no response. The units at the motel in Hyannis reported two dead in the shooting. Stasiak swiped a hand across his face, wondering what had happened. He had to get to a telephone and call someone and see what the hell was going on. Then came a report of car in a ditch off Collins Road in Truro.

Warren saw the rear end of the Ford pitched upward and sitting at an angle in a narrow ravine on the side of the road. He pulled over, shut off the engine, and got out, carrying one pistol and putting the other in his waist. It was Father Boyle's car, as near as he could tell. There was no one inside it. He had been driving blindly, looking for a phone booth or even a door to knock on when he heard a report that a car had gone off of nearby Collins Road. It was remote here, nothing around for miles. One of the murdered boys was found out this way. He tried to examine the foliage for signs of people passing through but it was useless. Grieving now, on the point of hysteria, Warren walked into the forest and up an incline. *"Mike!"* he screamed.

Stasiak came on Heller's unmarked suddenly. It was pulled over to the side of the road near another car, which was partially on its side in a ditch. The tan Ford belonging to the priest had two wheels in the air. He got out and unholstered his .38. Far off, he heard a shout. He followed the sound into the forest. He refused to believe Warren was out here. Warren, by now, was in half a dozen pieces and on his way out to sea. But someone was driving Heller's car, someone whose voice sounded like Warren's. It must be one of Grady's guys, he thought. Things might have gotten rough with Warren. He was no kind of a man, in Stasiak's estimation, but he was wound tight enough that Stasiak could see him getting crazy. And the priest was with a kid, and somewhere in the vicinity. It seemed too good to be true.

Stasiak experienced that euphoric confidence, that almost supernatural perception that he had felt at Iwo Jima. His eyes slid left and right as he moved among the trees. If he could catch the priest out here with a kid, this whole thing was over. He heard a faint shout again from far up the incline. He picked up his pace, preternaturally aware.

50

Father Boyle stood before Michael Warren. The boy sat there, weeping, his blanket wrapped around him. The priest was unsure of how to proceed. He looked around at the stars showing through holes in the cloud cover. When he'd brought Perry Boggs out here, it had rained heavily. He had prayed over the boy, who had wailed and gritted his teeth in the teeming downpour. Father Boyle cried himself. He cast his eyes skyward. He did not know what kind of incantation was called for or what kind of prayer he should say. In the end he just held Perry Boggs's wet, slick head in both his hands and shrieked at the clouds, *"Please! Please!"*

Stasiak followed the voice. A man was screaming, "Mike," somewhere up ahead. He went through a deep fir forest that was so black he had to feel his way through with his hands and then came upon a region of low woods where the stars were suddenly visible. He could smell the ocean. The man cried out, not a word this time, but something incoherent, a shriek. He emerged from the tree line where the woods gave way to sandy meadow. He walked toward the sound. Ahead, on his knees in the middle of a path, was a man screaming, *"God help me!"* Stasiak headed down toward him. *"Please! God help me!"*

It was Warren. Stasiak instantly raised his pistol. How in the name of Christ, he wondered. Where the hell were Heller and the rest of them? How did Warren get out of it and wind up with Heller's car all the way the hell out here?

In his agony and grief, on all fours in the sandy track, Warren raised his head. Through his tears, he saw a large figure approaching. He was so transported by his anguish, he wasn't sure where he was. The apparition now before him was like gossamer in his vision, wavering and ethereal. Then it solidified and began to take on qualities he recognized. He raised his revolver.

They fired at each other simultaneously. A plume of sand shot up and stung Warren's face. His neck felt like it had been whipped with nettles.

Stasiak heard a round howl past him, its pitch fading in the distance. He lay prone in the sand and watched Warren move across the moor-like landscape. He guessed that he would try to make his way back to the car. He had to keep him in sight. Stasiak would either beat him to the road or surprise him along the way. He got up, clearheaded, infused with an energy so intense he almost felt high. He ambled lightly back into the woods, transported by a sensation that was very nearly joy.

Warren ran through the trees, suppressing the cries of grief that rose from his throat. He would never be able to identify Mike's body. He would never be able to live through this. It was just a matter of how to die. He stopped running and stood panting in the forest. He drew the pistol out of his waistband and looked at it. He could do it now, he thought. No. He would do it once they discovered the body. As soon as he got word, he would go out and do it. He plodded on through the woods until he could see the road ahead. With the weapon hanging loosely by his side, he walked toward the car.

The impact was tremendous. It jarred his vision. Stasiak must have hit him at a dead run. Nothing else could explain a force like that. They slammed to the ground, Stasiak's arms clamped around him, his full weight crushing him. His femur felt like it had been dislodged from its socket. Stasiak wrenched the pistol out of his hands and flung it off to the side. He stood Warren up and hooked an arm around his neck from behind. He placed his other hand on the side of his jaw and started to push. Warren knew what he was doing and knew that it would only take a good hard shove to snap his neck. He reached around and clawed at Stasiak's face. He tried for his eyes, elbowed and lashed out any way he could. His hand suddenly fell on Stasiak's holstered revolver. He tried to grab it and Stasiak had to commit a hand to stopping him. Stasiak hooked one of his legs around Warren's and propelled them both to the ground. On top of Warren again, Stasiak tried to get his hands around his neck. Warren squirmed desperately and managed to get his right arm free. He punched Stasiak as hard as he could in the side of the face once, then again. Warren managed to twist free and get on his feet.

Now the state policeman came at him, wide and hulking, moving like a boxer. Warren welcomed it. He hoped Stasiak killed him. Warren let him come on and struck quickly. He hit Stasiak in the mouth and gashed his knuckle open on one of his teeth. Stasiak backed Warren down into the ravine and up against Father Boyle's car. He pressed a forearm against Warren's throat and pinned him against the vehicle. Again, Stasiak tried to force his head to the side and snap his neck. Warren scratched his flesh and tried to gouge his eyes, but Stasiak was determined. Warren grasped the car's radio antenna and snapped it off. He tried to use it like a knife, stabbing at Stasiak's arms and shoulders, but it had no effect. Something snapped in his neck and red swirls appeared behind his eyes. He reached further with the broken shaft of the antenna, swinging with all his strength, trying to hit Stasiak in a place that would make him stop.

Suddenly, he was free. His neck was all searing pain and his vision was strange, but he could see Stasiak a few feet away holding a hand to his face. There was a dark liquid dripping off his elbow, like oil. Stasiak reached for his weapon and Warren lunged at him. He had one hand on Stasiak's wrist. In the other he held the broken antenna. Stasiak grabbed him by the throat and squeezed. Warren stuck him in the side of the neck, and when Stasiak only made a face—almost a demonic grin, his teeth red with blood—he did it again. Stasiak let go of him then and fell on one knee. He fired his pistol blindly and struck the side of the car. Warren circled around behind him. Stasiak was unaware, holding the side of his neck. He tried to see where Warren was, rotating stiffly at the waist. He fell on his back, then rolled over and tried to get up on his elbows, but could not. Warren tore the pistol from Stasiak's grip. Blood was pumping from a hole in his neck. Warren secured the weapon, then tore a section of Stasiak's shirt free and wadded it up. He pressed it into the wound and watched as the head-lights of an oncoming car lit the ravine.

Driving down the dark roads on his way home from the late shift at a radio station down Cape, the disc jockey slowed as a bloodied figure emerge from the woods. He rolled his window down just far enough to speak. "Did you wreck?"

The man seemed unable to speak.

"Get in. I'll take you to the hospital."

"It's not me. There's another man. He's got a neck injury. He's bleeding to death."

Stasiak's weight was nearly more than they could bear. Warren kept a thumb pressed against the puncture wound in his neck. If he released it, blood shot out in great squirts. They fell twice, Stasiak tumbling to the ground like a stuffed dummy. His body was slick with blood and difficult to hold on to. By the time they got him to the pavement, all three were covered.

They loaded Stasiak into the backseat and sped toward Hyannis, the driver looking back at them in the rearview mirror. "How's he doing?" he asked as they blew through Chatham. Warren didn't answer. He sat there with his hand pressed hard against Stasiak's neck, his head hanging down, weeping quietly.

The highway lights glistened off their blood-slick skin, their clothes giving off a sheen. The car smelled of it. The driver opened a window and spat. "How did you come to be out this way?" he asked. There was no response from the backseat. He shook his head. "Strange things happening tonight," he said. "Coast Guard's been running a cutter up and down the coast. Running in real close, too. Drug interdiction. They been doing it all summer. And that boy. That boy they found way up the hell in the middle of nowhere."

Warren raised his head. "What did you say?"

"The boy. Coast Guard helicopter spotted a boy in Wellfleet, all by himself, way up the middle of nowhere. Must have wandered off or something, but that's way far away from anywhere, up there. How the hell they could see him in the middle of the night, I don't know."

"Is he alive?"

"Oh, he's alive. They sent somebody down to get him."

When they arrived at the hospital, the shooting victims from the Kismet had just arrived. The emergency room entrance was crowded with police cruisers and a group of state troopers and Barnstable cops stood outside. The disc jockey got out and approached them. "I've got two men hurt in the backseat. One of them really bad. I don't even know if he's alive."

The cops converged on the vehicle. It took them a moment to recognize Stasiak but when they did, the state police instantly coalesced into an aggressive, fanatically protective clan. Shock, anger, disbelief. They shoved back at the reporters, who rushed the car when they heard the name. They commandeered the emergency room and hustled the doctors out to the apron. Stasiak was carried inside, limp and bloody, the sight of him eliciting an outraged gasp from the officers.

Alone in the backseat, Warren closed his eyes. Mike was alive. Was he? The man said a little boy. They spotted a little boy. Could it be a different little boy? His breath started coming fast and he felt like he might hyperventilate. A Barnstable cop peered in. "Lieutenant?" he said, and then, to others, "Hey. This is one of ours."

Hands reached in and gripped him gently.

"Can you move?"

"Were you in a wreck, lieutenant?"

They helped Warren out of the car. "You guys listen to me. Come here." They gathered close around him so they could hear Warren's weakened voice. "You have to get me out of here. I have to find my son. He's lost. I think the Coast Guard might have located him out in the woods down Cape in Wellfleet somewhere. He's missing."

He saw the skepticism in their faces. "Sir," one of them said, "you're hurt."

"I need to know if the Coast Guard found a kid out there in Wellfleet. Michael Warren. He's got red pajamas on. He has blond hair, a crew cut. He's seven years old."

Suddenly Welke was there. He spoke in a low voice. "Break it up. Break it up, fellas. Let me see him." He looked over the top of the car at the state cops gathered around the entrance. "I need to talk to the lieutenant. Gimme some room."

"He's hurt, Welke," one of them said. "He needs a doctor."

"I know he's hurt. Just give me a minute with him." He took Warren by the elbow and led him to one of the cruisers. "What happened?"

"Welke, you have to help me. I have to get out of here."

"What the hell is going on?"

"I can't get into all that right now. How about you drive me to the Coast Guard station?"

"You look awful. What happened to your neck? Looks like somebody tried to hang you."

"Welke, please."

They pulled away from the hospital in Welke's cruiser, Warren slouched in the passenger seat. They drove for a long time in silence before Welke said, "I know everything."

Warren didn't say anything. He avoided looking at Welke.

"I know about Stasiak. I know about the rackets he's involved in. I know a lot."

"How . . ."

"Jenkins. I made him tell me. It's not his fault. I figured some of it out on my own and I confronted him and he agreed to let me in on it."

"Where is Jenkins?"

"I don't know. Some suit met him at the motel and they drove off somewhere. FBI. That's what I heard. I don't know what that's about yet."

"What motel?"

"There was a gun battle at this motor lodge on 28. Me and Jenkins and the staties had it out with a bunch of guys from the Elbow Room. We killed two of them."

"How did all that happen?"

"I don't know yet. Jenkins went out there for some reason and that's when it started."

Welke called ahead to the Coast Guard station and they were met at the gate by a petty officer who confirmed that they had picked up Mike in the bluffs a short distance from the shore in Truro. The officer escorted them past two parked helicopters and an amphibious aircraft to a two-story concrete building. "It's a lucky thing we spotted him," he said. "We weren't even looking for him. We were running an interdiction patrol up the coast—narcotics."

Inside, they directed Warren down a corridor and at the far

end he saw Mike sitting in an office with a cookie in one hand and a carton of milk in the other, his feet swinging back and forth. He put them down and got up, running out to meet his father. Warren fell to his knees and embraced his son, his hand on the back of the boy's head, pushing it into his shoulder. The release, the gratitude was ecstatic. For a moment he was not in the world but somewhere else, drifting, subsumed by an unfamiliar bliss, his father somehow present, peaceful, smiling, blessing the moment.

51

As news about what had happened at the Kismet came out, the men at the Elbow Room decided to dismantle everything and shut the place down. They nearly succeeded but were still working at it when Baldesaro and his team of FBI agents showed up. They had stripped the walk-in completely but all their equipment was in the trunks of their cars. Betting slips, money, lists, records, and everything else that identified the Elbow Room as a bookmaking operation were discovered intact.

Jenkins went with another group of agents to the house on Depot Road, where they arrested a number of people and found illegal weapons and a large quantity of cash. Brinkman's yielded paper records related to bookmaking, but Stasiak's house near the beach was absolutely clean.

In Boston, FBI agents raided the bar Ava had revealed and discovered that it was serving as a back-alley bank and money laundering service for Grady Pope's network of bookmakers, exchanging cash for the checks Frank Semanica delivered weekly. This made it possible for bettors to pay with checks written out to fictitious recipients and to bet larger amounts than would be possible in an all-cash system.

An FBI agent picked Warren and Mike up at the Coast Guard air station and drove them back to General Patton Drive. When they pulled up to the house, Grayson and James from Antiquitus came out and walked toward them. "Thank

God you're all right," said Grayson. "My God, what did they do to you?"

The agent looked at them. "Who are you people?"

"We're friends," said James.

"Everybody get inside."

Warren put Mike in the shower, then wrapped him in a towel and put him in his bed. Then he got under the water himself, his cuts and abrasions stinging. James and Grayson sat at the dining room table talking with Henry Sherman. The FBI man told them all to stay away from the telephone and took up vigil at a front window. When Warren got out of the shower he walked stiffly to his room and found Mike in his bed. He pulled the shades and lay down beside his son, who said, "What are we going to do now, Dad?"

Warren was already almost asleep. "We're going to take a nap, Mike."

"And then what?"

"We'll be together."

The boy slung an arm across his father's chest and they drifted off to the low, soft voices in the house.

When information began leaking out to the public, the press descended on the Cape. No one seemed to know what the story was: a gunfight at a run-down motel in Hyannis, a celebrated state policeman who'd had a stroke during emergency surgery for a stab wound to his neck, another found shot to death at some abandoned cottages, a boy abducted by a priest who was a suspect in the child murders and, miraculously, found unharmed. As reporters were struggling to put everything together, news came of a federal raid that exposed an extensive gambling and extortion racket that had been operating on the Cape for six months, and not only that, but that certain state police officers were involved, prominent among them Captain Dale Stasiak.

Lieutenant Colonel John Fitzgerald, head of the state police, was temperate in his response. He asked the Department of Justice to refrain from speaking to the media until more was known. The one name that kept coming up in all of this—William Warren—who was he? By now it was known that he had shot Heller and maimed Stasiak. They wanted him. Fitzgerald called the US attorney and said as much.

"He's our primary witness and he risked a great deal to help us," the attorney responded. "We're not going to honor that request."

"He murdered a state trooper, counselor."

"In self-defense."

"So he says."

"Warren won't be going anywhere. You file whatever you have to file but access to him is FBI only."

Fitzgerald said, "Senator Kennedy will be having a meeting with the attorney general down in DC. The complexion of this whole thing may change after that."

Detective Ferrell of the state police was designated the head of the task force on the child killings. Father Boyle, it seemed, had completely disappeared from the woods where Mike was found. They combed the area for days, even had the Coast Guard fly over the outer Cape but he was nowhere to be found. The prevailing theory was that he walked into the ocean and drowned.

Father Keenan and Mrs. Gonsalves hunkered down in the house as autumn deepened. The archdiocese of Boston sent an attorney and two priests to help him get through the daily business of running a parish. Worshippers saw a different man on the altar than the one they knew. Father Keenan moved slowly, uncharacteristically grave and fragile.

Detective Ferrell interviewed Mike about the night of his

abduction. Baldesaro was present along with a lawyer from the US attorney's office. "Now, Detective Ferrell," said the attorney. "We understand you're here to speak with Michael Warren regarding the events of October 4, specifically his kidnapping from his house and experience related to that."

"Correct."

"There will be no discussion of the current investigation into certain members of the Massachusetts state police or of Mr. Warren's actions on the night of October 4 or the search warrants executed on October 5."

"No."

"Go ahead, then."

Ferrell had Mike walk him through what happened. "So, after the Dairy Queen, was that when the car went 'crooked,' as you say?"

"Yes, and it went 'bang' too. Real loud."

"Did you get hurt?"

"No, I was just scared. I cried."

"And what happened then?"

"We walked in the woods and then we were in a big field."

"Did he hurt you?"

"No."

"What did he do when you were in the field?"

"He prayed."

"He prayed?"

"Uh-huh. He put his hands on my head like this."

"And what else?"

"He cried."

"He cried."

"Yup. He cried when the light came."

"Now, what light was that?"

Mike put his hand up and made a motion to indicate the entire room. "A big light," he said. "All around like that and that. And . . . just bright."

"Did he hurt you at all? Did he touch you any place he shouldn't have, like your private area?"

"No. He's nice to me. He wouldn't do that. Can I ask a question?"

"Sure."

"Do you know where he went?"

"That's what we're trying to find out."

Warren attributed the changes in his son's behavior to the trauma of recent events. He was pensive and quiet, taking note of things around him with an attentiveness his father found unsettling somehow. What was unusual was the stillness. When Warren spoke to the boy, he looked back at him in the most peculiar way, an unfamiliar quality to his eyes.

The remarkable thing about Mike's account of what happened out in Truro was that it never changed. He did not know what to make of the boy's account of a sudden light. Warren suggested that perhaps it was the helicopter Mike was describing but he was firm in his claim that the helicopter came after the light. Father Boyle was standing by him, he said, when the light came.

"And then what?" Warren asked.

"And then it was like I took a nap. On the grass. I was lying down. I woke up and Father Boyle was gone. And then I heard the helicopter."

A doctor came down from Children's Hospital in Boston and met with Warren at Nazareth Hall. They sat alone in one of the classrooms. "Where are the sisters?" Warren asked.

"I'd just as soon we keep the sisters out of this for the time being," the doctor said. "There have been some changes in your son and they're . . . quite dramatic, for lack of a better description. The sisters are pragmatic, in general. But we don't want to encourage any kind of . . . Well, we don't want any mystery around what is likely a very explicable event."

Warren searched for ways to explain the differences he saw

in his son. The inscrutable quirkiness, the impenetrable aspect of his personality had disappeared, and while it had been endearing in its way, it represented uncountable miles between son and father, the gulf between an impaired mind and the rest of the world, a distance that love would never bridge. The truth was Mike shocked him daily now with comments and observations that indicated a perceptiveness that thrilled and bewildered his father at the same time. Mike seemed to be growing, blooming before his very eyes.

His attempts to convey this to the doctor did not seem to be satisfactory. The doctor frowned and looked at his notes, at test results, at the contents of Mike's file, which was spread across his desk. Warren tried to grasp the entire strange situation in his mind and wound up saying, "I don't know what's happening."

After the meeting, he was pulling out of the driveway when Sister John Frances lumbered down the steps, black skirts flowing. She leaned into his window and pressed a scapular of St. Jude into his hand and then closed it with both of her own. "God has a special place in his heart for you, Mr. Warren," she said. She released his hand and turned and went back up the steps without another word.

In mid-October, Phil Dunleavy went missing. His wife and sons said he had gone off to work as usual but he never came home. His office at the police station was as he had left it the day before. His unmarked was discovered on a service road near a cranberry bog ten miles outside New Bedford. Not long afterward, he was indicted for what the FBI alleged was his role in Stasiak's and Pope's illicit activity on the Cape. They had recruited him early, using him to keep them apprised of what Warren and Jenkins were up to, feeding them information.

Warren was sitting at home, reading the story in the *Boston*

Globe when he got a call from Grayson and James at Antiquitus about the work they had discussed before all the trouble started. With ceremony and a hint of intrigue, James revealed their plans to convert the barn into a bed-and-breakfast. Their well-heeled clientele, taken with the property and its quaint environs, often asked about places to stay, where to eat, and what to visit. The converted barn would be a natural draw, rustic, intentionally suspended at the edge of dilapidation but chic and comfortable. Their proposal was for Warren to manage the renovation. He and Mike could live there while the work was going on. When it was finished, they wanted him to stay on as caretaker for the property in general.

One morning in mid-October, Warren walked up the steps to the rectory at St. Clement's. Mrs. Gonsalves answered his knock. There was a visible reaction in her face when she recognized him. "Is Father Keenan here?" he asked.

She held the door open for him. "I'm sorry," she said. "Your son."

Warren nodded.

"He is O.K.?"

"Yes, thank you. He's fine."

"I will get Father."

In a few minutes, Father Keenan appeared. They went into what looked like a seldom-used parlor that appeared to have been furnished and decorated in another century. Father Keenan said, "It's a good thing Mr. Wiggins is not here."

"Mr. Wiggins?"

"The attorney from the archdiocese. We're not speaking to anyone, officially. But he's out running errands. I *must* speak with you. I owe it to you. Before you say anything, let me tell you how sorry I am for what you and your son have gone through. If you believe I am at fault in any way, please tell me, and tell me how I can make it right because I never intended for this to happen. I will make amends to you in any way I can. And please understand that I am truly sorry for what Father Boyle did."

Warren sat back in his chair. He had not expected this kind of candor or humility. "I'm not sure why I'm here, to be absolutely honest with you."

"It's understandable. You want answers. You are no longer with the police force, is that correct?"

"Yes."

"You know they're after Father Boyle. I can't see him harming children—murdering them—but that's what they're saying."

"His activities have been very suspicious."

"Indeed they have."

"They say my son was unharmed. He wasn't molested in any way."

Father Keenan closed his eyes. "Thank God. Thank God."

"Did you have doubts?"

"There has been such a confluence of strange events. And they're saying all kinds of things. I don't know what will come out next. No, I don't believe Terry would ever have touched your son. He was completely incapable of such things, the man I knew."

"Why do you suppose he took my son?"

"I'm sure he had some reason that made sense to him at the time, however wrong it was. He was mentally ill. He was an alcoholic as well. He once told me that people didn't know what to make of him, but I did. He had a hole in him that he couldn't fill. I think taking your son out to Wellfleet had something to do with that condition.

"There was a boy in Belmont. A very sick boy, terminally ill with cancer. Father Boyle had found a place that seemed . . . I don't know. Miraculous. To him, anyway. It was during one of his unwell periods. He took that boy out there—with no one's permission, with no explanation—and it was an awful scandal.

The Church managed to avoid legal action, but shortly afterward, Father Boyle attempted suicide. He nearly succeeded. He went into the sanctuary at Our Lady of Good Counsel, knelt there, and shot himself in the chest. The bullet narrowly missed his aorta. There was nerve damage, numbness in one of his legs, and chest pain that always bothered him afterwards.

In any event, they shipped him out of Belmont and sent him here. He felt terrible guilt after the suicide attempt. He believed he would never be forgiven. Terry found it hard to live, just to *live.*"

A tear ran down the side of the priest's nose and he wiped it away.

"You talk about him as if he's gone."

"I believe he is gone. I like to think I'll see him again, but . . . He was too good. And completely unnoticed. Everywhere he went, he was the biggest heart and the smallest presence."

Father Keenan was crying openly now. "He is in God's arms now. He should be. If he isn't, then I'm in the wrong racket."

Warren chuckled at the comment.

"I take it you are a fellow who doesn't smile much," said Father Keenan.

"Not much."

"Well, Terry is surely with us then."

The medical examiner determined that the woman who was found in a dilapidated cottage in Truro had been dead for nearly two weeks. Syringes were found in the room along with heroin residue. The body was too decomposed to lift fingerprints. The death was a small story amidst the sensational events that were being reported daily in 72-point type.

In a wall space, local police found an expired driver's license belonging to one Ava Kittredge, along with a set of keys, a wedding band, and a photograph of an infant boy.

When the news found its way to the FBI, they sent a team of agents to the cottage. The place had been wiped nearly clean of fingerprints. But a metal box on the side of the house that contained the telephone connection from the street produced a thumbprint belonging to Dale Stasiak.

One of the agents asked Baldesaro if he thought they should tell Warren the details of the squalid little cottage, of Stasiak's presence there. "No," he said. "There's no need to do that."

When Warren got the call he was saddened; he couldn't say grief-stricken, just saddened. He didn't want to know anything about the body in the cottage. The years of uncertainty about her whereabouts had been easier than knowing. He liked to think that she might be out there somewhere, not because he wanted her to come back but because he harbored a foolish hope that she would be living somewhere, joyous, irreverent, passionate, inaccessible, as he remembered her. For all her faults she had good in her.

52

Warren watched as James threw a bundle of sticks into the woodstove, straightened, and surveyed Mike. They were helping him with his Halloween costume: A pair of scarlet pantaloons, sequined slippers, and on his head a gold turban. "We're definitely getting there," James said. "You're looking more royal by the minute."

Grayson appeared from behind one of the columns that supported the second floor, the structural member itself hung with every type of oddity and relic that would fit until it resembled a folk totem of some kind. "I can't find the ermine," he said. "What's a king without an ermine mantle?" He looked at Mike. "He looks very arabesque at this point. He'd be better off with chain mail and a scimitar."

"Honestly. It's about make-believe, Grayson. Mike, what do *you* think?" James stood him in front of the full-length mirror.

"I think I look good."

"There you go, Grayson."

"He looks like a Moorish warrior. Your doing."

"Then the fur will be superfluous. Or add it if you want. It doesn't have to be historically accurate."

It was clear to Warren that Mike, or someone like him, was something that Grayson and James had desperately wanted, and as strange as it seemed to him—he was still getting used to the fact of two men living together the way they did—it moved him all the same.

He and Mike had been living on the property now for two

weeks, staying in the big barn. Mike had been at Osterville elementary school for a month without any setbacks. In the mornings he often walked across the property and found James and Grayson in the shop, setting up for the day. They came up with endless ways to use Mike's fascination with their inventory as a vehicle for practical instruction. They conducted make-believe transactions with Mike and showed him how to do the sums on the stylized receipt paper they used, small slips that read, "Antiquitus" in calligraphy.

As Warren carried on the solitary work of fixing up Grayson and James's property, there was something that intruded on his thoughts with increasing persistence. Seeing the name "Clyde" scrawled on the defaced artwork in Dr. Hawthorne's house had triggered a nagging familiarity. Its origins, he felt, were somewhere in the early days of the investigation. He pored over the information that he'd cajoled Jenkins into getting for him, their own record of the short-lived Lefgren investigation, and the Truro police department's notes on the Gilbride murder.

Some calls had come in from outside jurisdictions in the days after the Lefgren killing. Police in Maine called about a truck driver with a record of accosting young girls. There was a mental patient from Pittsburgh with ties to the New England area. In a margin he had written, "carnival/Lee." He was lucky Jenkins had included Dunleavy's legible and more detailed notes. There, the detective had recorded that in mid-June, police in the Western Massachusetts town of Lee had questioned a man named Clyde Pommering. This was where he had heard the name, the source of the familiarity that had been bothering him.

He called the Lee police department and learned that Pommering was noticed at a carnival that was passing through, loitering around the Tilt-A-Whirl and leering at the kids. The police drove Pommering out to the Mass Turnpike and told him to disappear.

One afternoon, Warren took a break from reshingling the roof on the barn and telephoned the Lee police department. The chief remembered the incident. He described Pommering as gangly and homely. "He was a real oddball," the chief said. "And an awful young guy to have a heart problem."

"How's that?"

The chief explained that when Pommering was picked up for questioning, officers found amyl nitrite capsules in his possession. Pommering claimed that they were prescribed to him by his doctor for a heart condition. The doctor—Reese Hawthorne of Provincetown—corroborated Pommering's story, though the chief said he was not convincing. "He didn't sound happy about it," he said. "It sounded to me like he was just going along with the story."

Warren left Grayson, James, and Mike to their costume-making and went into the side office and called Jenkins.

"What are you doing, Ed?"

"Me and Gladys are watching *Jackie Gleason*, that's all. What about you?"

"Nothing much."

"Settling into the new place O.K.?"

"Yes. Mike loves it here. Listen, Ed, did you ever talk to Ferrell about Dr. Hawthorne?"

"I did."

"And what did he say?"

"He was decent about it."

"Decent?"

"He wasn't interested but he didn't try to make me look like an idiot, either."

"He's an O.K. guy."

"He is."

"What do you think?" asked Warren.

"About what?"

"About Hawthorne."

"I think Hawthorne is ten pounds of shit in a five-pound bag." Warren heard Jenkins mutter, "Sorry, hon," off to the side.

"What do you think about taking another trip out there?"

"To P-town?"

"Yes. Drop in on Dr. Hawthorne one last time."

"You gonna go back into police work, lieutenant?"

"No."

"They'd hire you back, I bet."

"I wouldn't take the job."

"Well, at some point, you've got to adjust to the fact that you're a civilian now."

"I'm adjusting."

"I can see that. Lieutenant, it's done. Sooner or later they're going to find evidence that will pin all this on Boyle. The rest of it is just . . . strangeness."

"You're probably right. But I've been doing a little calling around and there are some things I want to look into. I can explain it to you on the way out there."

"O.K. When?"

"How about tomorrow afternoon about five?"

"Tomorrow's Halloween. Aren't you taking Mike out trick or treating?"

"I'm sure he'd be happy to go with Grayson and James."

"All right. See you tomorrow."

Dusk was falling in Provincetown when Warren and Jenkins arrived. The air was still and a bluish gray light had come down on the peninsula, the ocean flat and faintly luminescent, the white on the buildings glowing with the vestiges of the day's dying light. Lights were on in the houses, shops, and bars. Throngs of people walked beneath the glowing plastic pumpkins and grinning witches' heads that were strung across Commercial Street.

They found Hawthorne's house in darkness. No one

answered when they knocked. "Let's go talk to the neighbors," said Jenkins. They walked to the house across the street and knocked on the door. A man appeared with a package of Mint Juleps in his hand, a surprised expression on his face.

Jenkins said, "Police."

"Yes?"

"Do you know Dr. Hawthorne across the way?"

"Kind of. He doesn't live there anymore as far as I can tell."

"When did he leave?"

"A couple of weeks ago. His renter might still be there, I think."

"He has a renter?"

"Well, I'm not sure the man was renting. He was living there at any rate."

"What's his name?"

"I don't know. But sometimes there's a light on in the cellar of Dr. Hawthorne's house. It comes and goes."

They looked across the street. Hawthorne's house was a dark, silent mass. "Any idea why Hawthorne might have left?"

"No."

Jenkins took a card out of his wallet and handed it to the man. "I'm going to give you a number to call. If you see Hawthorne around . . ."

"*There.*"

They looked at the neighbor.

"Right there," he said. "The light."

Jenkins and Warren turned. A faint glow was coming from a cellar window, partially concealed by shrubbery. Without a word, they crossed the street and headed toward Hawthorne's house. They both got down and peered through the glass. There, dressed in an adult's skeleton suit—black fabric with white bones—was Edgar Cleve. His lips were moving but there appeared to be no one in the cellar with him. Nearby stood the oil burner and next to it a cot with a pillow and a balled-up blanket. He held a white cloth to his chest, rubbing it back and forth across himself, talking, though they could not hear what he said.

"Edgar Cleve," Jenkins whispered.

Warren looked at him through the smudged glass, recalling the strange-looking gangly man who had sat across from him in Jenkins's office the day of the Lefgren murder.

"Let's see if we can get him to come out of there," Warren said.

"You bring a weapon?"

"No. You?"

Jenkins shook his head.

"We could call the state police," said Warren.

"They're not going to come out here for this. This guy is nobody to them."

Cleve took the cloth he was holding, spread it out in front of his face, and put his nose into the fabric. It was clear then that what he held was a pair of boys' underwear.

"You see that?" Jenkins whispered. "You see what he's got?"

Warren was silent, nodding.

Cleve let the underwear drop to the floor and sat there, rubbing his thighs, looking around the cellar. His eyes went to the window and he stopped, motionless. He took the skeleton mask that was hanging around his neck by its elastic cord, brought it up over his face, then dashed out of sight. A moment later, the cellar went dark.

"Go around back," Warren said. "Yell if he comes out that way."

Warren stood on the sidewalk in front of the house. A small band of costumed children went by. In the backyard, Jenkins kept his eyes on the darkened porch, watching for movement.

They remained at their posts for ten minutes. Jenkins came around from the back. "He's not coming out," he said. "He's probably watching us from one of the windows."

"Why don't you see if you can find a cop down on Commercial Street. Tell them Barnstable wants him for questioning and you have reason to believe he'll resist."

Jenkins went down Daggett Lane the way the trick-or-treaters had gone. Warren stood in the shadow of a big yew bush across the street. Cleve did not come out, nor did any lights go on. At some point during his vigil, Warren turned toward Commercial Street to look for Jenkins and saw a black-clad figure step out of a hedge and onto the sidewalk, the long, high, exaggerated motion of the leg like a bit of physical comedy, a Chaplinesque version of stealth. There was Cleve, creeping out of the adjacent yard.

Warren watched him head down to Commercial Street. He counted to ten, then began following. Cleve's head was swiveling all around, looking for pursuers. He didn't see Warren, who at one point ducked into the trellised entrance of a front yard. A short distance from Commercial Street, Cleve suddenly turned and caught Warren in the open. Cleve froze for a moment, standing stock-still beneath a street light, the bones on his black suit brightly articulated, the black sockets of the skull mask and the grinning teeth staring back at Warren. Warren pointed at him. "You," he said. "Come here." Cleve took off at a sprint.

A twinge of pain shooting through his ribs at every pounding step, Warren pursued Cleve into Commercial Street. He saw him crash into the stream of reveling pedestrians and saw their reaction, like a shock wave radiating outward from the intersection with Daggett Lane. Warren pursued; Jenkins appeared out of nowhere and fell in behind him, both of them shouting and shoving their way through.

Cleve turned right into a wide break between the buildings. Warren and Jenkins made the turn and saw him headed toward the water. Some people were standing nearby, a small group looking at the lights on the harbor. Startled, they watched as Cleve ran past them and straight into the water. Warren yelled,

"Stop that man!" To his amazement, two of the bystanders suddenly moved into action. They were about waist deep when they jumped on Cleve's back. He went under and out of sight briefly. They all came up, thrashing. The bystanders got hold of his arms but he was a kicking, biting fury. Warren splashed out to them and joined the struggle and though Cleve launched ferocious bursts of resistance, they managed to drag him ashore.

There was a crowd now, and they parted as a Provincetown police cruiser crawled toward the docks. The officers handcuffed Cleve and dragged him to the car. Jenkins turned to Warren and said, "I think you better make yourself scarce, being a civilian and all." He handed Warren the keys to his car. "Go on back. I'll get a ride from one of the locals. Do me a favor, though. Would you call Gladys and tell her I'm tied up?"

"O.K."

"I'll call you as soon as I know more."

Warren sidled into the crowd and vanished.

Detective Ferrell had just returned from his weekly run to the grocery store, setting his bags down in the kitchen of his rented apartment in South Yarmouth, when the phone rang.

"Is this Detective Ferrell?" asked the voice on the other end.

"It is. Who's this?"

"It's Ed Jenkins. Barnstable police."

"What is it, Jenkins?"

"Remember I told you about a Dr. Reese Hawthorne in Provincetown? The sexual deviance specialist?"

"Yeah."

"I'm standing in his house right now and you need to get out here."

"Why?"

"We've got the guy who did the murders. Are you there? Ferrell?"

"Yeah, yeah. I'm here."

"Did you hear what I just said?"

"Yes, and I'm at a loss for words. *We've* got the guy, Jenkins."

"No, you don't."

"Not in custody, no, but we've got the guy. We know who he is."

"You need to come out here. We've got someone in custody. He was living in Hawthorne's house."

There was a pause, and then Jenkins heard Ferrell sigh. "O.K. This is what I'm going to do. I'm going to come out there. Alone. I'm not going to say anything to anyone. And whatever the big discovery is you made out there, when it turns out to be unrelated, I'm not going to say anything about that, either. It's a good thing I like you, Jenkins."

"You can tell anyone you damn well please. I just want to see your face when you see what we've got here."

53

Hidden in a small duffel bag that had been stuffed into the lowest drawer of an old bureau in Dr. Hawthorne's cellar, Jenkins and the Provincetown police found items of clothing belonging to several of the murdered boys. A bloodied T-shirt and a pair of shorts were found concealed in the floor joists.

Their suspect, whose true name was Clyde Pommering, sat handcuffed in the kitchen, refusing to speak. Detective Ferrell entered the house, was directed to the cellar, where he met Jenkins, and said absolutely nothing while he examined the clothing. Jenkins watched him struggle with the shock of it, then went back upstairs, leaving Ferrell alone.

Jenkins sat down across from Clyde Pommering. He was dripping wet, looking straight ahead, an impassive expression on his face. "Are you going to tell me why you've got the clothing of four murdered kids in your possession?"

Pommering looked at Jenkins with wide, owllike eyes. The sound of Ferrell's feet clumping slowly up the stairs reached them in the kitchen. Ferrell stood there and studied Pommering for a moment, then turned to Jenkins. "Come outside."

They stood in the darkness on the front lawn. A few neighbors were out in their yards, watching. "Christ," Ferrell said. "How did you come on this?"

"I told you . . ."

"I mean the whole thing. From the start."

Standing in the window of a seventh-floor office building on Tremont Street, Karl Althaus looked out across downtown Boston. Seated at a table behind him were the corporate counsel for Luxor Laboratories, the company's CEO, and its chief financial officer. Althaus turned from the glass and said, "I don't know where Hawthorne is now."

"Would he have been prudent enough to remove company documents from the house before it was searched?"

"I'm sure he would have."

"But we're not certain. After all, he left in a hurry."

"And they're looking for him," said the CEO. "If he's in trouble, he might trade information about Luxor for certain considerations in the other thing. Sit down, Karl. You're making me nervous."

One of the lawyers said, "Tell us everything you know. In case all this starts coming back in our direction."

Althaus told them about his periodic trips to Cape Cod, acting as the liaison between Luxor and his old friend and colleague who was being paid to conduct illicit experiments with new drugs. Living at the house in Provincetown with the doctor was a man named Edgar Cleve. Hawthorne had discovered him through a research project he had been working on at Bridgewater State Hospital. Cleve was one of several patients to whom Hawthorne had administered an experimental antipsychotic drug that Luxor was developing—seropromazine—though it showed little promise and they abandoned it. Hawthorne said he was treating Cleve, but it was often difficult to tell what the doctor's relationship was with the patients he took in. Althaus happened to know that Cleve was not the first. There had been trouble when Hawthorne was working in New York, something to do with an offender he'd been keeping around. Althaus wasn't clear on the details.

Hawthorne was a prominent mind in the field of sexual deviance and Althaus believed he was investigating some therapeutic techniques with Cleve, but he also suspected that Hawthorne was keeping him as a curiosity, an accoutrement to his bohemian existence on Daggett Lane.

Hawthorne was vague about Cleve's tendencies, but there was an insinuation that he was dangerous, a subtle boast on the part of the doctor about his own capabilities. Hawthorne had given him the spare bedroom downstairs and engaged him in various therapeutic exercises. The doctor confided to Althaus that staying with him was a condition of Cleve's freedom and intimated that he had either enough knowledge or enough influence to have Cleve incarcerated, which he held over his tenant—along with forced medications—as a means of behavior modification. Althaus suspected that while Cleve was initially grateful for the situation, he eventually bristled under the doctor's authority and began asserting himself.

Cleve occasionally worked on a fishing boat that did day runs out of Provincetown Harbor. He frequently wandered off on foot and came back dirty and hyperactive. Althaus asked Hawthorne what he thought his patient was up to and the doctor said that he was probably looking for work, but Althaus could see that Hawthorne was uneasy.

It was about that time that Hawthorne tried to find some kind of artistic outlet for Cleve. He showed no interest in drawing or painting, but was mildly intrigued by collages. This devolved into defacing photographs of people in magazines, erasing their eyes and mouths and drawing pupils and teeth with a ballpoint pen. The effect was either comical or sinister, depending on his mood, which had a predominant tendency to the latter.

Althaus was a bit startled during a subsequent visit when he saw that Cleve had introduced an X-ACTO knife to his magazine work. Althaus saw the pages wadded into balls, hurled across the porch, scribbled on and sliced with such a frenzy the tabletop was scarred. Hawthorne would choose one of the ruined magazines from a pile on the floor, lead Cleve into the study, and close the door so they could discuss what it meant.

Hawthorne let him borrow his car. The new freedom had a calming effect. He was gone much of the time, a yard job, a painting job, washing dishes at a restaurant. Hawthorne didn't use the car much, seeing his patients there at the house on Daggett Lane. The child murders hit a crescendo in that month.

And there was Althaus's final visit to the house on Daggett Lane. Hawthorne was away in Boston at a psychiatric conference and he'd invited Althaus to use the house for the weekend. He came down to the kitchen in the morning and while gazing out the window, he saw a shower of earth erupt from the mass of untended hollyhocks growing by the stockade fence. Partially concealed by the growth, Cleve was hunched over a short spade. He straightened, dropped the shovel, then held up a pair of children's shorts. He rubbed them on his chest and throat before he threw them down and picked up the spade again.

Althaus stepped away from the window and that's when he noticed the kitchen sink. The basin and faucets were stained with what he believed was blood.

The CEO of Luxor said, "Why didn't you come to us with this earlier?"

"Because it was all speculation at the time."

"You saw blood in Hawthorne's house in September. It's November now."

"We don't have another Hawthorne. You know that as well as I do. You know how valuable Hawthorne was to us. He couldn't just be replaced by running an ad."

"Well we're going to have to replace him. And in the meantime, hope he doesn't lead them back to us. For purposes of the public record, Karl, your association with Hawthorne was strictly personal. Understand?" He spoke to everyone in the room. "If anyone is contacted by authorities, notify me immediately. All records of business with Dr. Hawthorne are to be destroyed."

In a guarded room at Massachusetts General Hospital, Stasiak lay in his bed, his one good eye staring, unfocused. His face had thinned, his once formidable mass reduced somehow under the childlike gown, light blue with jolly little geometric shapes dancing across the fabric. Lieutenant Colonel John Fitzgerald walked in. He was wearing civilian clothes, a suit and tie, beige overcoat, and carrying a gift-wrapped shaving kit. He stood at the foot of the bed and looked at Stasiak, whose eye moved to take him in. "How are you doing?" Fitzgerald said. Stasiak continued to look at him for a moment, then his eye shifted away.

"I'm damn sorry about all of this," Fitzgerald said. "Damn sorry." He looked around the room. "I'm going to do everything I can for you but I told you to stop. When you went down there, I thought we all understood it was over and we were just going to sit back and count our money. I don't know if you'll ever talk again but if you do . . ." A nurse came in and removed the tray from beside Stasiak's bed. Fitzgerald smiled at her. When she was gone, he said, "If you do, you'd better choose your words carefully."

He put the gift down on Stasiak's end table. "You're very vulnerable now. You'll be easy to find. I know your mother and father still live in Charlestown. You want them to live out their golden years without any more heartbreak." He looked around the room. "Well, that's it for now. Keep your chin up."

Warren and his son spent the frigid autumn nights in their single beds with the woodstove hissing and ticking between them. They talked in the complete darkness up in the loft of the former barn, which was like a tree house, the upper branches of the big elms and the stars beyond visible through the large window in the gable. One night, they saw a shooting star arc through the black universe. Mike said, "Was that Sputnik?"

"I don't know," Warren yawned. "Maybe it was a meteorite."

Seconds passed. The wood shifted in the stove with a soft clunk.

"Maybe it was a Martian spaceship," Warren said.

"Maybe it was for us."

Warren looked up into the black, the rafters high above barely distinguishable. He spoke to his son. "What are you laughing at?"

"I'm not laughing."

"No?"

"I'm just smiling."

"At what?"

"At us, Dad."

In the morning, as Warren prepared breakfast, he saw James standing in the yard by the main house, talking with Ed Jenkins. He put his coat on and went outside. "There he is!" Jenkins said when he saw him. "I was just talking to Mr. Holbrooke here about the big renovation."

"And Thanksgiving," James added. "Grayson and I were talking last night and we decided we'd like to have a big Thanksgiving celebration and have lots of people come. You and Mike of course, and Officer Jenkins and his family. We'll decorate the house and we have a big table where everyone can sit—it hasn't been used in years—and if the weather is nice, we can set it up outside and maybe have a bonfire."

Warren looked at Jenkins, who was nodding, noncommittal, a functional smile on his face with which Warren was very familiar.

"You think about it, Officer Jenkins," said James. "But let us know so we know how many are coming."

"All right."

"Now, would you like to see our shop? We don't give the tour to just anyone, you know."

"Yeah," he said. "*Yeah*. That would be terrific."

James led the way toward the house. Jenkins turned to Warren. "I'll catch you on the way out," he said. "I gotta see this."

Warren was on his way back to the barn when a car pulled up and parked out front. He watched in astonishment as Fred Sibley got out. He spotted Warren and waved. They met in the yard. "Warren, how are you?" he said.

"Surprised as hell. When did you get out?"

"A couple of days ago. I was going to go on a weeklong bender but that's not a good idea for me. How are you making out?"

"I'm great. I'm glad to see you."

This took Sibley aback. "Well, yeah, I . . . Between the FBI and your ex-wife, the US attorney convinced a judge to get right on it. I understand she didn't make it, your wife."

"She didn't."

"I'm sorry. If it's any consolation, she screwed them pretty good. Especially the bit about the place in Boston and the check-cashing scheme they had going. I guess you know the feds hit that and came up big. That was thanks to her."

Warren was silent.

"You went through a hell of an ordeal, I understand," Sibley said. "I'd like to hear about it sometime."

Warren shrugged. He crossed his hands in front of him.

"You went head-to-head with Stasiak," said Sibley.

"I was lucky."

"I don't know, Warren. You're a New England stoic."

"Mr. Sibley, luck is the only reason I'm standing here right now."

Sibley's eyes went off toward the barn. Warren turned to see Mike approaching.

"Or something," said Sibley. "I've heard about your son."

Warren detected a drop in Sibley's tone of voice, an inflection that seemed to suggest this was a new, much less transparent subject.

"Let's leave that alone," Warren said.

"I'm a journalist. I don't believe in fairy tales but they make for a hell of a story line."

"Speaking of which, what are you going to do? Hire on with another newspaper?"

"There isn't one on the East Coast that would hire me. I could go out West but these things have a way of following you around. I'm planning to write a book."

"What about?"

"About Pope and Stasiak. About what happened here this summer. About you and Jenkins. Would you be willing to sit down with me and talk about it?"

"I don't know, Mr. Sibley. That's not the kind of thing . . ."

Jane Myrna's '48 DeSoto pulled into the drive. Mike ran across the grass and into her arms. A young man got out with her, slender, good-looking. Jane was radiant as she walked toward them, her hair parted on the side and pinned up in the back, a colorful scarf tied around her throat. She looked directly into Warren's face as she approached, put her arms out, and hugged him. Warren stood stiffly with his arms by his sides, then brought them up and patted her clumsily on the back with his hands. He hadn't seen her since just before everything happened. "Mr. Warren," she whispered, her mouth close to his ear. He could smell her perfume. The house on General Patton Drive used to carry faint traces of it. It was like she was still there even when she had gone, bringing on spells of evening melancholy.

"Jane, it's so good to see you."

They talked, brought each other up-to-date on what had happened since they'd seen each other, avoiding the obviously painful. She introduced her fiancé, who embarrassed Warren by saying, "Sir, it's an honor."

Jane said, "I'd love to spend some time with Mike. I've missed him."

"We'll be living here now," said Warren. "Any time you want to stop in, you're welcome. We'd love to see you."

"I'll be going back to work soon," she said. "I'll be seeing Mike in school. Right, Mike?"

The boy had Fred Sibley off to the side, engaged in conversation. The journalist stood there with a slightly flummoxed expression.

The side door to the house opened and Jenkins and James came out. Jane looked up, saw Jenkins, and her eyes welled with tears. "Hey!" he shouted, "look who's here!"

She talked to Jenkins for a long time, both of them in quiet voices, Jane frequently brushing tears away and wiping her nose. Sometimes she laughed at what Jenkins said. Watching them, Warren felt the same sensation he got when he used to pick up stray signs of her in the house: loneliness, loss, an invincible grey twilight before him.

Sibley came over to Warren. "So how about the book? Would you be willing?"

"I don't want to be the subject of a book, Mr. Sibley."

"You wouldn't be the subject . . ." Mike reappeared at Sibley's side and the reporter moved to put Warren between him and the boy. "Christ, Warren. Did you teach this kid how to give the third degree? I've never seen a kid ask so many questions in my life."

"What are you doing for Thanksgiving?" Warren asked him.

"Thanksgiving?" Sibley looked shocked. "I never do anything on Thanksgiving. I haven't done anything for Thanksgiving for the past five years."

"If you want to come here on Thanksgiving, we're having

dinner. The Grady Pope trial starts next week, so there's not a whole lot I can say."

"Preliminary," Sibley said. "That's all. Preliminary discussion."

Grayson came up the walk with the mail. "My goodness," he said. "A convention." He handed a thick envelope to Warren, who glanced at the official-looking print and froze once he made the words out: Federal Bureau of Investigation, Washington, DC. He held the envelope down by his leg and introduced Grayson to Jenkins, Sibley, Jane, and her fiancé. "Are they all coming for Thanksgiving?" Grayson asked.

"I'll be with my family," Jane said. "But I can come afterward."

Grayson took her by the arm. "You'd better, darling. I don't want to be the only pretty face at the table."

Mike said, "What's in the envelope, Dad?"

"Kid asks more questions than Joe McCarthy," Sibley muttered. "What *is* in the envelope, Warren? It looks official."

"I applied to the FBI some time ago," Warren said. "It's probably a rejection letter."

"Rejection letters don't come in envelopes like that."

Jenkins walked over and shook Sibley's hand but did not look at him. "Jail not agree with you, Sibley?'

"You're Detective Jenkins, right?"

"That's right."

"I remember you from the East End Lodge."

Jenkins nodded. "Hell of a thing. Bad bunch of bastards you got on the wrong side of."

"I heard about the Kismet."

Jenkins did not respond. "What are you doing now?" he asked.

"Nothing," said Sibley. "Listen, are you coming to this Thanksgiving thing?"

Jenkins squinted. He looked at Warren. Sibley said, "Well, I hope you do come. I'd love to sit down and talk with you."

"Come on, Ed," said Warren. "Bring Gladys and the boys."

Jenkins said, "I don't suppose I could convince you to take the chief's job, could I?"

"I don't think so."

"They asked me but I don't want it. You take the chief's job, I'll come for Thanksgiving."

Jane walked up, reaching into her purse for something. "Mr. Warren, I almost forgot to give this to you. I was reading it at your house. How I wound up with it, I don't know." She took out the small yellow book. Warren snatched it out of her hand a little too eagerly. "I have to go now," Jane said. She kissed Warren on the cheek, then Jenkins. She shook Sibley's hand. "Goodbye, Mr. Sibley."

"Bye."

"Will I be seeing you all here on Thanksgiving?"

Warren said, "We'll be here."

"You too, Jenkins?"

"Yeah, kid. I'll be here with the missus."

She left then, she and her fiancé driving off. The three men looked after her. "Pretty girl," Sibley said. He looked over at the book that Warren was holding, along with the letter, so that its title wasn't visible. Sibley didn't need to see the title. He looked out across the road and muttered, more to himself than anyone else, *"Pictures of the Gone World."* He shook his head quickly. "Whew. I've got to go. I'll see you on Thanksgiving."

When he was gone, Warren walked Jenkins to his car. "So, you're doing good?" Jenkins asked.

"Yes. I'm doing fine."

"Jury selection for the Pommering trial starts next week."

"The Pope thing'll be going when they start that."

"We're going to be busy," Jenkins said.

Warren watched his friend, whose face was closed yet intensely occupied, like he was trying to figure something that eluded him. He followed Jenkins's gaze up the drive to where

Mike was talking with Grayson and James. The detective fidgeted with his keys and looked down at the ground. "It's been a crazy time, hasn't it?"

Before Warren could speak, Jenkins said, "Think about the chief thing, will you?" And with that he got into his car, avoiding Warren's eyes. He drove off and held a hand up in parting.

Warren took the envelope back to the barn and placed it on a weathered old table that stood just inside the door. He and Mike walked through the former apple orchard, stepping around the fruit that lay on the ground, its smell rich and intoxicating, carrying with it some old quality of autumn, a brief reappearance, in the burnished sunlight, of the past, a suggestion of promise. They wandered to the edge of the herring run. Mike said, "Do you think there are any fish in there?"

"Not this time of year. Wait till the spring. It'll be full of them."

Warren sat down on the bank and watched his son play at the edge of the stream. The swift moving water made glinting arcs and crystalline spouts as it flowed over boulders and branches, its liquid sound delicate and alluring. It glinted beyond Mike's form so that Warren could only see him as a silhouette, ageless, featureless, simply a presence. There was an object in his coat pocket that he had assumed was a piece of Kleenex, except that now he felt a string. He pulled it out and discovered that it was the St. Jude scapular that Sister John Frances had given him. He was sure he had stuffed it into the ashtray of the car. "Mike," he called. "Did you put something in my pocket?" He held the scapular up. It swung from his fingers. He could not see his son's expression. Mike spoke as if a figure in a dream. "It's for you, Dad."

Warren lay back on the grass and closed his eyes. What was this feeling? He was changed, freed, grief and suffering no longer in his blood, though he would always have a religious devotion to these things. At night he saw Ava. The dead children spoke to him. He paced the house at General Patton Drive in some perpetual extreme hour that never ended. But morning brought this new life, consistently, without disappointment. His son. The miracle of his son. The word he would never utter to a single soul: *Miracle*. The blood in his veins, the warmth of his own bed. Warren closed his eyes and lay silent and still. For a moment he thought he felt sleep stealing over him, its soft narcotic grip, friendly, welcome, but it wasn't sleep. He interlaced his fingers over his chest, opened his eyes. He looked up at the sky and understood that he was overwhelmed with gratitude.

ABOUT THE AUTHOR

Joe Flanagan was born in Hyannis, Massachusetts. He has worked as a freelance writer, a speechwriter, and a magazine editor. His fiction has appeared in the anthology *Glimmer Train*. He lives in Alexandria, Virginia.